tiny tit

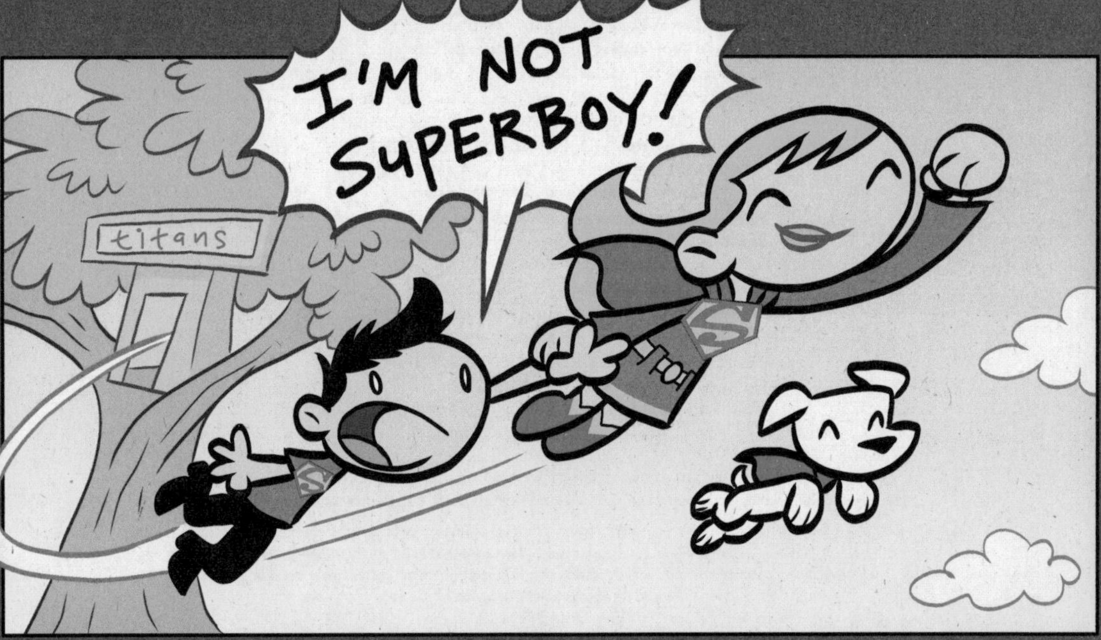
I'M NOT SUPERBOY!
titans

THE TREEHOUSE AND BEYOND!

Art Baltazar & Franco
Writers

Art Baltazar
Artist & Letterer

Chynna Clugston Flores Kristy Quinn Editors – Original Series
Ian Sattler Director – Editorial, Special Projects and Archival Editions
Robin Wildman Editor
Robbin Brosterman Design Director – Books

Eddie Berganza Executive Editor
Bob Harras VP – Editor-in-Chief

Diane Nelson President
Dan DiDio and **Jim Lee** Co-Publishers
Geoff Johns Chief Creative Officer
John Rood Executive VP – Sales, Marketing and Business Development
Amy Genkins Senior VP – Business and Legal Affairs
Nairi Gardiner Senior VP – Finance
Jeff Boison VP – Publishing Operations
Mark Chiarello VP – Art Direction and Design
John Cunningham VP – Marketing
Terri Cunningham VP – Talent Relations and Services
Alison Gill Senior VP – Manufacturing and Operations
David Hyde VP – Publicity
Hank Kanalz Senior VP – Digital
Jay Kogan VP – Business and Legal Affairs, Publishing
Jack Mahan VP – Business Affairs, Talent
Nick Napolitano VP – Manufacturing Administration
Sue Pohja VP – Book Sales
Courtney Simmons Senior VP – Publicity
Bob Wayne Senior VP – Sales

TINY TITANS: THE TREEHOUSE AND BEYOND!
Published by DC Comics. Cover, text and compilation Copyright © 2011 DC Comics. All Rights Reserved.

Originally published in single magazine form in TINY TITANS 33-38. Copyright © 2010, 2011 DC Comics. All Rights Reserved.
All characters, their distinctive likenesses and related elements featured in this publication are trademarks of DC Comics.
The stories, characters and incidents featured in this publication are entirely fictional.
DC Comics does not read or accept unsolicited ideas, stories or artwork.

DC Comics, 1700 Broadway, New York, NY 10019
A Warner Bros. Entertainment Company
Printed by RR Donnelley, Willard, OH, USA. 11/11/11. First Printing.
ISBN: 978-1-4012-3310-5

SUSTAINABLE
FORESTRY
INITIATIVE
Certified Fiber Sourcing
www.sfiprogram.org
Fiber used in this product line meets the
sourcing requirements of the SFI program.
www.sfiprogram.org SGS-SFI/COC-US10/81072

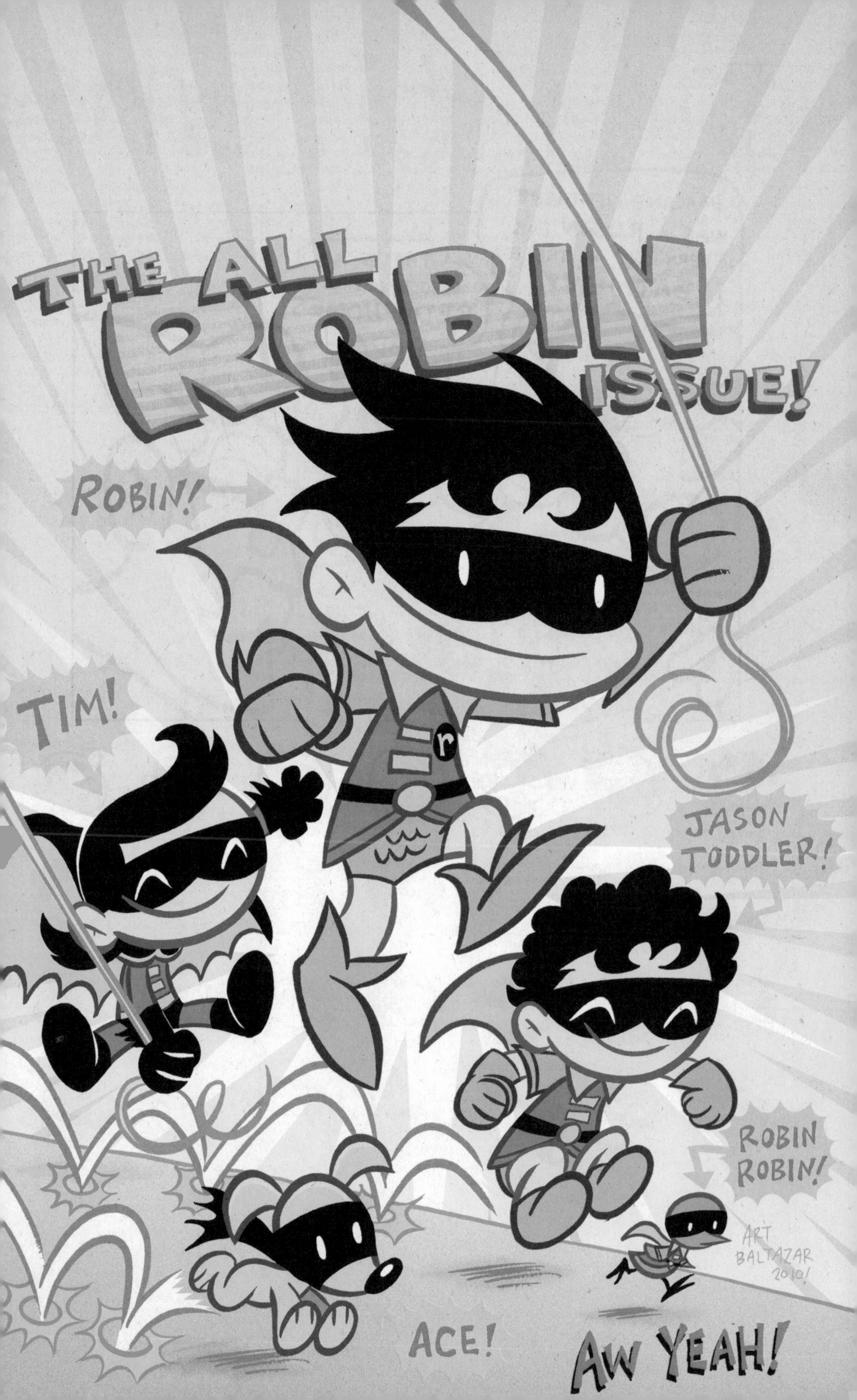
THE ALL ROBIN ISSUE!
ROBIN!
TIM!
JASON TODDLER!
ROBIN ROBIN!
ART BALTAZAR 2010!
ACE!
AW YEAH!

tiny titans

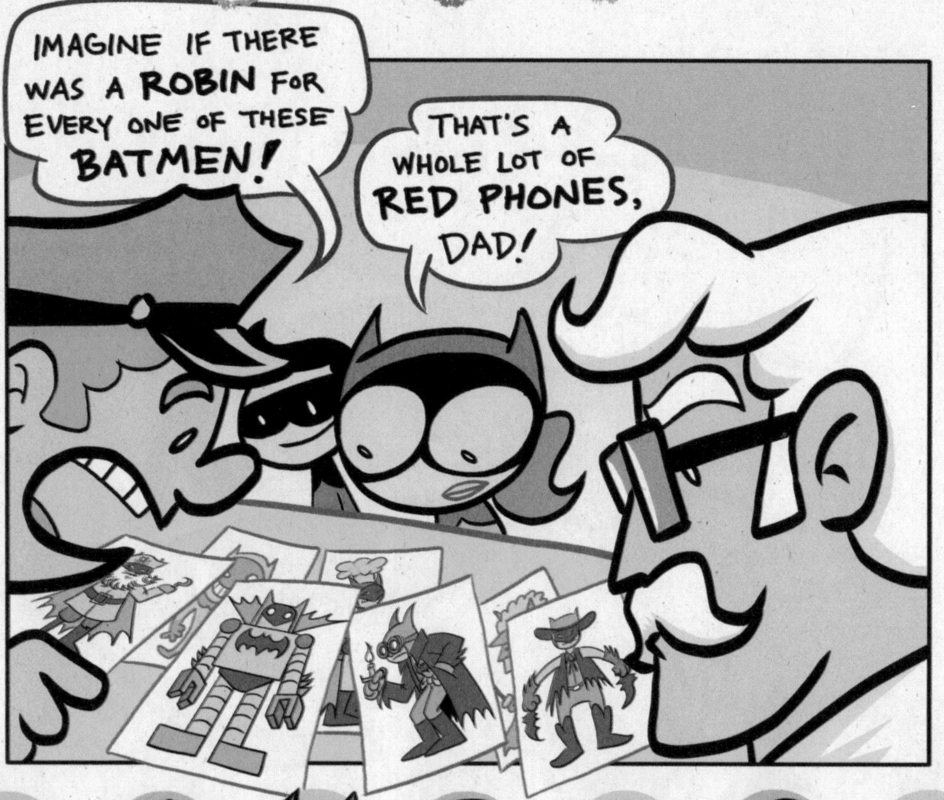
IMAGINE IF THERE WAS A ROBIN FOR EVERY ONE OF THESE BATMEN!
THAT'S A WHOLE LOT OF RED PHONES, DAD!

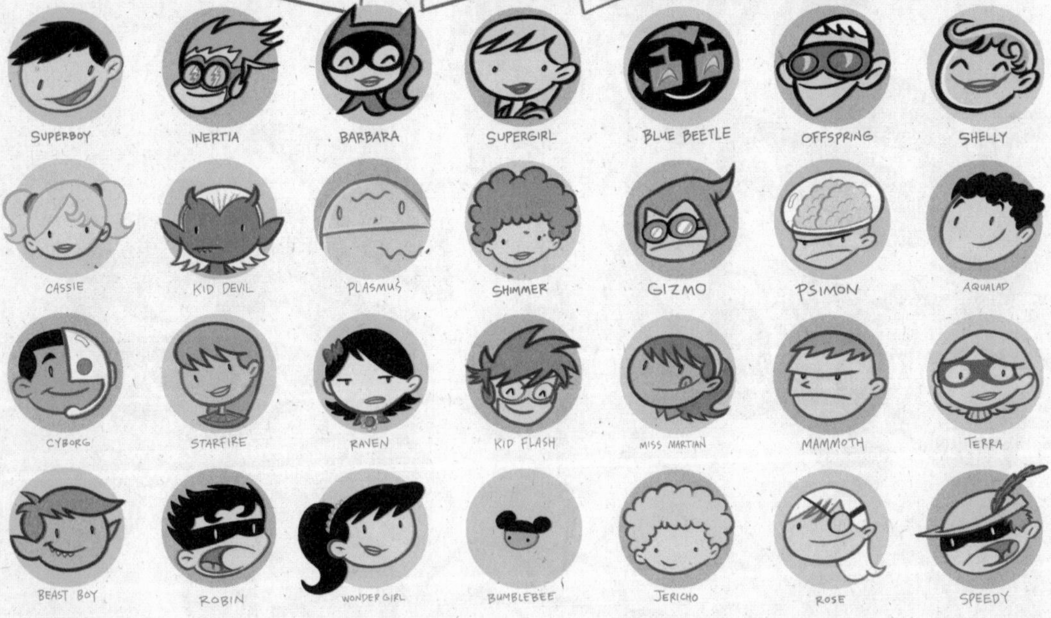
SUPERBOY
INERTIA
BARBARA
SUPERGIRL
BLUE BEETLE
OFFSPRING
SHELLY
CASSIE
KID DEVIL
PLASMUS
SHIMMER
GIZMO
PSIMON
AQUALAD
CYBORG
STARFIRE
RAVEN
KID FLASH
MISS MARTIAN
MAMMOTH
TERRA
BEAST BOY
ROBIN
WONDER GIRL
BUMBLEBEE
JERICHO
ROSE
SPEEDY

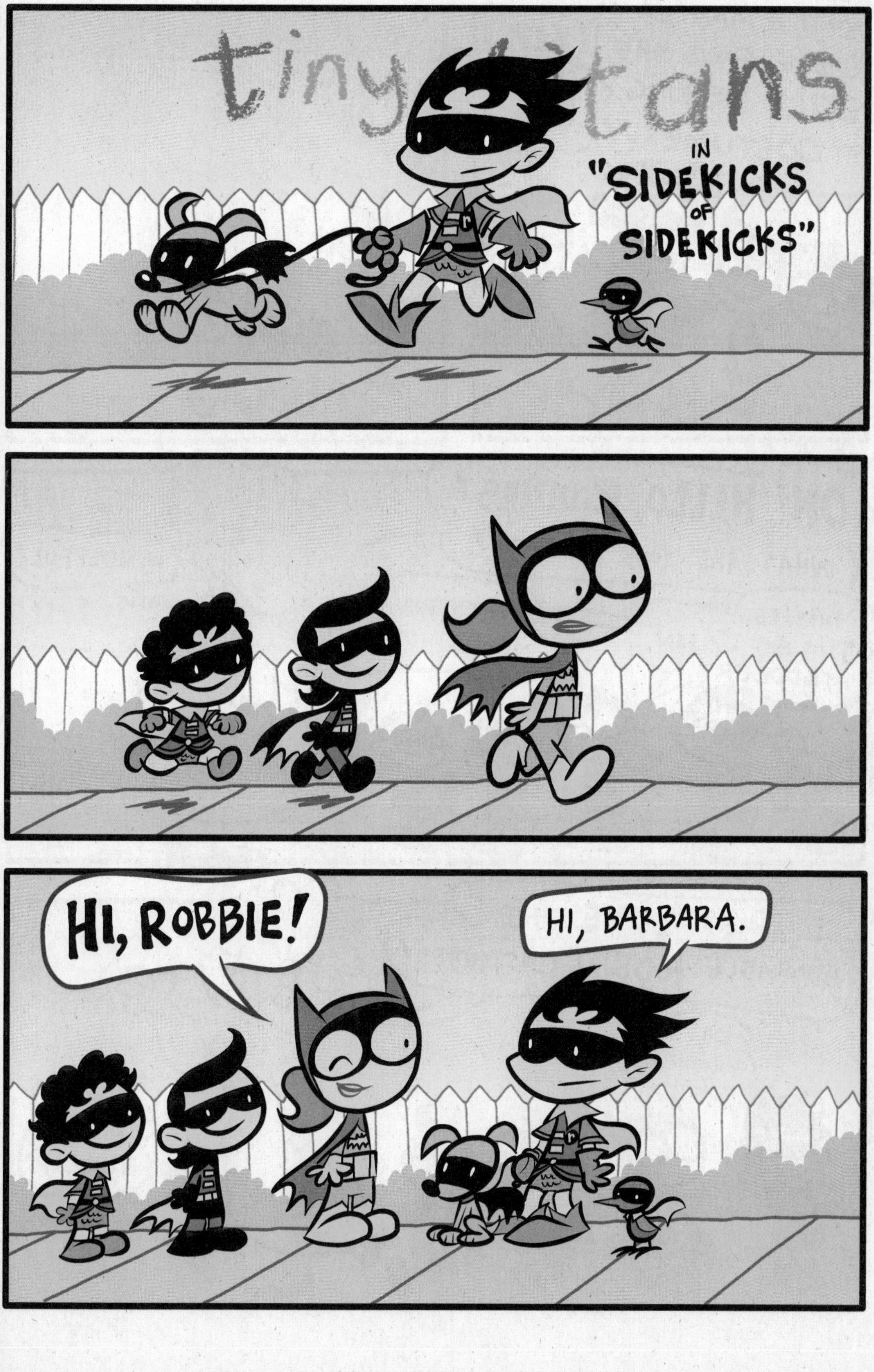
tiny titans
IN "SIDEKICKS OF SIDEKICKS"
HI, ROBBIE!
HI, BARBARA.

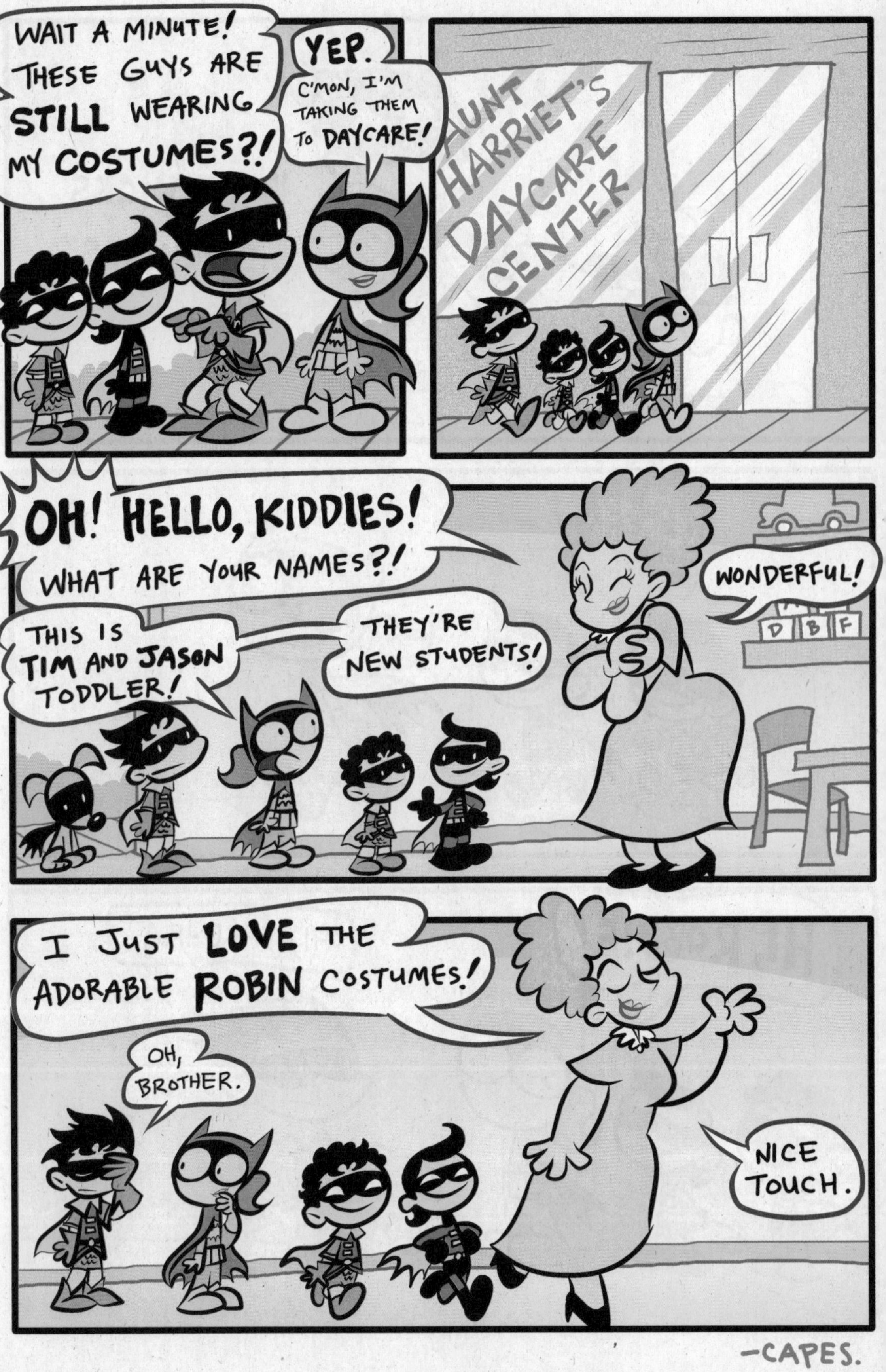
WAIT A MINUTE! THESE GUYS ARE STILL WEARING MY COSTUMES?!
YEP.
C'MON, I'M TAKING THEM TO DAYCARE!
AUNT HARRIET'S DAYCARE CENTER
OH! HELLO, KIDDIES! WHAT ARE YOUR NAMES?!
THIS IS TIM AND JASON TODDLER!
THEY'RE NEW STUDENTS!
WONDERFUL!
D B F
I JUST LOVE THE ADORABLE ROBIN COSTUMES!
OH, BROTHER.
NICE TOUCH.

–CAPES.

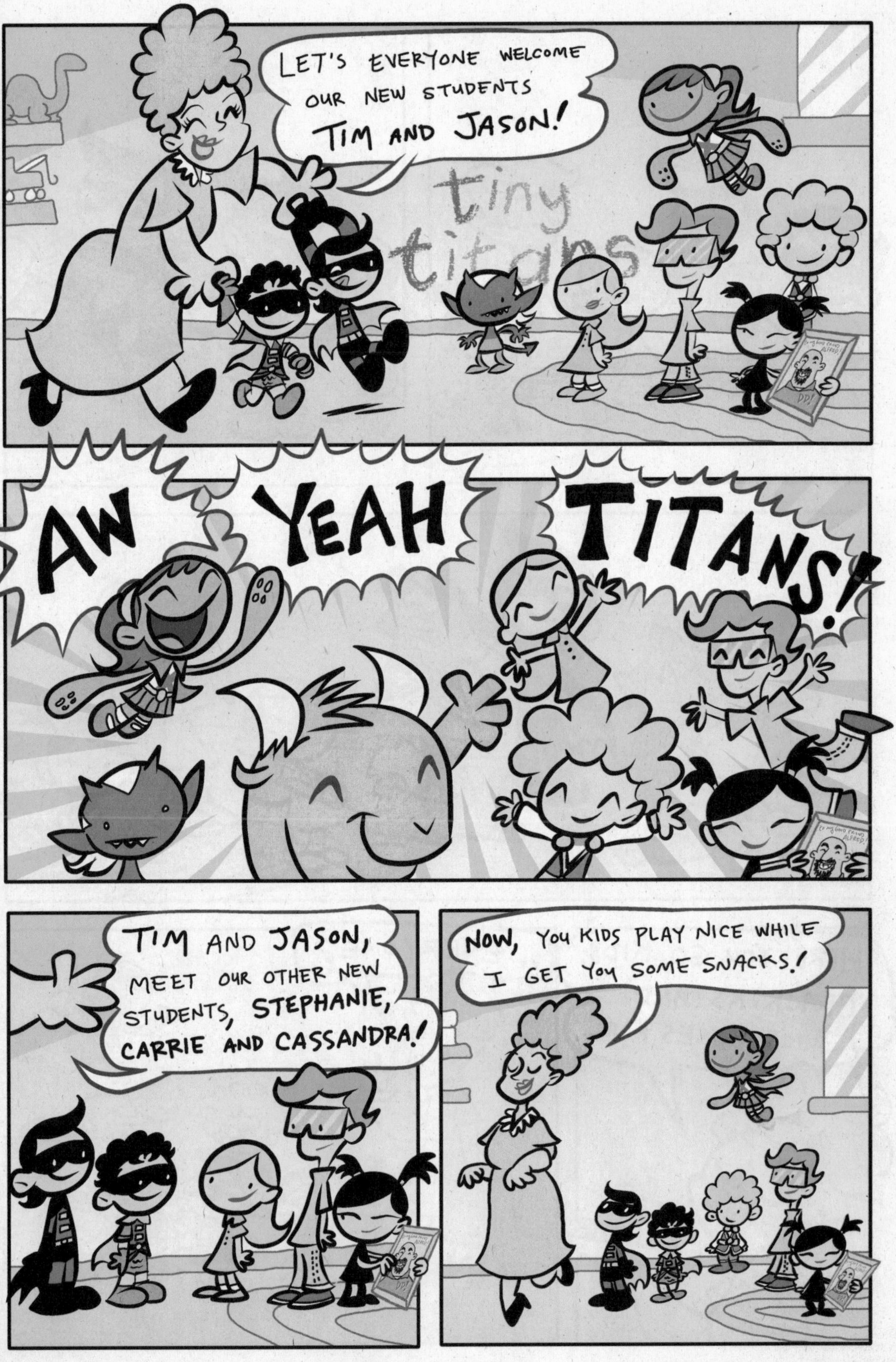
LET'S EVERYONE WELCOME OUR NEW STUDENTS TIM AND JASON!
tiny titans
AW YEAH TITANS!
TIM AND JASON, MEET OUR OTHER NEW STUDENTS, STEPHANIE, CARRIE AND CASSANDRA!
NOW, YOU KIDS PLAY NICE WHILE I GET YOU SOME SNACKS!

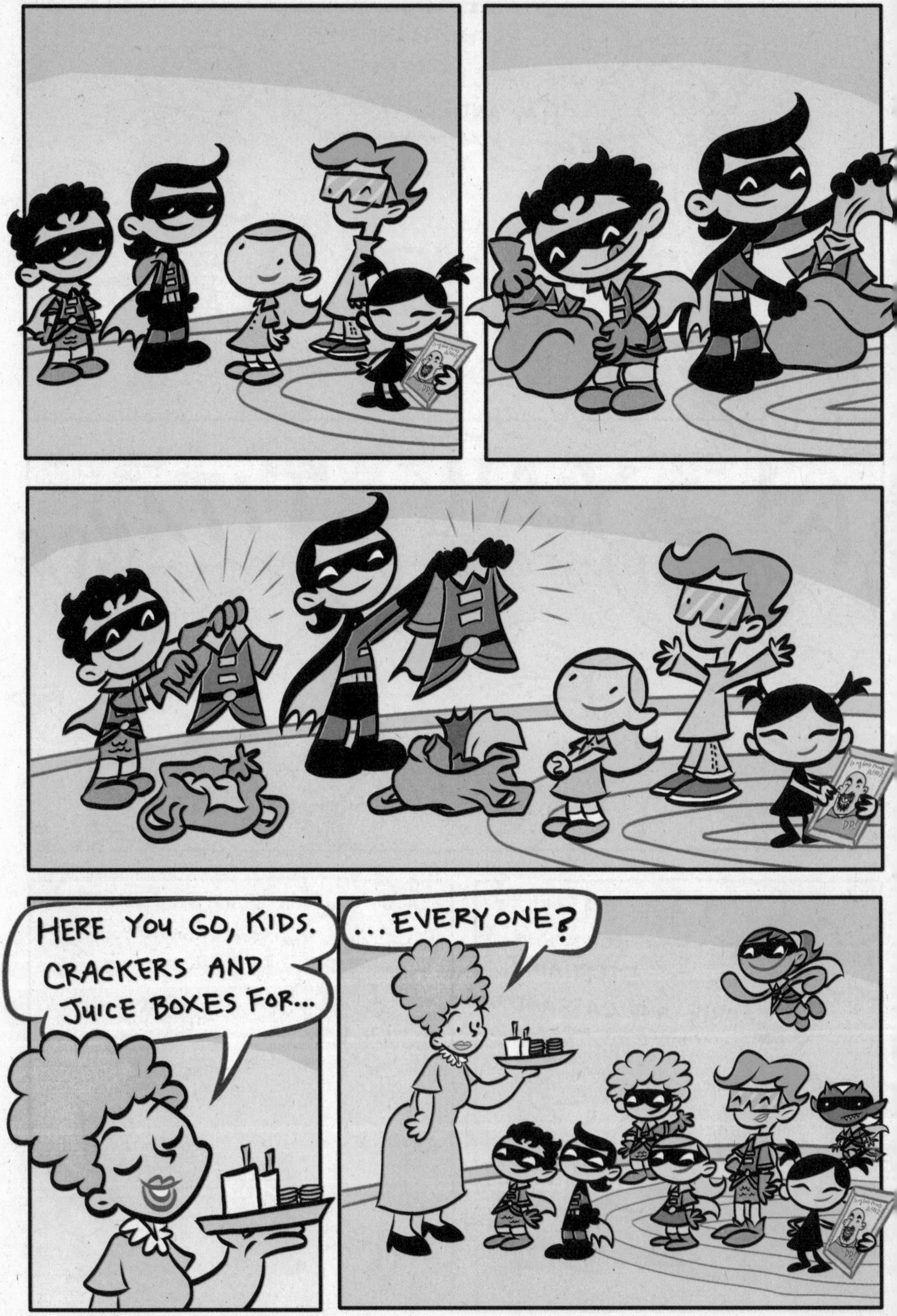
HERE YOU GO, KIDS. CRACKERS AND JUICE BOXES FOR...
...EVERYONE?

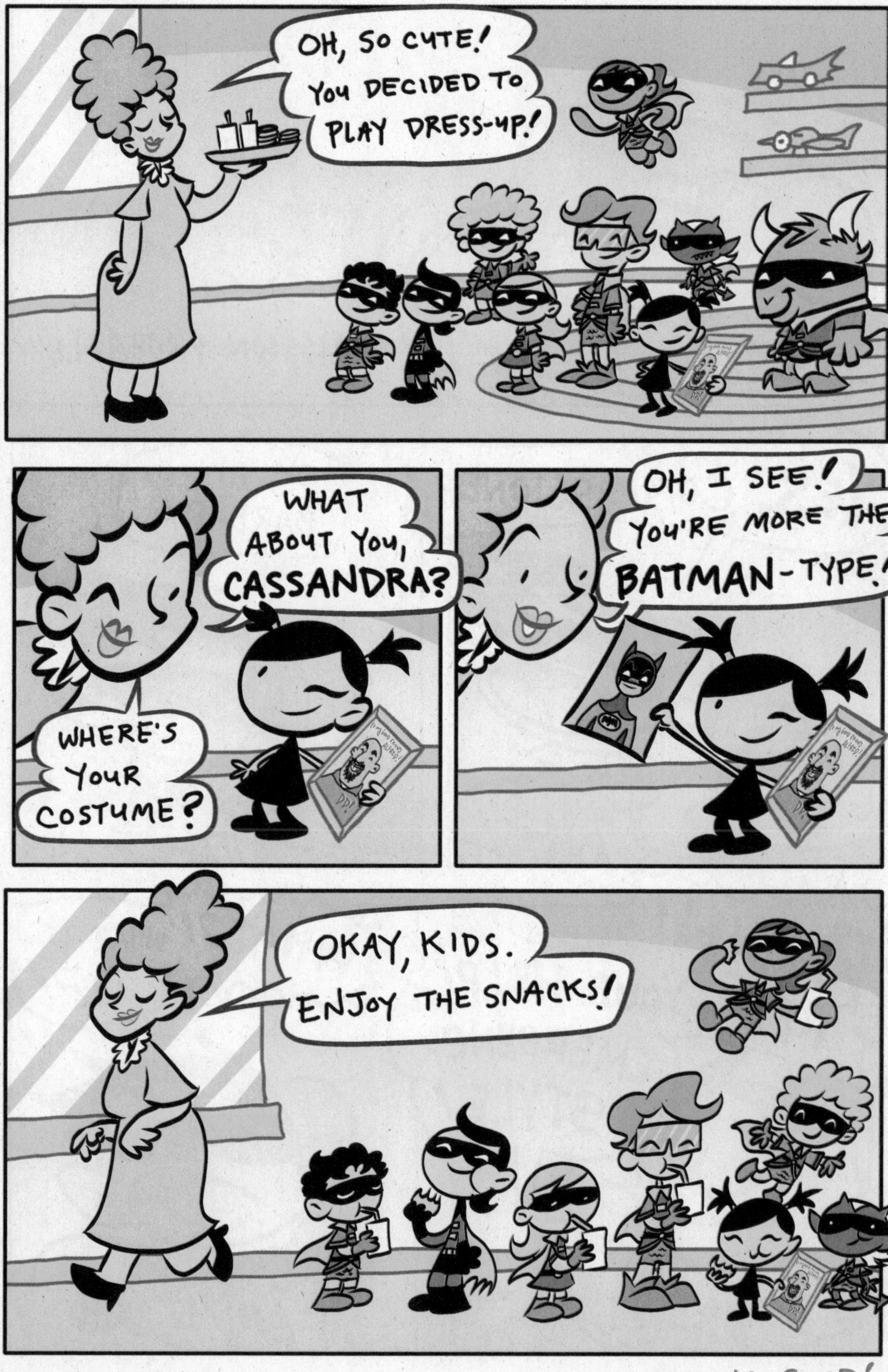
OH, SO CUTE! YOU DECIDED TO PLAY DRESS-UP!
WHAT ABOUT YOU, CASSANDRA?
WHERE'S YOUR COSTUME?
OH, I SEE! YOU'RE MORE THE BATMAN-TYPE!
OKAY, KIDS. ENJOY THE SNACKS!

—LOOKING GOOD!

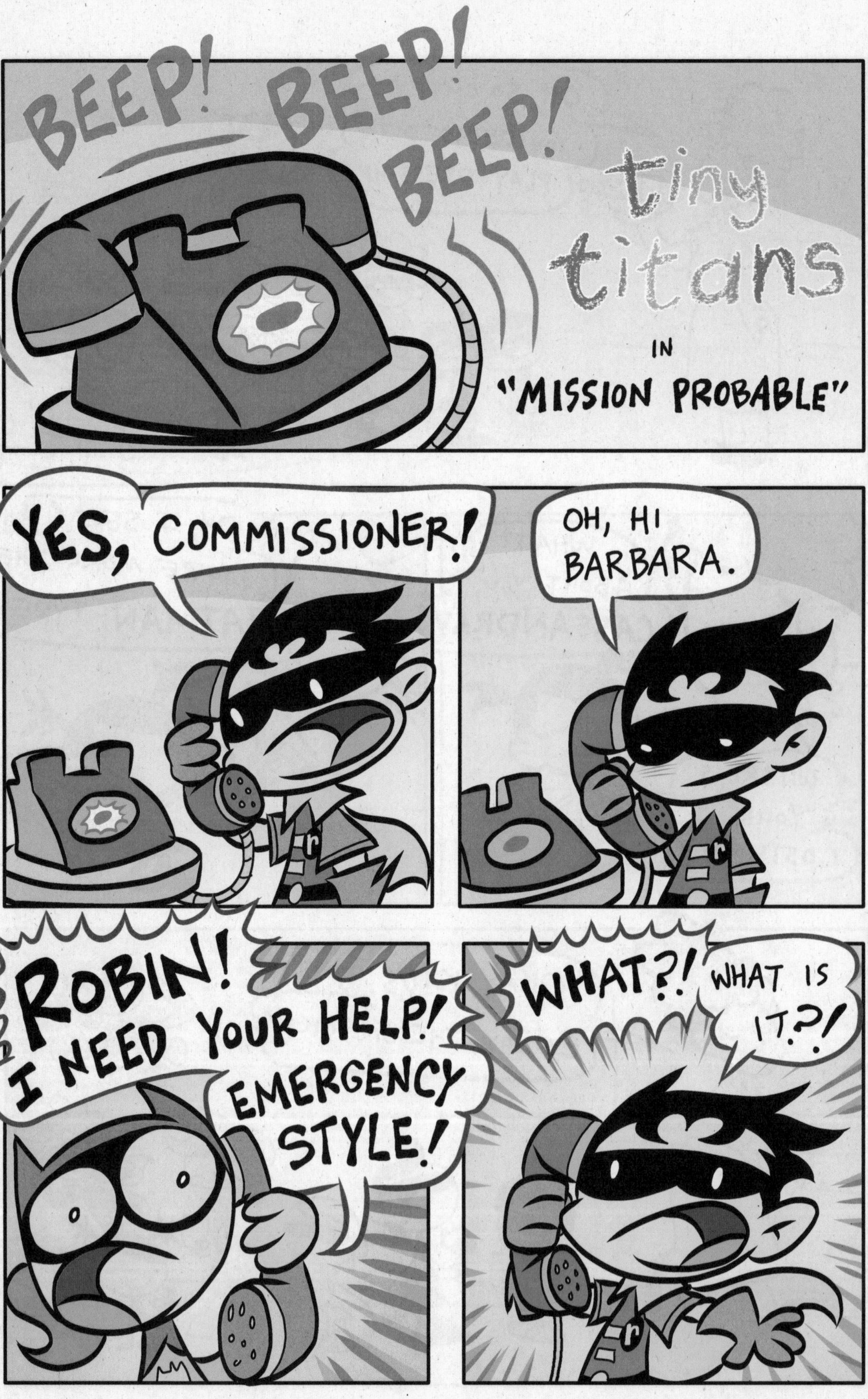
BEEP! BEEP! BEEP!
tiny titans
IN
"MISSION PROBABLE"
YES, COMMISSIONER!
OH, HI BARBARA.
ROBIN! I NEED YOUR HELP!
EMERGENCY STYLE!
WHAT?!
WHAT IS IT?!

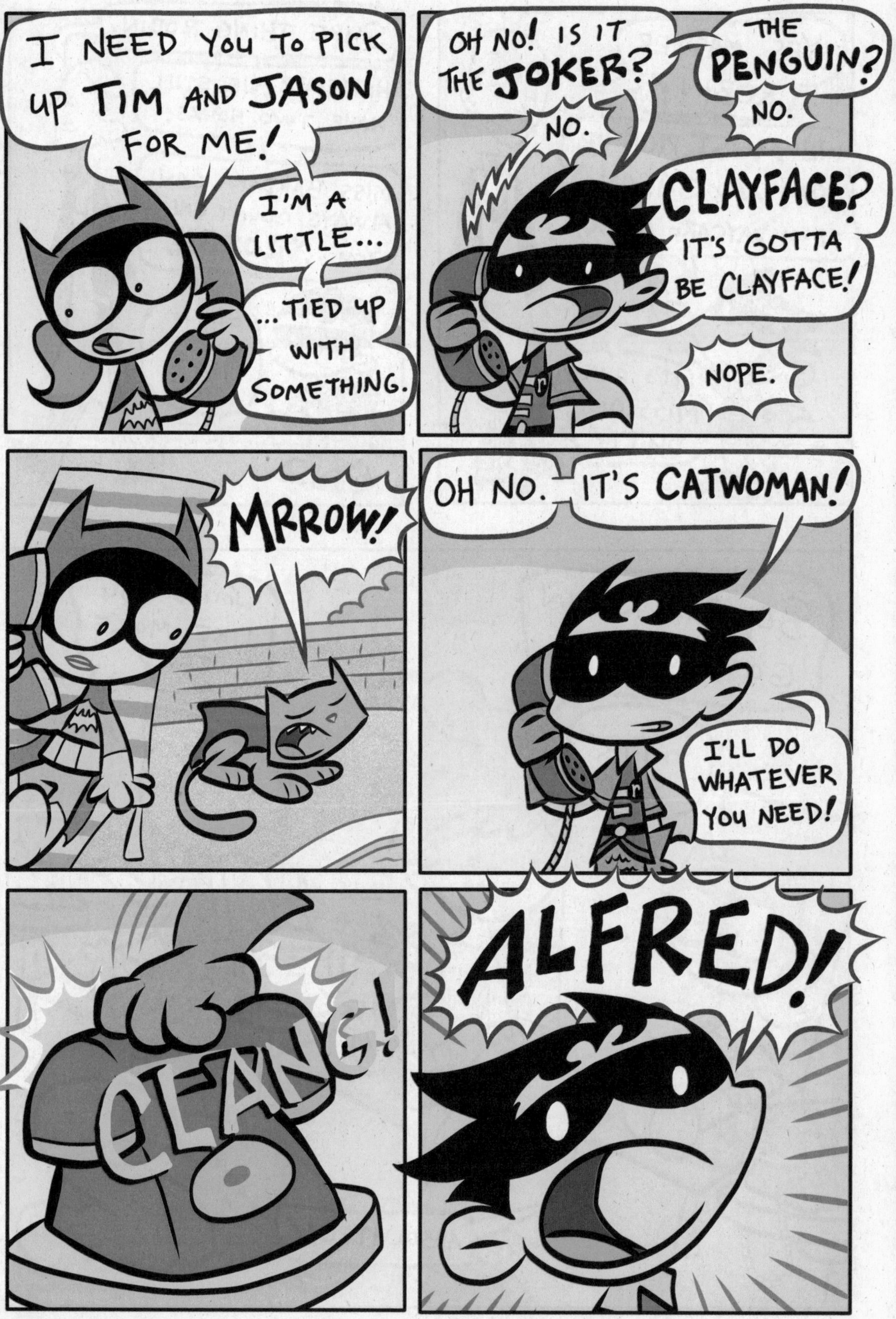
I NEED YOU TO PICK UP TIM AND JASON FOR ME!
I'M A LITTLE...
...TIED UP WITH SOMETHING.
OH NO! IS IT THE JOKER?
NO.
THE PENGUIN?
NO.
CLAYFACE? IT'S GOTTA BE CLAYFACE!
NOPE.
MRROW!
OH NO.
IT'S CATWOMAN!
I'LL DO WHATEVER YOU NEED!
CLANG!
ALFRED!

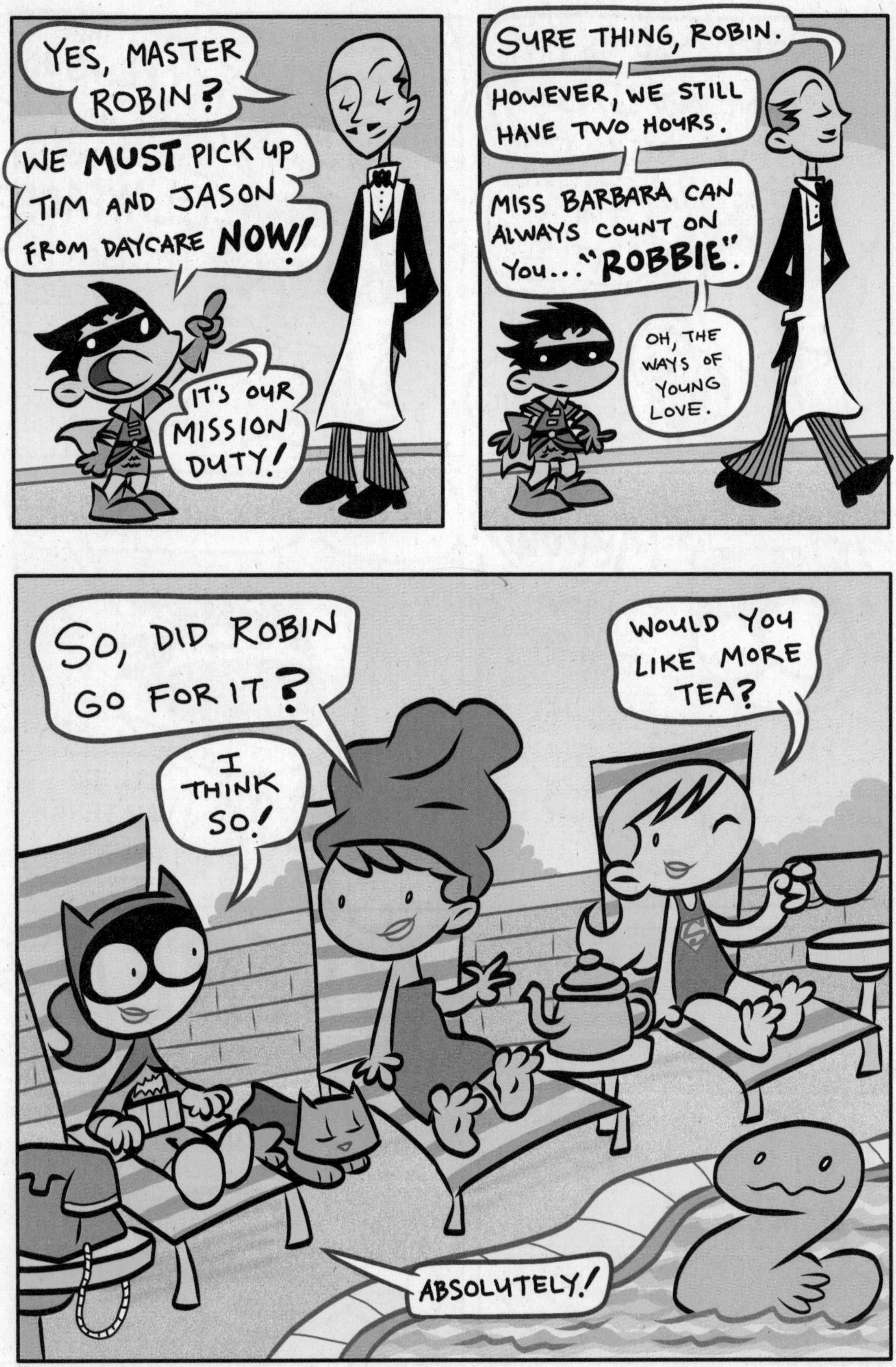
YES, MASTER ROBIN?
WE MUST PICK UP TIM AND JASON FROM DAYCARE NOW!
IT'S OUR MISSION DUTY!
SURE THING, ROBIN.
HOWEVER, WE STILL HAVE TWO HOURS.
MISS BARBARA CAN ALWAYS COUNT ON YOU... "ROBBIE".
OH, THE WAYS OF YOUNG LOVE.
SO, DID ROBIN GO FOR IT?
I THINK SO!
WOULD YOU LIKE MORE TEA?
ABSOLUTELY!

-BREW SOME.

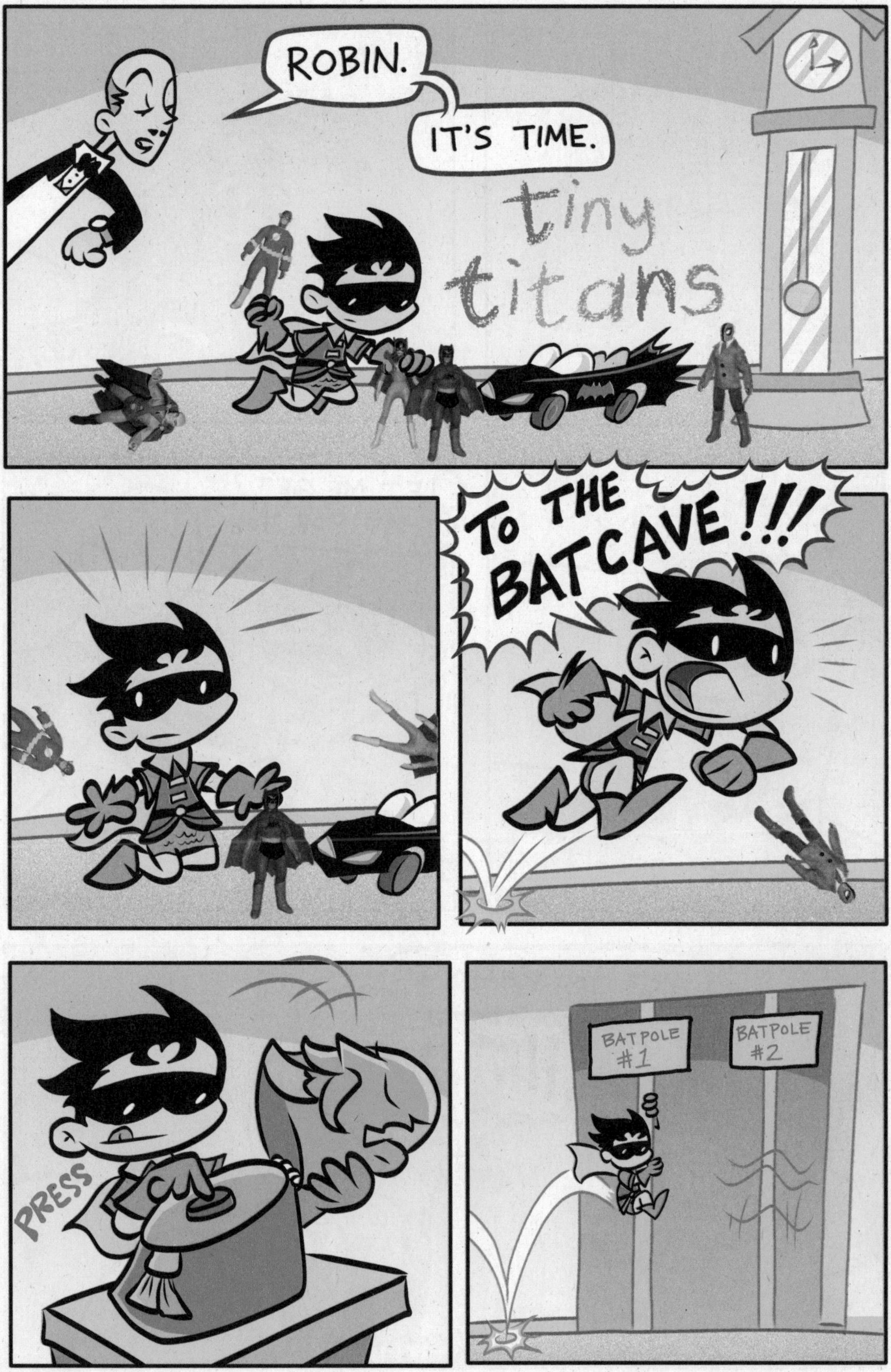
ROBIN.
IT'S TIME.
tiny titans
TO THE BATCAVE!!!
PRESS
BATPOLE #1
BATPOLE #2

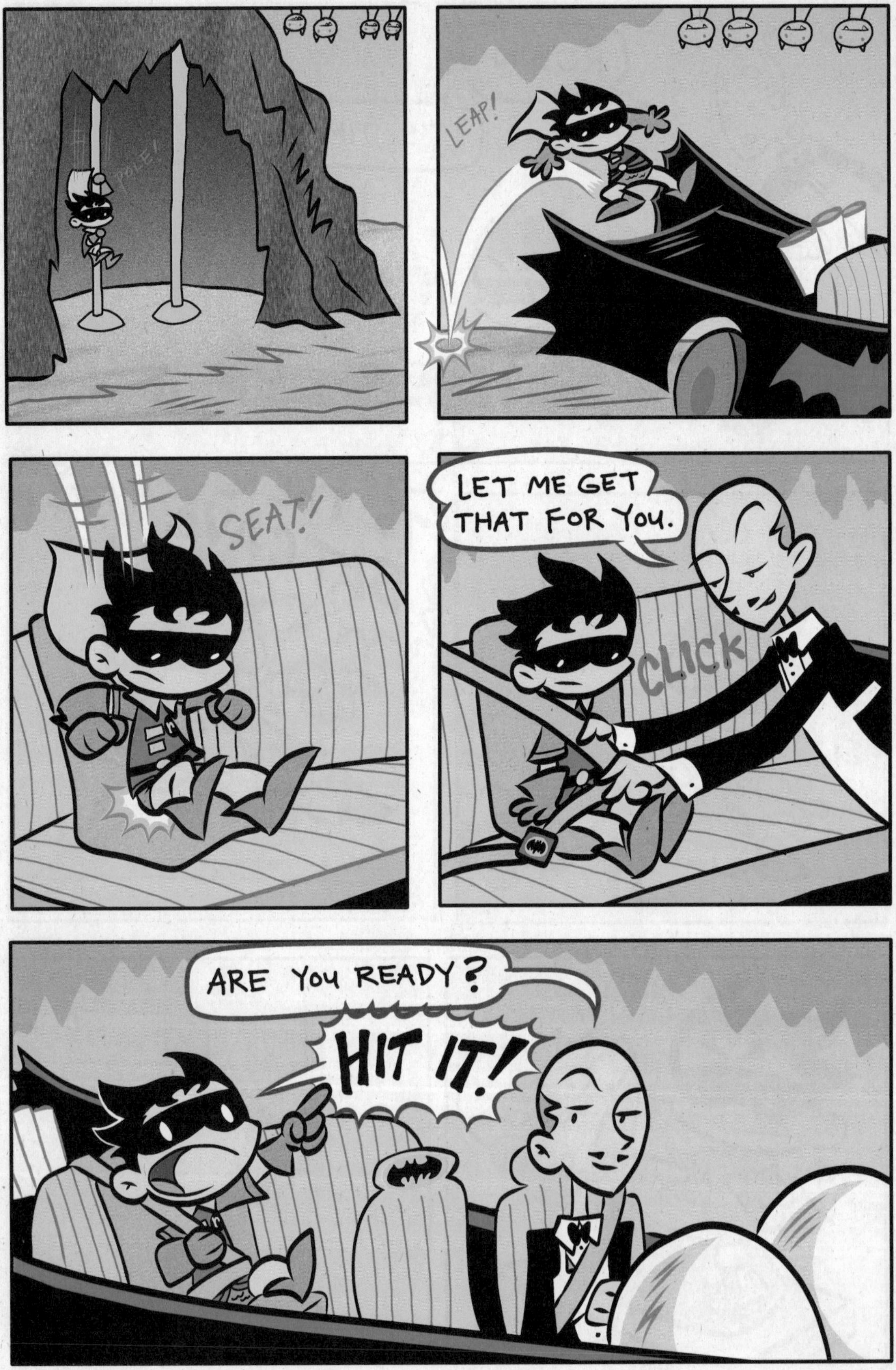
POLE!
LEAP!
SEAT!
LET ME GET THAT FOR YOU.
CLICK
ARE YOU READY?
HIT IT!

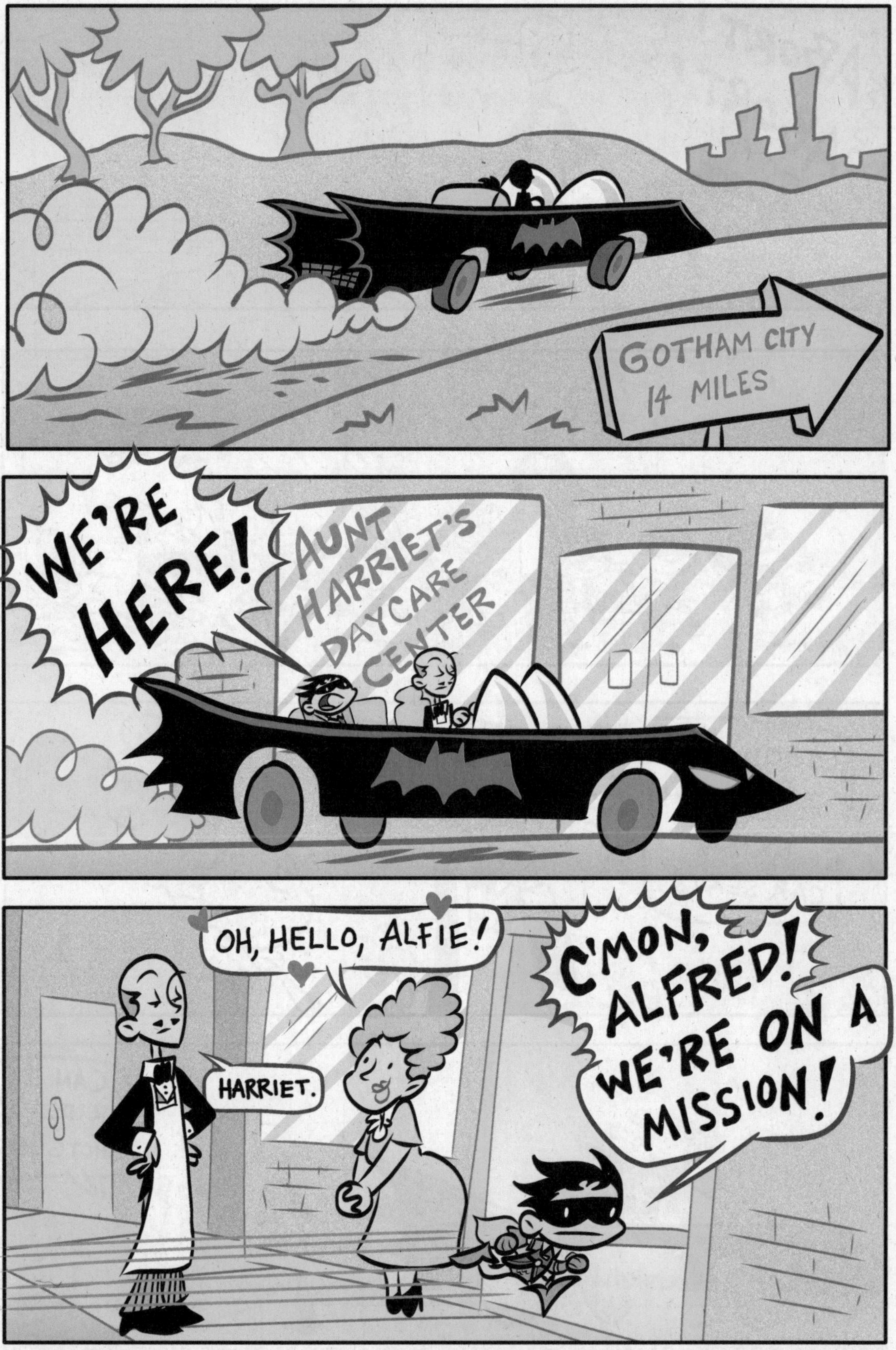
GOTHAM CITY
14 MILES
WE'RE HERE!
AUNT HARRIET'S DAYCARE CENTER
OH, HELLO, ALFIE!
HARRIET.
C'MON, ALFRED! WE'RE ON A MISSION!

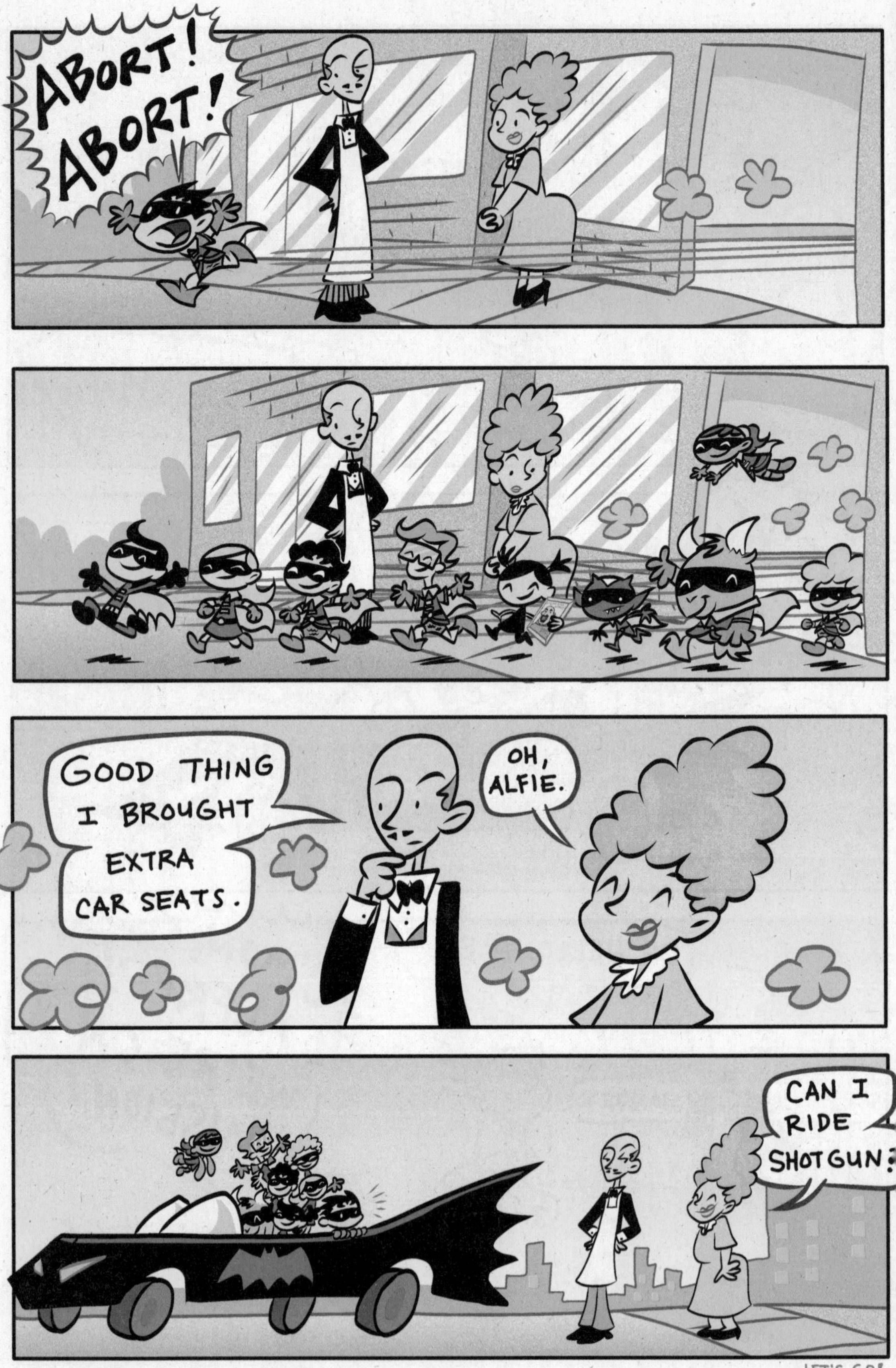
ABORT! ABORT!
GOOD THING I BROUGHT EXTRA CAR SEATS.
OH, ALFIE.
CAN I RIDE SHOTGUN?

-LET'S GO!

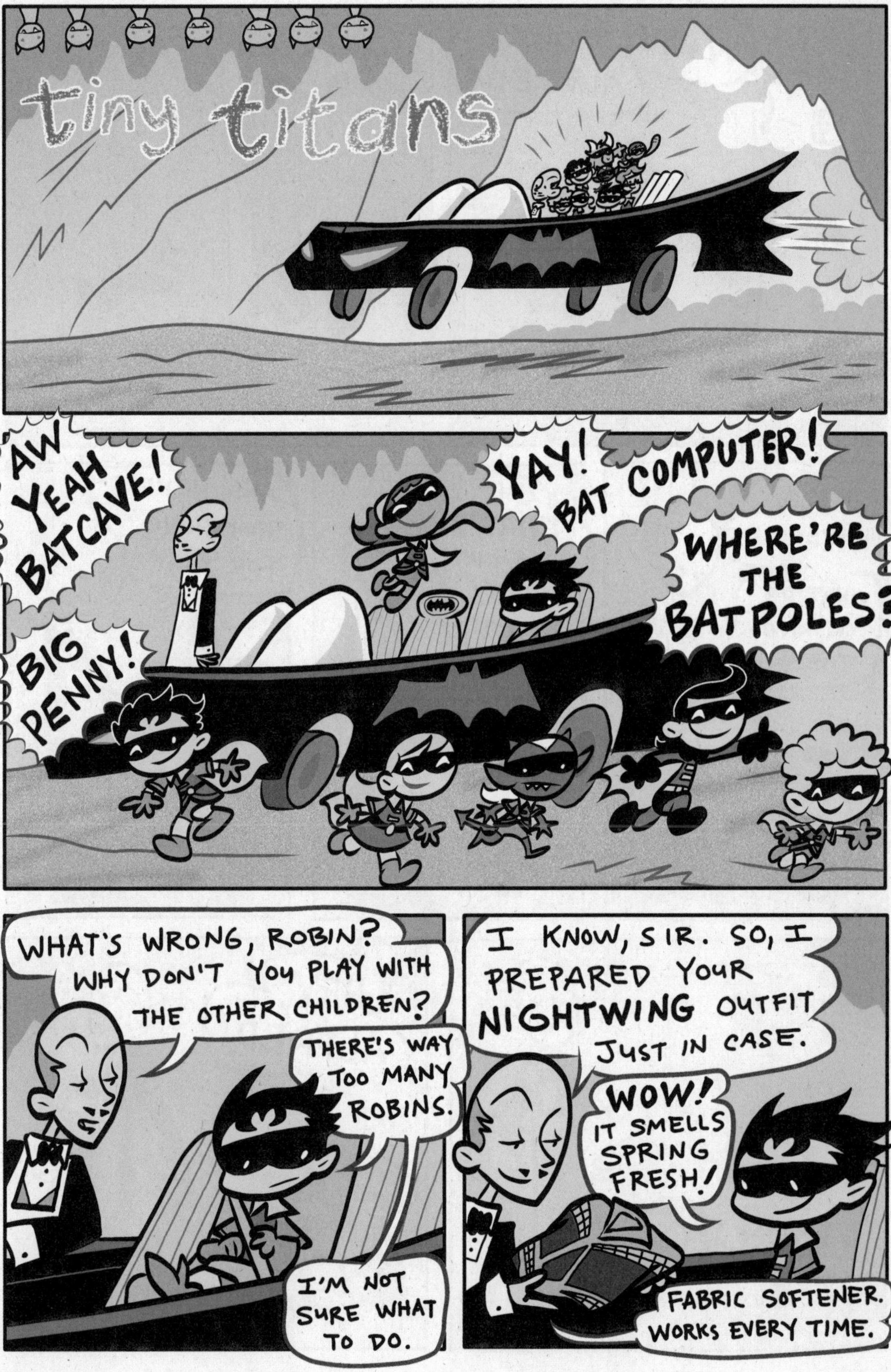
tiny titans
AW YEAH BATCAVE!
YAY!
BAT COMPUTER!
WHERE'RE THE BATPOLES?
BIG PENNY!
WHAT'S WRONG, ROBIN? WHY DON'T YOU PLAY WITH THE OTHER CHILDREN?
THERE'S WAY TOO MANY ROBINS.
I'M NOT SURE WHAT TO DO.
I KNOW, SIR. SO, I PREPARED YOUR NIGHTWING OUTFIT JUST IN CASE.
WOW! IT SMELLS SPRING FRESH!
FABRIC SOFTENER. WORKS EVERY TIME.

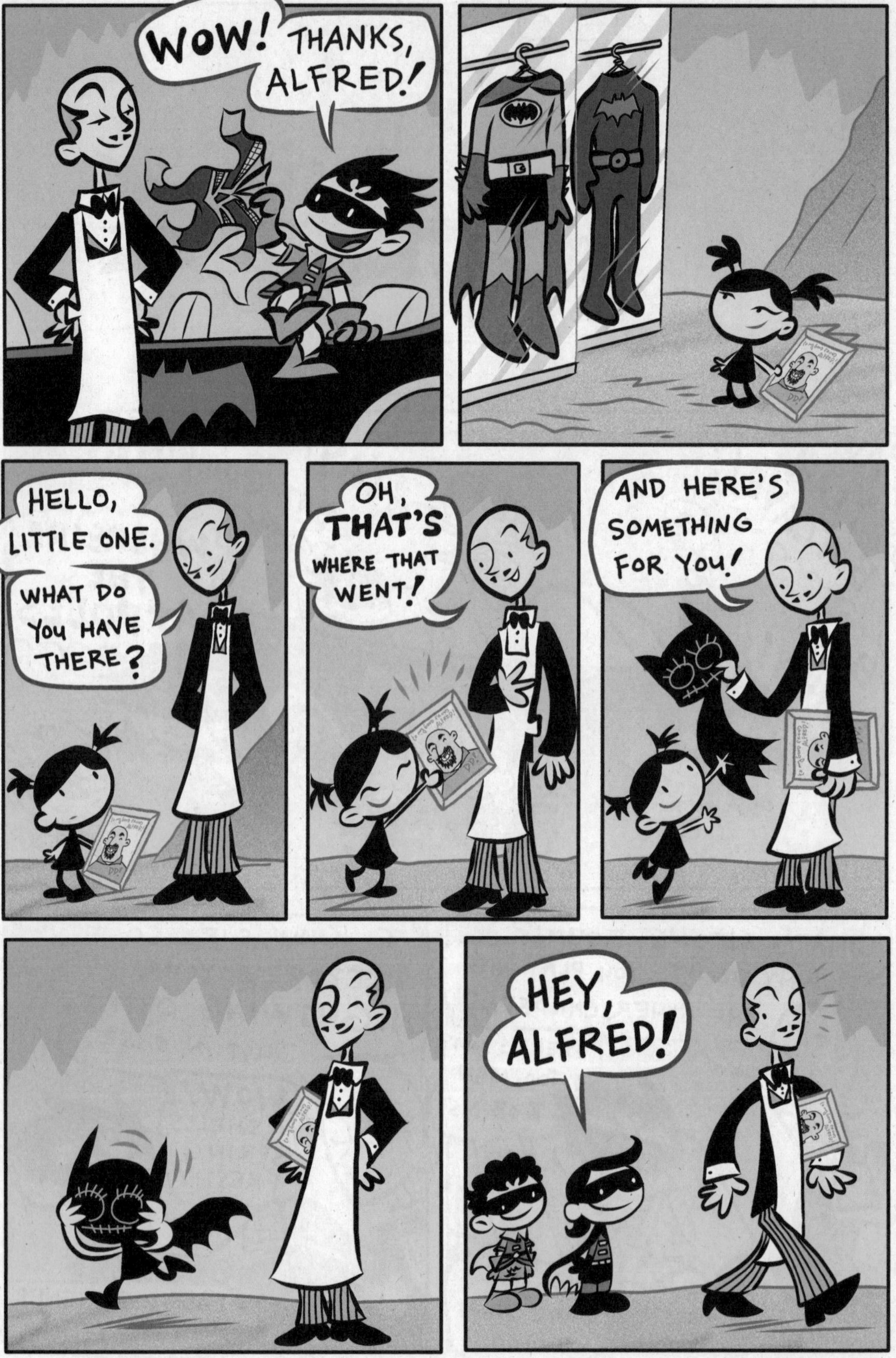
WOW! THANKS, ALFRED!
HELLO, LITTLE ONE.
WHAT DO YOU HAVE THERE?
OH, THAT'S WHERE THAT WENT!
AND HERE'S SOMETHING FOR YOU!
HEY, ALFRED!

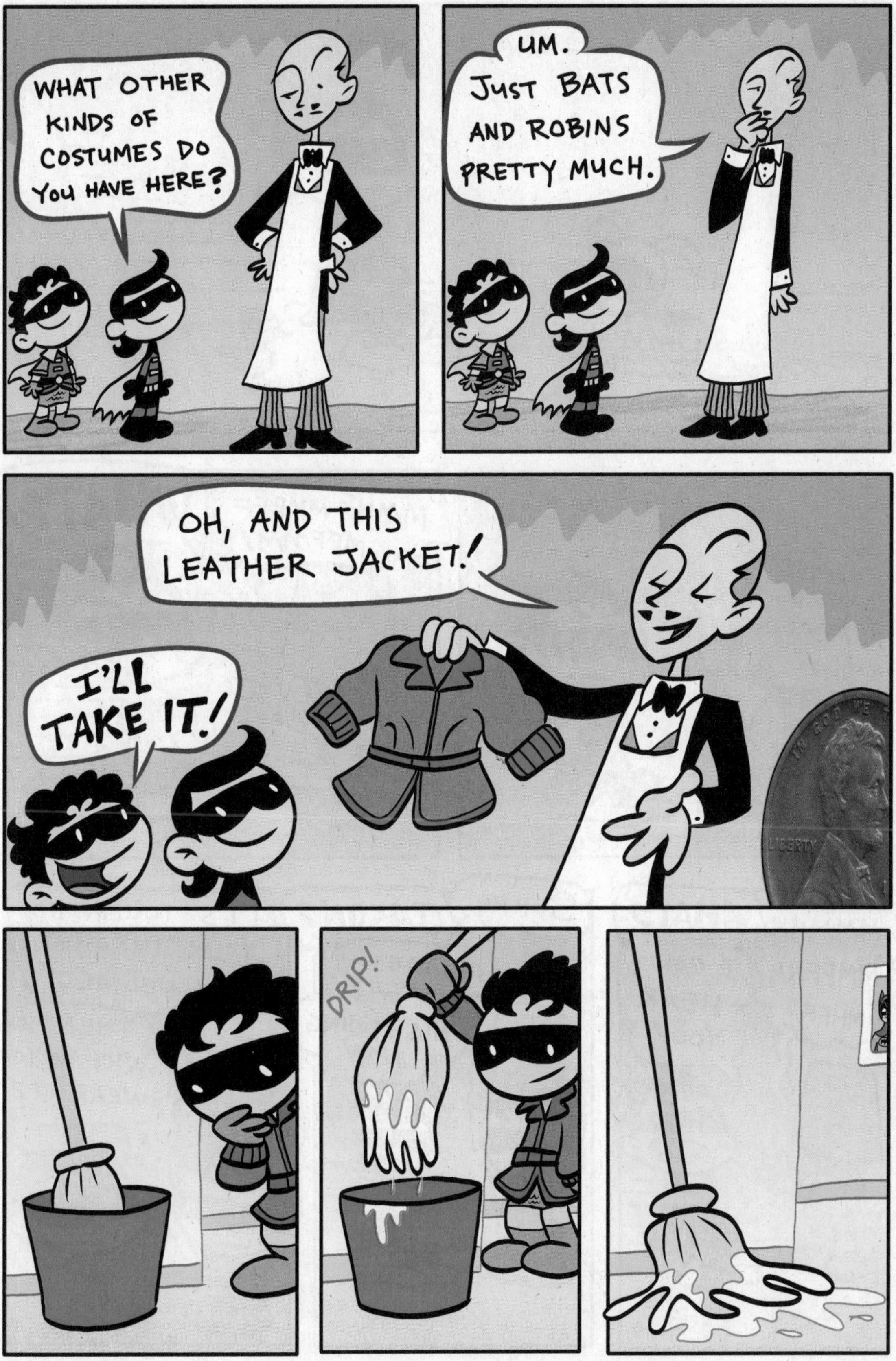
WHAT OTHER KINDS OF COSTUMES DO YOU HAVE HERE?
UM. JUST BATS AND ROBINS PRETTY MUCH.
OH, AND THIS LEATHER JACKET!
I'LL TAKE IT!
IN GOD WE
LIBERTY
DRIP!

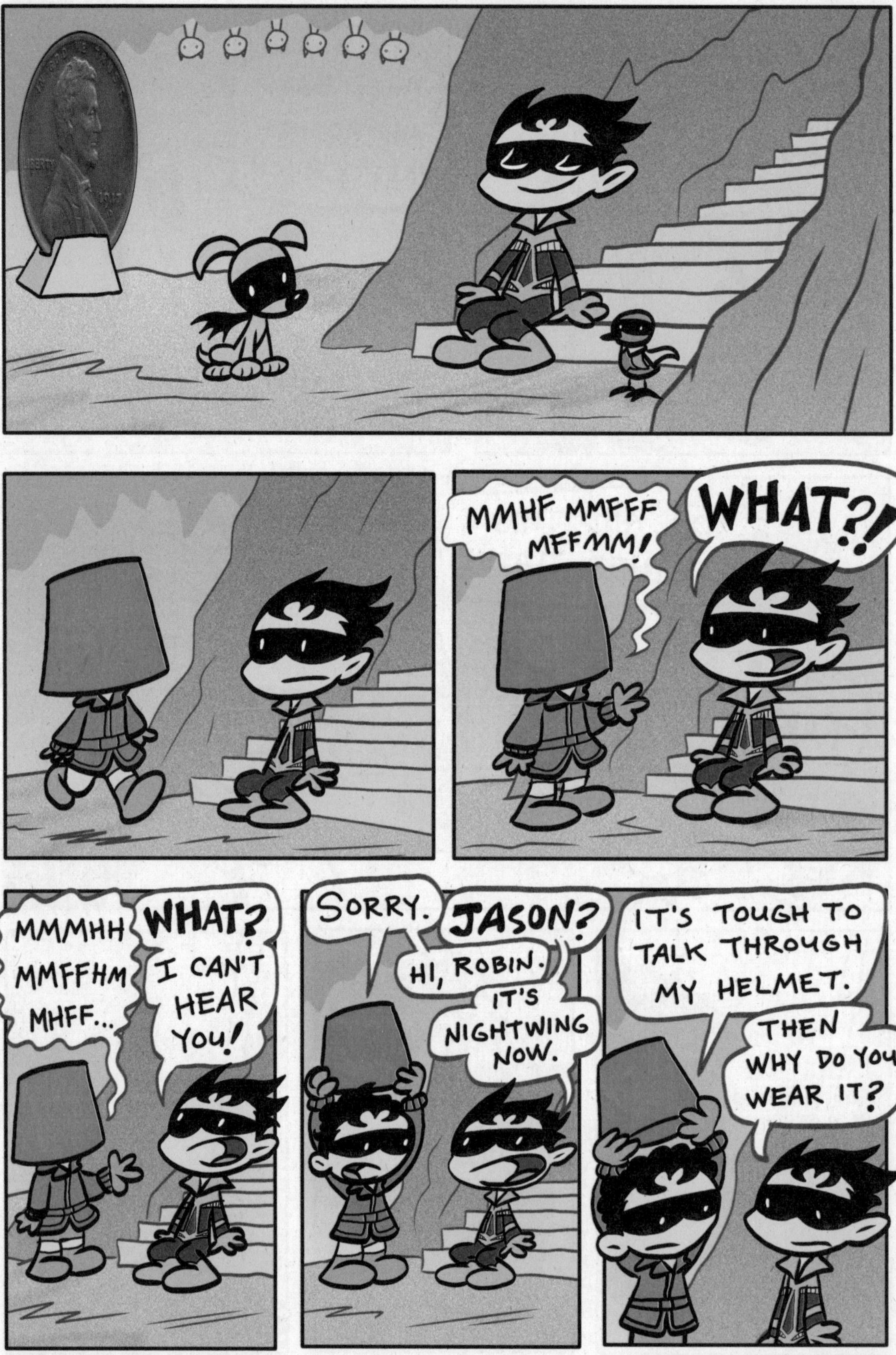
MMHF MMFFF MFFMM!
WHAT?!
MMMHH MMFFHM MHFF...
WHAT? I CAN'T HEAR YOU!
SORRY.
JASON?
HI, ROBIN.
IT'S NIGHTWING NOW.
IT'S TOUGH TO TALK THROUGH MY HELMET.
THEN WHY DO YOU WEAR IT?

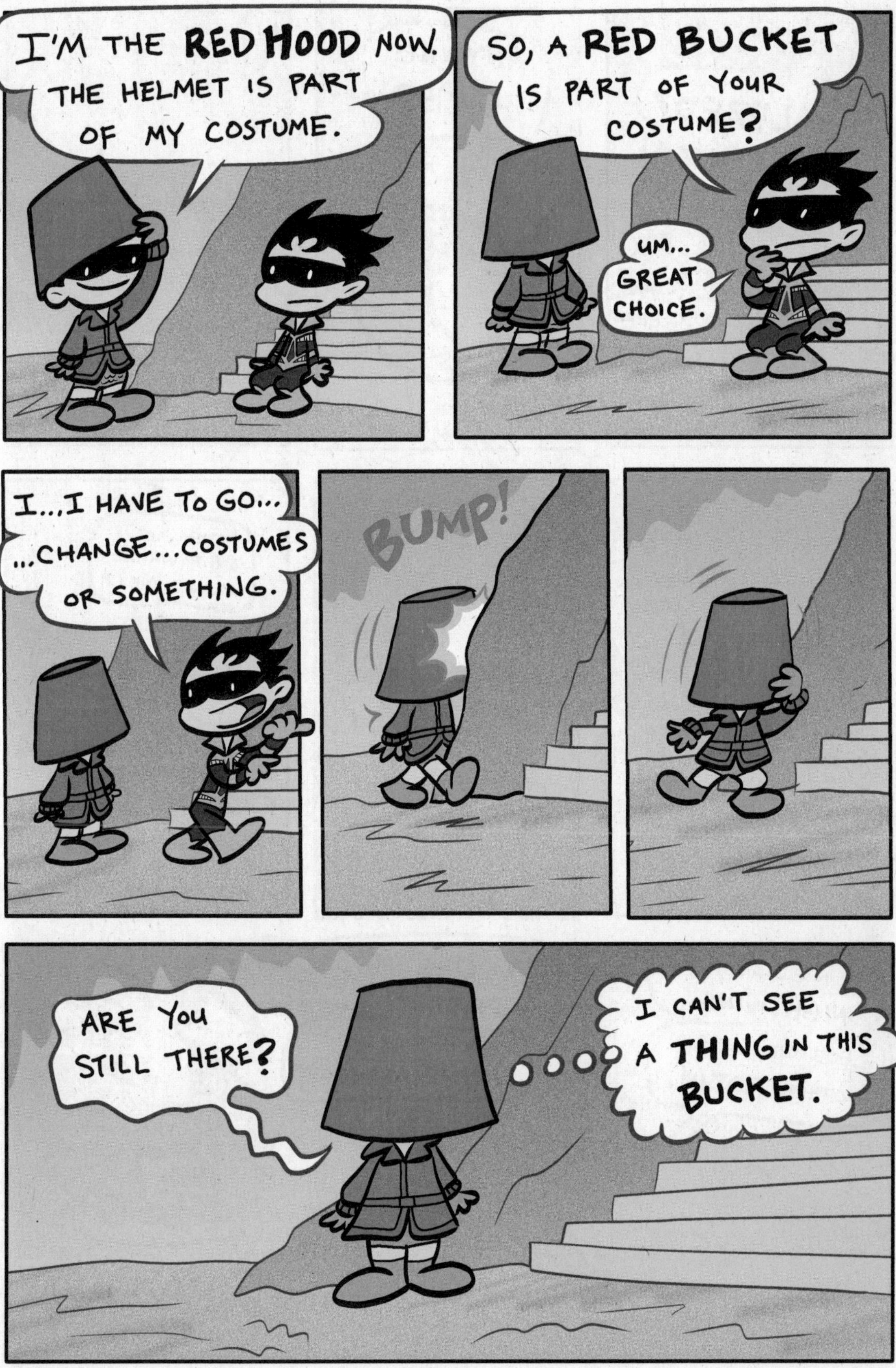
I'M THE RED HOOD NOW. THE HELMET IS PART OF MY COSTUME.
SO, A RED BUCKET IS PART OF YOUR COSTUME?
UM... GREAT CHOICE.
I...I HAVE TO GO... ...CHANGE...COSTUMES OR SOMETHING.
BUMP!
ARE YOU STILL THERE?
I CAN'T SEE A THING IN THIS BUCKET.

—MOP & GLOW.

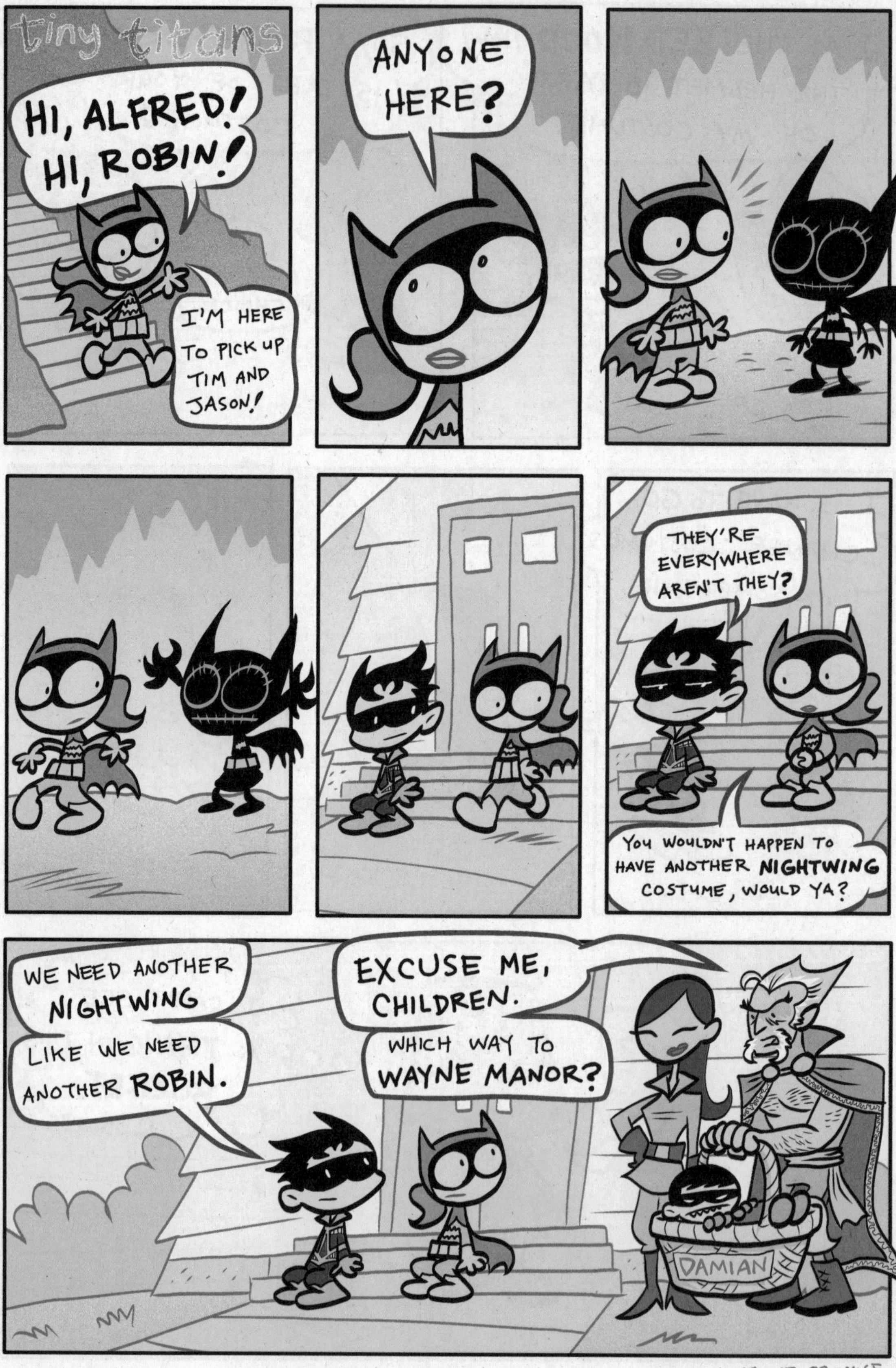
tiny titans
HI, ALFRED! HI, ROBIN!
I'M HERE TO PICK UP TIM AND JASON!
ANYONE HERE?
THEY'RE EVERYWHERE AREN'T THEY?
YOU WOULDN'T HAPPEN TO HAVE ANOTHER NIGHTWING COSTUME, WOULD YA?
WE NEED ANOTHER NIGHTWING
LIKE WE NEED ANOTHER ROBIN.
EXCUSE ME, CHILDREN.
WHICH WAY TO WAYNE MANOR?
DAMIAN

—LAST ONE. PROMISE.

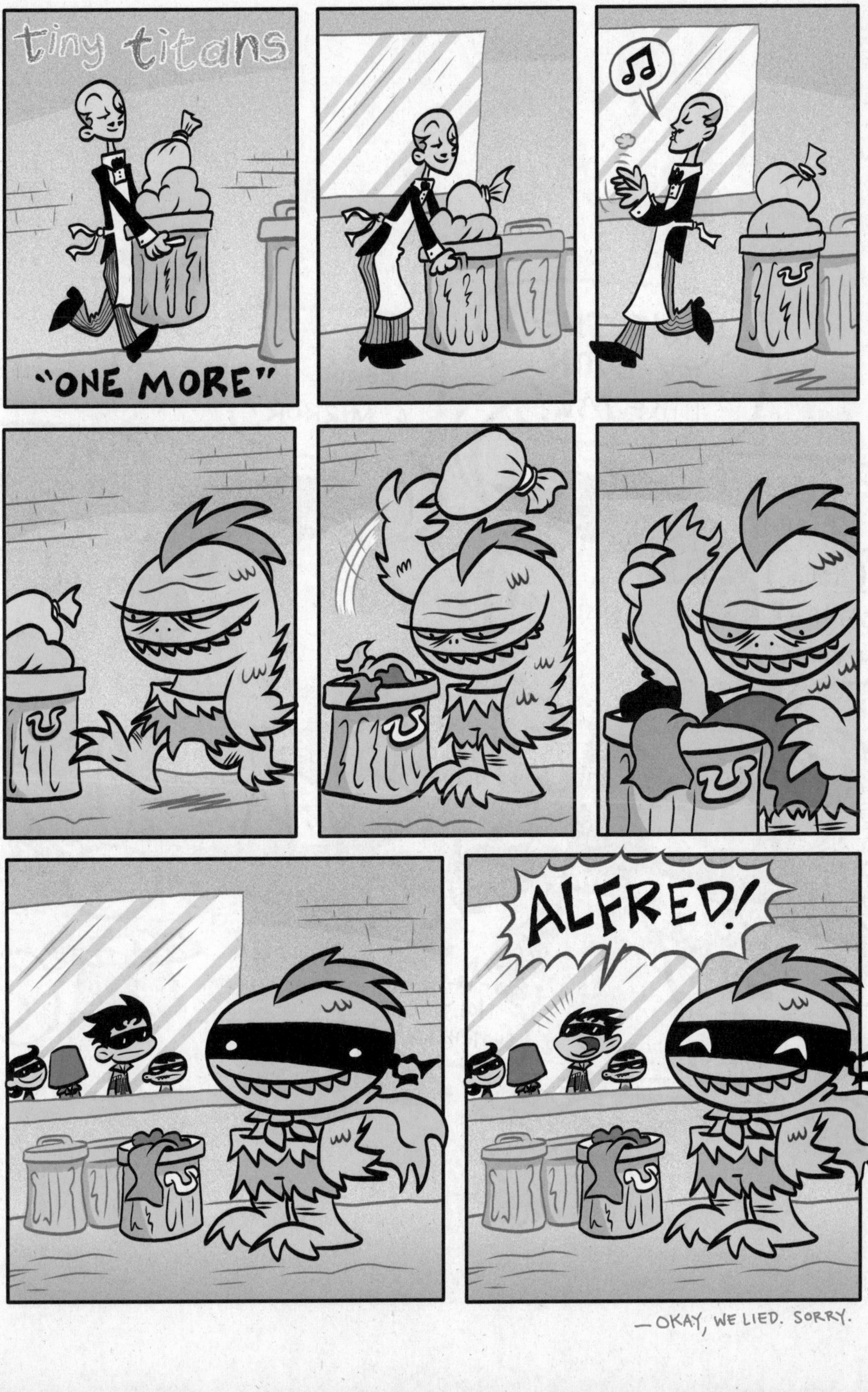
tiny titans
"ONE MORE"
ALFRED!
— OKAY, WE LIED. SORRY.

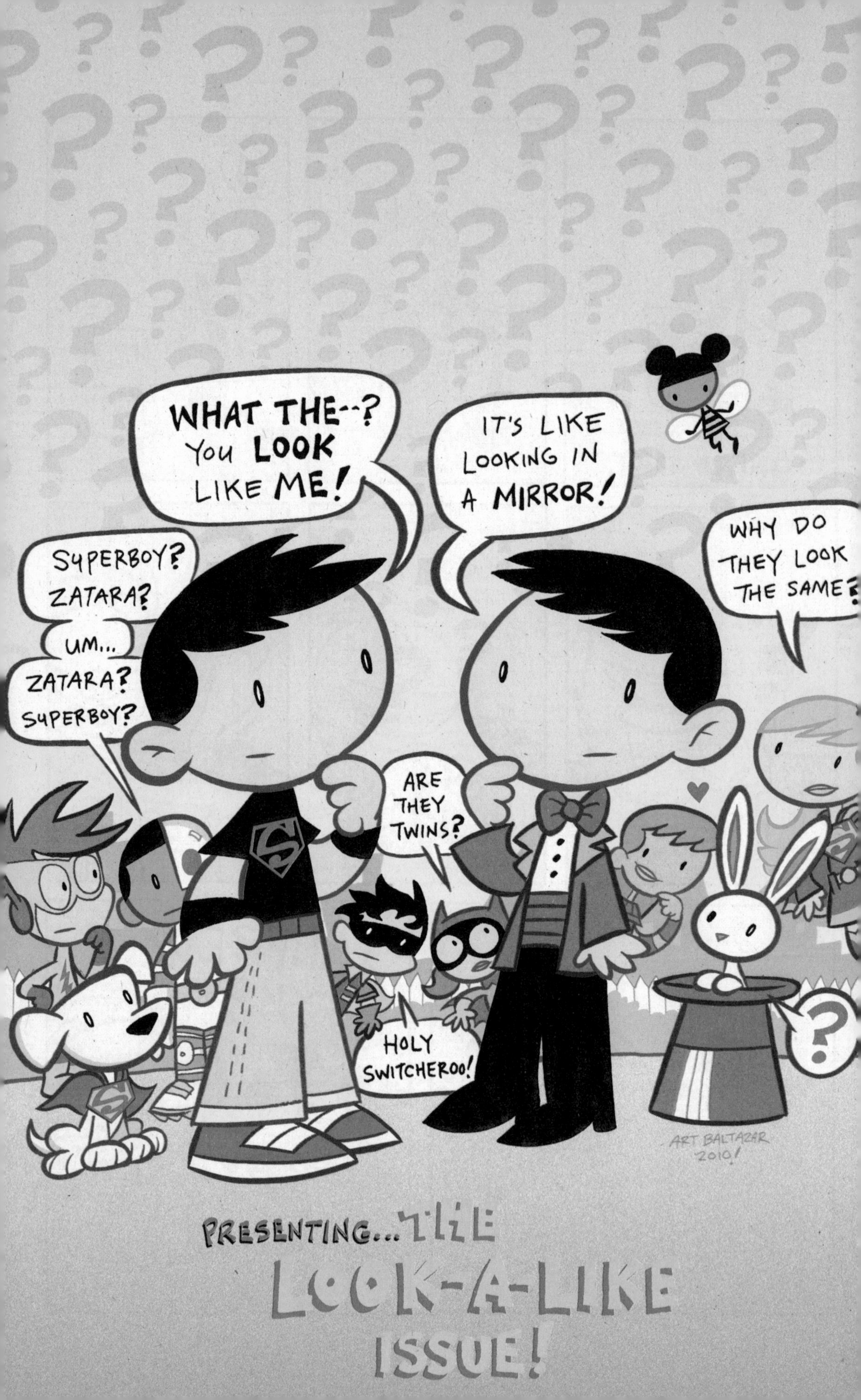

WHAT THE--? YOU LOOK LIKE ME!
IT'S LIKE LOOKING IN A MIRROR!
SUPERBOY? ZATARA?
UM...
ZATARA? SUPERBOY?
WHY DO THEY LOOK THE SAME?
ARE THEY TWINS?
HOLY SWITCHEROO!
?
ART BALTAZAR 2010!
PRESENTING... THE LOOK-A-LIKE ISSUE!

tiny titans

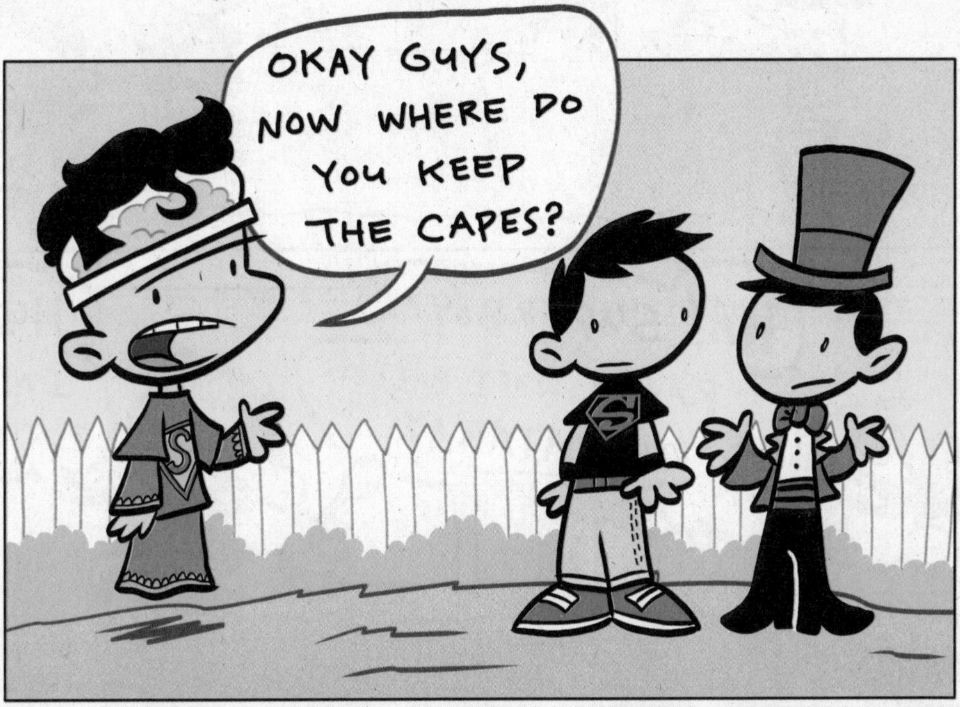
OKAY GUYS, NOW WHERE DO YOU KEEP THE CAPES?

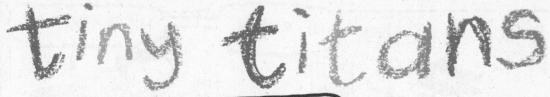

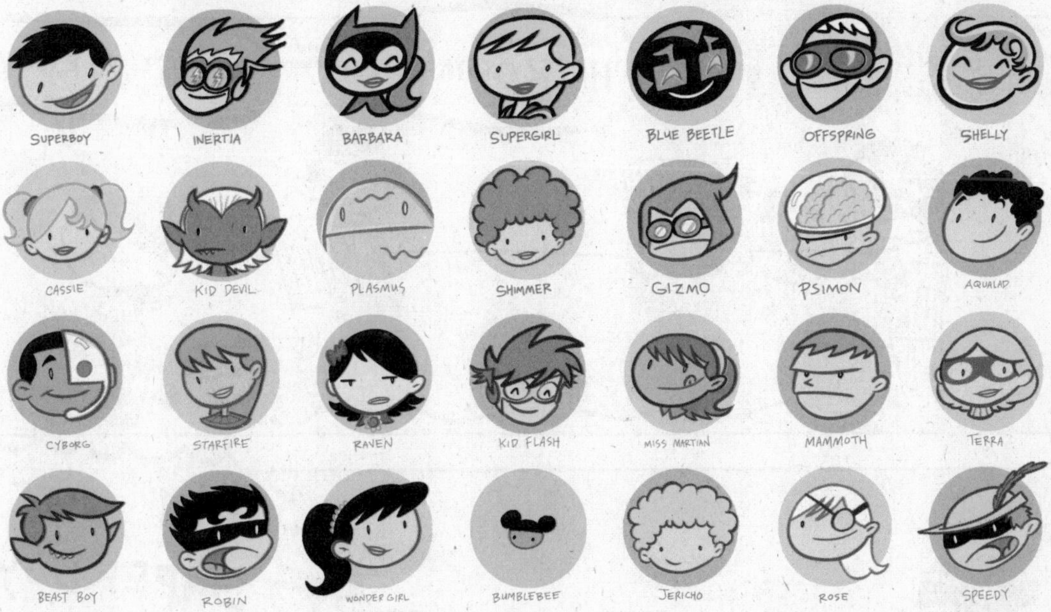
SUPERBOY
INERTIA
BARBARA
SUPERGIRL
BLUE BEETLE
OFFSPRING
SHELLY
CASSIE
KID DEVIL
PLASMUS
SHIMMER
GIZMO
PSIMON
AQUALAD
CYBORG
STARFIRE
RAVEN
KID FLASH
MISS MARTIAN
MAMMOTH
TERRA
BEAST BOY
ROBIN
WONDER GIRL
BUMBLEBEE
JERICHO
ROSE
SPEEDY

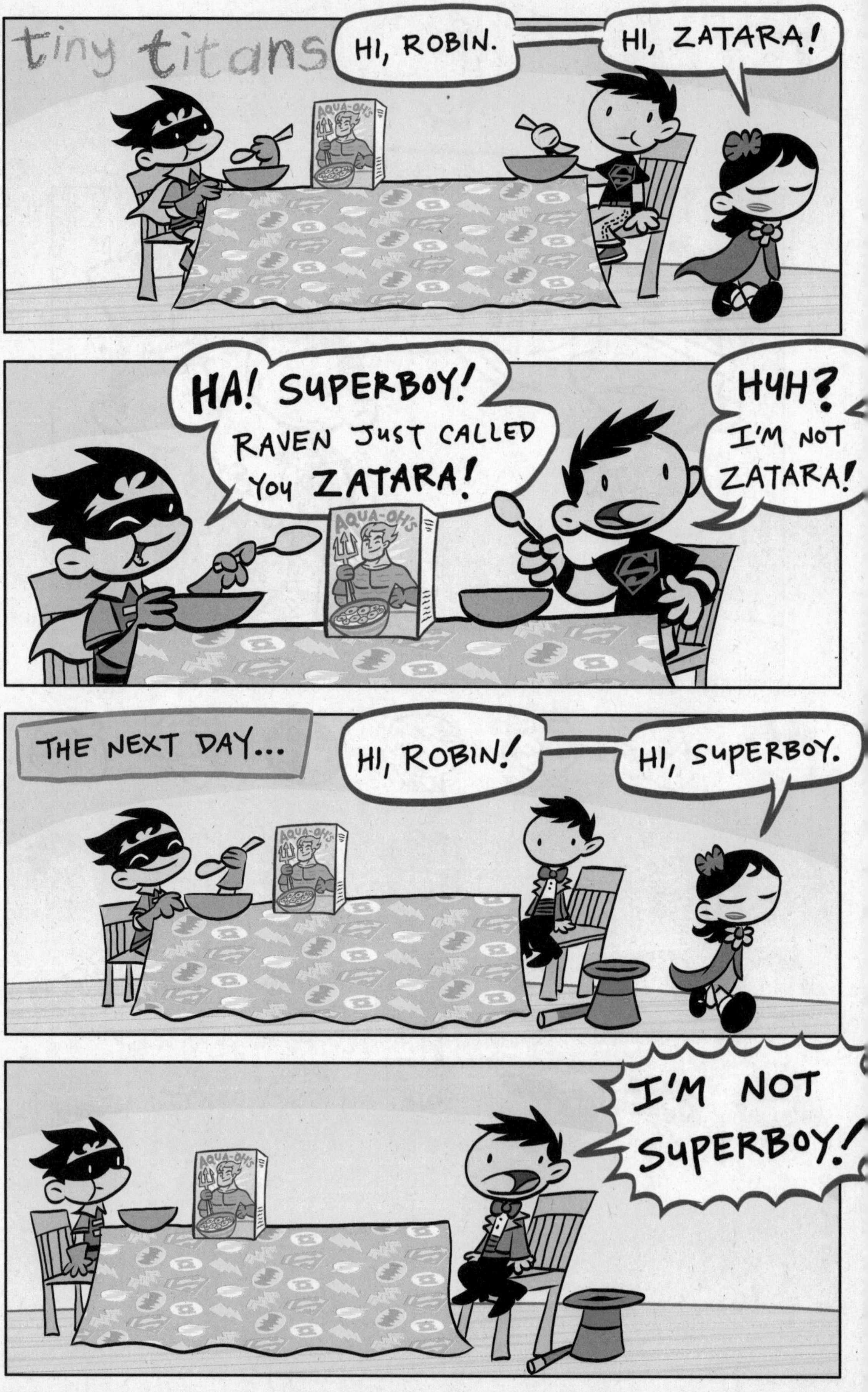
tiny titans
HI, ROBIN.
HI, ZATARA!
HA! SUPERBOY! RAVEN JUST CALLED YOU ZATARA!
HUH? I'M NOT ZATARA!
AQUA-OH'S
THE NEXT DAY...
HI, ROBIN!
HI, SUPERBOY.
I'M NOT SUPERBOY!

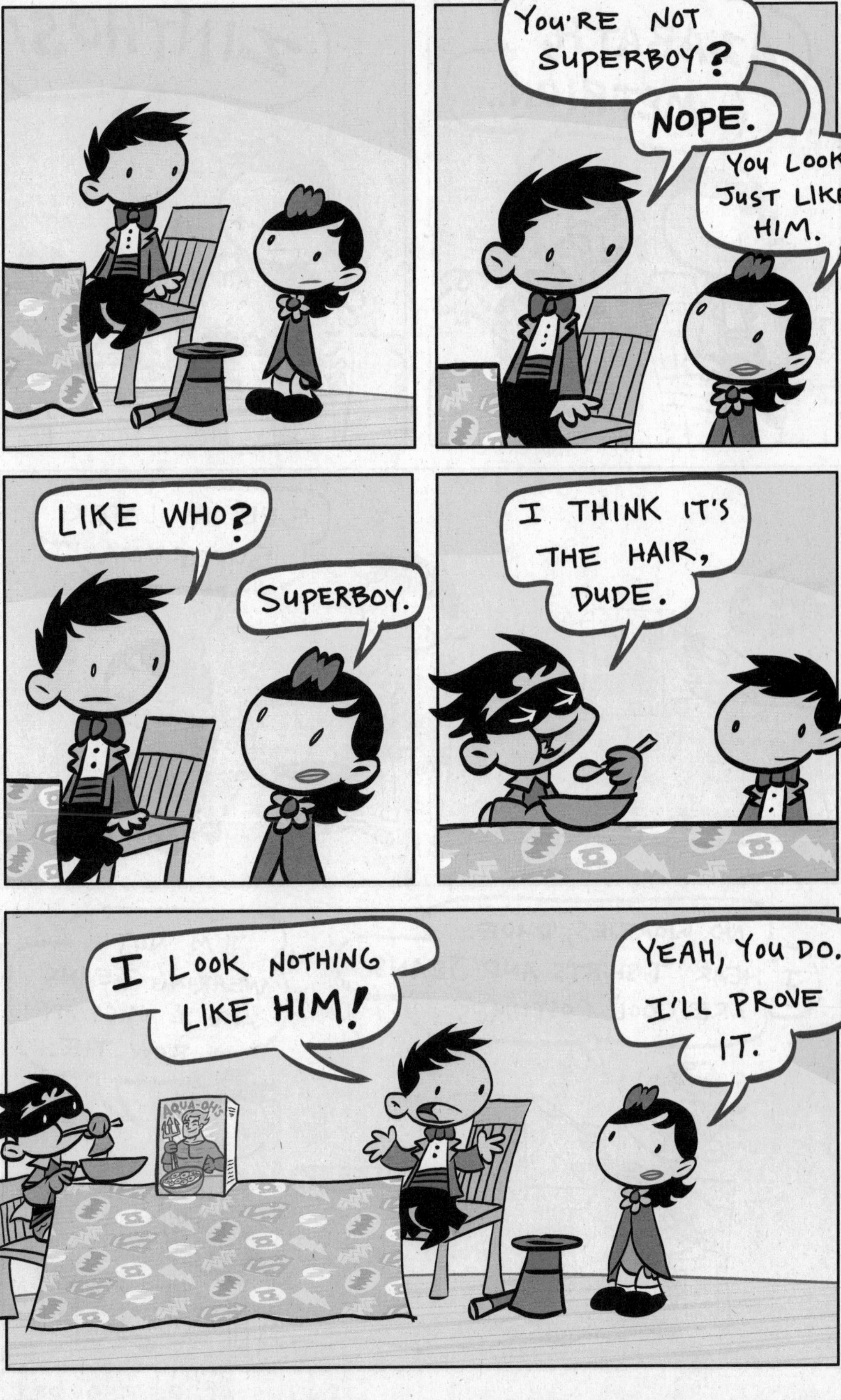

YOU'RE NOT SUPERBOY?
NOPE.
YOU LOOK JUST LIKE HIM.
LIKE WHO?
SUPERBOY.
I THINK IT'S THE HAIR, DUDE.
I LOOK NOTHING LIKE HIM!
YEAH, YOU DO. I'LL PROVE IT.
AQUA-OH'S

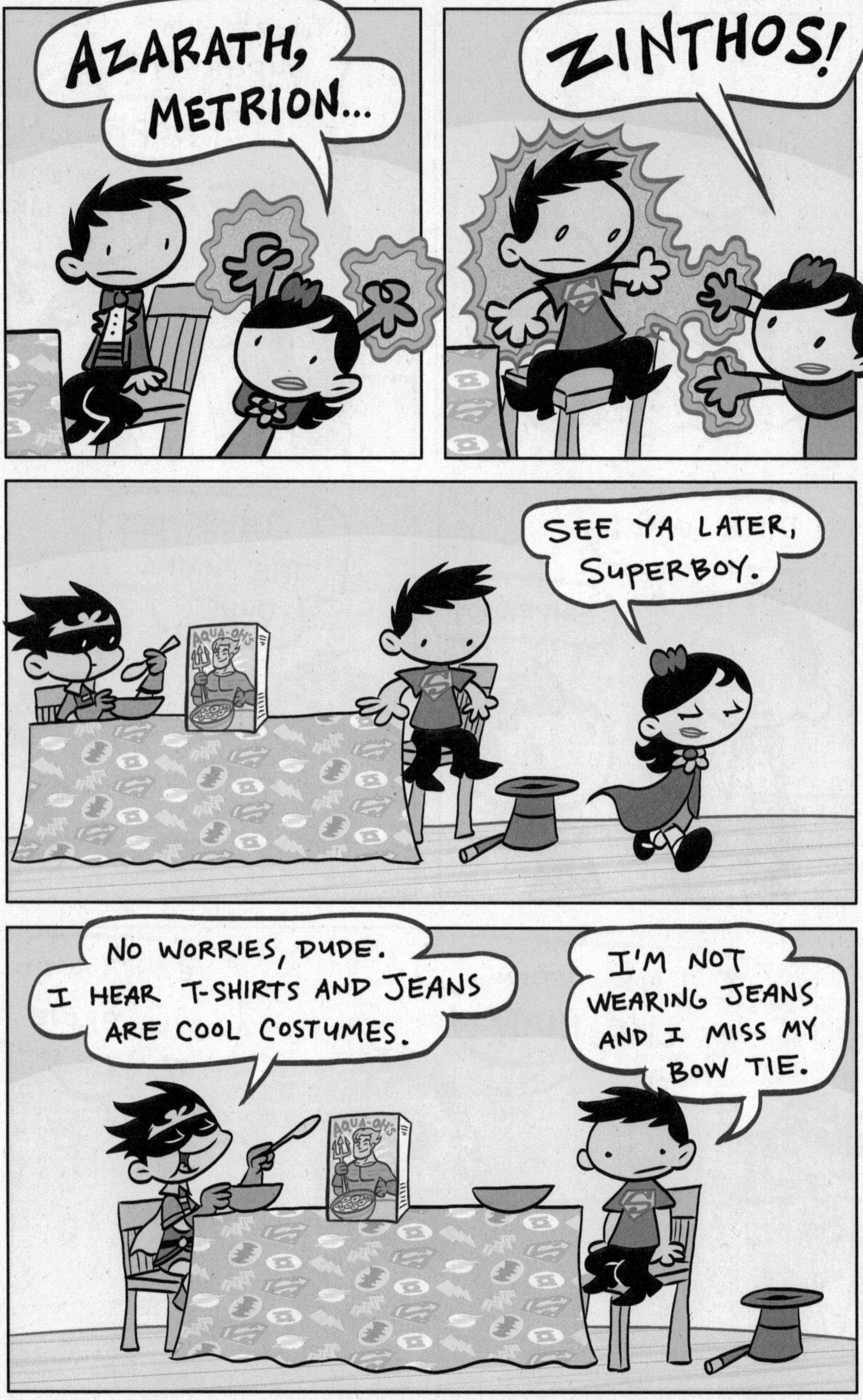
AZARATH, METRION...
ZINTHOS!
SEE YA LATER, SUPERBOY.
AQUA-OH'S
NO WORRIES, DUDE. I HEAR T-SHIRTS AND JEANS ARE COOL COSTUMES.
I'M NOT WEARING JEANS AND I MISS MY BOW TIE.

—FORMAL ATTIRE REQUIRED.

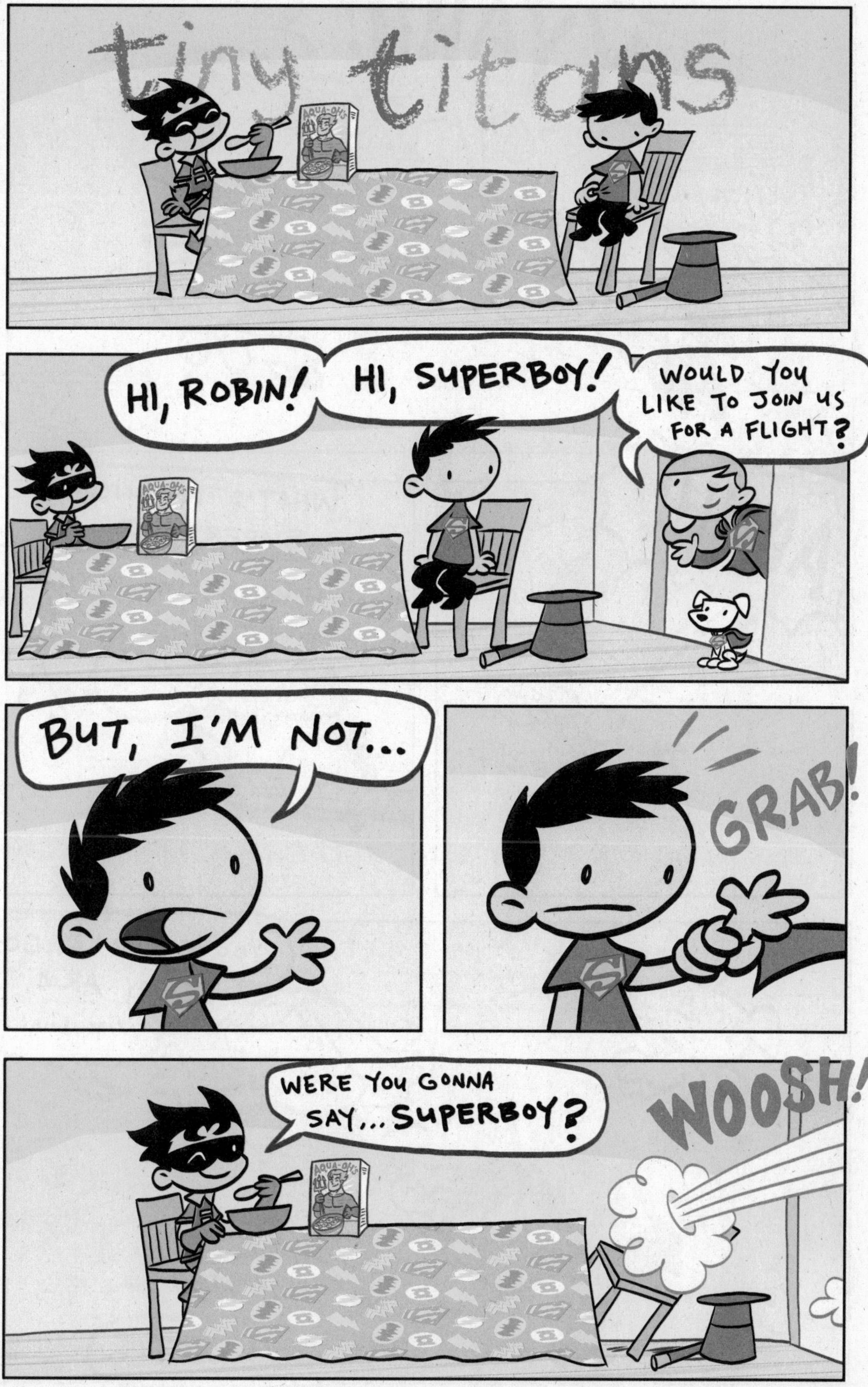
tiny titans
AQUA-OH'S
HI, ROBIN!
HI, SUPERBOY!
WOULD YOU LIKE TO JOIN US FOR A FLIGHT?
BUT, I'M NOT...
GRAB!
WERE YOU GONNA SAY... SUPERBOY?
WOOSH!

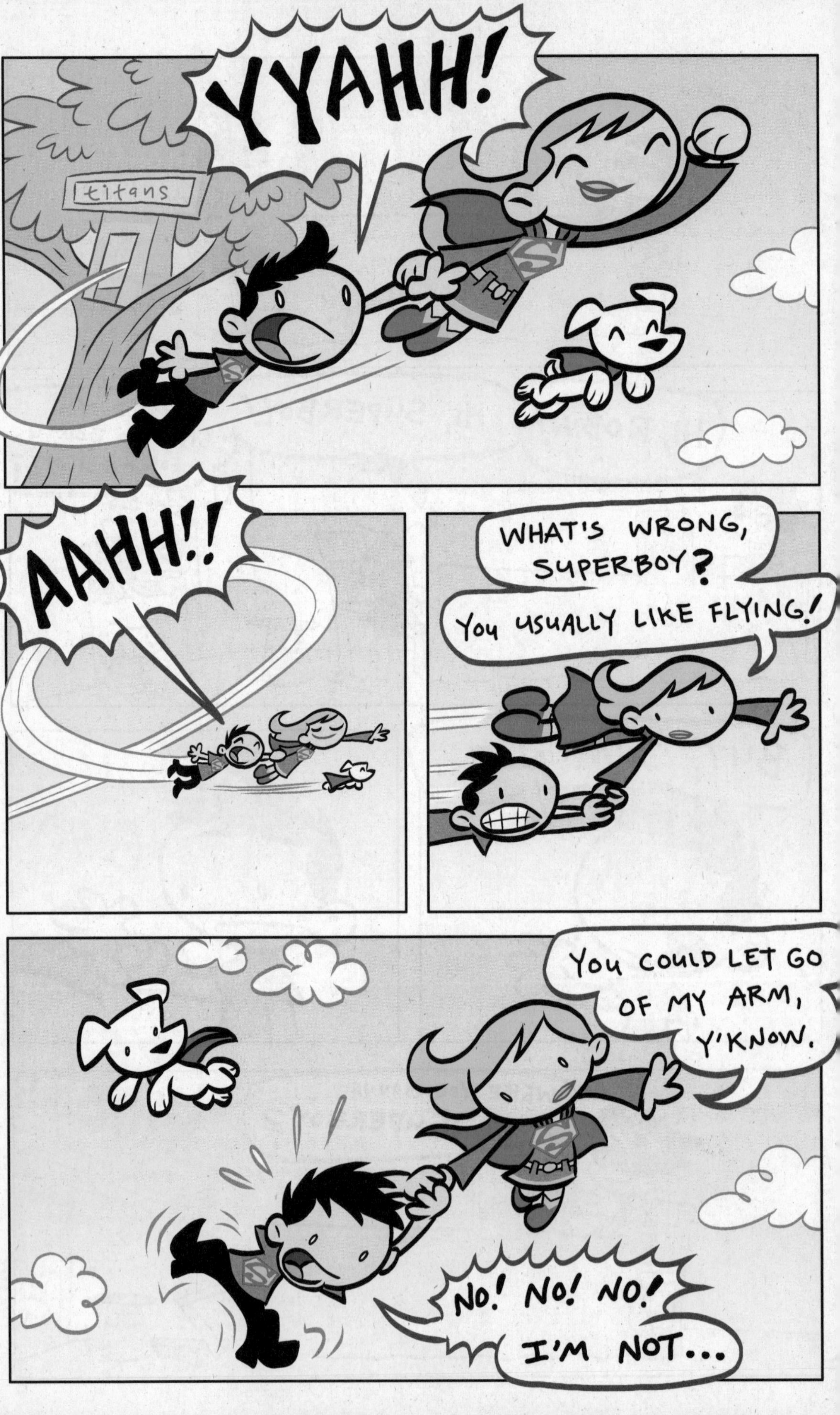

YYAHH!
titans
AAHH!!
WHAT'S WRONG, SUPERBOY?
YOU USUALLY LIKE FLYING!
YOU COULD LET GO OF MY ARM, Y'KNOW.
NO! NO! NO!
I'M NOT...

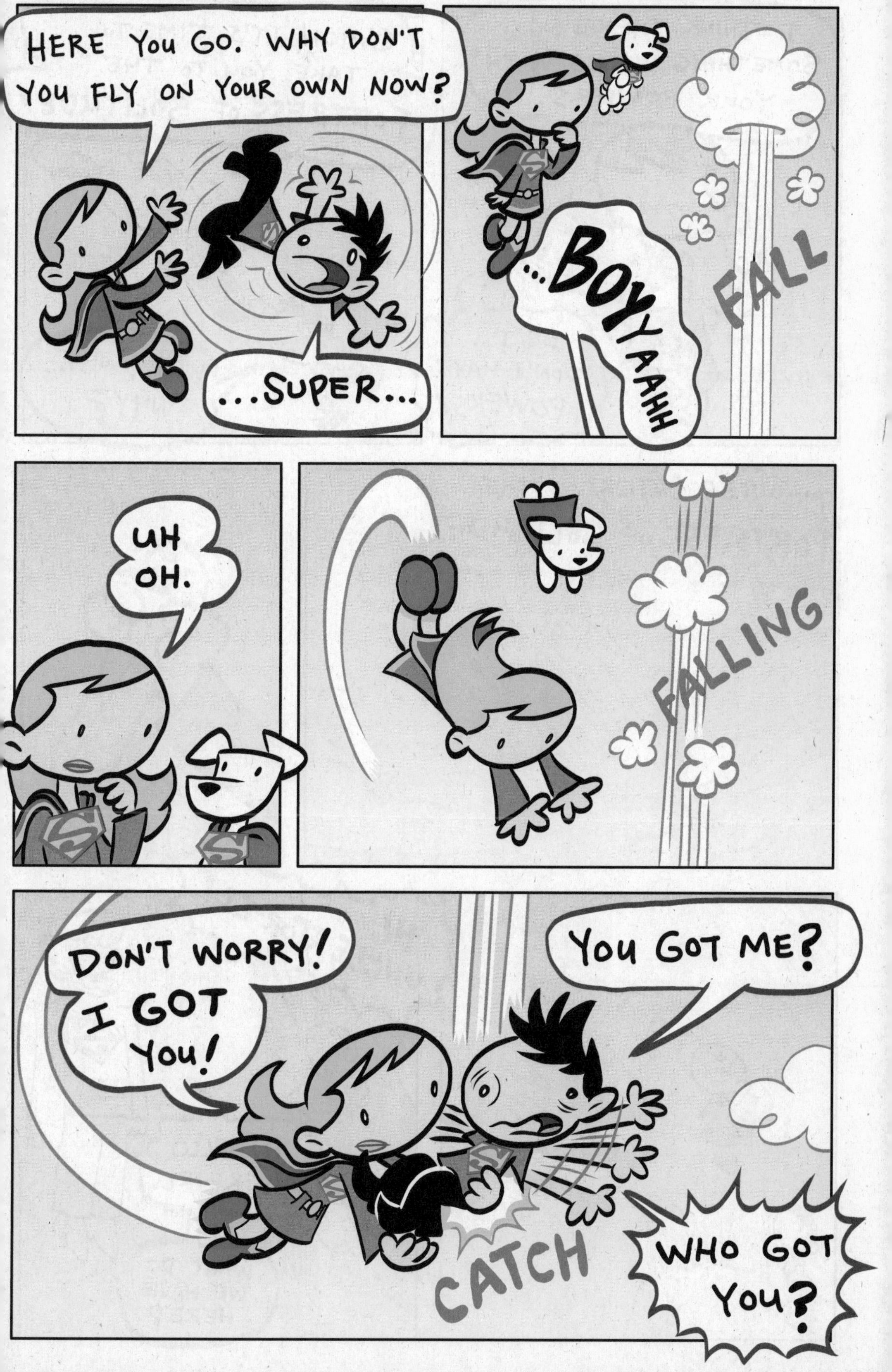

HERE YOU GO. WHY DON'T YOU FLY ON YOUR OWN NOW?
...SUPER...
...BOYYAAHH
FALL
UH OH.
FALLING
DON'T WORRY! I GOT YOU!
YOU GOT ME?
CATCH
WHO GOT YOU?

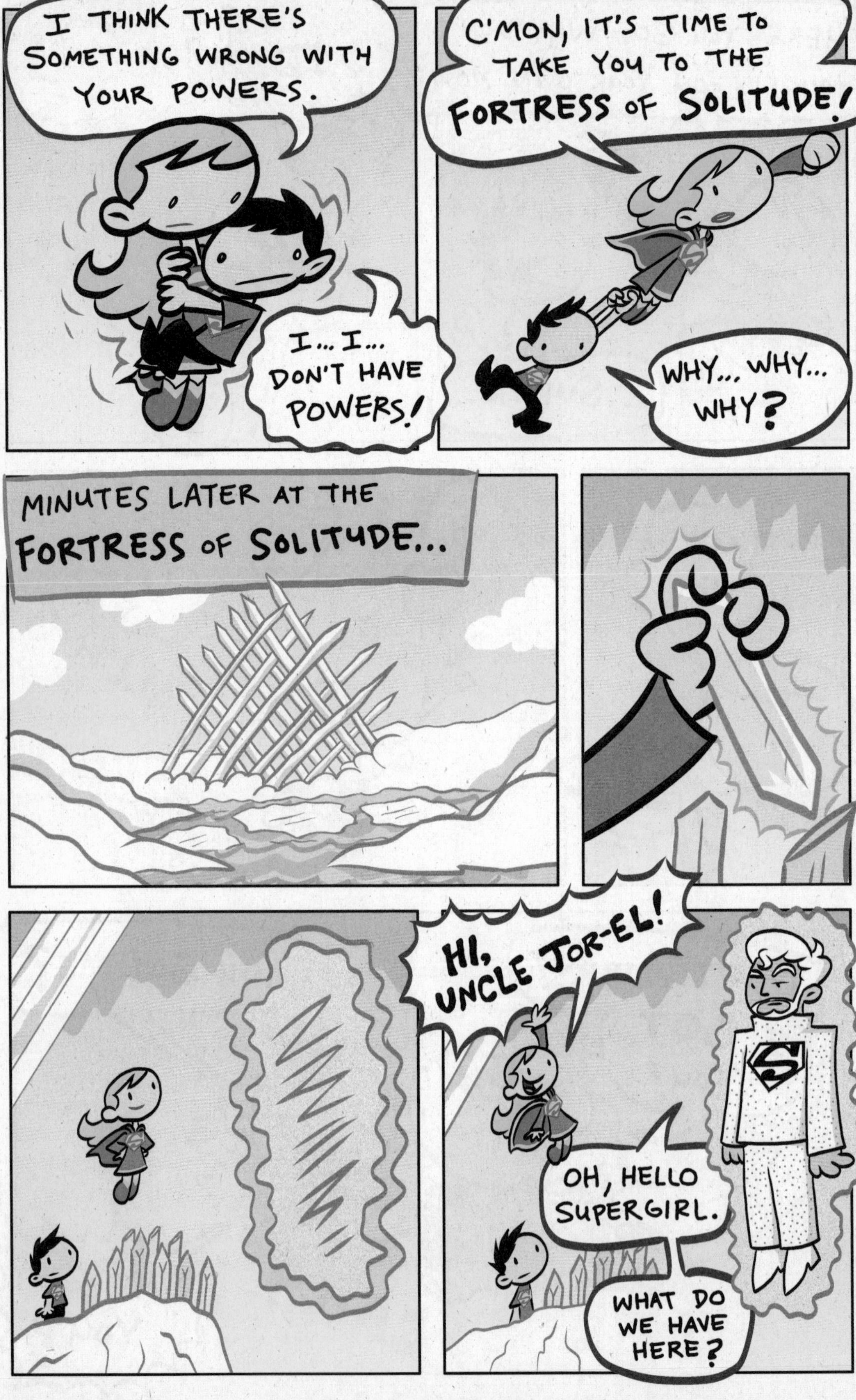
I THINK THERE'S SOMETHING WRONG WITH YOUR POWERS.
I... I... DON'T HAVE POWERS!
C'MON, IT'S TIME TO TAKE YOU TO THE FORTRESS OF SOLITUDE!
WHY... WHY... WHY?
MINUTES LATER AT THE FORTRESS OF SOLITUDE...
HI, UNCLE JOR-EL!
OH, HELLO SUPERGIRL.
WHAT DO WE HAVE HERE?

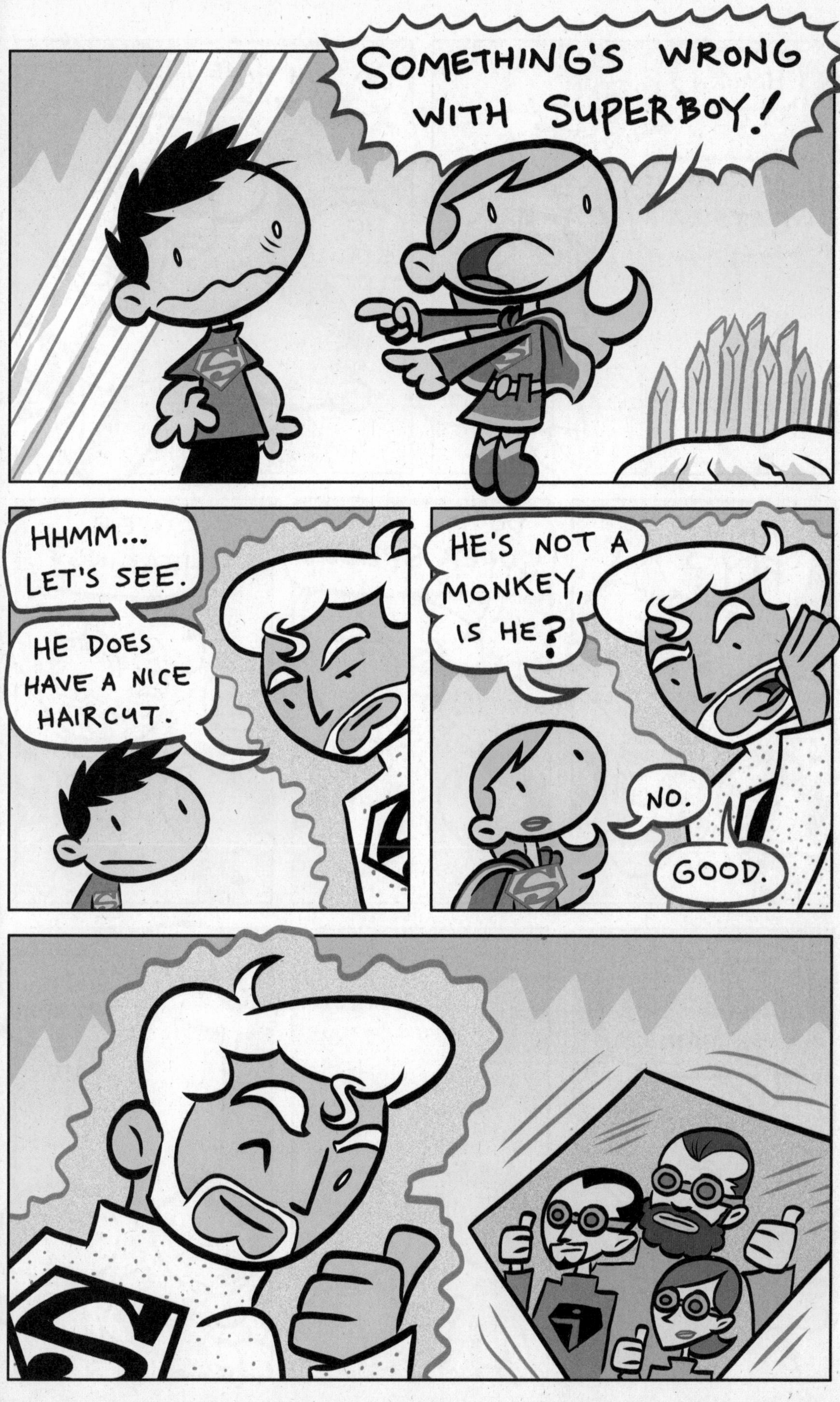
SOMETHING'S WRONG WITH SUPERBOY!
HHMM... LET'S SEE.
HE DOES HAVE A NICE HAIRCUT.
HE'S NOT A MONKEY, IS HE?
NO.
GOOD.

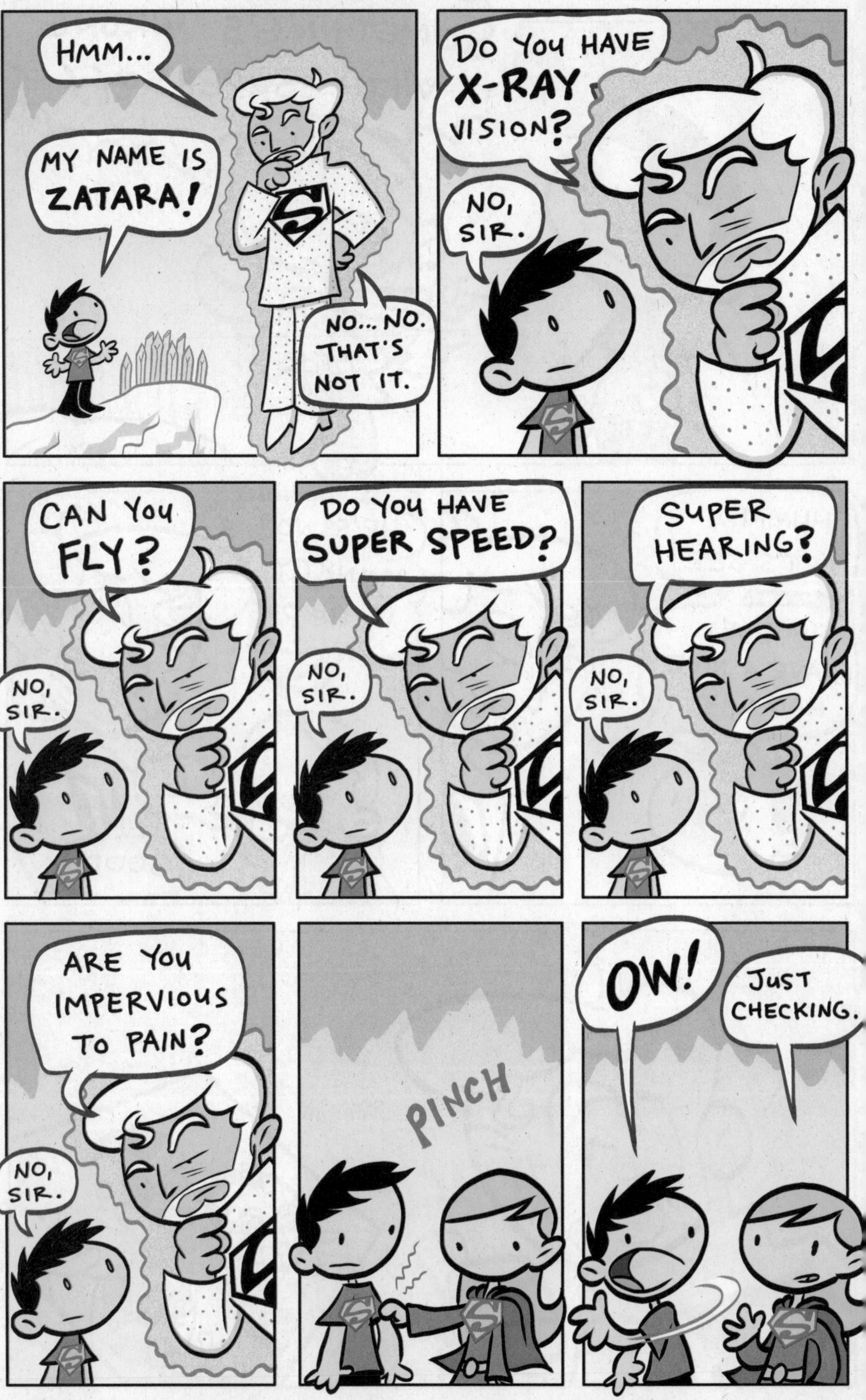
HMM...
MY NAME IS ZATARA!
NO... NO. THAT'S NOT IT.
DO YOU HAVE X-RAY VISION?
NO, SIR.
CAN YOU FLY?
NO, SIR.
DO YOU HAVE SUPER SPEED?
NO, SIR.
SUPER HEARING?
NO, SIR.
ARE YOU IMPERVIOUS TO PAIN?
NO, SIR.
PINCH
OW!
JUST CHECKING.

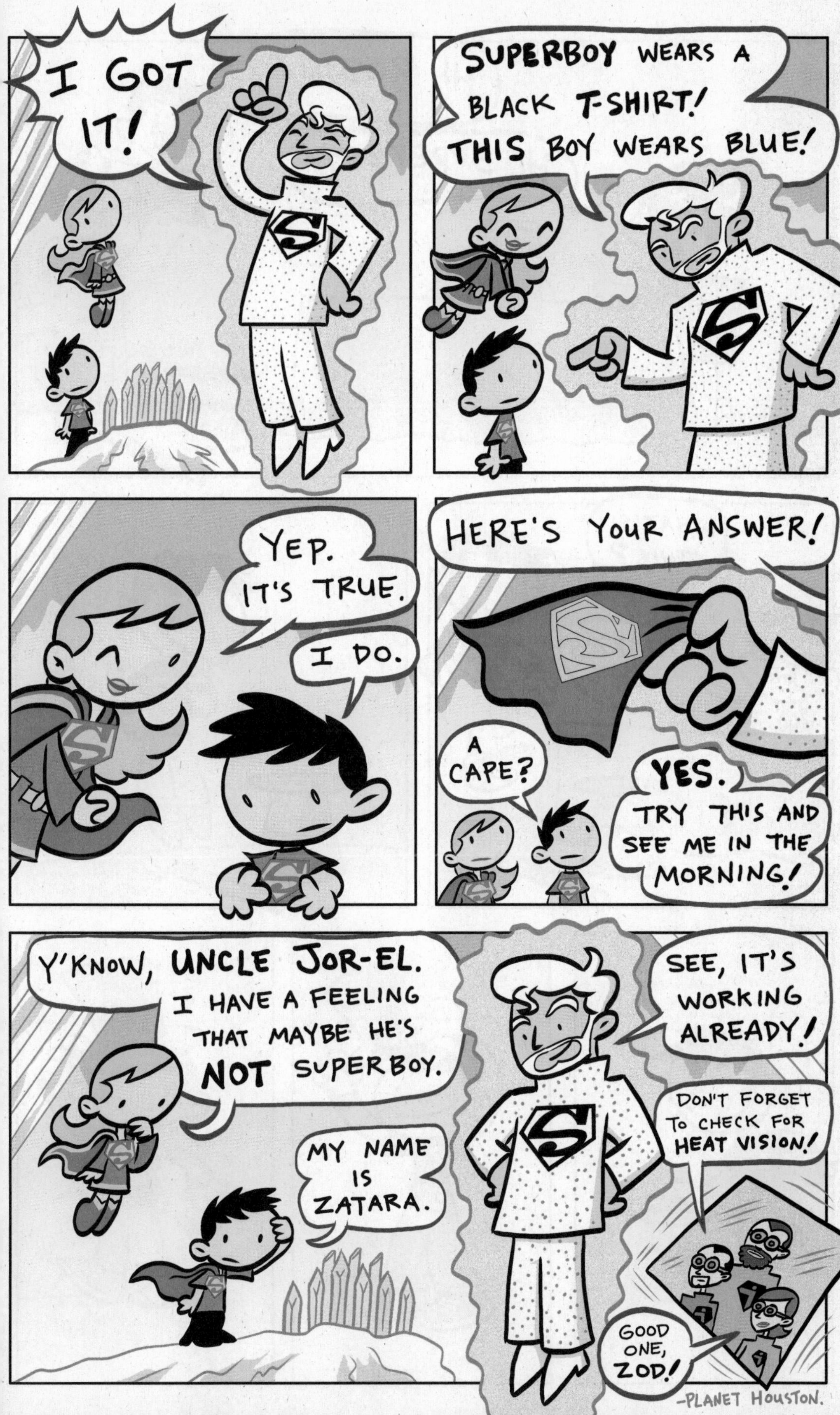

I GOT IT!
SUPERBOY WEARS A BLACK T-SHIRT! THIS BOY WEARS BLUE!
YEP. IT'S TRUE.
I DO.
HERE'S YOUR ANSWER!
A CAPE?
YES. TRY THIS AND SEE ME IN THE MORNING!
Y'KNOW, UNCLE JOR-EL. I HAVE A FEELING THAT MAYBE HE'S NOT SUPERBOY.
MY NAME IS ZATARA.
SEE, IT'S WORKING ALREADY!
DON'T FORGET TO CHECK FOR HEAT VISION!
GOOD ONE, ZOD!
-PLANET HOUSTON.

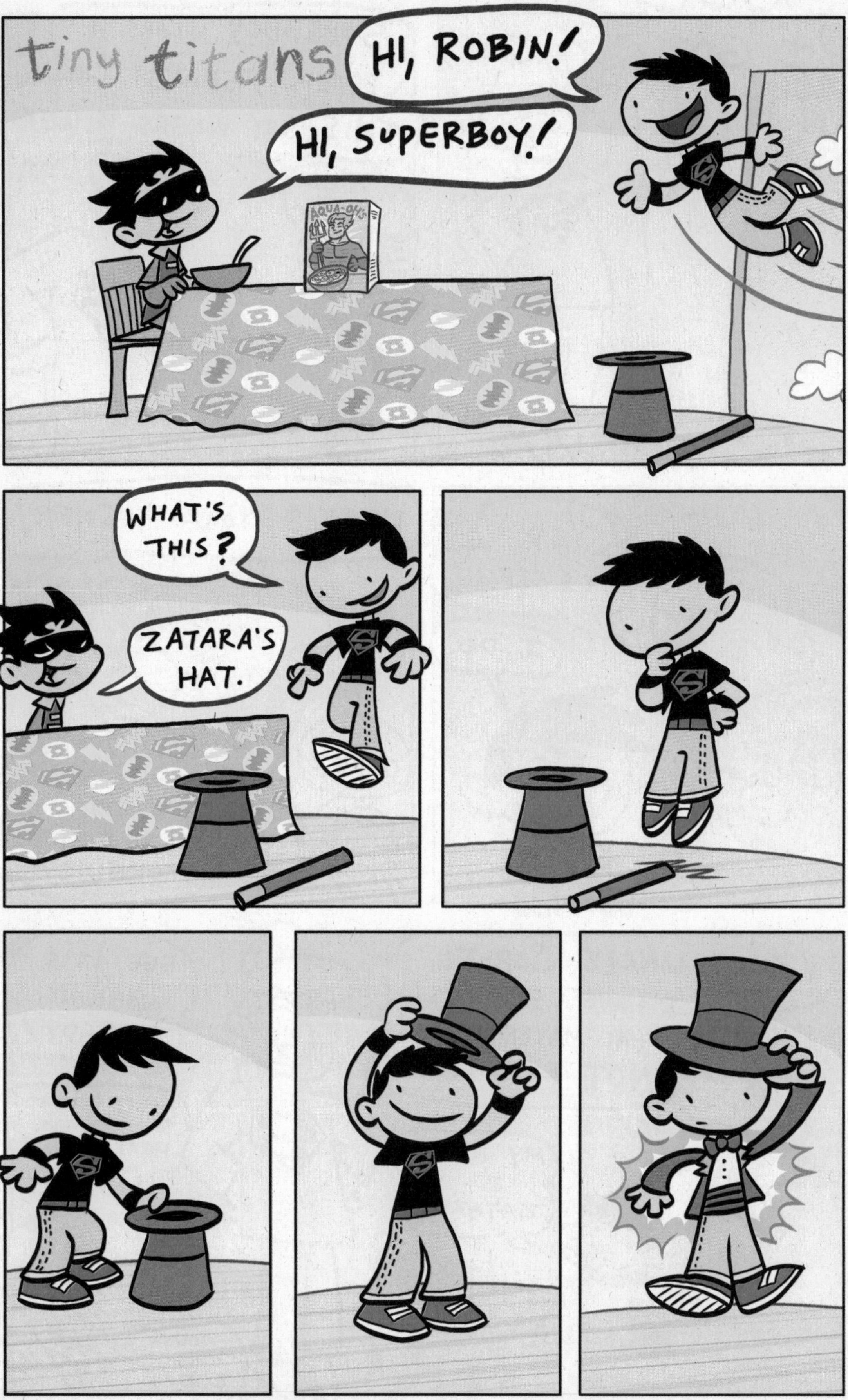
tiny titans
HI, ROBIN!
HI, SUPERBOY!
AQUA-OHS
WHAT'S THIS?
ZATARA'S HAT.

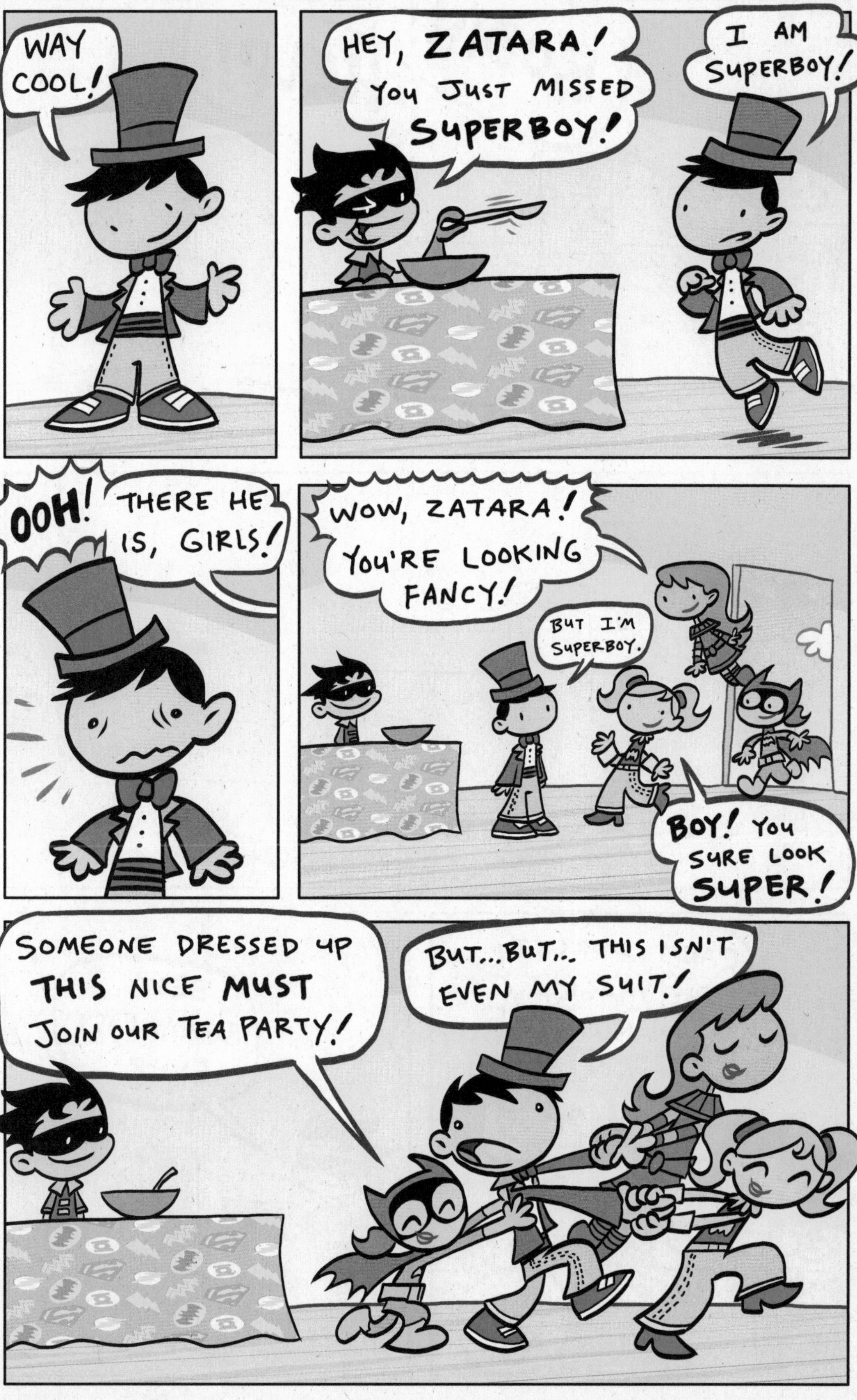
WAY COOL!
HEY, ZATARA! YOU JUST MISSED SUPERBOY!
I AM SUPERBOY!
OOH!
THERE HE IS, GIRLS!
WOW, ZATARA! YOU'RE LOOKING FANCY!
BUT I'M SUPERBOY.
BOY! YOU SURE LOOK SUPER!
SOMEONE DRESSED UP THIS NICE MUST JOIN OUR TEA PARTY!
BUT...BUT... THIS ISN'T EVEN MY SUIT!

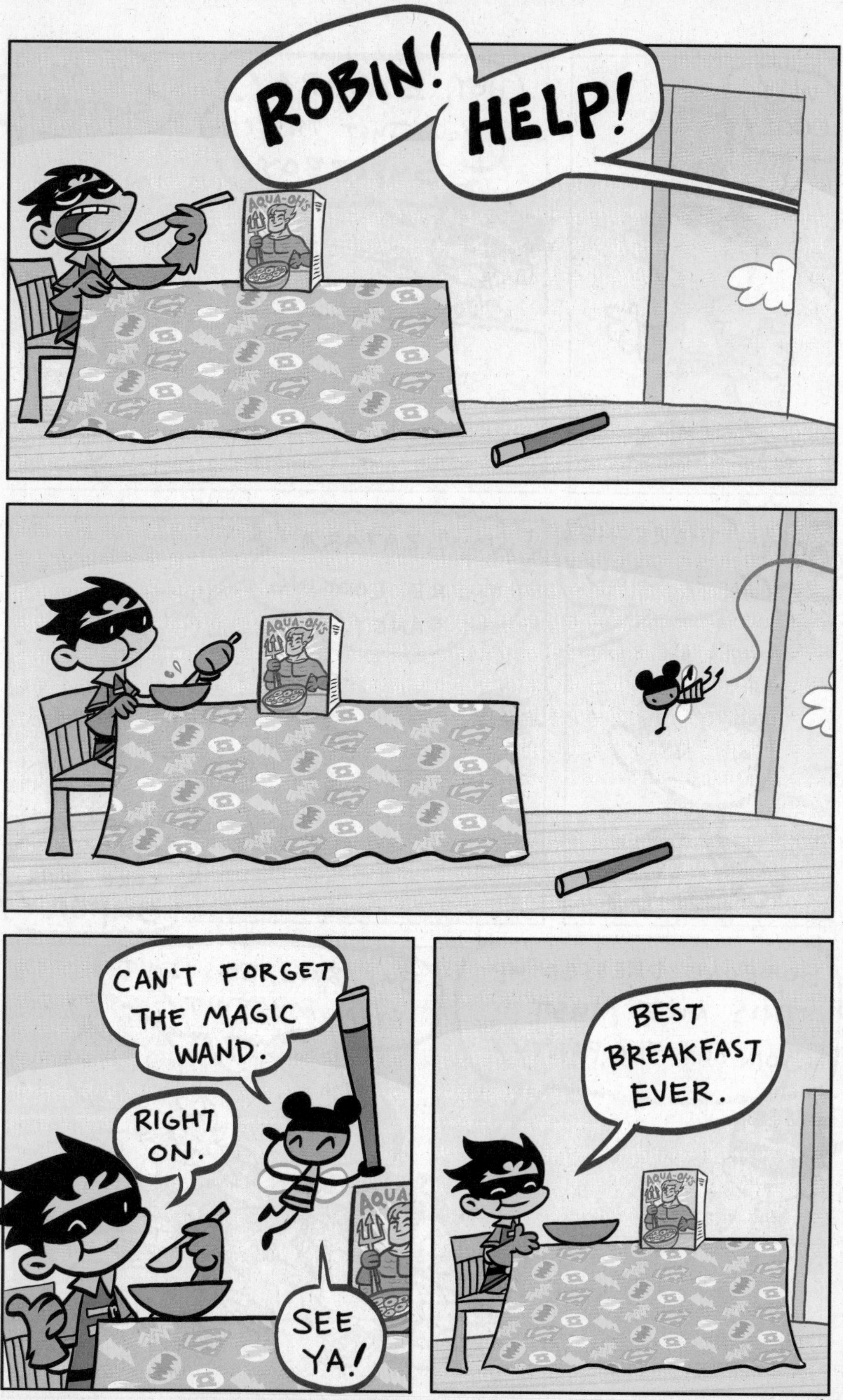
ROBIN! HELP!
AQUA-OH'S
AQUA-OH'S
CAN'T FORGET THE MAGIC WAND.
RIGHT ON.
SEE YA!
BEST BREAKFAST EVER.
AQUA-OH'S

—PASS THE JELLY.

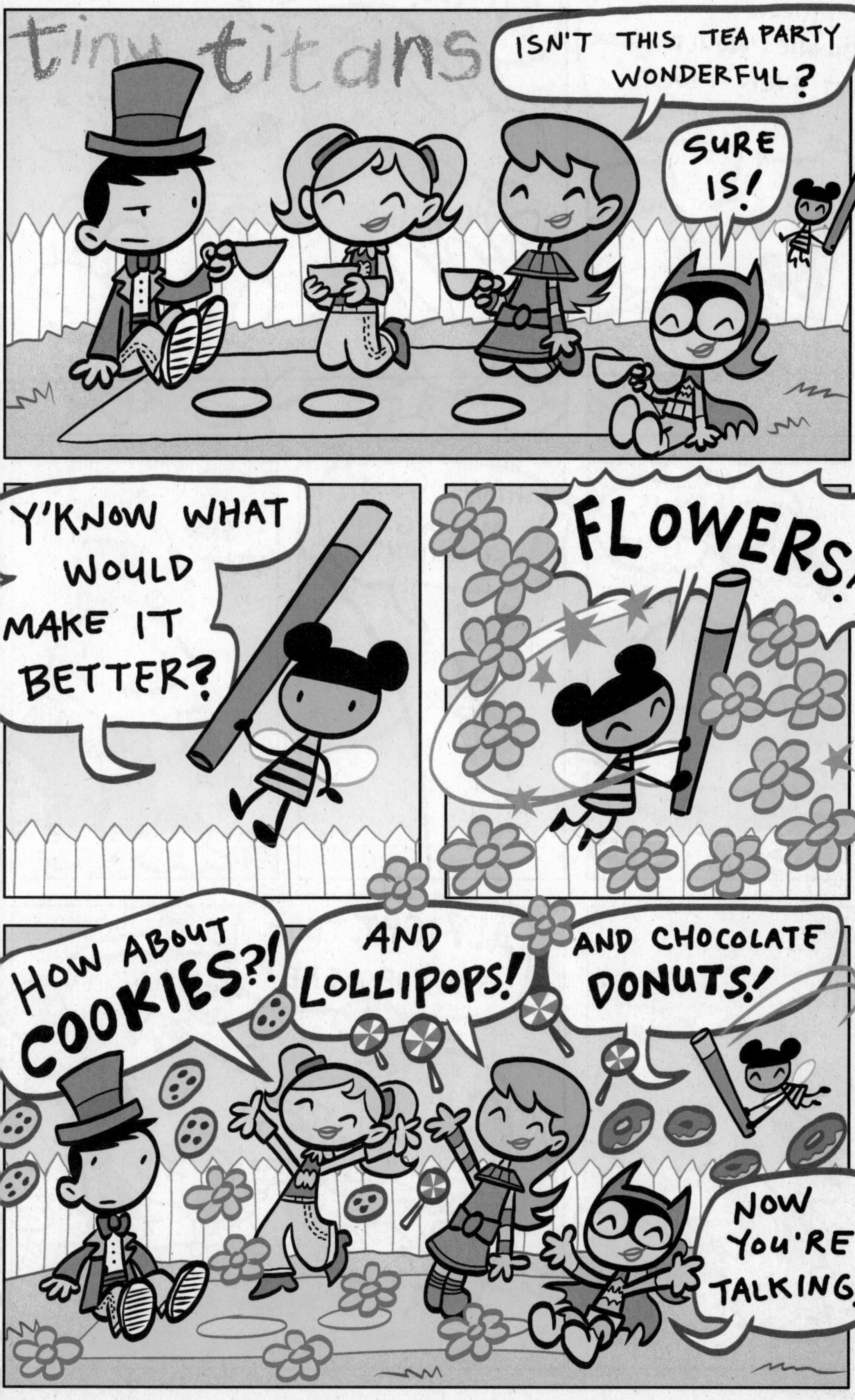
tiny titans
ISN'T THIS TEA PARTY WONDERFUL?
SURE IS!
Y'KNOW WHAT WOULD MAKE IT BETTER?
FLOWERS!
HOW ABOUT COOKIES?!
AND LOLLIPOPS!
AND CHOCOLATE DONUTS!
NOW YOU'RE TALKING!

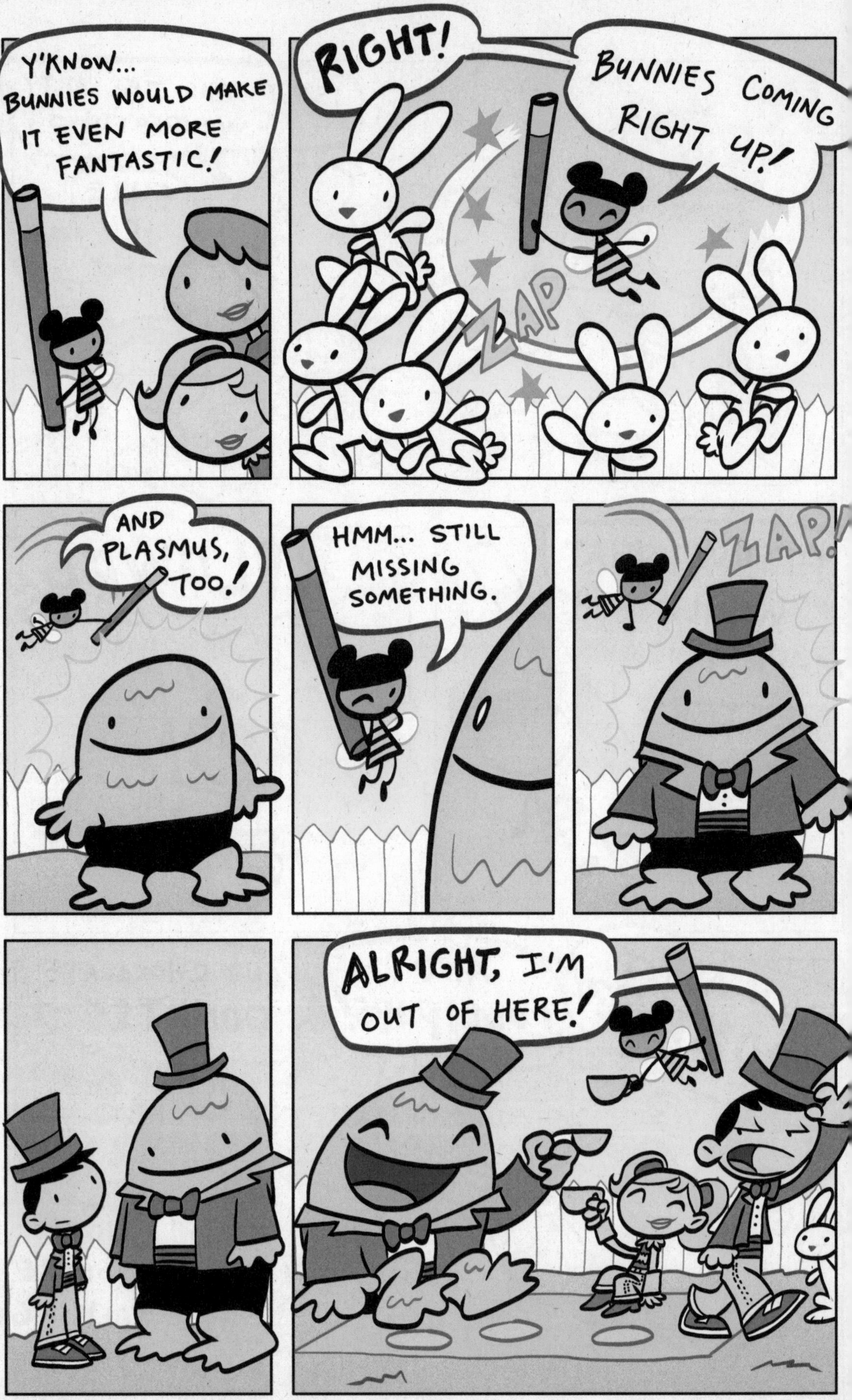
Y'KNOW... BUNNIES WOULD MAKE IT EVEN MORE FANTASTIC!
RIGHT!
BUNNIES COMING RIGHT UP!
ZAP
AND PLASMUS, TOO!
HMM... STILL MISSING SOMETHING.
ZAP!
ALRIGHT, I'M OUT OF HERE!

—PERFECT!

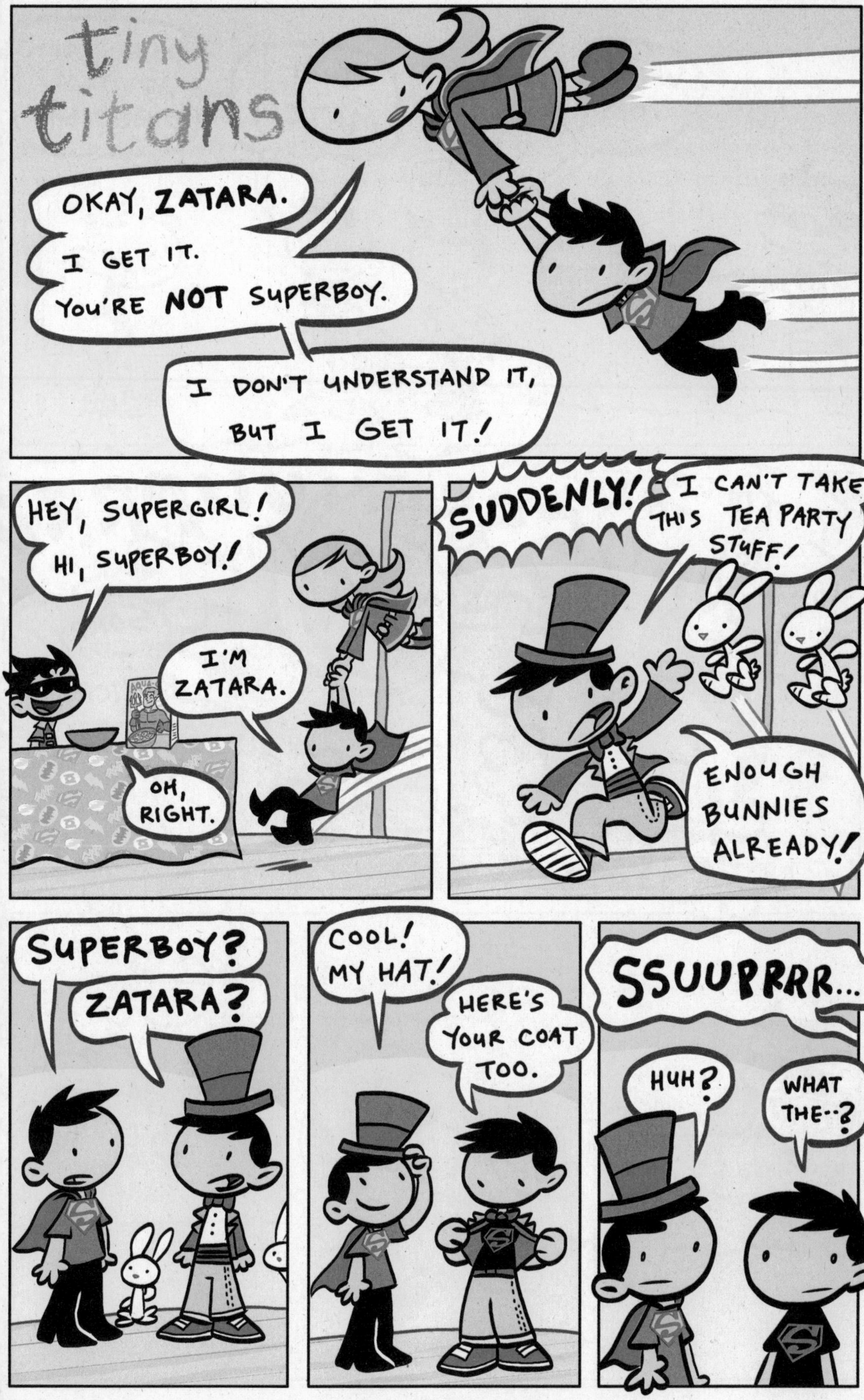
tiny titans
OKAY, ZATARA.
I GET IT.
YOU'RE NOT SUPERBOY.
I DON'T UNDERSTAND IT, BUT I GET IT!
HEY, SUPERGIRL!
HI, SUPERBOY!
I'M ZATARA.
OH, RIGHT.
SUDDENLY!
I CAN'T TAKE THIS TEA PARTY STUFF!
ENOUGH BUNNIES ALREADY!
SUPERBOY?
ZATARA?
COOL! MY HAT!
HERE'S YOUR COAT TOO.
SSUUPRRR...
HUH?
WHAT THE--?

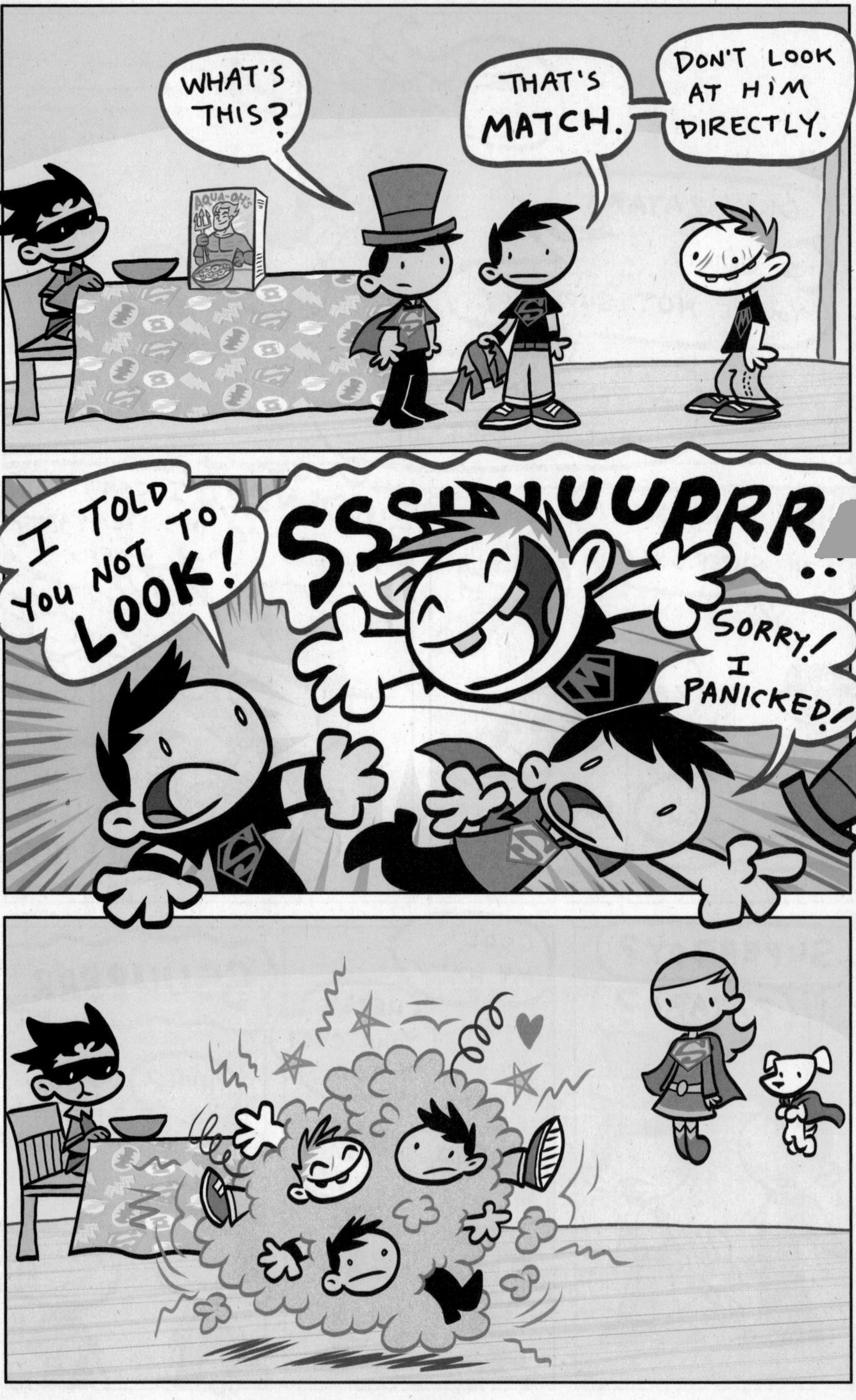
AQUA-OH'S
WHAT'S THIS?
THAT'S MATCH.
DON'T LOOK AT HIM DIRECTLY.
I TOLD YOU NOT TO LOOK!
SORRY! I PANICKED!

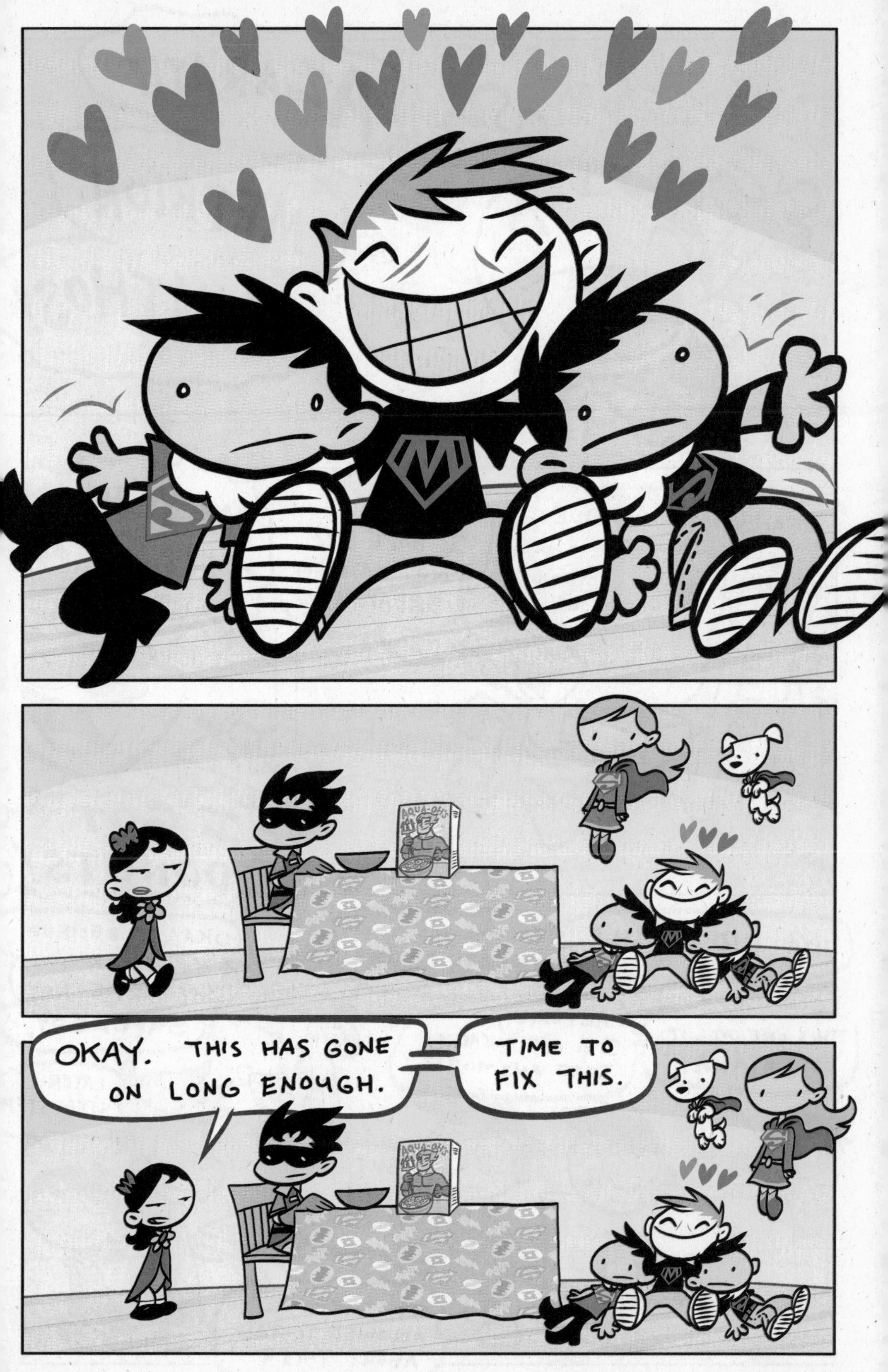
AQUA-OH'S
OKAY. THIS HAS GONE ON LONG ENOUGH.
TIME TO FIX THIS.

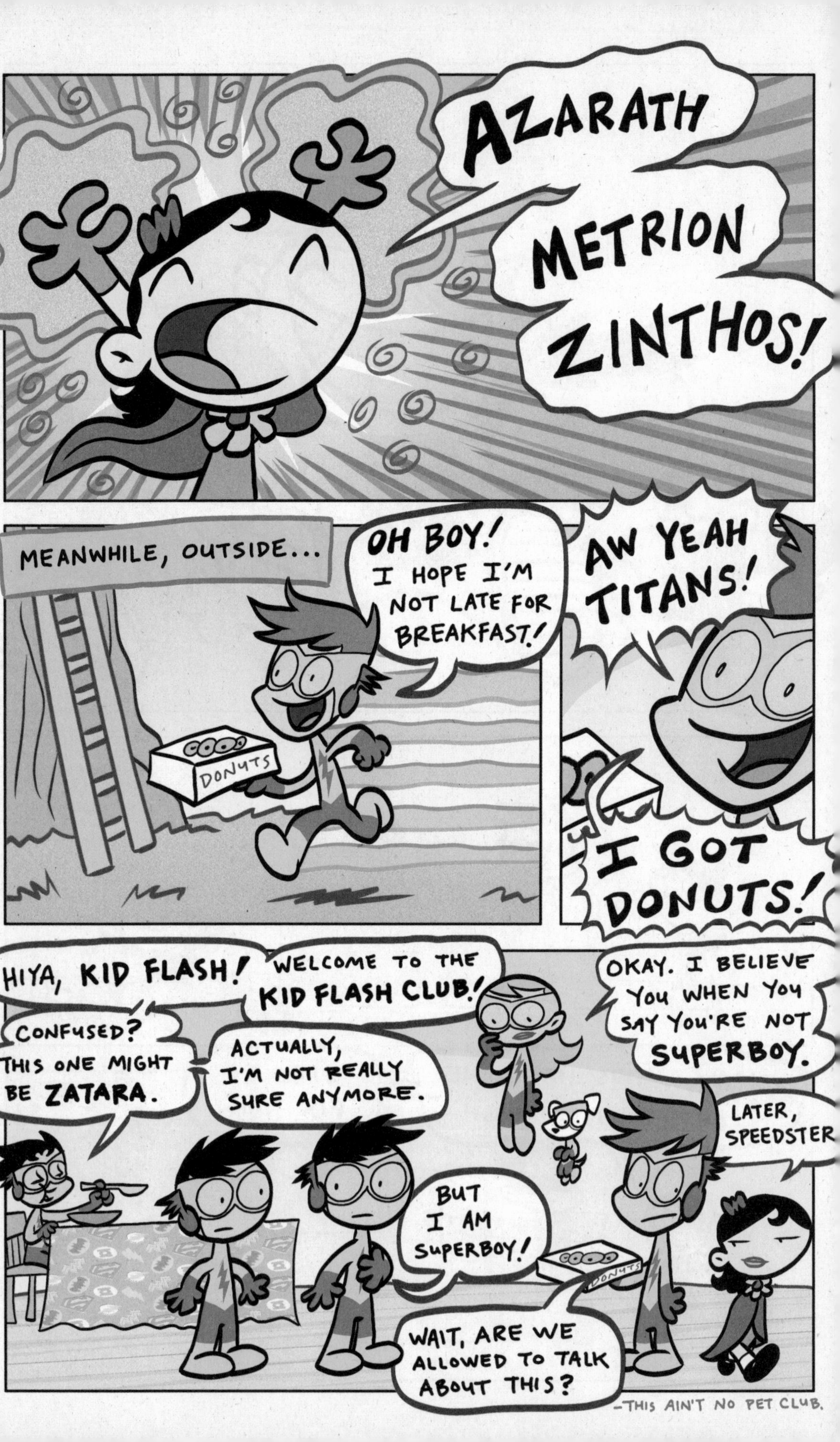
AZARATH
METRION
ZINTHOS!
MEANWHILE, OUTSIDE...
OH BOY! I HOPE I'M NOT LATE FOR BREAKFAST!
DONUTS
AW YEAH TITANS!
I GOT DONUTS!
HIYA, KID FLASH!
WELCOME TO THE KID FLASH CLUB!
CONFUSED? THIS ONE MIGHT BE ZATARA.
ACTUALLY, I'M NOT REALLY SURE ANYMORE.
OKAY. I BELIEVE YOU WHEN YOU SAY YOU'RE NOT SUPERBOY.
LATER, SPEEDSTER
BUT I AM SUPERBOY!
DONUTS
WAIT, ARE WE ALLOWED TO TALK ABOUT THIS?
-THIS AIN'T NO PET CLUB.

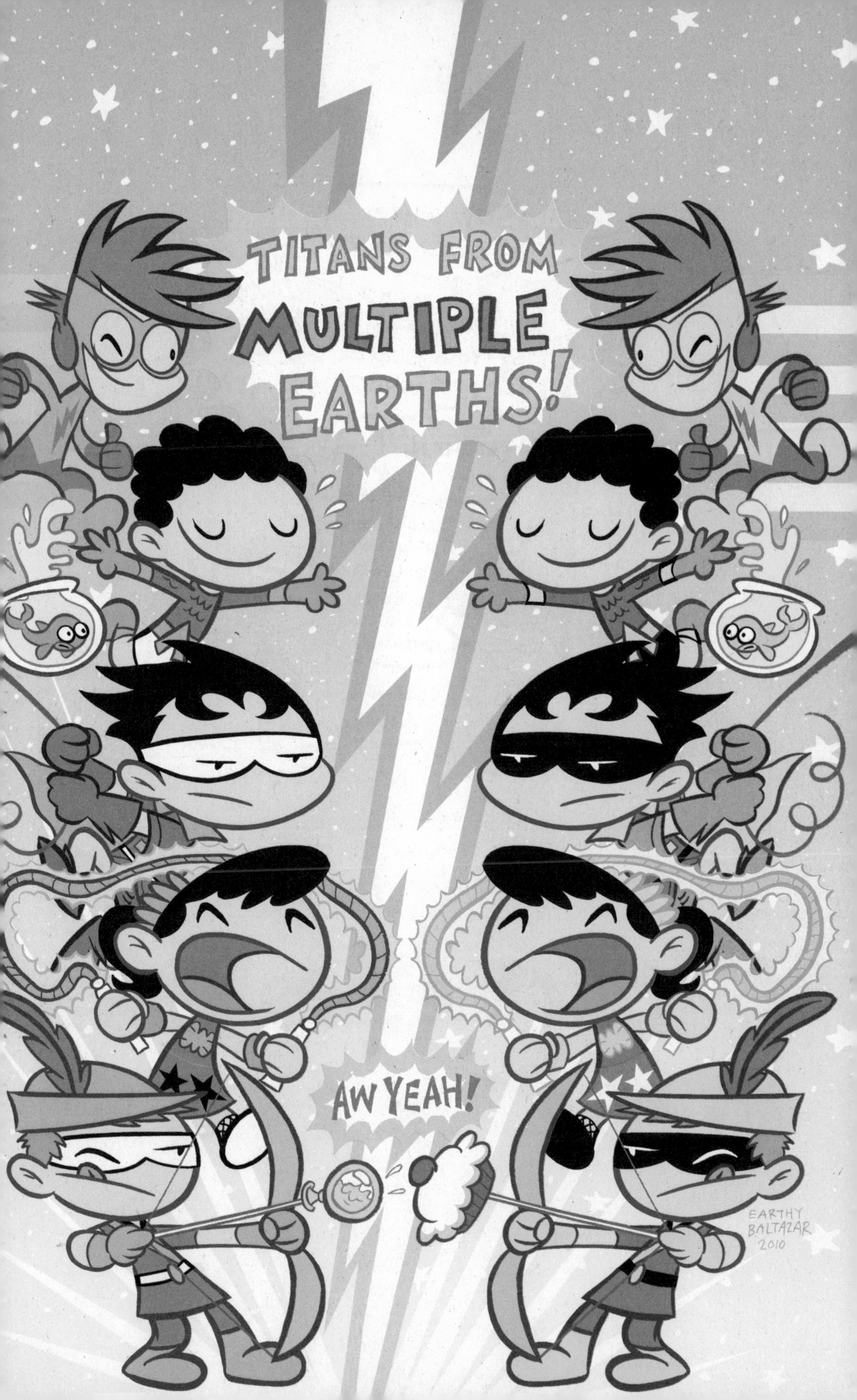
TITANS FROM MULTIPLE EARTHS!
AW YEAH!
EARTHY BALTAZAR 2010

tiny titans

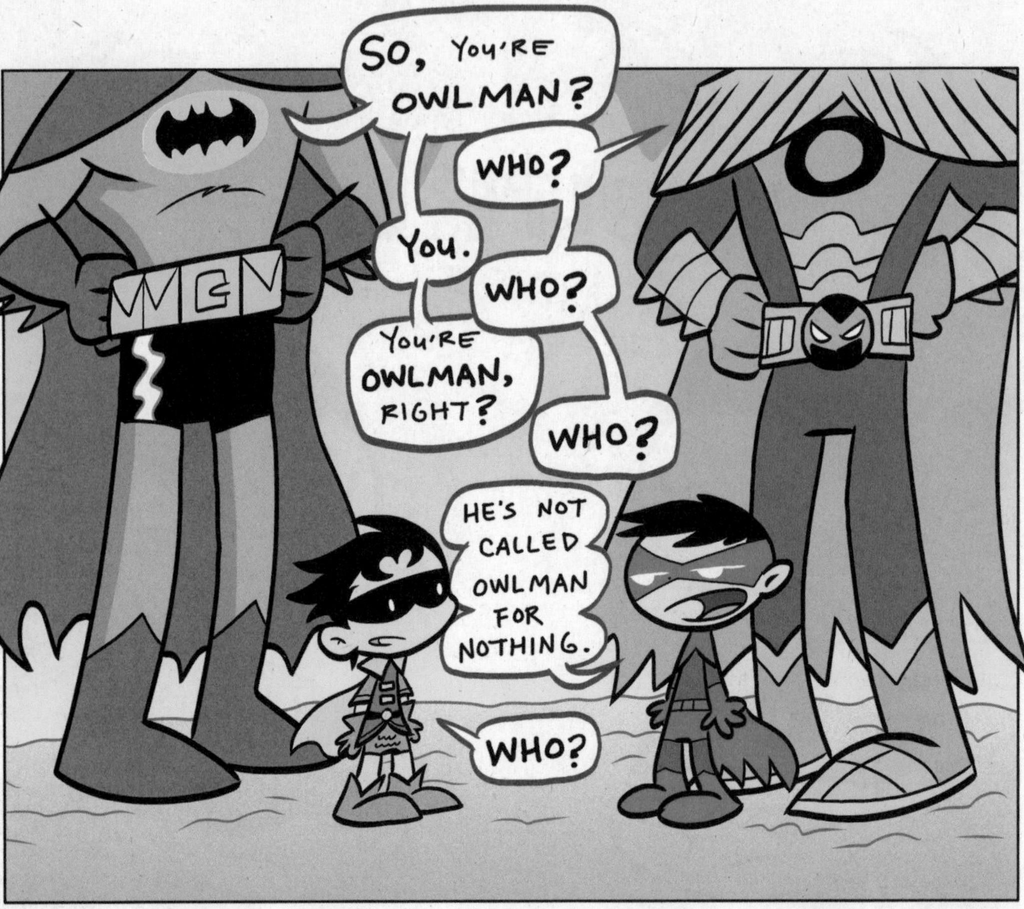
SO, YOU'RE OWLMAN?
WHO?
YOU.
WHO?
YOU'RE OWLMAN, RIGHT?
WHO?
HE'S NOT CALLED OWLMAN FOR NOTHING.
WHO?

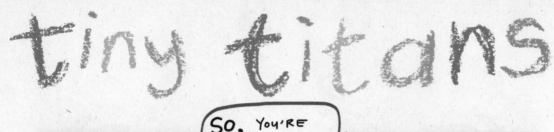

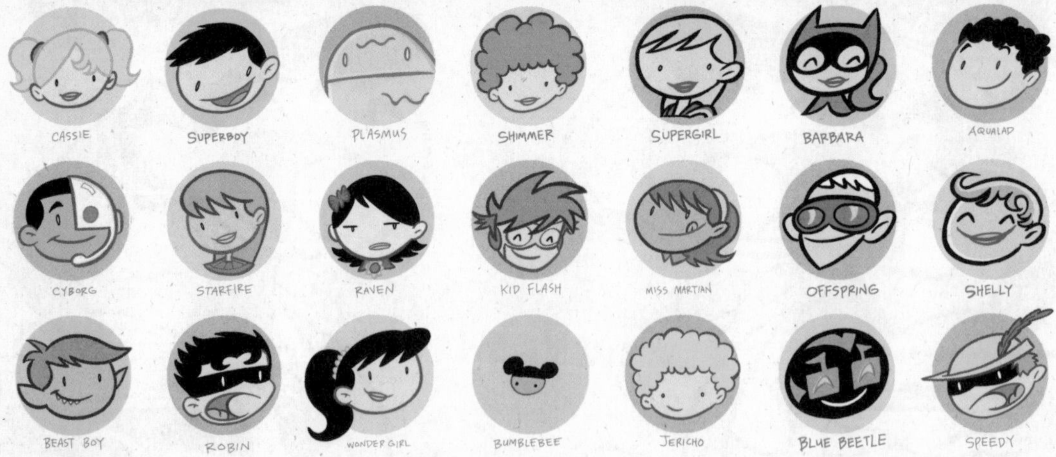
CASSIE
SUPERBOY
PLASMUS
SHIMMER
SUPERGIRL
BARBARA
AQUALAD
CYBORG
STARFIRE
RAVEN
KID FLASH
MISS MARTIAN
OFFSPRING
SHELLY
BEAST BOY
ROBIN
WONDER GIRL
BUMBLEBEE
JERICHO
BLUE BEETLE
SPEEDY

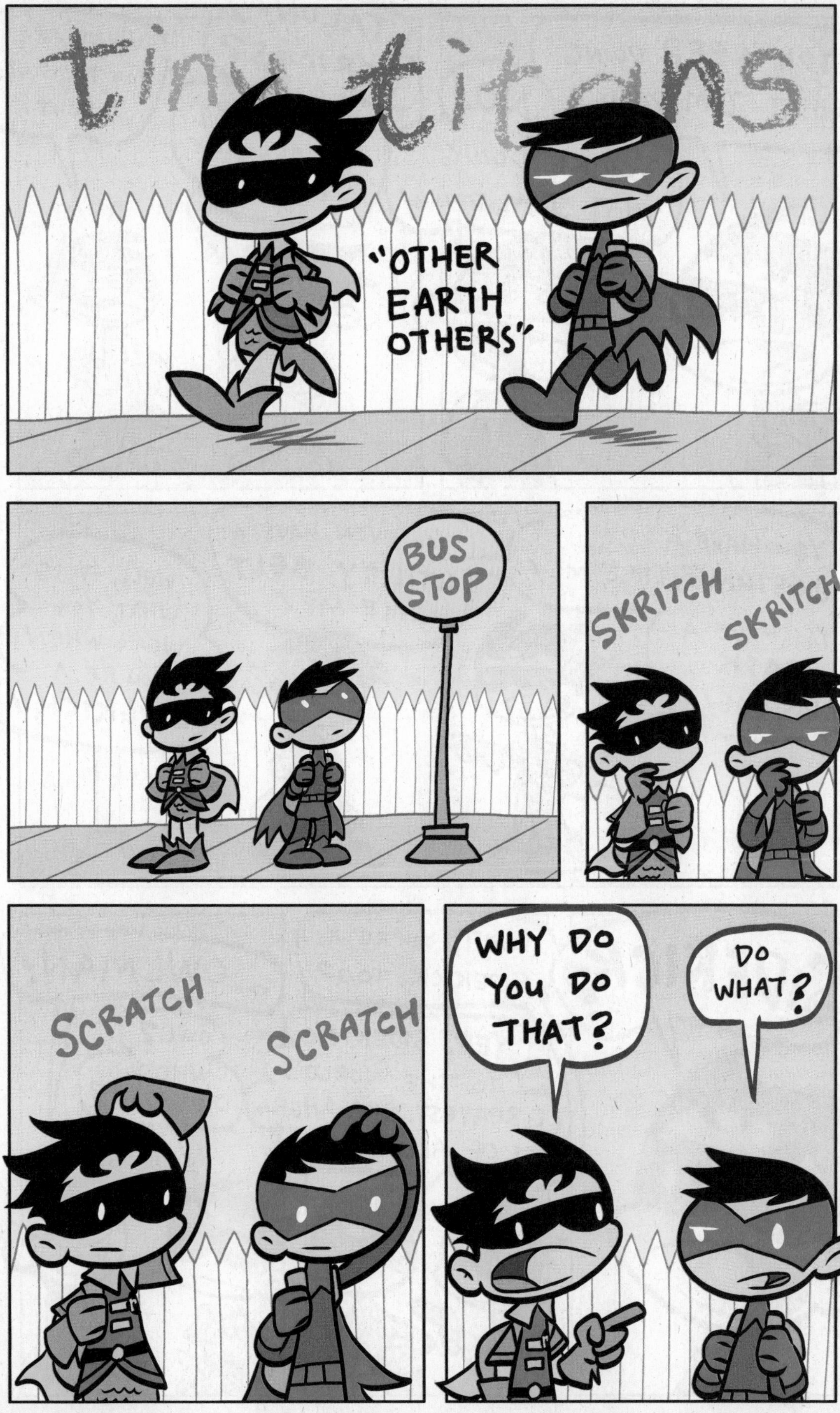
tiny titans
"OTHER EARTH OTHERS"
BUS STOP
SKRITCH
SKRITCH
SCRATCH
SCRATCH
WHY DO YOU DO THAT?
DO WHAT?

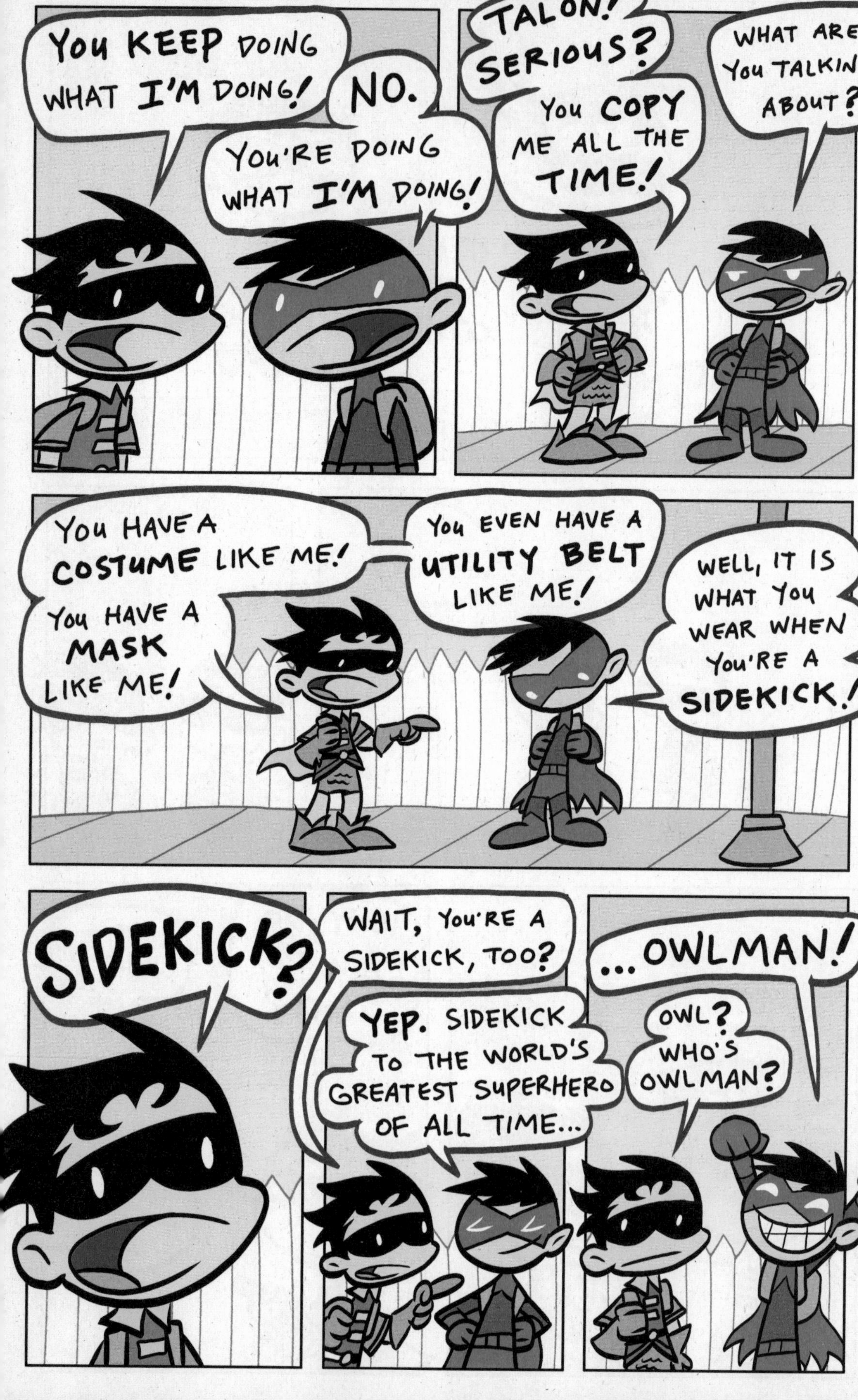
YOU KEEP DOING WHAT I'M DOING!
NO.
YOU'RE DOING WHAT I'M DOING!
TALON! SERIOUS?
YOU COPY ME ALL THE TIME!
WHAT ARE YOU TALKING ABOUT?
YOU HAVE A COSTUME LIKE ME!
YOU HAVE A MASK LIKE ME!
YOU EVEN HAVE A UTILITY BELT LIKE ME!
WELL, IT IS WHAT YOU WEAR WHEN YOU'RE A SIDEKICK!
SIDEKICK?
WAIT, YOU'RE A SIDEKICK, TOO?
YEP. SIDEKICK TO THE WORLD'S GREATEST SUPERHERO OF ALL TIME...
...OWLMAN!
OWL? WHO'S OWLMAN?

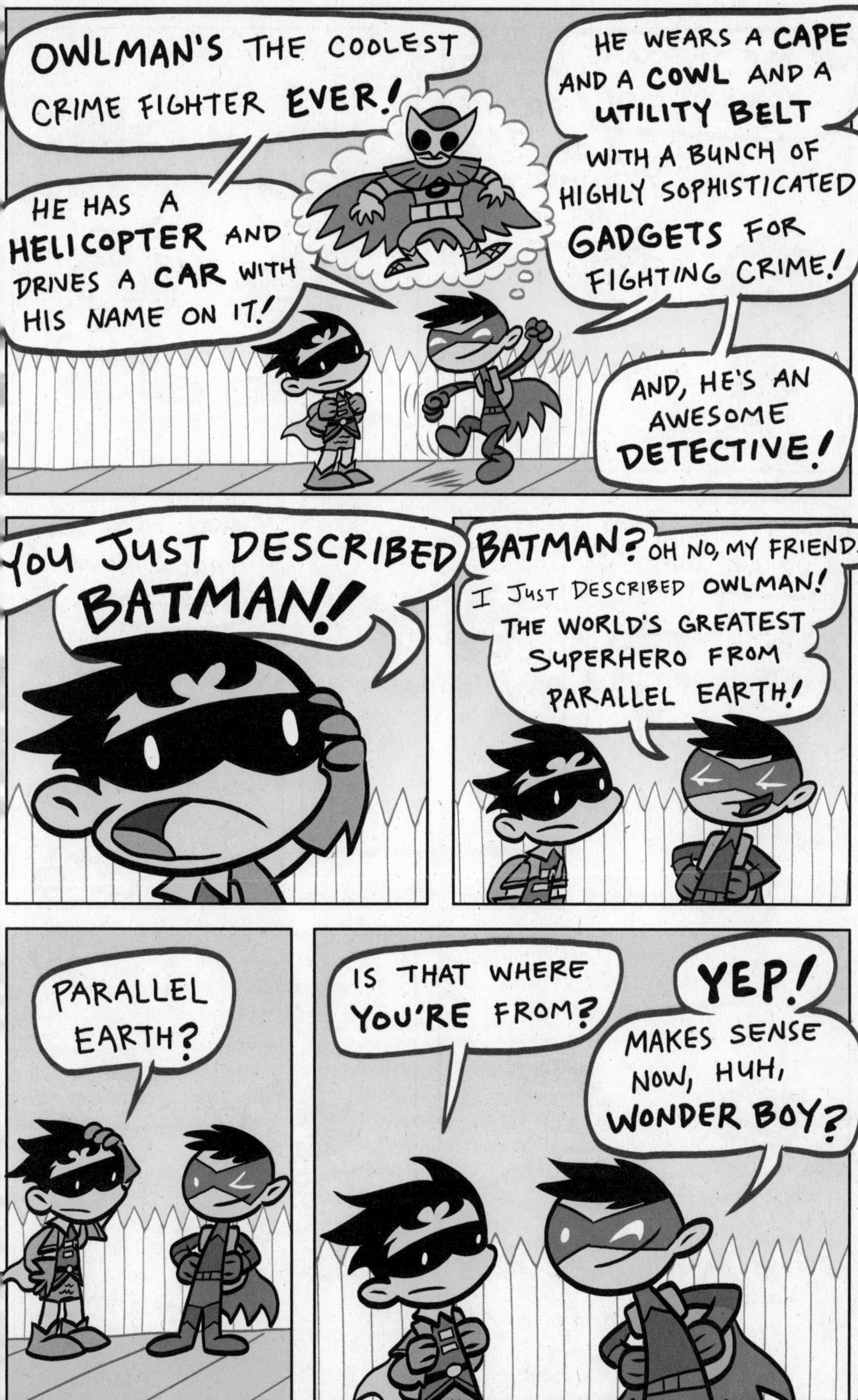
OWLMAN'S THE COOLEST CRIME FIGHTER EVER!
HE HAS A HELICOPTER AND DRIVES A CAR WITH HIS NAME ON IT!
HE WEARS A CAPE AND A COWL AND A UTILITY BELT WITH A BUNCH OF HIGHLY SOPHISTICATED GADGETS FOR FIGHTING CRIME!
AND, HE'S AN AWESOME DETECTIVE!
YOU JUST DESCRIBED BATMAN!
BATMAN? OH NO, MY FRIEND. I JUST DESCRIBED OWLMAN! THE WORLD'S GREATEST SUPERHERO FROM PARALLEL EARTH!
PARALLEL EARTH?
IS THAT WHERE YOU'RE FROM?
YEP!
MAKES SENSE NOW, HUH, WONDER BOY?

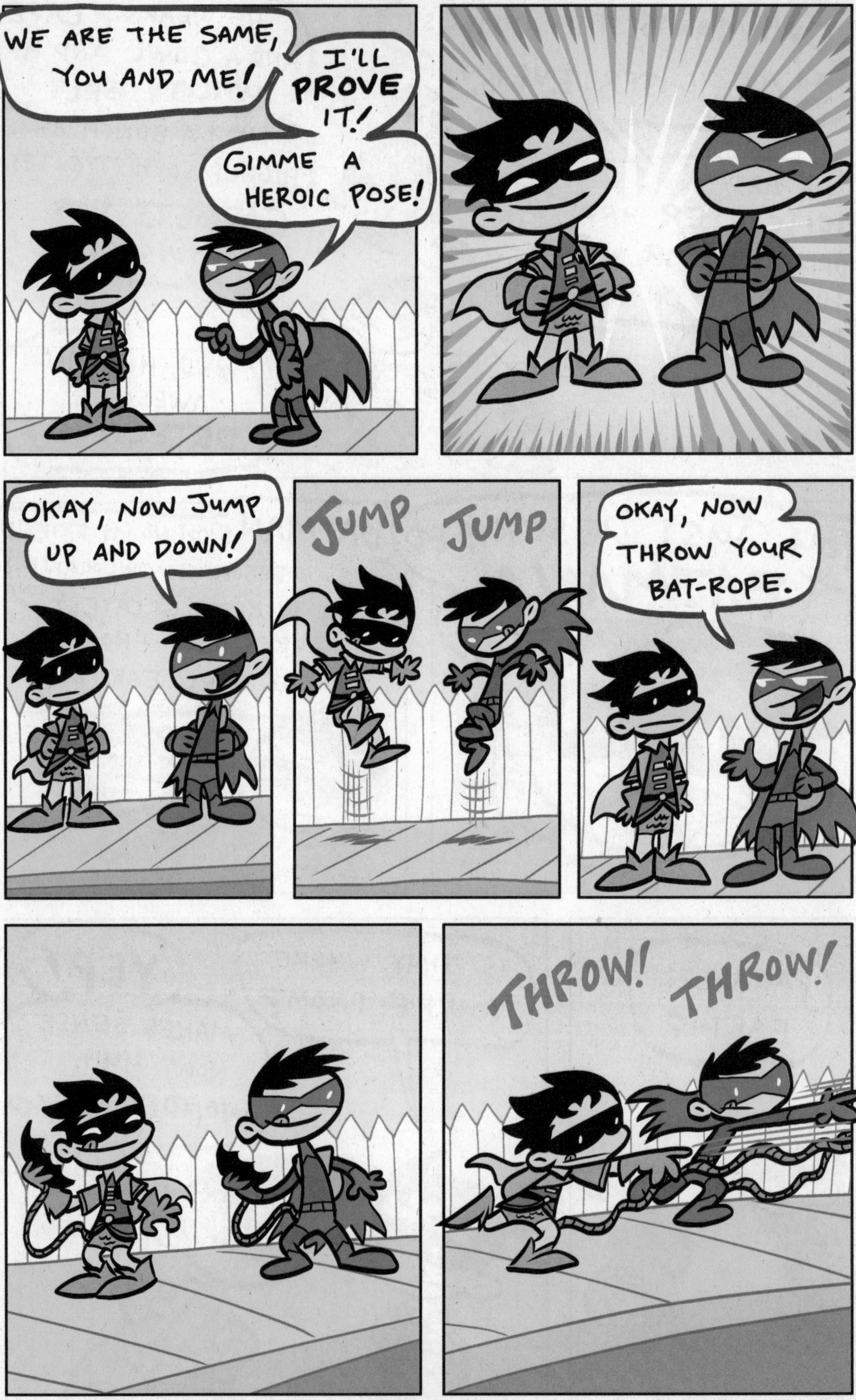
WE ARE THE SAME, YOU AND ME!
I'LL PROVE IT!
GIMME A HEROIC POSE!
OKAY, NOW JUMP UP AND DOWN!
JUMP
JUMP
OKAY, NOW THROW YOUR BAT-ROPE.
THROW!
THROW!

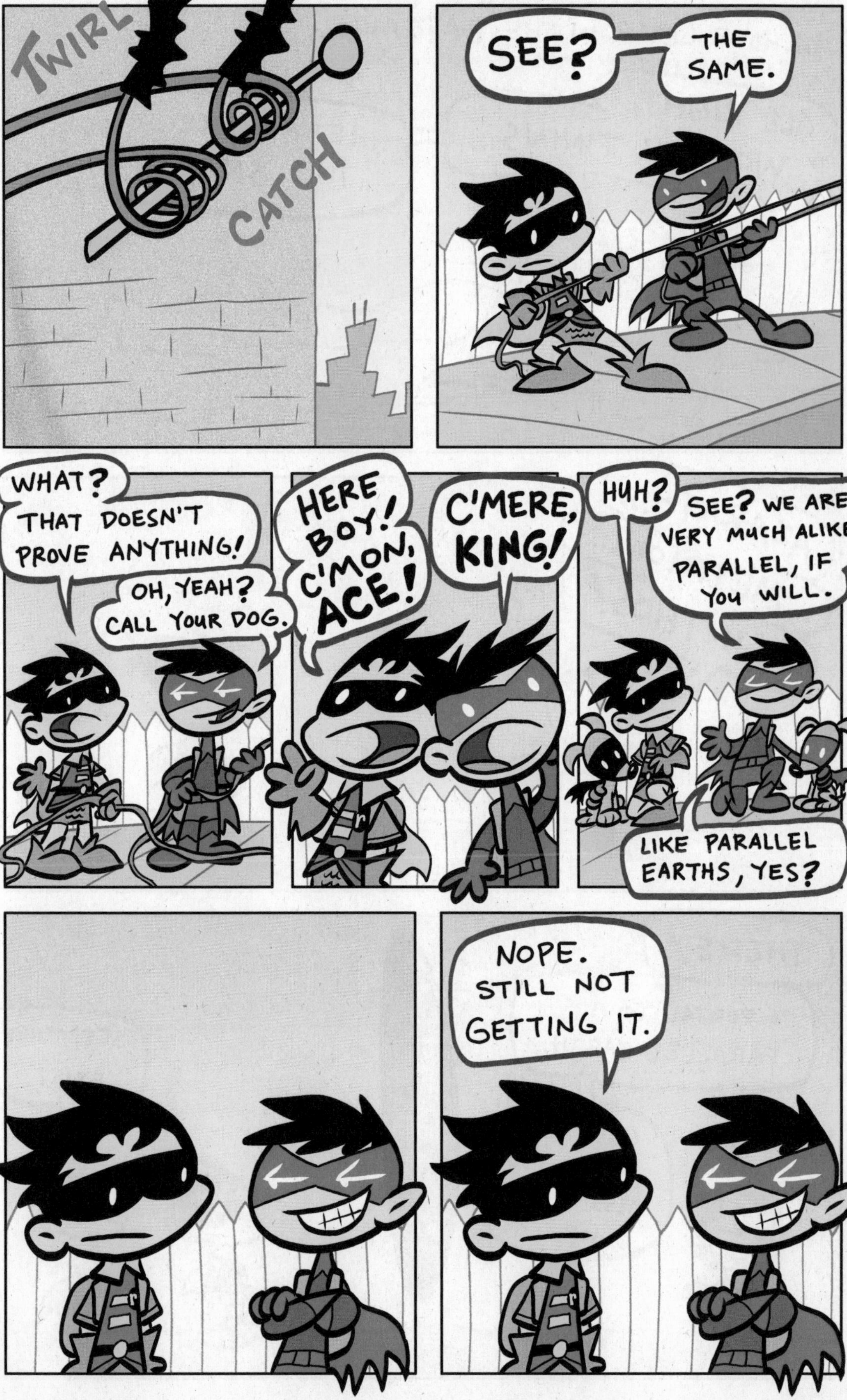

TWIRL
CATCH
SEE?
THE SAME.
WHAT? THAT DOESN'T PROVE ANYTHING!
OH, YEAH? CALL YOUR DOG.
HERE BOY! C'MON, ACE!
C'MERE, KING!
HUH?
SEE? WE ARE VERY MUCH ALIKE. PARALLEL, IF YOU WILL.
LIKE PARALLEL EARTHS, YES?
NOPE. STILL NOT GETTING IT.

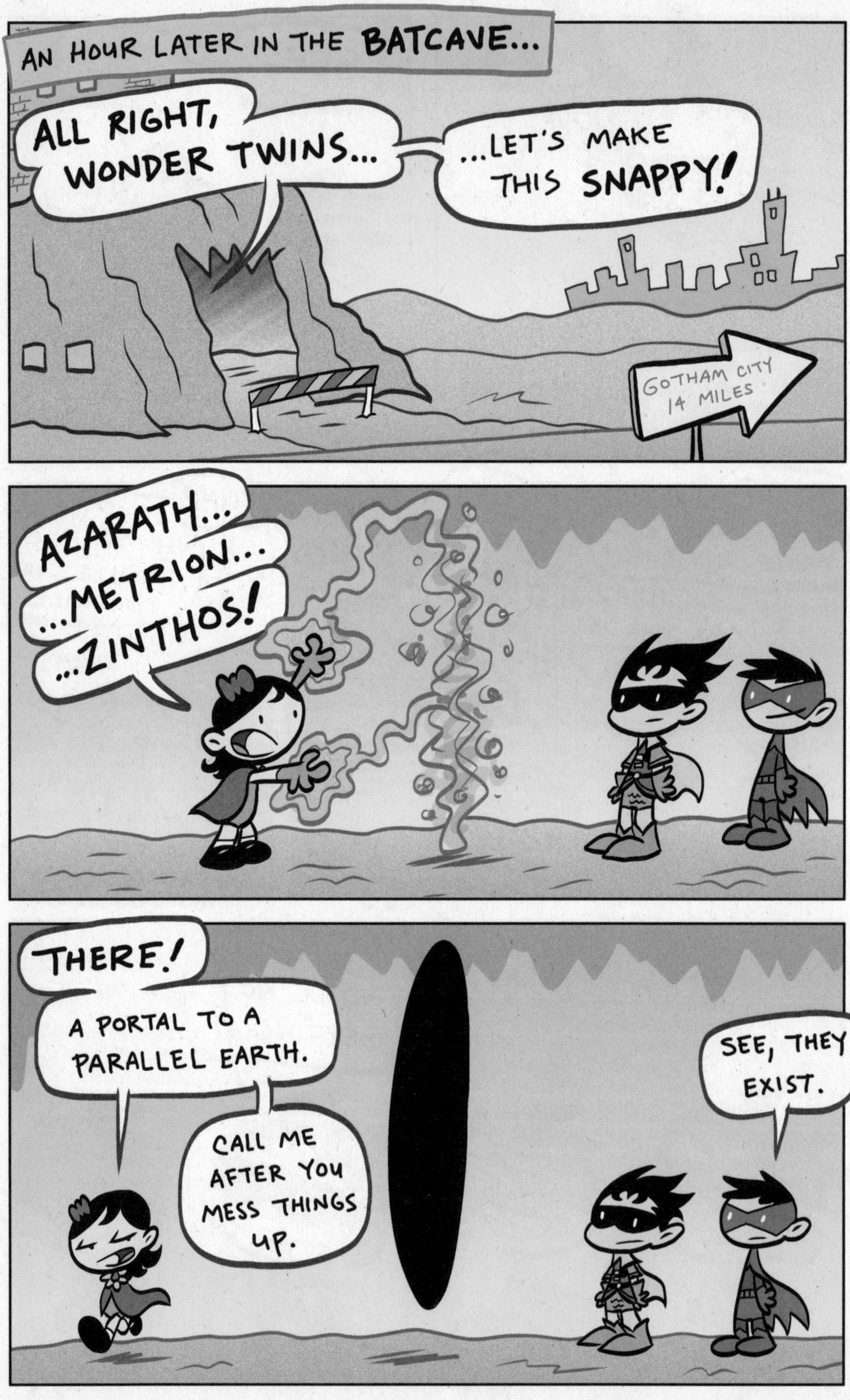
AN HOUR LATER IN THE BATCAVE...
ALL RIGHT, WONDER TWINS...
...LET'S MAKE THIS SNAPPY!
GOTHAM CITY 14 MILES
AZARATH...
...METRION...
...ZINTHOS!
THERE!
A PORTAL TO A PARALLEL EARTH.
CALL ME AFTER YOU MESS THINGS UP.
SEE, THEY EXIST.

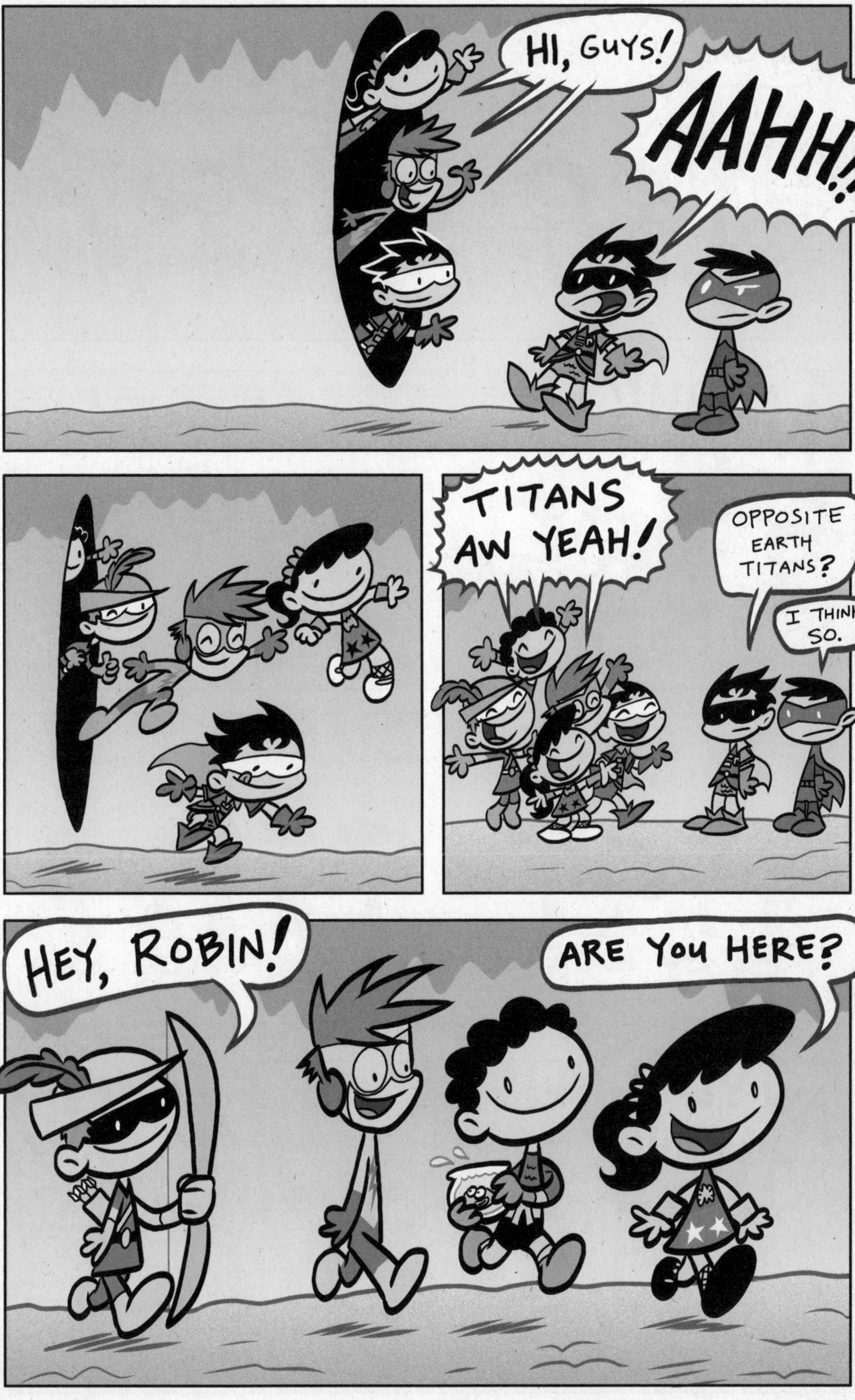
HI, GUYS!
AAHH!!
TITANS AW YEAH!
OPPOSITE EARTH TITANS?
I THINK SO.
HEY, ROBIN!
ARE YOU HERE?

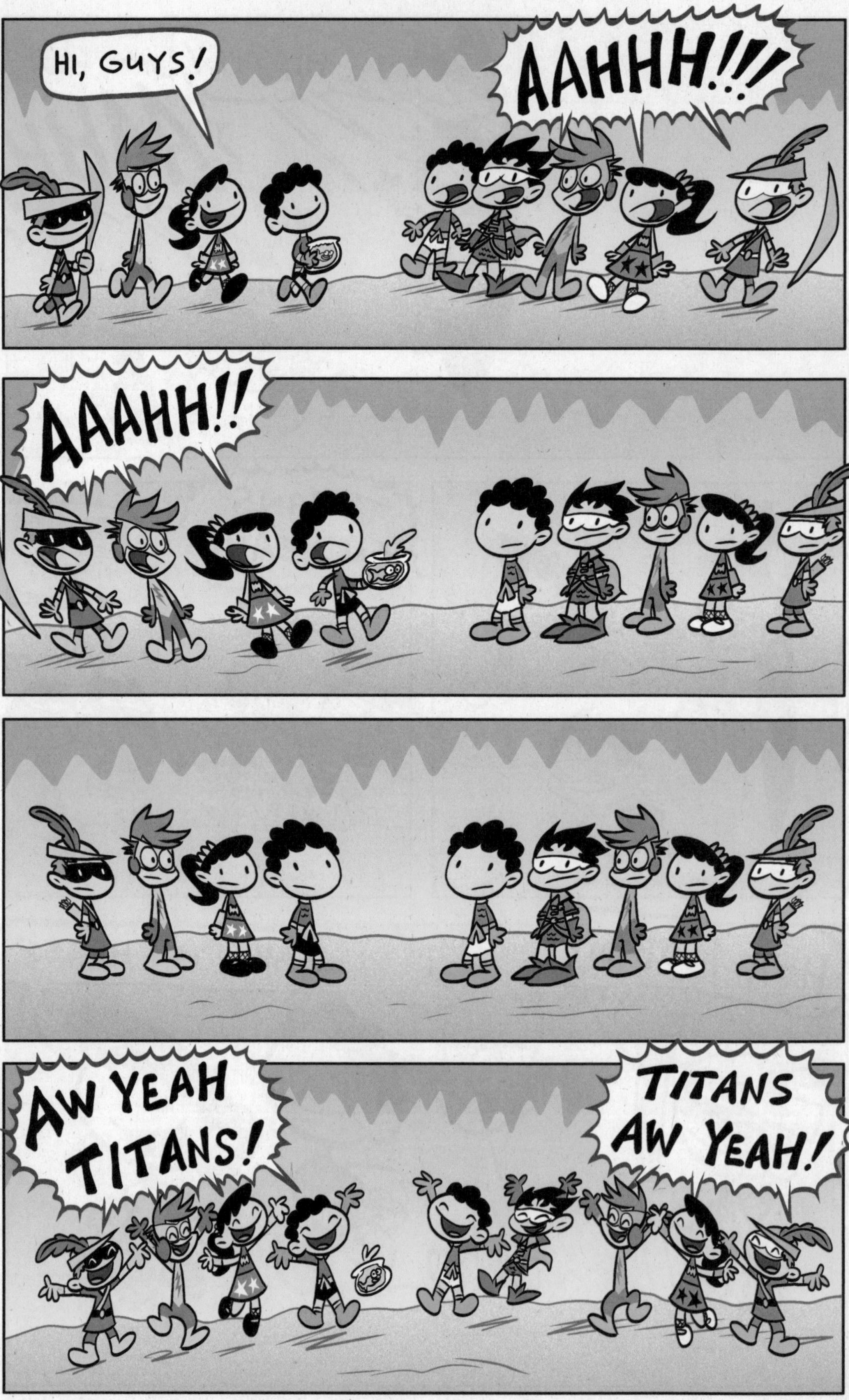
HI, GUYS!
AAHHH!!!
AAAHH!!
AW YEAH TITANS!
TITANS AW YEAH!

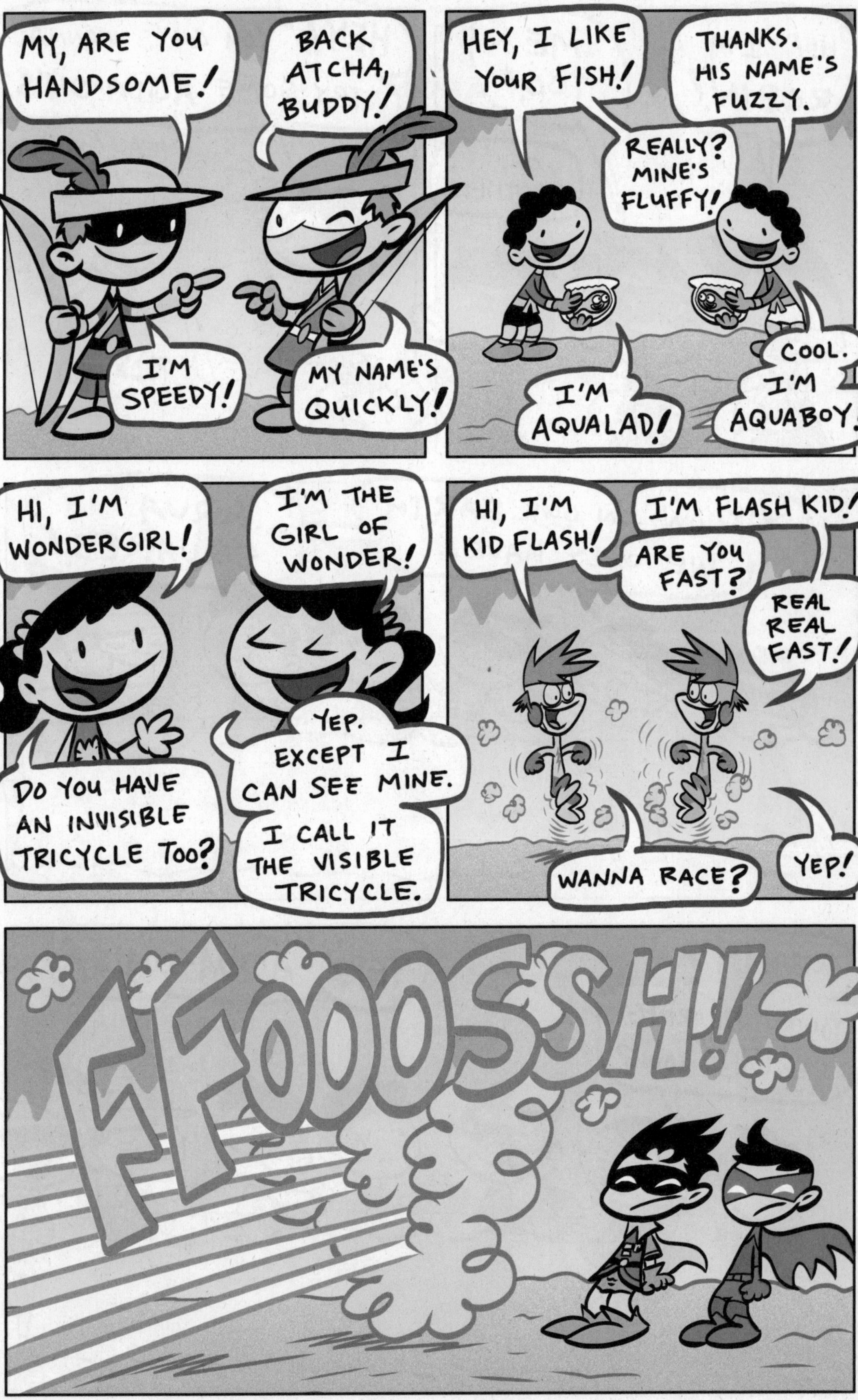
MY, ARE YOU HANDSOME!
BACK ATCHA, BUDDY!
I'M SPEEDY!
MY NAME'S QUICKLY!
HEY, I LIKE YOUR FISH!
THANKS. HIS NAME'S FUZZY.
REALLY? MINE'S FLUFFY!
I'M AQUALAD!
COOL. I'M AQUABOY!
HI, I'M WONDERGIRL!
I'M THE GIRL OF WONDER!
DO YOU HAVE AN INVISIBLE TRICYCLE TOO?
YEP. EXCEPT I CAN SEE MINE.
I CALL IT THE VISIBLE TRICYCLE.
HI, I'M KID FLASH!
I'M FLASH KID!
ARE YOU FAST?
REAL REAL FAST!
WANNA RACE?
YEP!
FFOOOSSH!

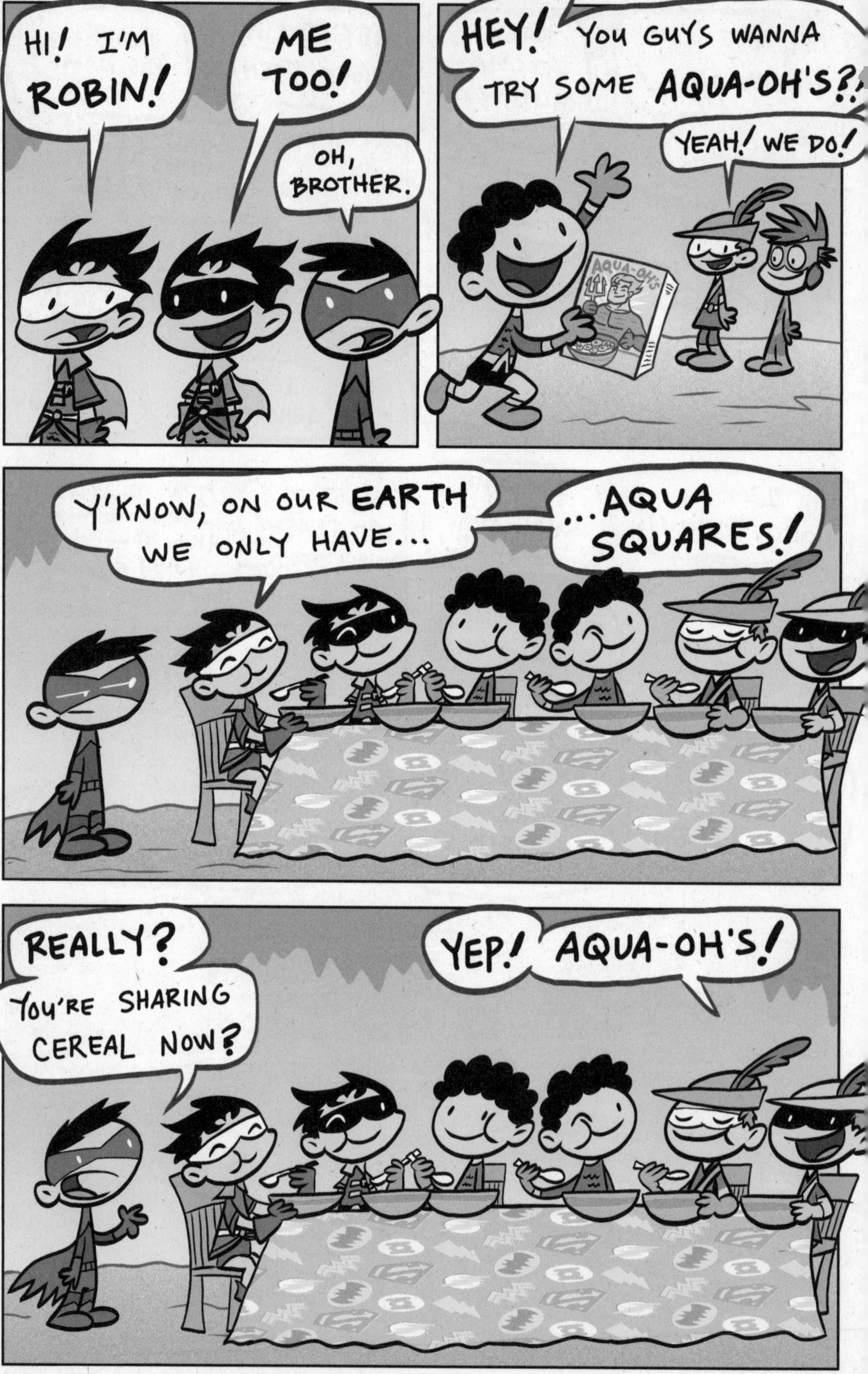
HI! I'M ROBIN!
ME TOO!
OH, BROTHER.
HEY! YOU GUYS WANNA TRY SOME AQUA-OH'S?!
YEAH! WE DO!
AQUA-OH'S
Y'KNOW, ON OUR EARTH WE ONLY HAVE...
...AQUA SQUARES!
REALLY? YOU'RE SHARING CEREAL NOW?
YEP! AQUA-OH'S!

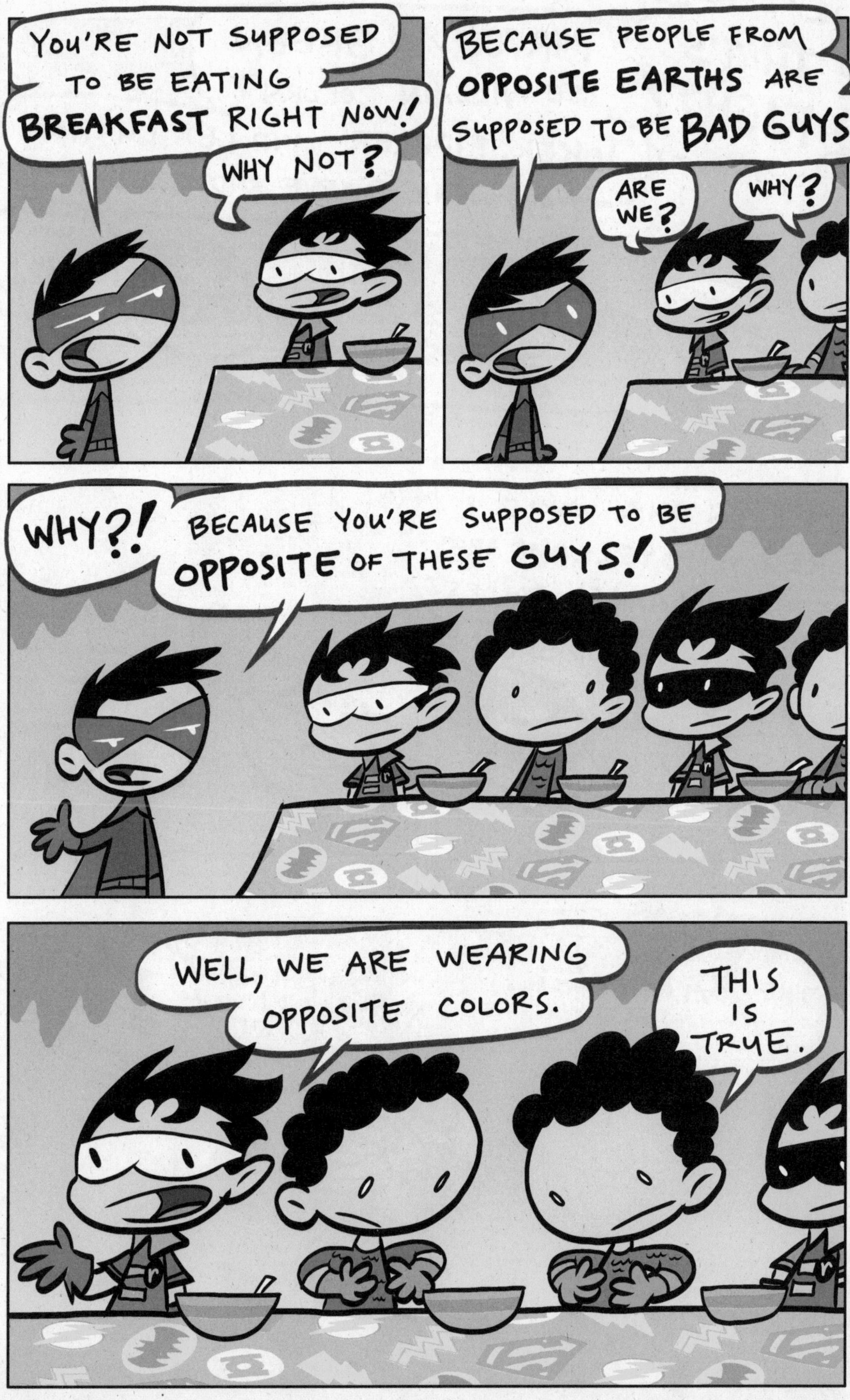
YOU'RE NOT SUPPOSED TO BE EATING BREAKFAST RIGHT NOW!
WHY NOT?
BECAUSE PEOPLE FROM OPPOSITE EARTHS ARE SUPPOSED TO BE BAD GUYS!
ARE WE?
WHY?
WHY?!
BECAUSE YOU'RE SUPPOSED TO BE OPPOSITE OF THESE GUYS!
WELL, WE ARE WEARING OPPOSITE COLORS.
THIS IS TRUE.

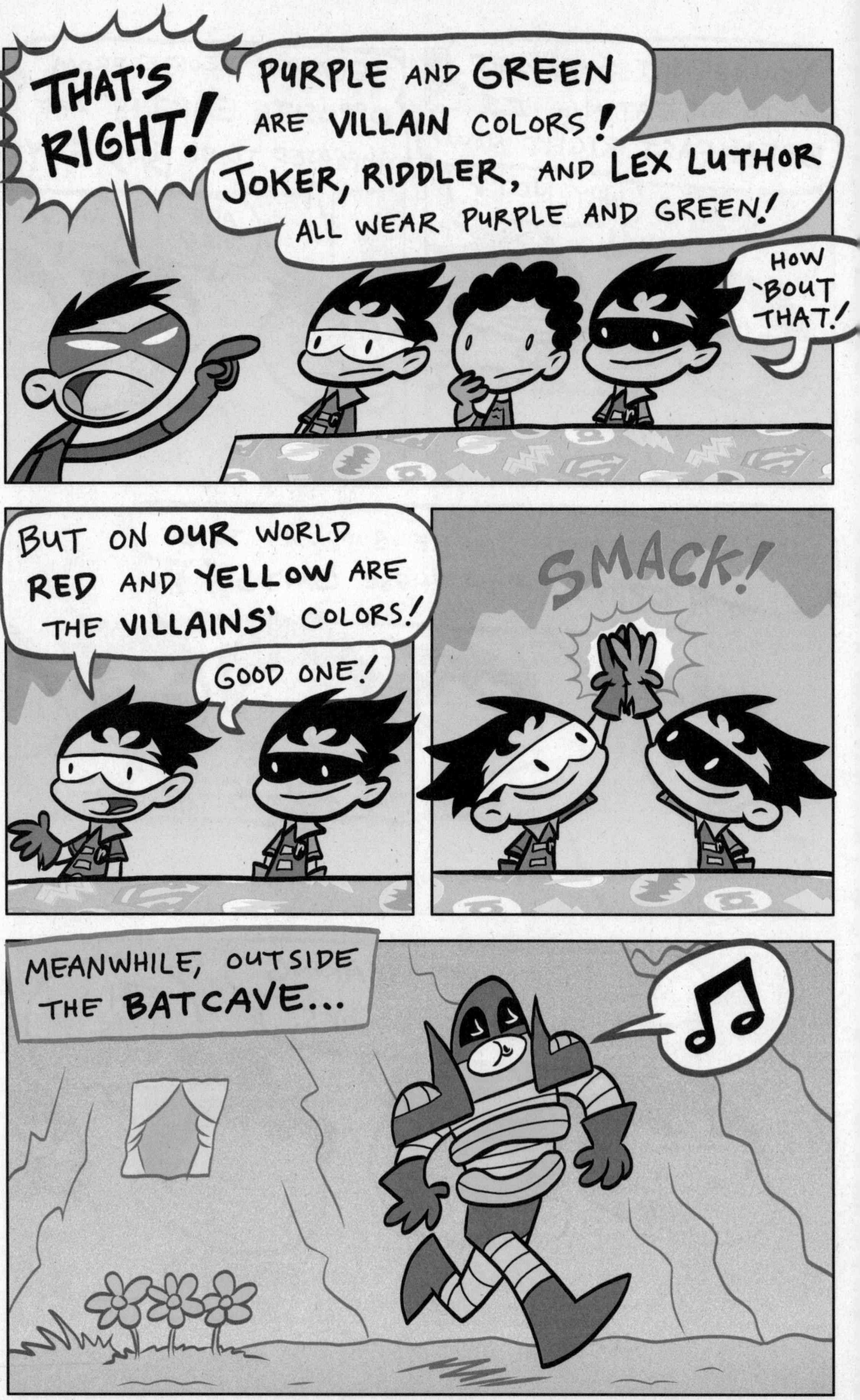
THAT'S RIGHT!
PURPLE AND GREEN ARE VILLAIN COLORS!
JOKER, RIDDLER, AND LEX LUTHOR ALL WEAR PURPLE AND GREEN!
HOW `BOUT THAT!
BUT ON OUR WORLD RED AND YELLOW ARE THE VILLAINS' COLORS!
GOOD ONE!
SMACK!
MEANWHILE, OUTSIDE THE BATCAVE...

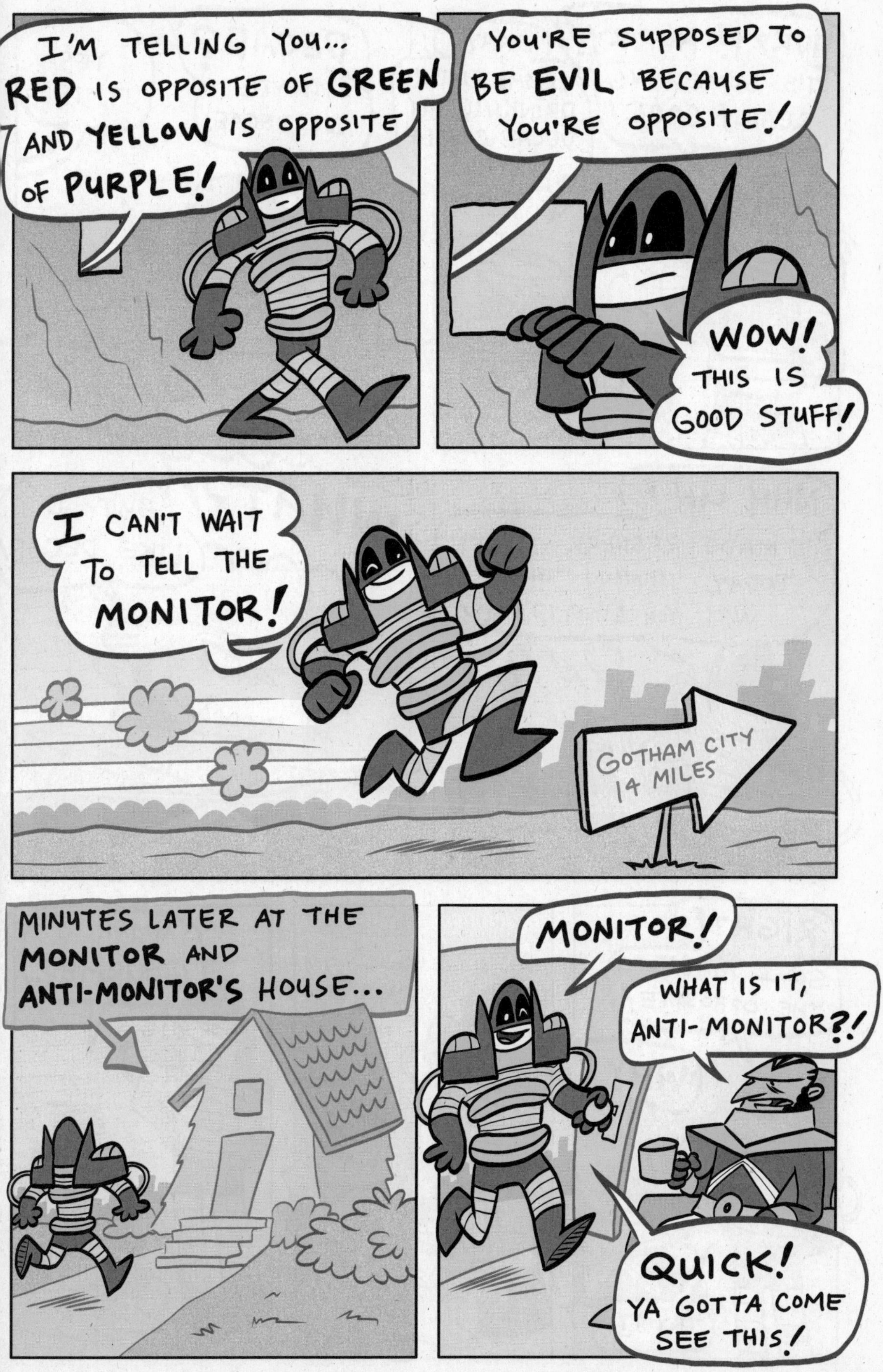
I'M TELLING YOU... RED IS OPPOSITE OF GREEN AND YELLOW IS OPPOSITE OF PURPLE!
YOU'RE SUPPOSED TO BE EVIL BECAUSE YOU'RE OPPOSITE!
WOW! THIS IS GOOD STUFF!
I CAN'T WAIT TO TELL THE MONITOR!
GOTHAM CITY 14 MILES
MINUTES LATER AT THE MONITOR AND ANTI-MONITOR'S HOUSE...
MONITOR!
WHAT IS IT, ANTI-MONITOR?!
QUICK! YA GOTTA COME SEE THIS!

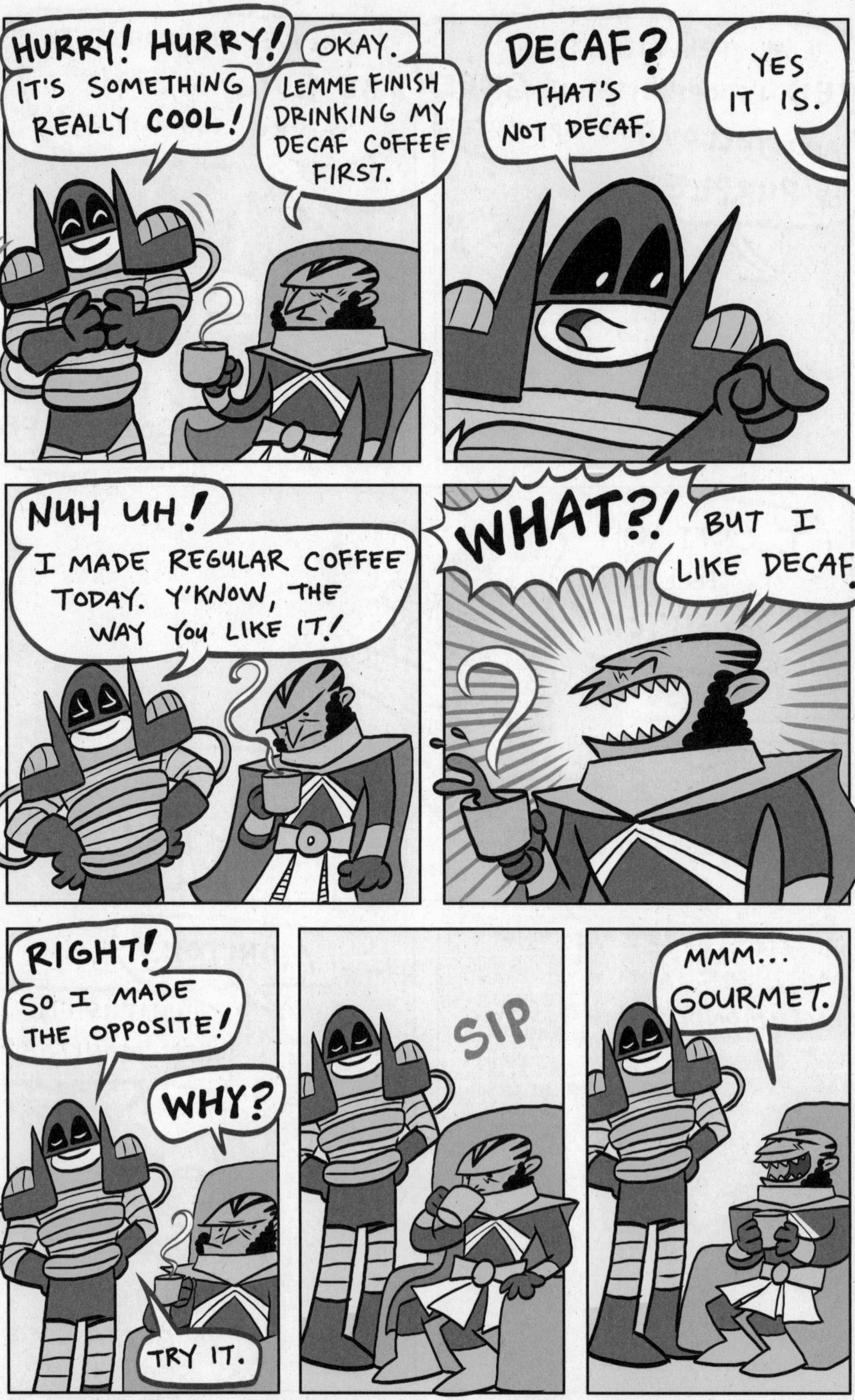
HURRY! HURRY! IT'S SOMETHING REALLY COOL!
OKAY. LEMME FINISH DRINKING MY DECAF COFFEE FIRST.
DECAF? THAT'S NOT DECAF.
YES IT IS.
NUH UH! I MADE REGULAR COFFEE TODAY. Y'KNOW, THE WAY YOU LIKE IT!
WHAT?!
BUT I LIKE DECAF!
RIGHT! SO I MADE THE OPPOSITE!
WHY?
TRY IT.
SIP
MMM... GOURMET.

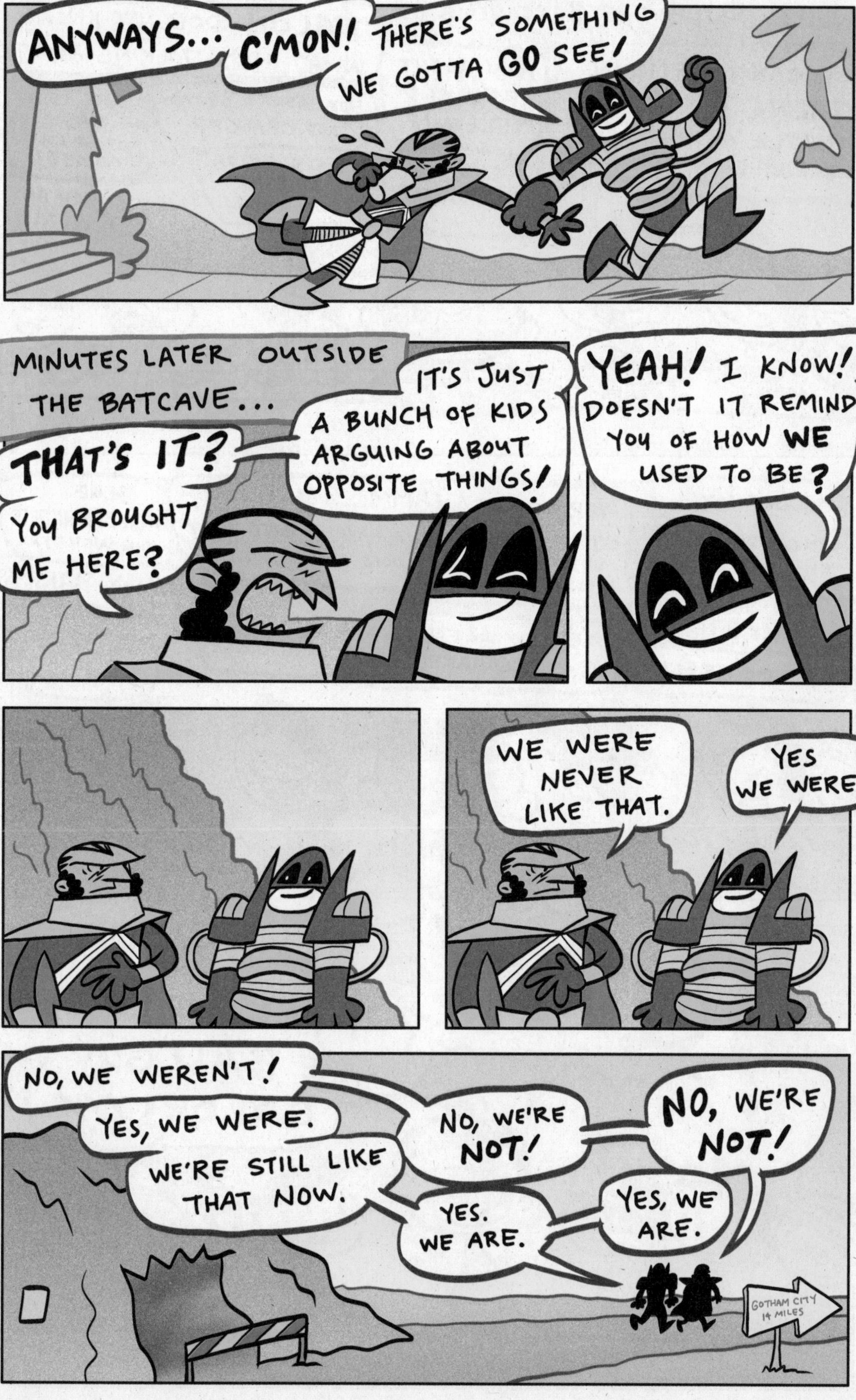
ANYWAYS... C'MON! THERE'S SOMETHING WE GOTTA GO SEE!
MINUTES LATER OUTSIDE THE BATCAVE...
THAT'S IT? YOU BROUGHT ME HERE?
IT'S JUST A BUNCH OF KIDS ARGUING ABOUT OPPOSITE THINGS!
YEAH! I KNOW! DOESN'T IT REMIND YOU OF HOW WE USED TO BE?
WE WERE NEVER LIKE THAT.
YES WE WERE.
NO, WE WEREN'T!
YES, WE WERE.
WE'RE STILL LIKE THAT NOW.
NO, WE'RE NOT!
YES. WE ARE.
NO, WE'RE NOT!
YES, WE ARE.
GOTHAM CITY 14 MILES

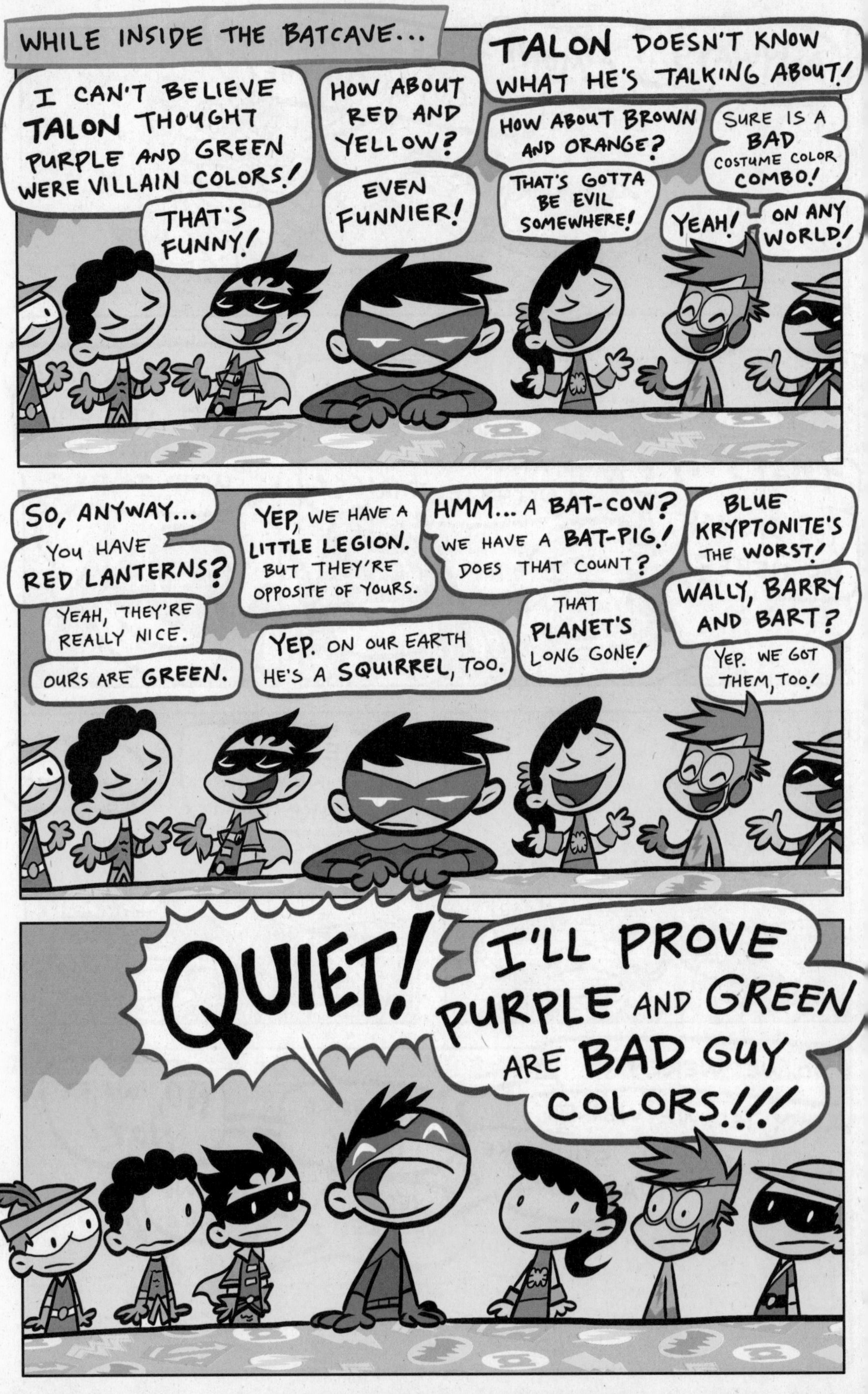
WHILE INSIDE THE BATCAVE...
I CAN'T BELIEVE TALON THOUGHT PURPLE AND GREEN WERE VILLAIN COLORS!
THAT'S FUNNY!
HOW ABOUT RED AND YELLOW?
EVEN FUNNIER!
TALON DOESN'T KNOW WHAT HE'S TALKING ABOUT!
HOW ABOUT BROWN AND ORANGE?
THAT'S GOTTA BE EVIL SOMEWHERE!
SURE IS A BAD COSTUME COLOR COMBO!
YEAH!
ON ANY WORLD!
SO, ANYWAY...
YOU HAVE RED LANTERNS?
YEAH, THEY'RE REALLY NICE.
OURS ARE GREEN.
YEP, WE HAVE A LITTLE LEGION. BUT THEY'RE OPPOSITE OF YOURS.
YEP. ON OUR EARTH HE'S A SQUIRREL, TOO.
HMM... A BAT-COW? WE HAVE A BAT-PIG! DOES THAT COUNT?
THAT PLANET'S LONG GONE!
BLUE KRYPTONITE'S THE WORST!
WALLY, BARRY AND BART?
YEP. WE GOT THEM, TOO!
QUIET!
I'LL PROVE PURPLE AND GREEN ARE BAD GUY COLORS!!!

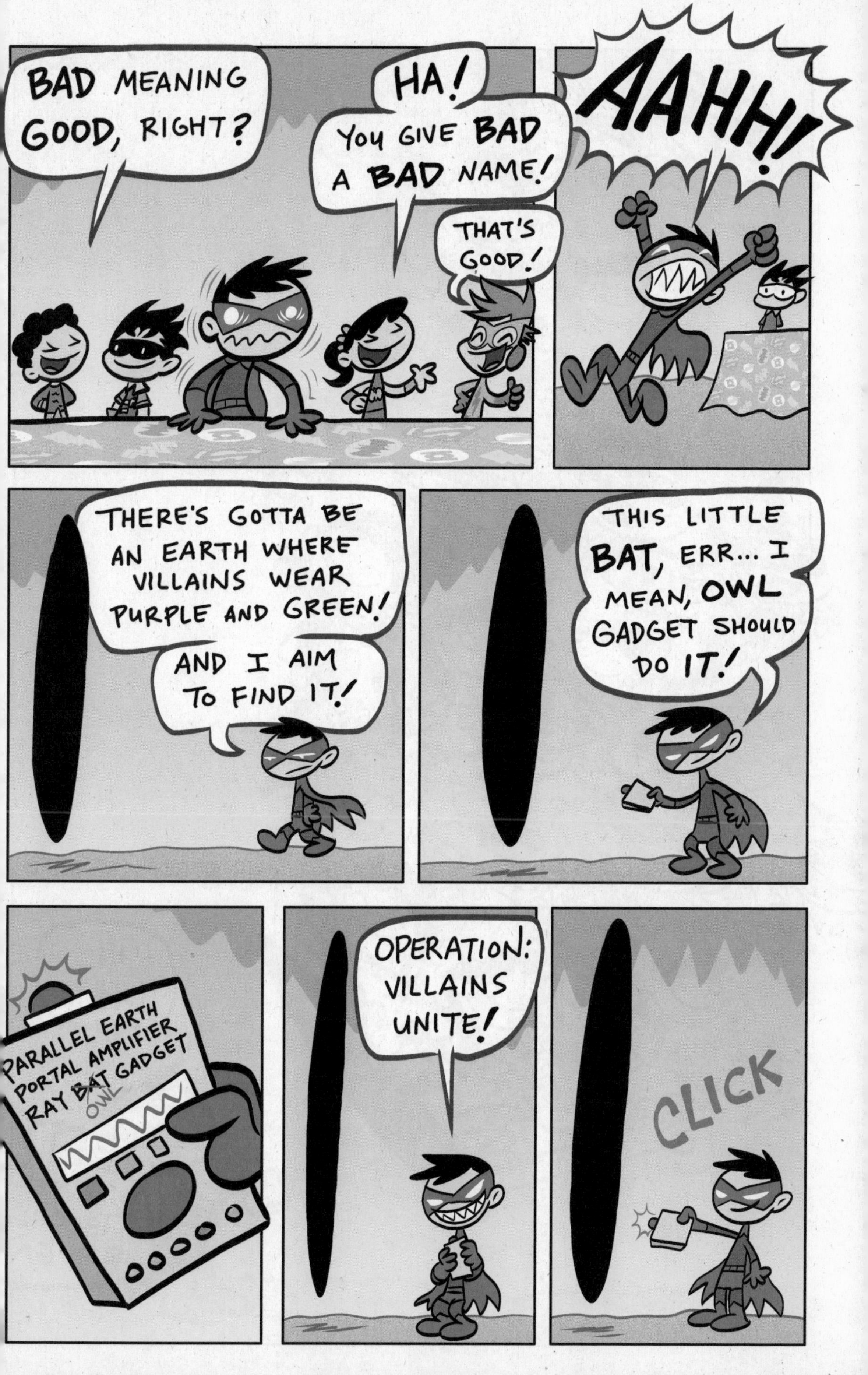
BAD MEANING GOOD, RIGHT?
HA! YOU GIVE BAD A BAD NAME!
THAT'S GOOD!
AAHH!
THERE'S GOTTA BE AN EARTH WHERE VILLAINS WEAR PURPLE AND GREEN!
AND I AIM TO FIND IT!
THIS LITTLE BAT, ERR... I MEAN, OWL GADGET SHOULD DO IT!
PARALLEL EARTH PORTAL AMPLIFIER RAY BAT OWL GADGET
OPERATION: VILLAINS UNITE!
CLICK

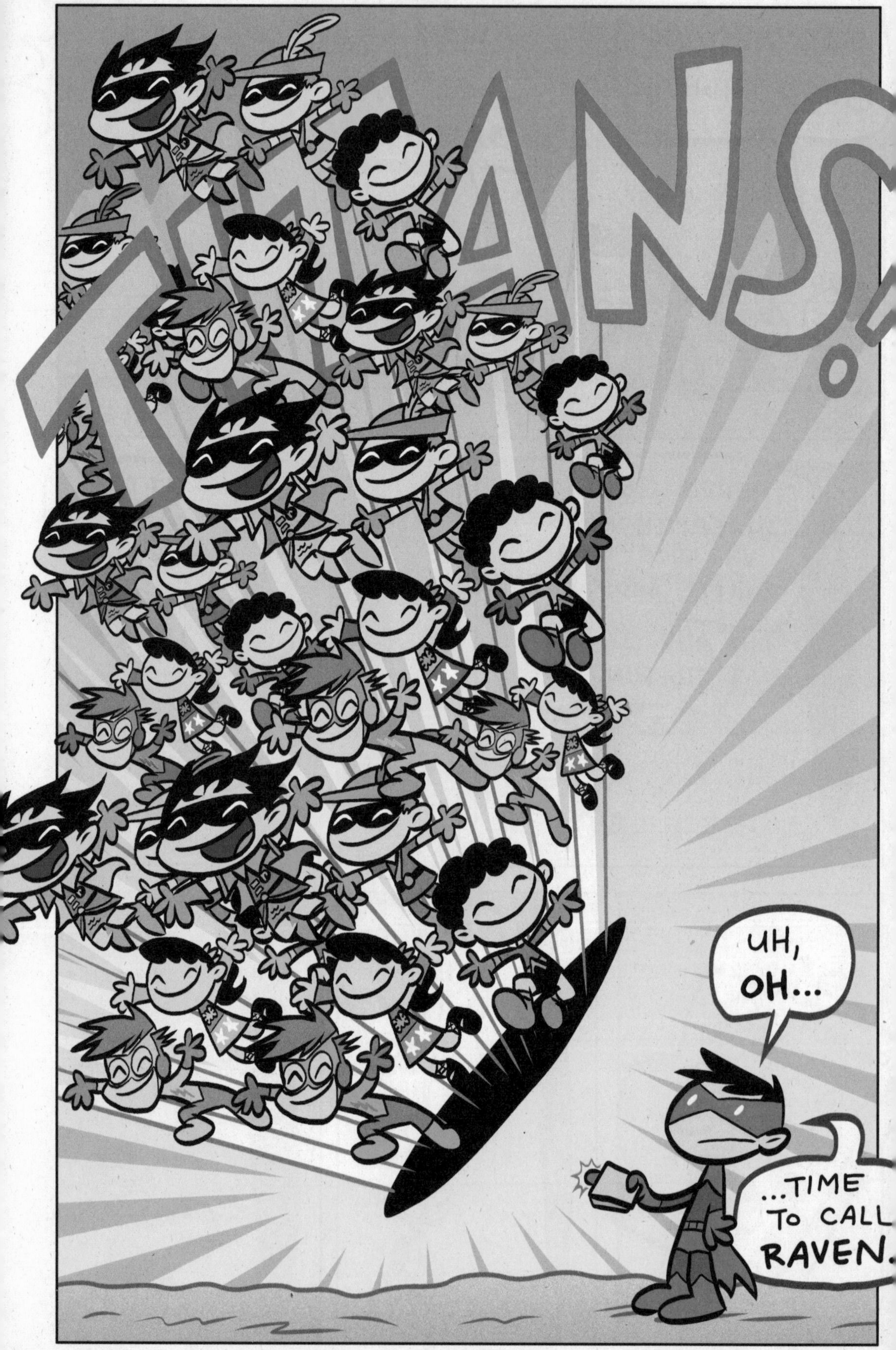
TITANS!
UH, OH...
...TIME TO CALL RAVEN.

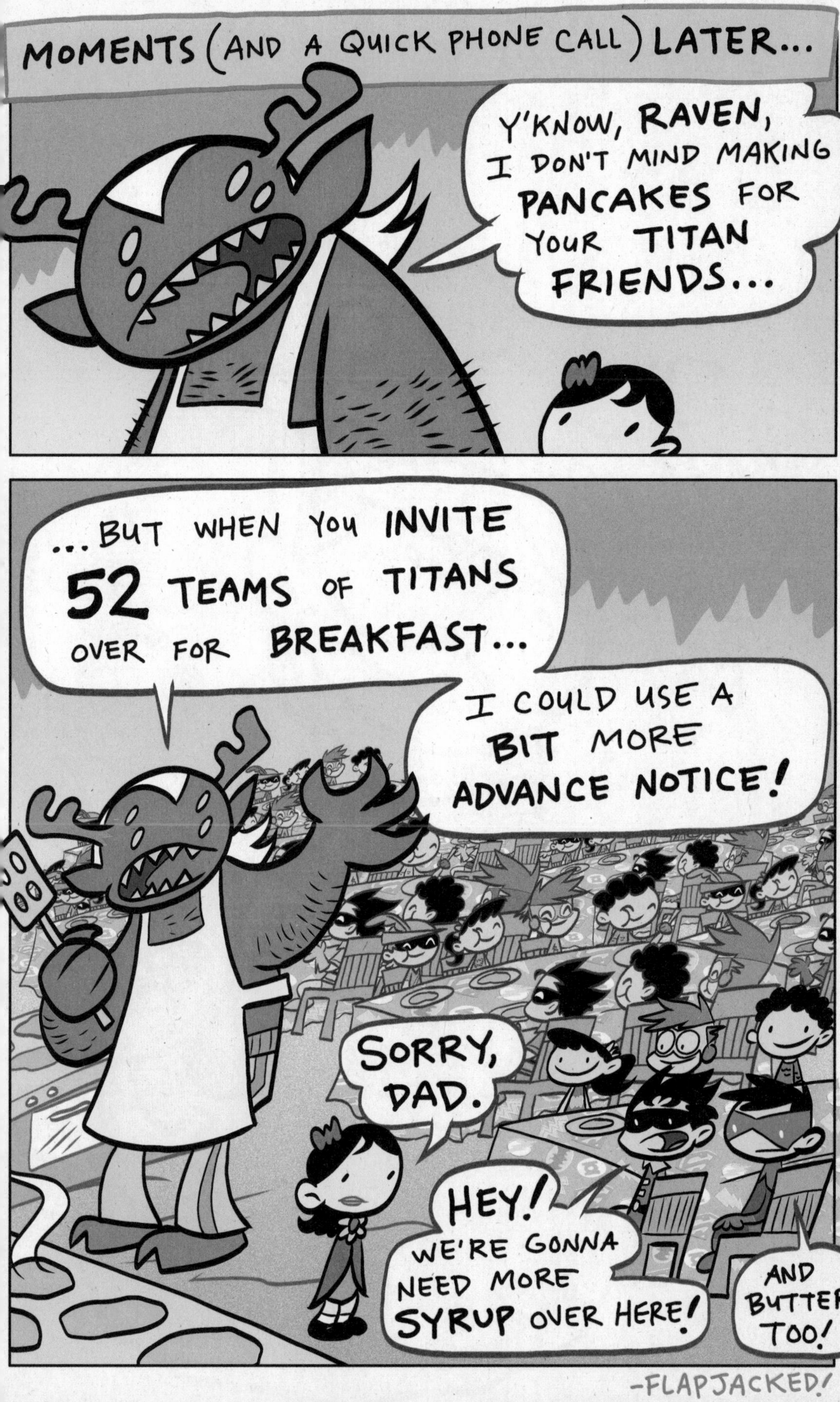
MOMENTS (AND A QUICK PHONE CALL) LATER...
Y'KNOW, RAVEN, I DON'T MIND MAKING PANCAKES FOR YOUR TITAN FRIENDS...
...BUT WHEN YOU INVITE 52 TEAMS OF TITANS OVER FOR BREAKFAST...
I COULD USE A BIT MORE ADVANCE NOTICE!
SORRY, DAD.
HEY! WE'RE GONNA NEED MORE SYRUP OVER HERE!
AND BUTTER, TOO!
-FLAPJACKED!

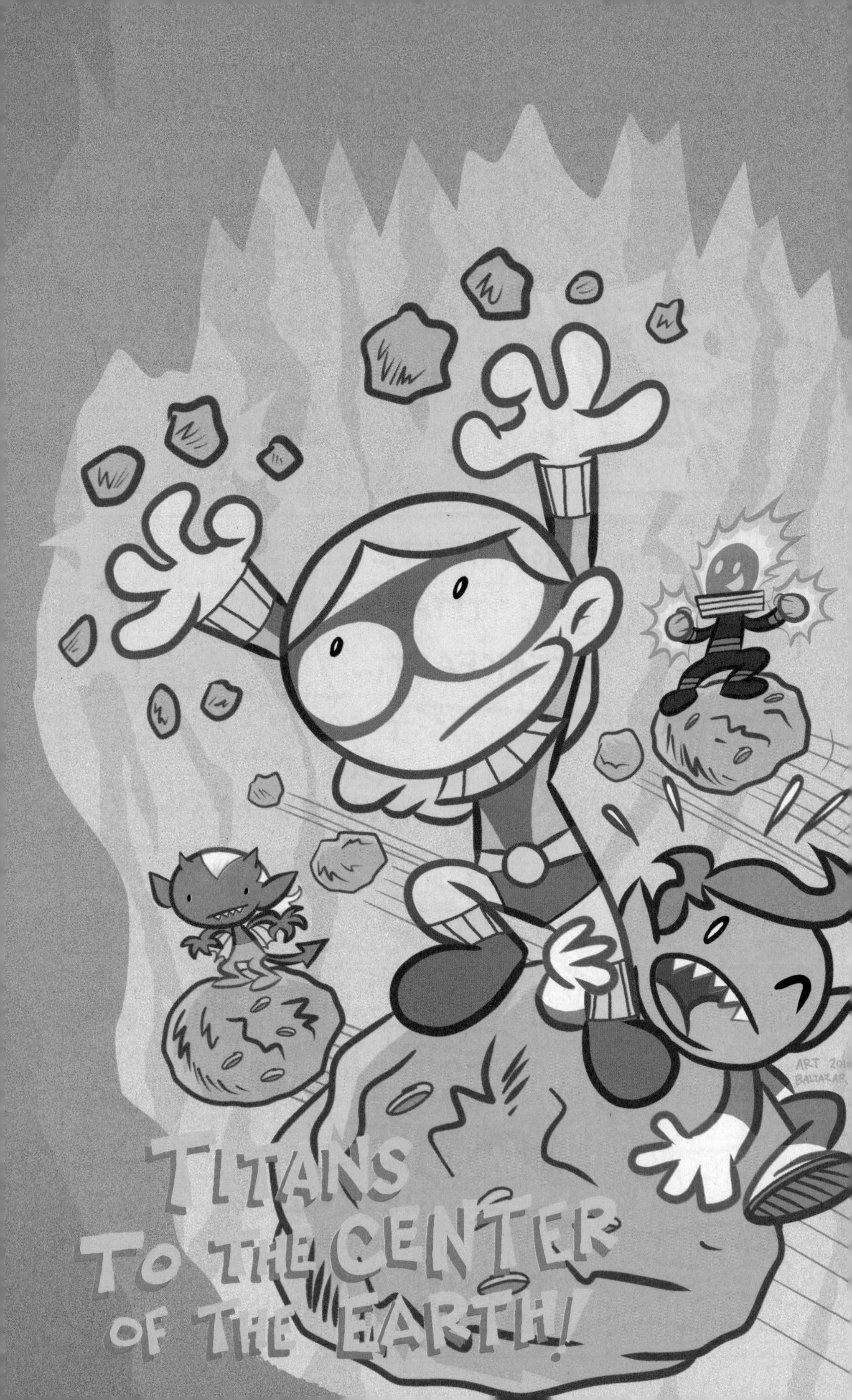

TITANS
TO THE CENTER
OF THE EARTH!
ART 2011
BALTAZAR

tiny titans

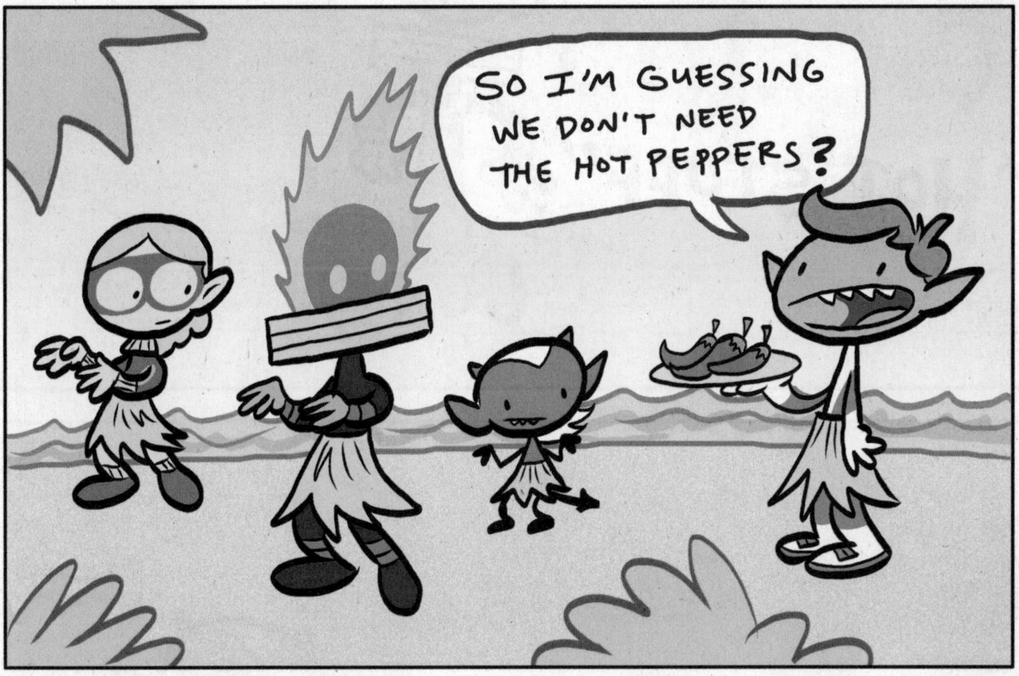
SO I'M GUESSING WE DON'T NEED THE HOT PEPPERS?

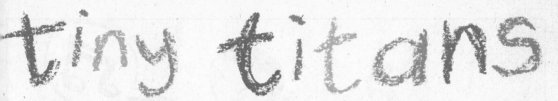

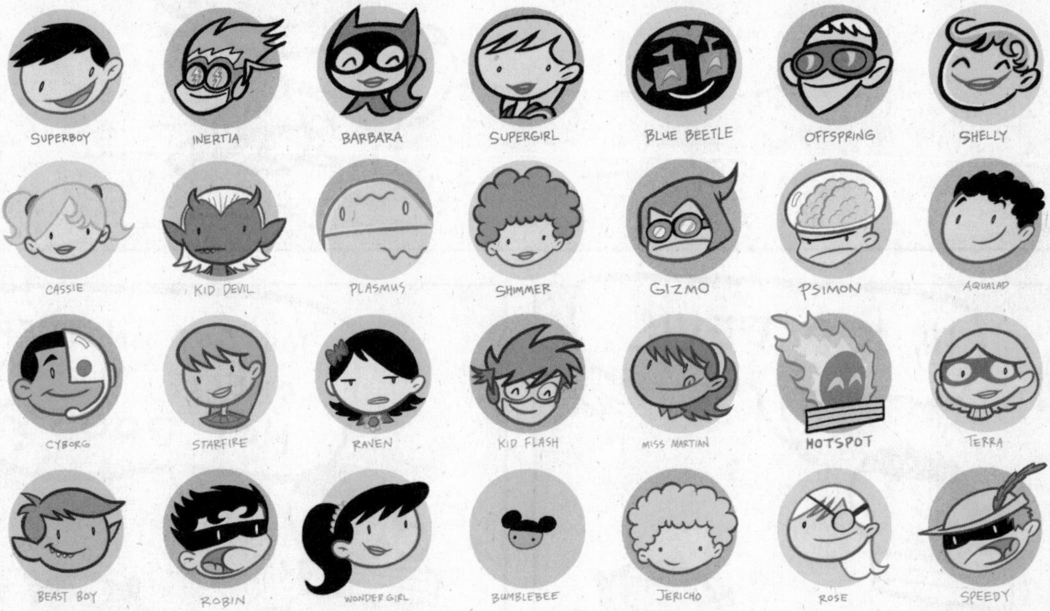
SUPERBOY
INERTIA
BARBARA
SUPERGIRL
BLUE BEETLE
OFFSPRING
SHELLY
CASSIE
KID DEVIL
PLASMUS
SHIMMER
GIZMO
PSIMON
AQUALAD
CYBORG
STARFIRE
RAVEN
KID FLASH
MISS MARTIAN
HOTSPOT
TERRA
BEAST BOY
ROBIN
WONDER GIRL
BUMBLEBEE
JERICHO
ROSE
SPEEDY

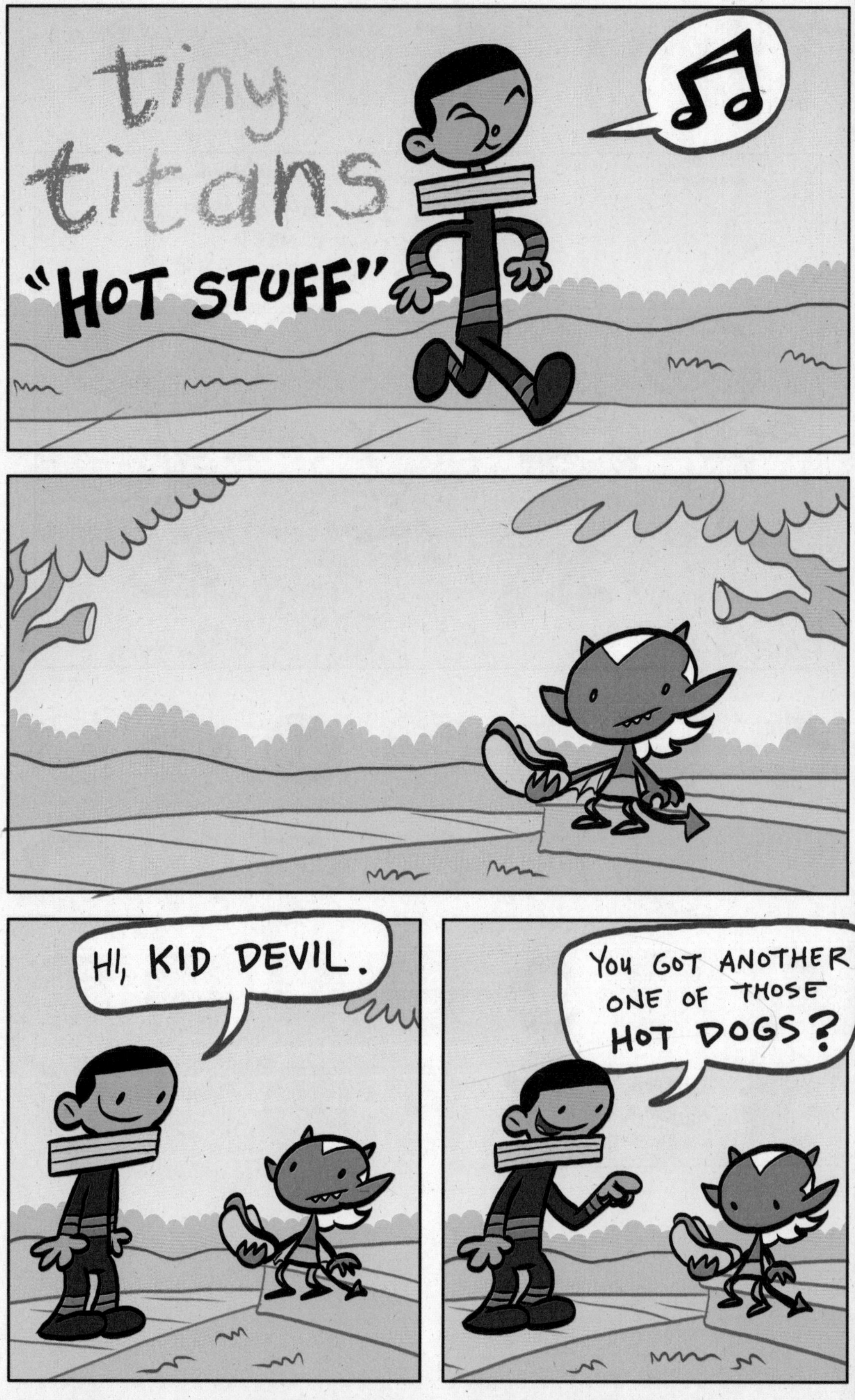
tiny titans
"HOT STUFF"
HI, KID DEVIL.
YOU GOT ANOTHER ONE OF THOSE HOT DOGS?

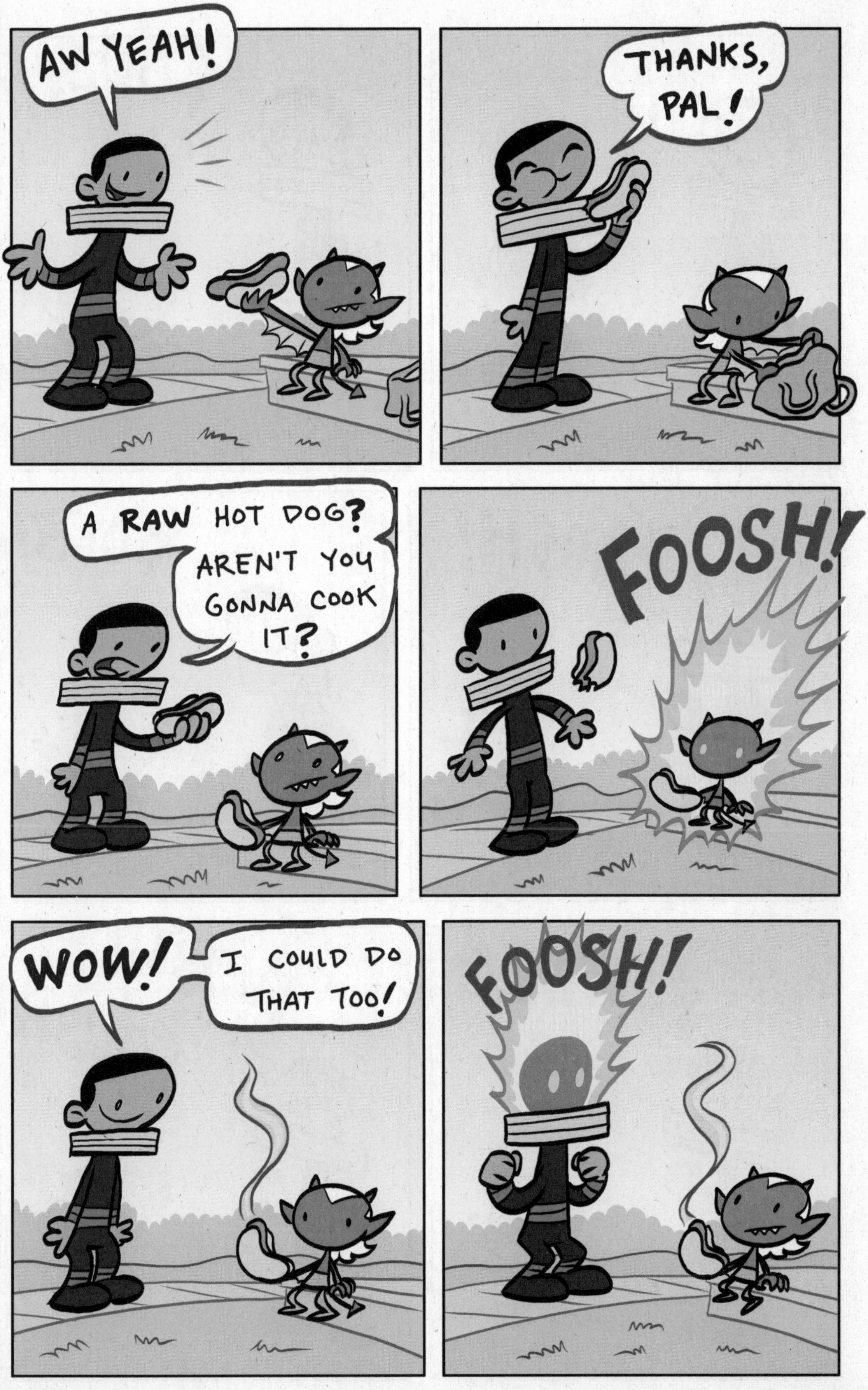
AW YEAH!
THANKS, PAL!
A RAW HOT DOG?
AREN'T YOU GONNA COOK IT?
FOOSH!
WOW!
I COULD DO THAT TOO!
FOOSH!

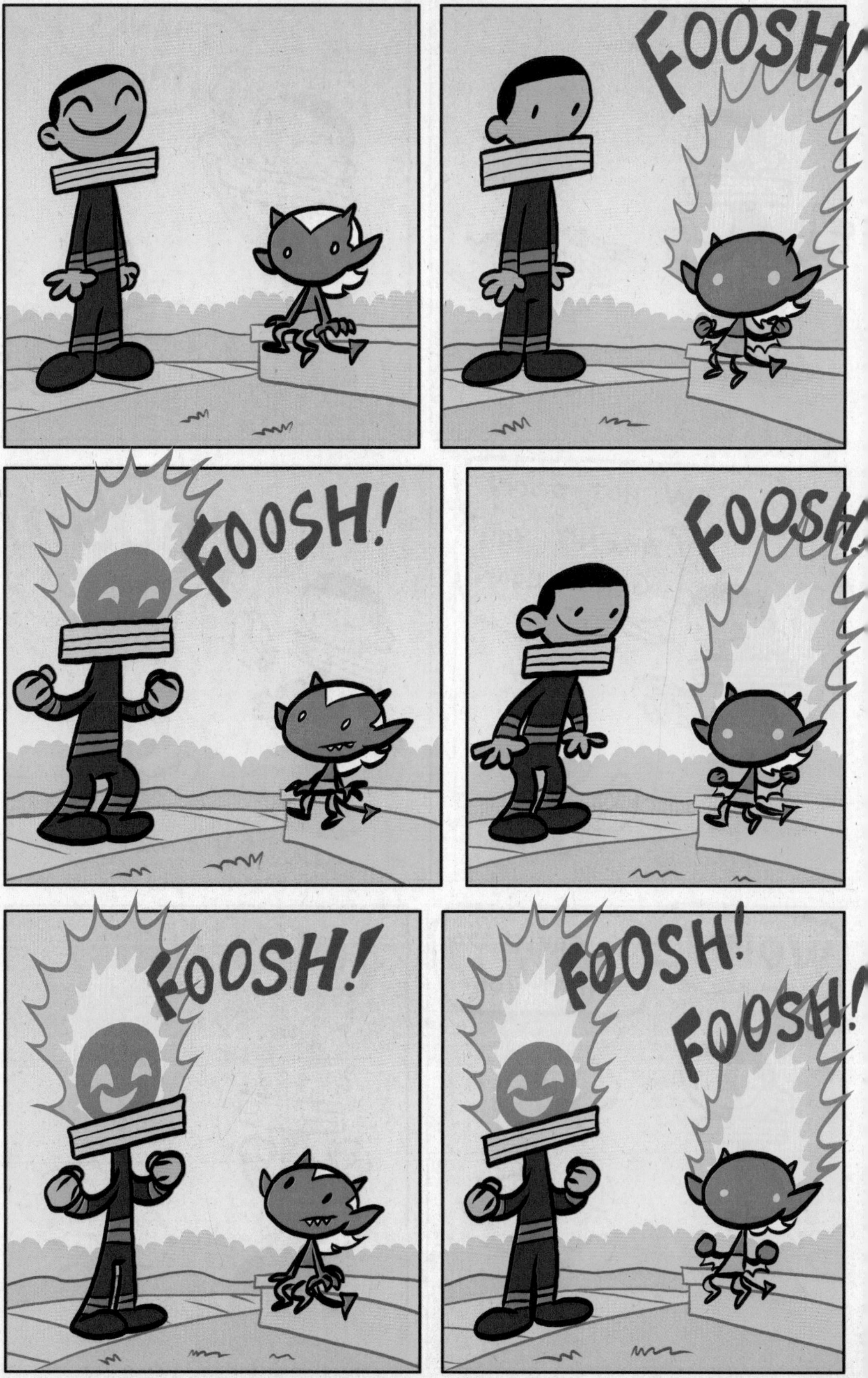
FOOSH!
FOOSH!
FOOSH!
FOOSH!
FOOSH!
FOOSH!

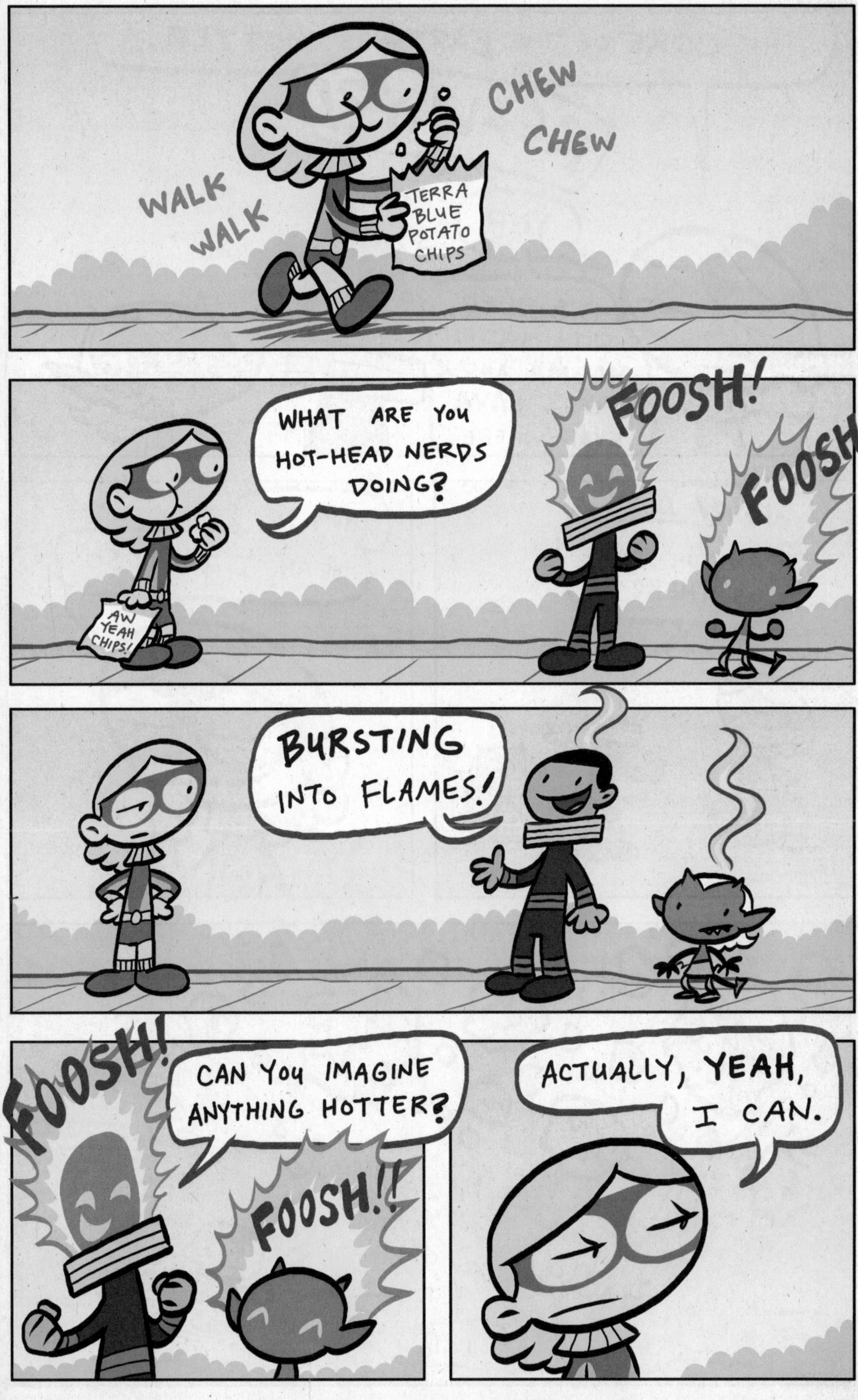
WALK
WALK
CHEW
CHEW
TERRA BLUE POTATO CHIPS
WHAT ARE YOU HOT-HEAD NERDS DOING?
AW YEAH CHIPS!
FOOSH!
FOOSH!
BURSTING INTO FLAMES!
FOOSH!
CAN YOU IMAGINE ANYTHING HOTTER?
FOOSH!!
ACTUALLY, YEAH, I CAN.

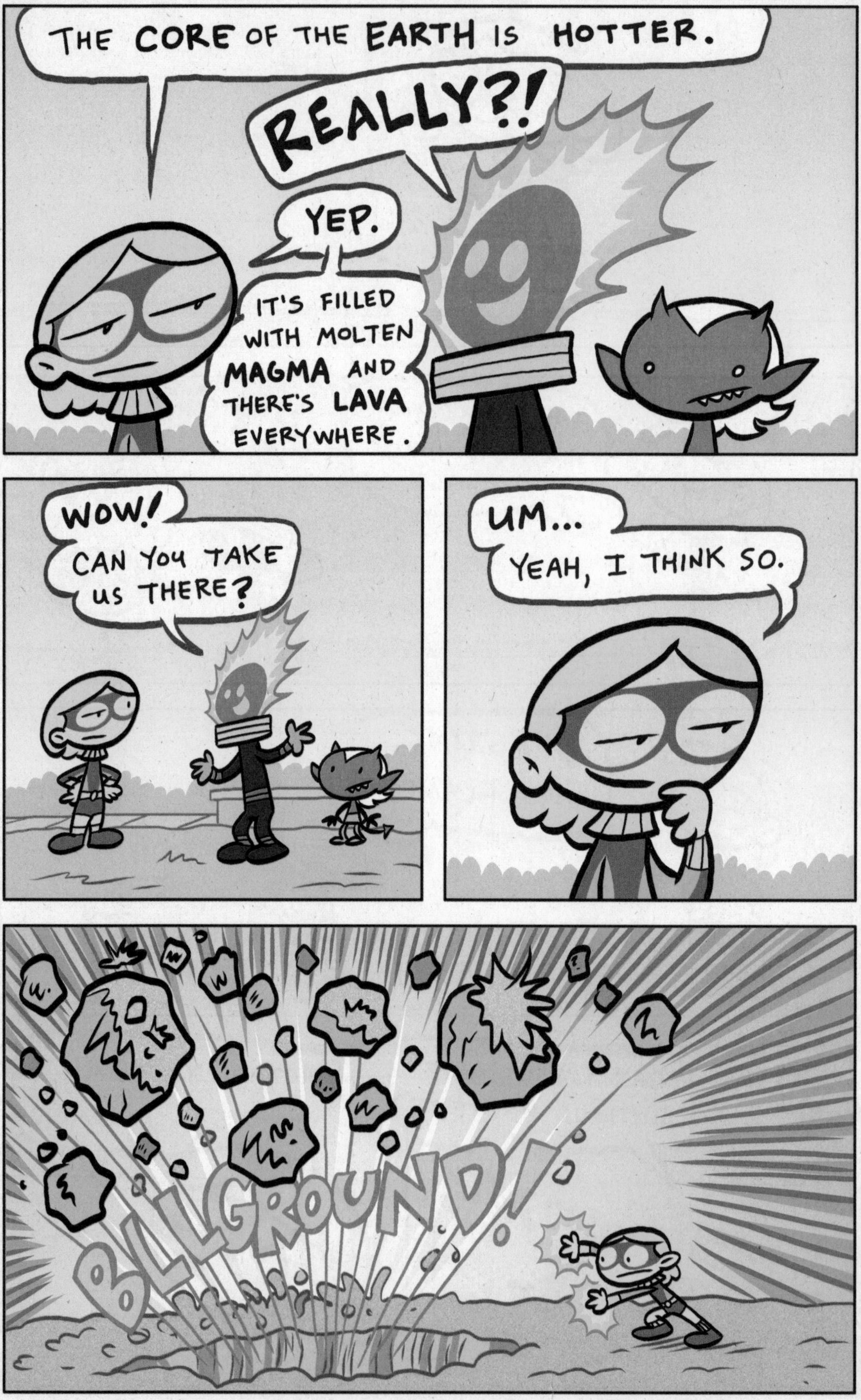
THE CORE OF THE EARTH IS HOTTER.
REALLY?!
YEP.
IT'S FILLED WITH MOLTEN MAGMA AND THERE'S LAVA EVERYWHERE.
WOW! CAN YOU TAKE US THERE?
UM... YEAH, I THINK SO.
BLLGROUND!

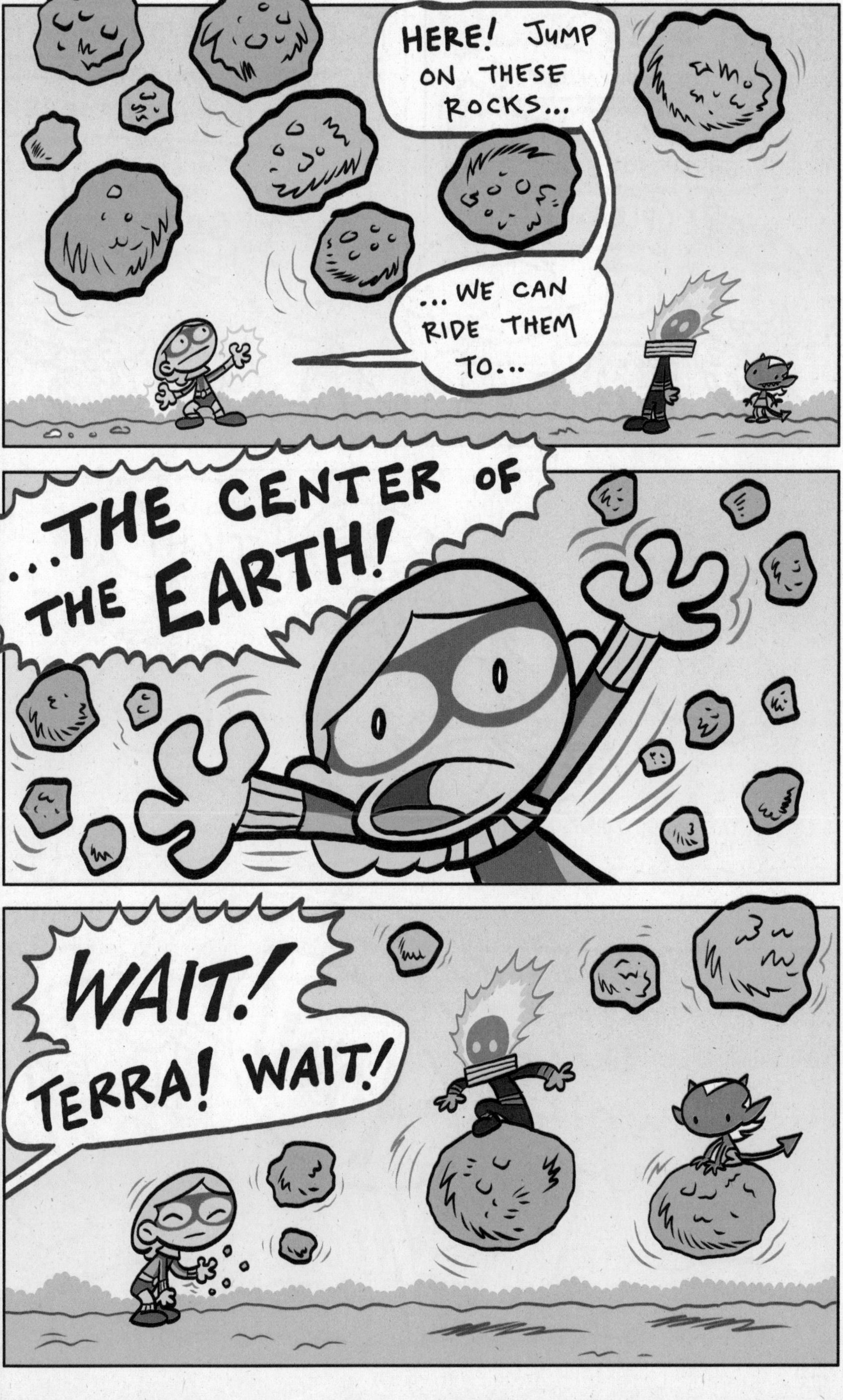
HERE! JUMP ON THESE ROCKS...
...WE CAN RIDE THEM TO...
...THE CENTER OF THE EARTH!
WAIT!
TERRA! WAIT!

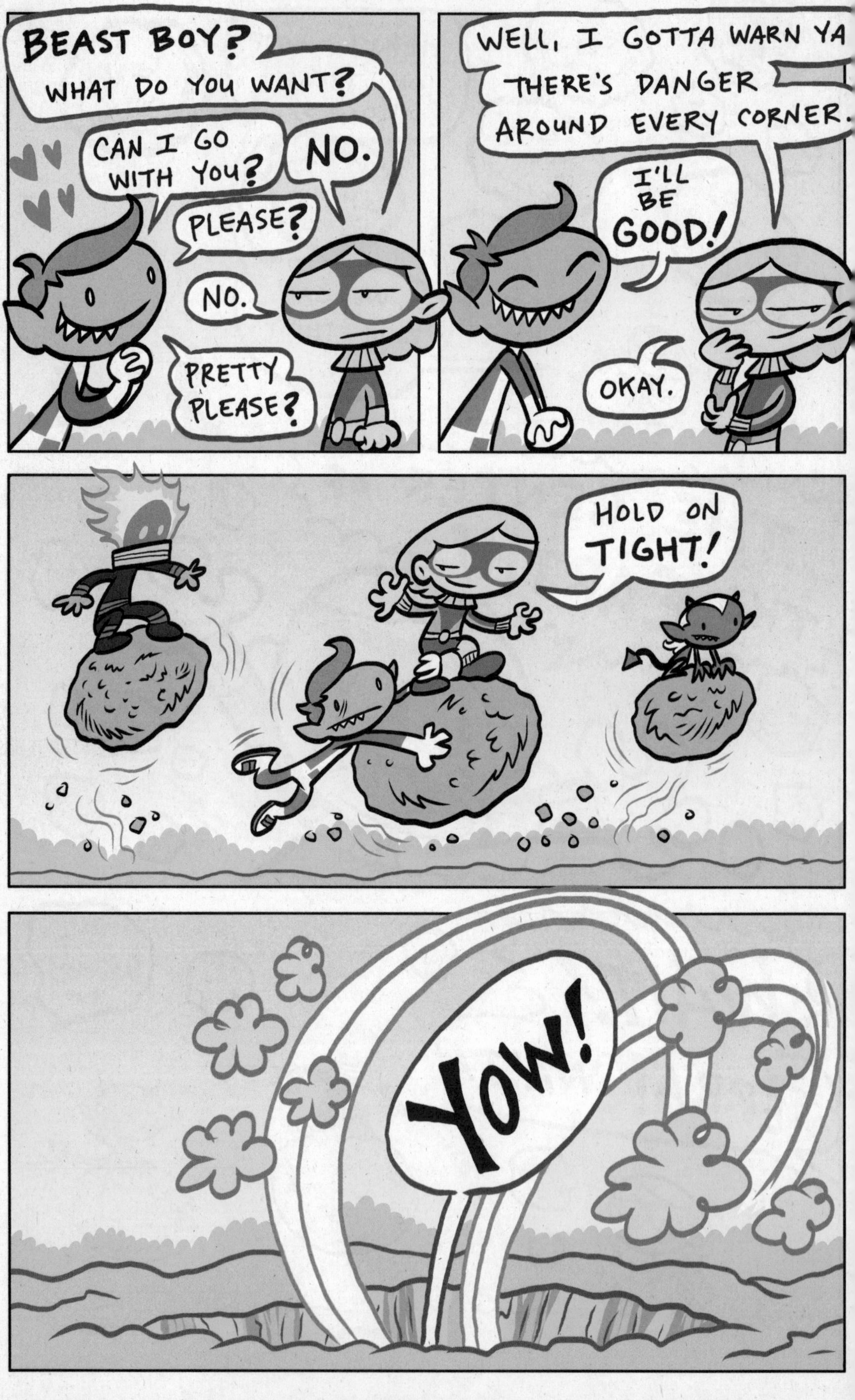
BEAST BOY? WHAT DO YOU WANT?
CAN I GO WITH YOU?
NO.
PLEASE?
NO.
PRETTY PLEASE?
WELL, I GOTTA WARN YA THERE'S DANGER AROUND EVERY CORNER.
I'LL BE GOOD!
OKAY.
HOLD ON TIGHT!
YOW!

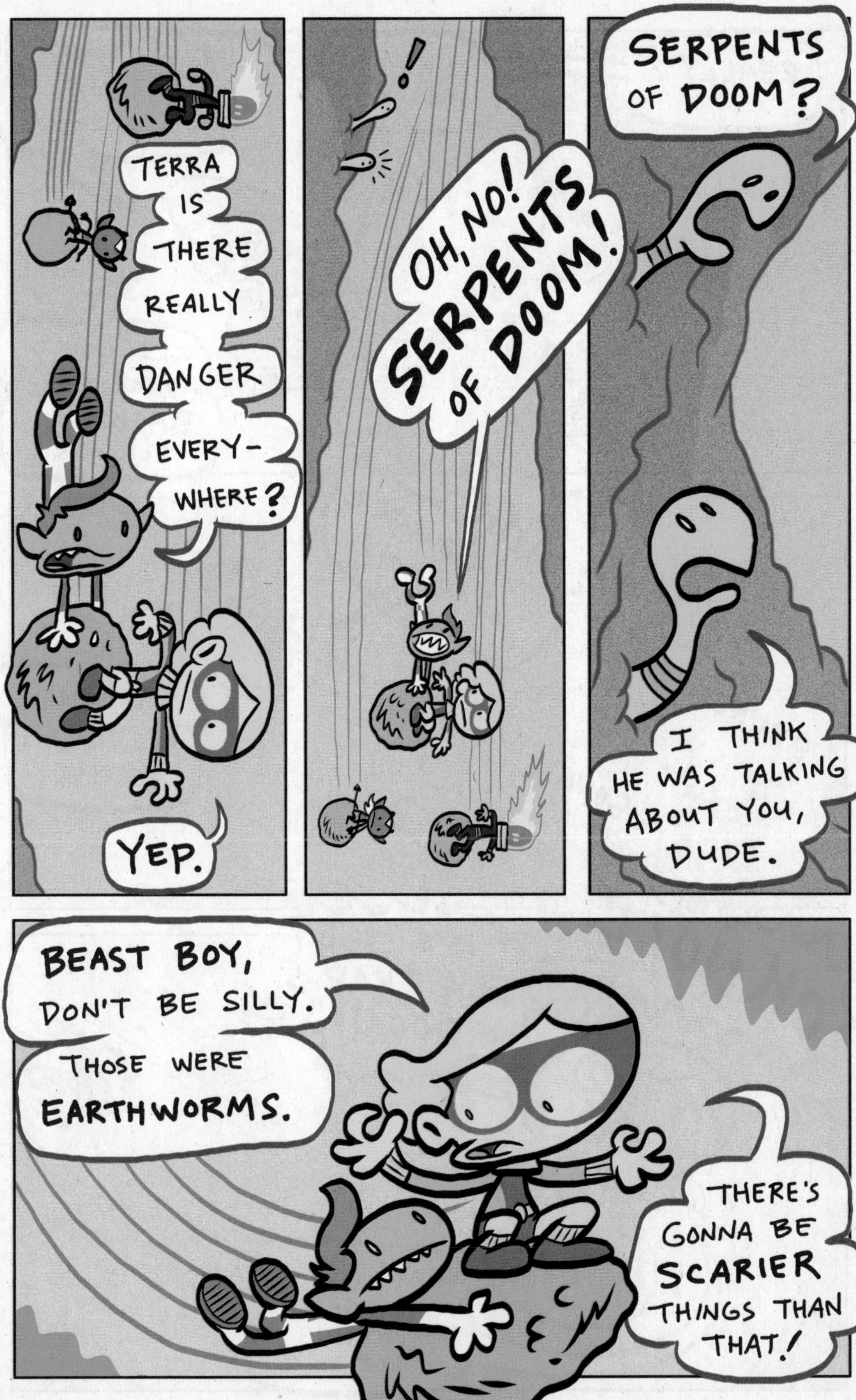
TERRA IS THERE REALLY DANGER EVERY-WHERE?
YEP.
!
OH, NO! SERPENTS OF DOOM!
SERPENTS OF DOOM?
I THINK HE WAS TALKING ABOUT YOU, DUDE.
BEAST BOY, DON'T BE SILLY.
THOSE WERE EARTHWORMS.
THERE'S GONNA BE SCARIER THINGS THAN THAT!

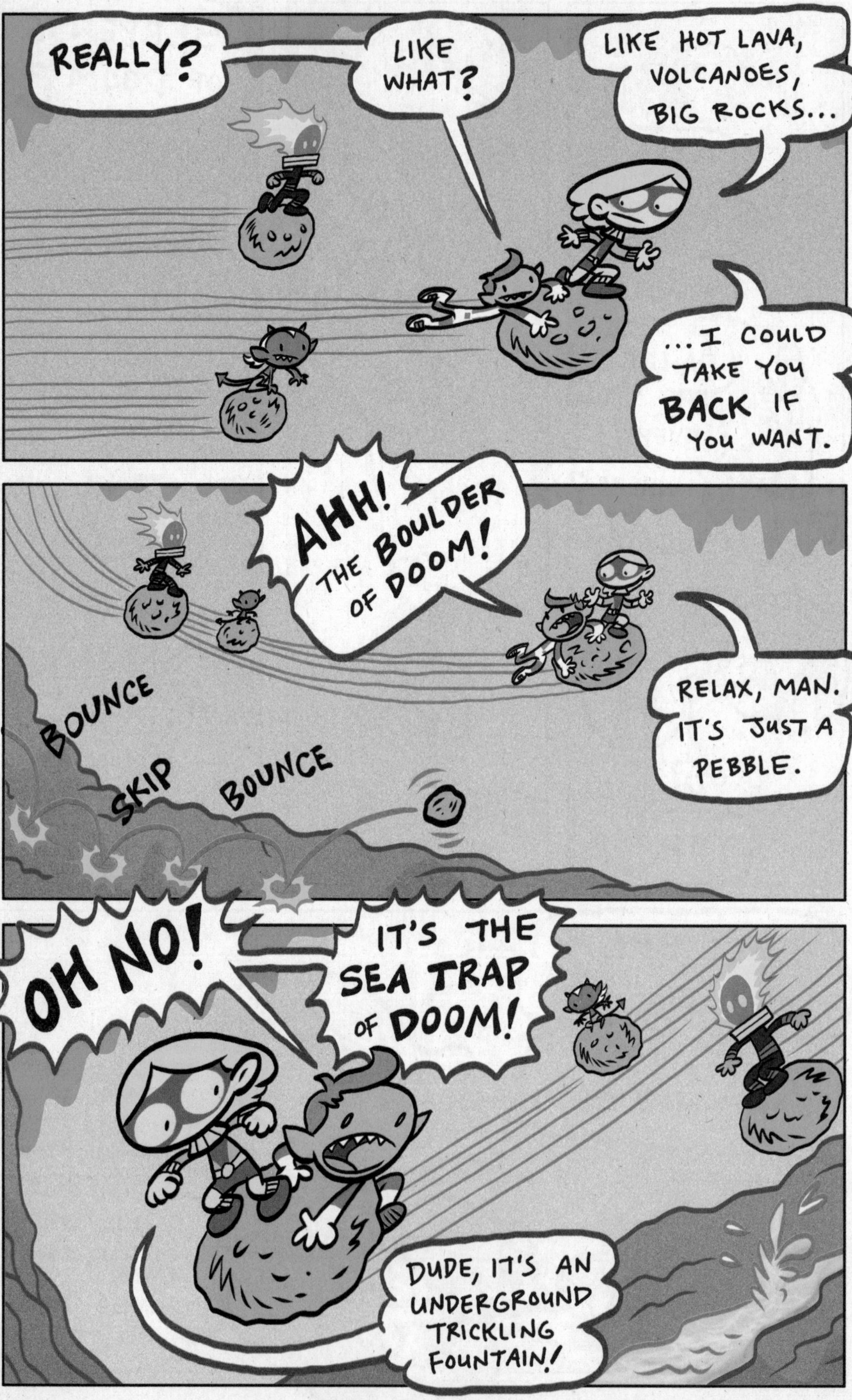
REALLY?
LIKE WHAT?
LIKE HOT LAVA, VOLCANOES, BIG ROCKS...
...I COULD TAKE YOU BACK IF YOU WANT.
AHH! THE BOULDER OF DOOM!
RELAX, MAN. IT'S JUST A PEBBLE.
BOUNCE
SKIP
BOUNCE
OH NO!
IT'S THE SEA TRAP OF DOOM!
DUDE, IT'S AN UNDERGROUND TRICKLING FOUNTAIN!

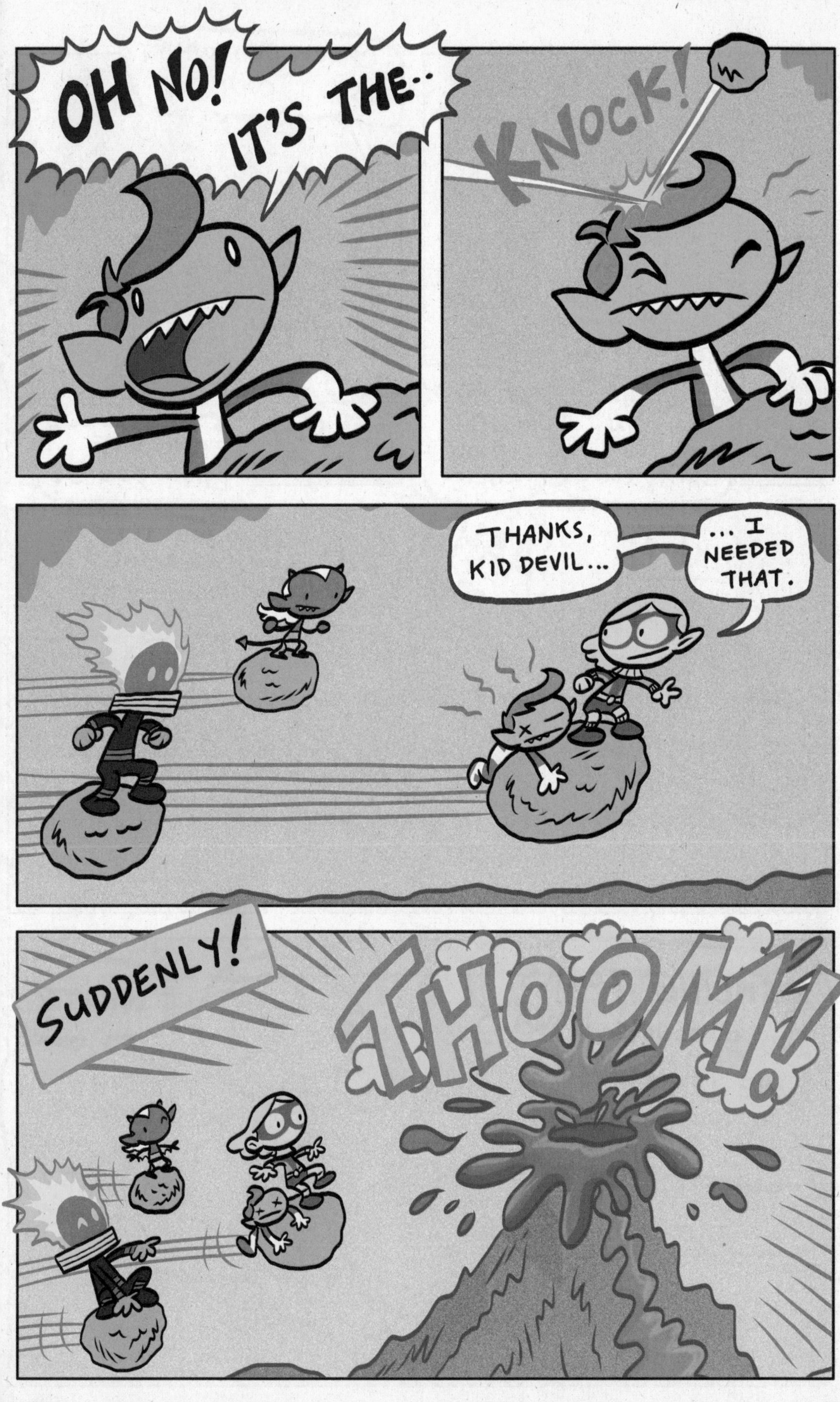
OH NO! IT'S THE..
KNOCK!
THANKS, KID DEVIL...
... I NEEDED THAT.
SUDDENLY!
THOOM!

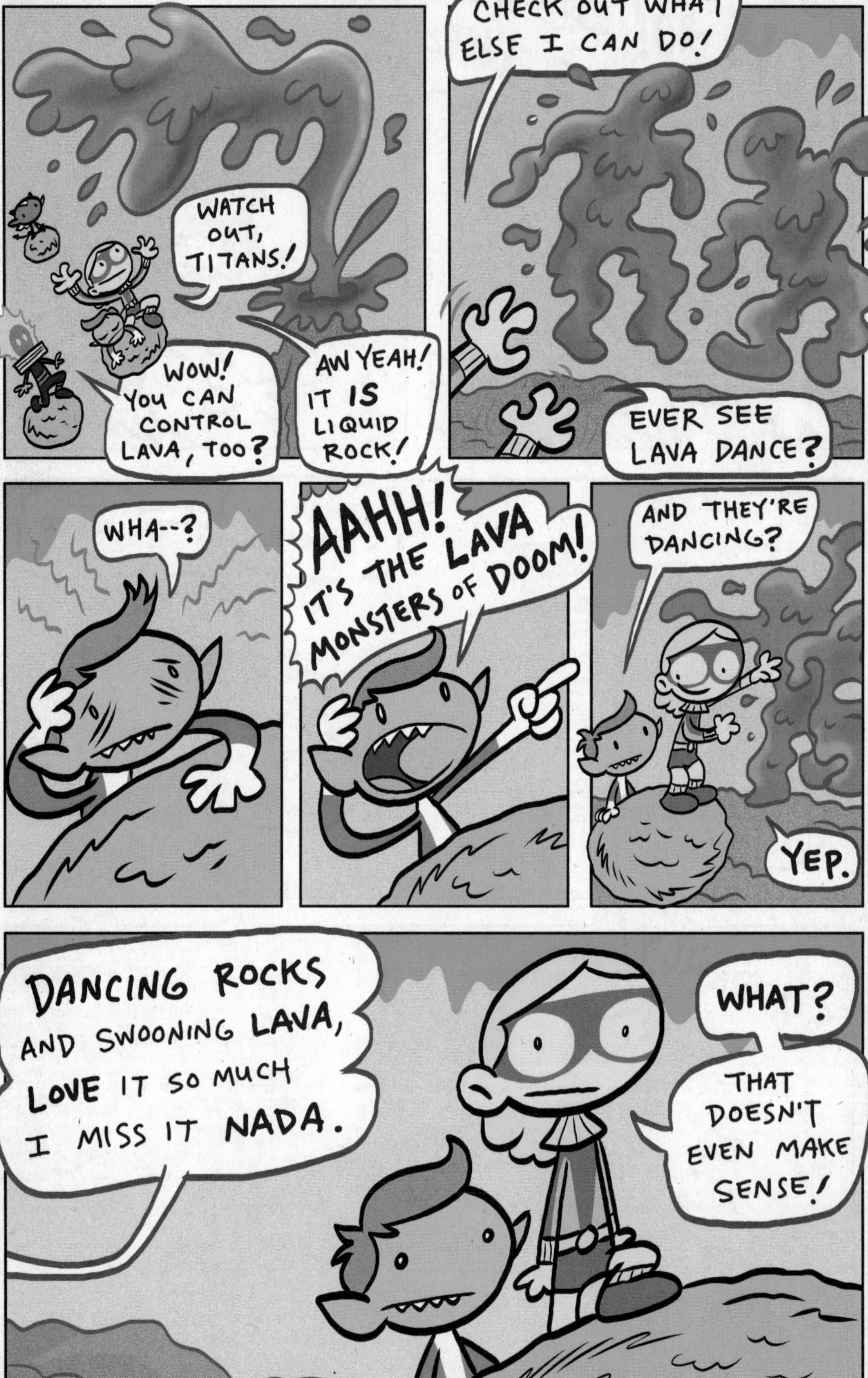
WATCH OUT, TITANS!
WOW! YOU CAN CONTROL LAVA, TOO?
AW YEAH! IT IS LIQUID ROCK!
CHECK OUT WHAT ELSE I CAN DO!
EVER SEE LAVA DANCE?
WHA--?
AAHH! IT'S THE LAVA MONSTERS OF DOOM!
AND THEY'RE DANCING?
YEP.
DANCING ROCKS AND SWOONING LAVA, LOVE IT SO MUCH I MISS IT NADA.
WHAT?
THAT DOESN'T EVEN MAKE SENSE!

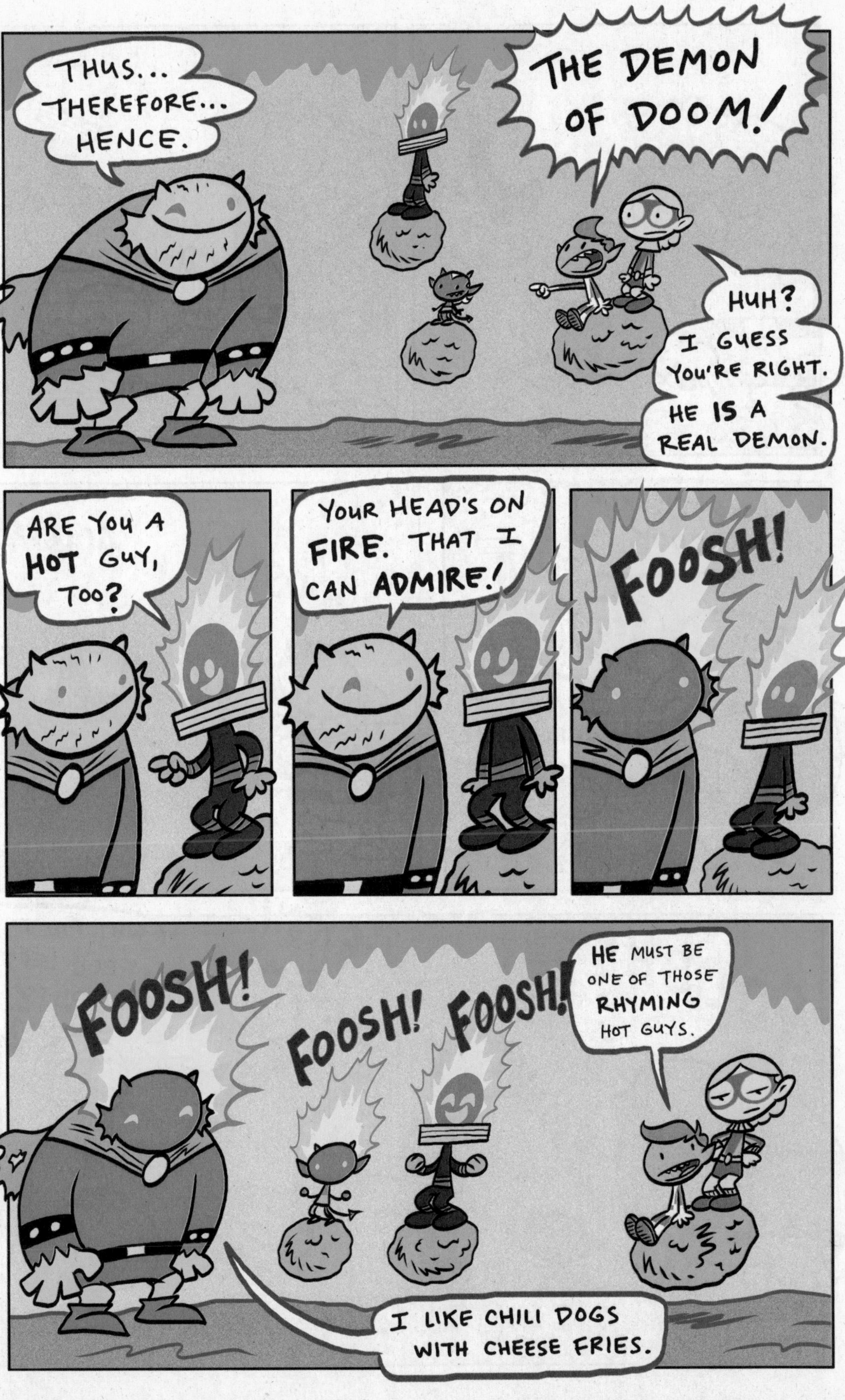
THUS... THEREFORE... HENCE.
THE DEMON OF DOOM!
HUH? I GUESS YOU'RE RIGHT.
HE IS A REAL DEMON.
ARE YOU A HOT GUY, TOO?
YOUR HEAD'S ON FIRE. THAT I CAN ADMIRE!
FOOSH!
FOOSH!
FOOSH!
FOOSH!
HE MUST BE ONE OF THOSE RHYMING HOT GUYS.
I LIKE CHILI DOGS WITH CHEESE FRIES.

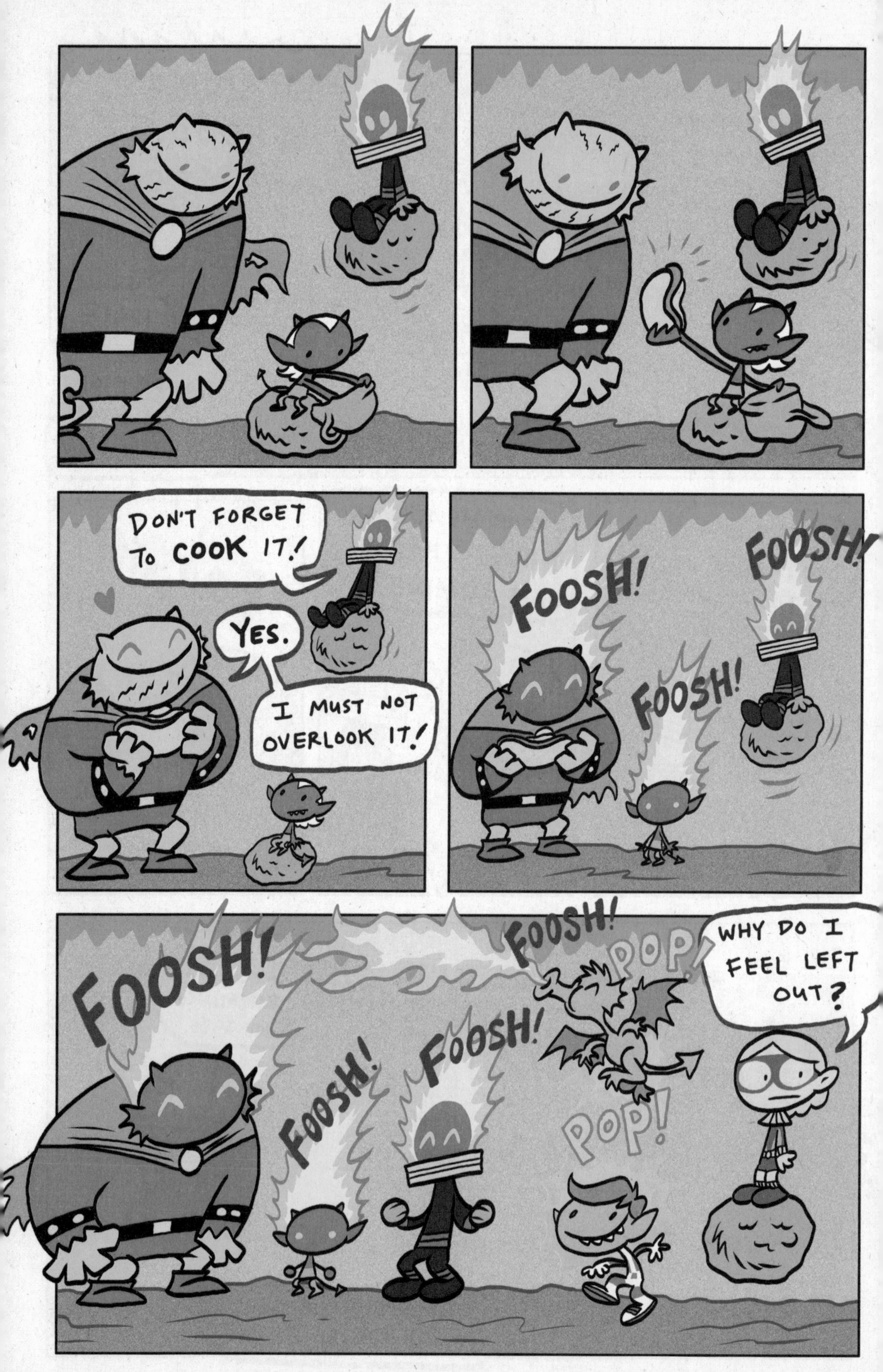
DON'T FORGET TO COOK IT!
YES.
I MUST NOT OVERLOOK IT!
FOOSH!
FOOSH!
FOOSH!
FOOSH!
FOOSH!
FOOSH!
FOOSH!
POP!
POP!
WHY DO I FEEL LEFT OUT?

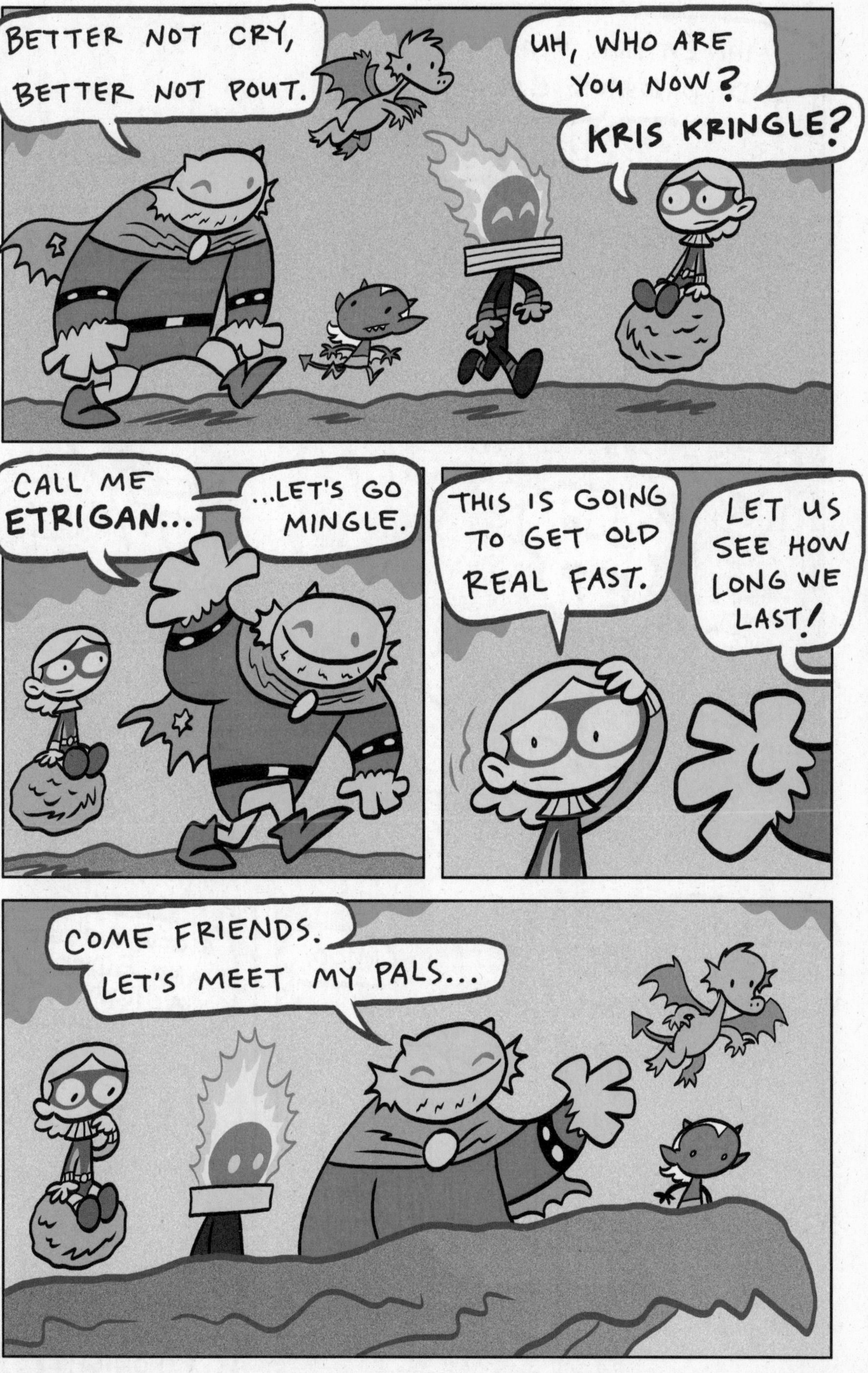
BETTER NOT CRY, BETTER NOT POUT.
UH, WHO ARE YOU NOW? KRIS KRINGLE?
CALL ME ETRIGAN...
...LET'S GO MINGLE.
THIS IS GOING TO GET OLD REAL FAST.
LET US SEE HOW LONG WE LAST!
COME FRIENDS. LET'S MEET MY PALS...

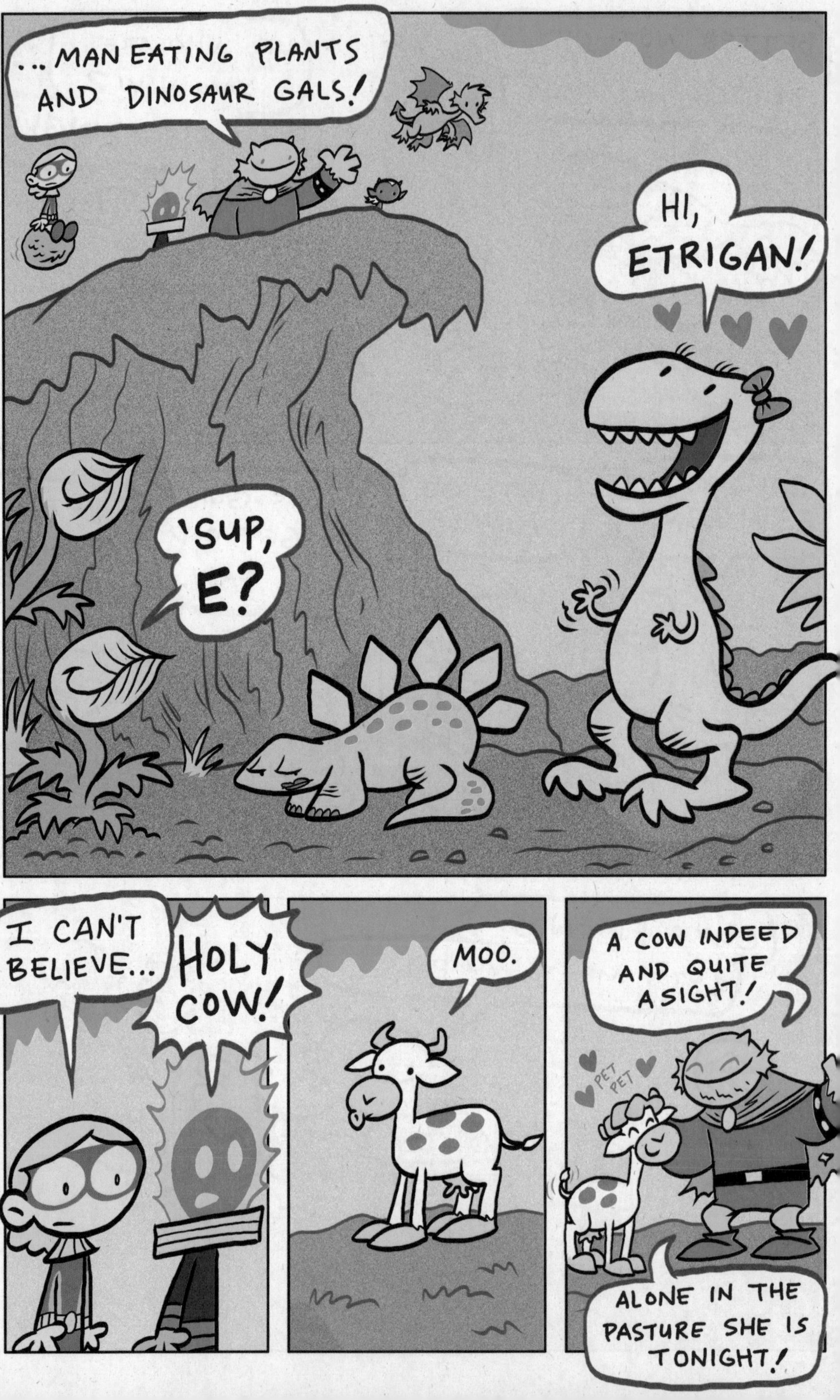
...MAN EATING PLANTS AND DINOSAUR GALS!
HI, ETRIGAN!
'SUP, E?
I CAN'T BELIEVE...
HOLY COW!
MOO.
A COW INDEED AND QUITE A SIGHT!
PET PET
ALONE IN THE PASTURE SHE IS TONIGHT!

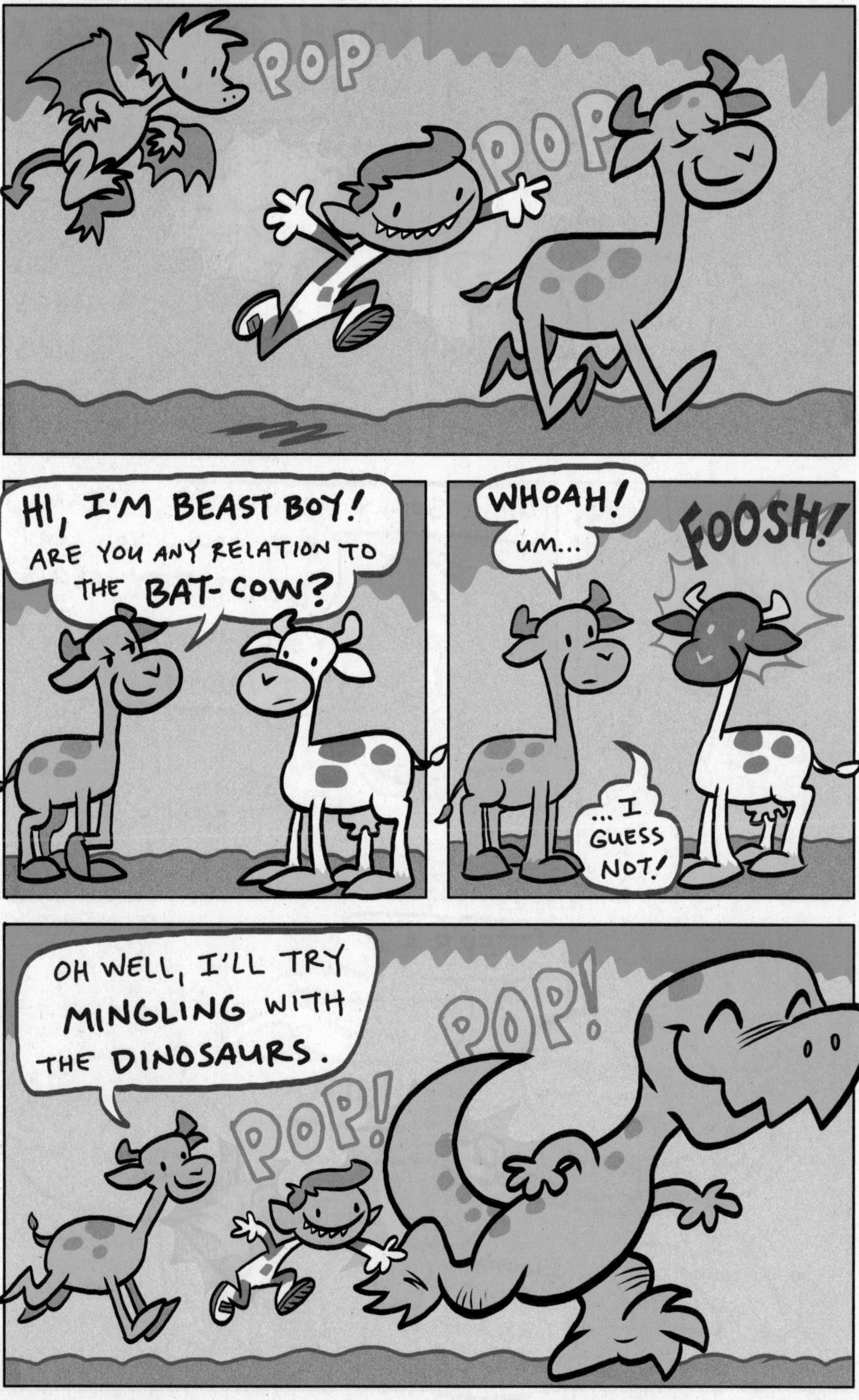
POP
POP
HI, I'M BEAST BOY! ARE YOU ANY RELATION TO THE BAT-COW?
WHOAH! UM...
FOOSH!
...I GUESS NOT!
OH WELL, I'LL TRY MINGLING WITH THE DINOSAURS.
POP!
POP!

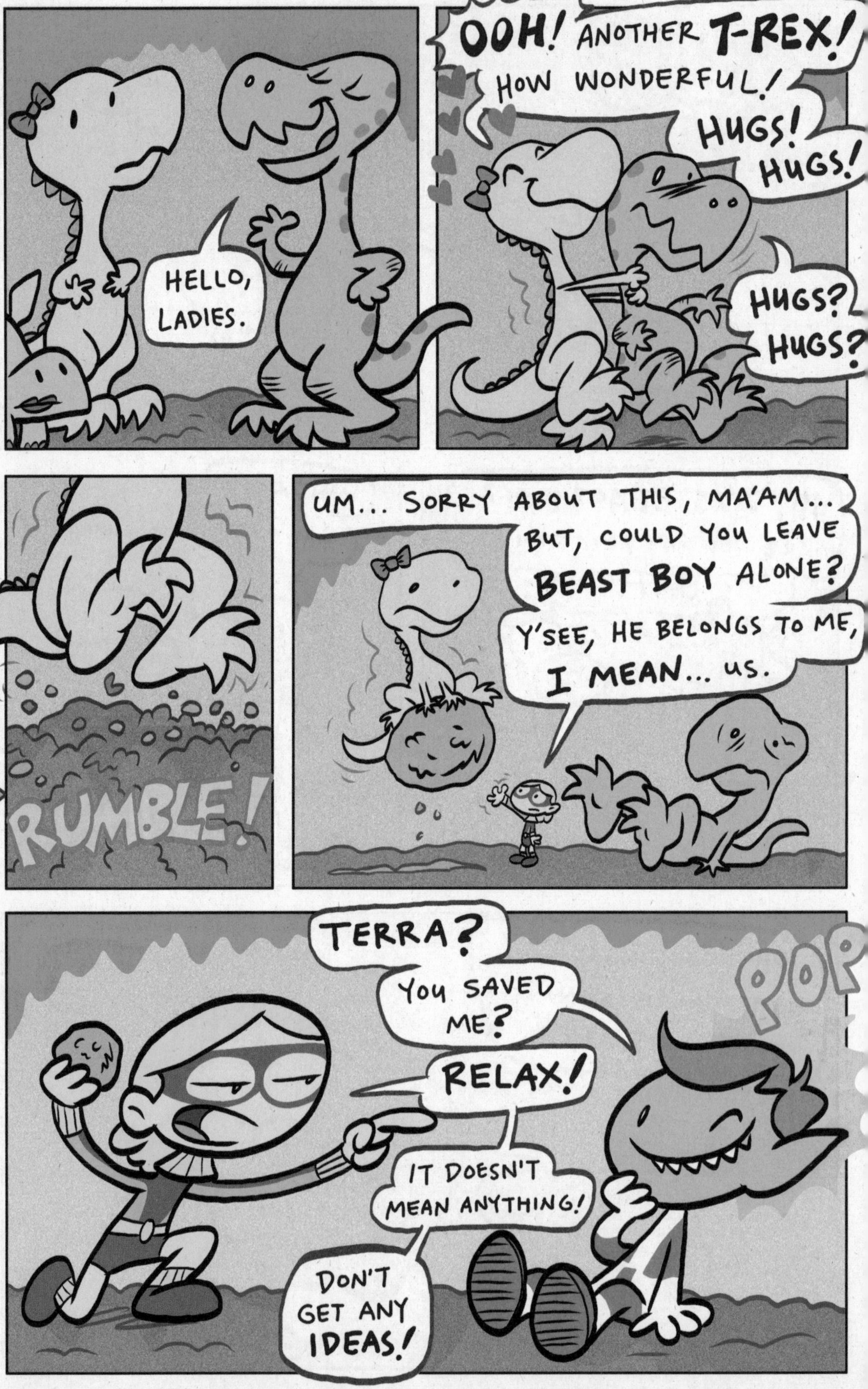
HELLO, LADIES.
OOH! ANOTHER T-REX! HOW WONDERFUL!
HUGS! HUGS!
HUGS? HUGS?
RUMBLE!
UM... SORRY ABOUT THIS, MA'AM... BUT, COULD YOU LEAVE BEAST BOY ALONE?
Y'SEE, HE BELONGS TO ME, I MEAN... US.
TERRA?
YOU SAVED ME?
POP
RELAX!
IT DOESN'T MEAN ANYTHING!
DON'T GET ANY IDEAS!

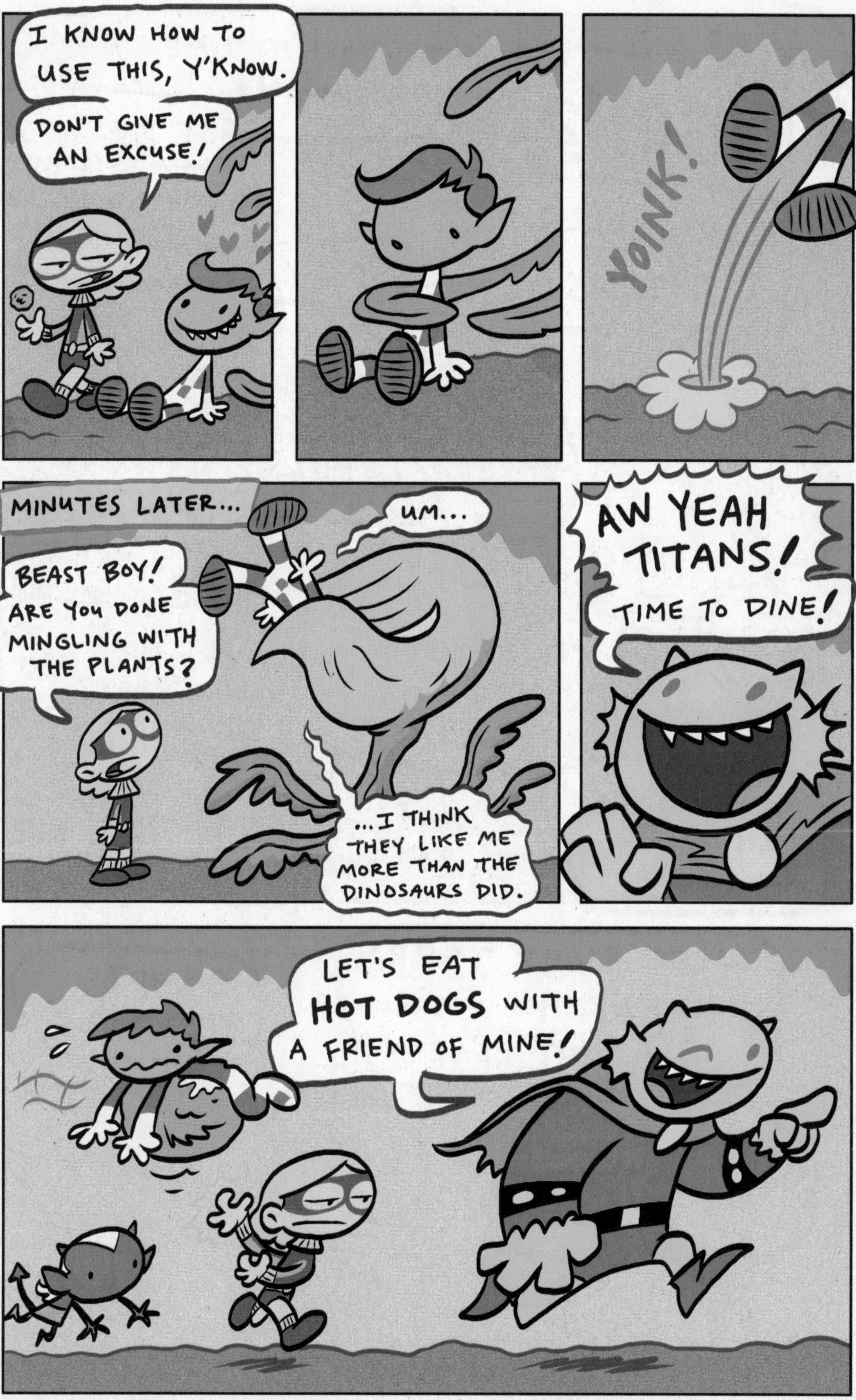
I KNOW HOW TO USE THIS, Y'KNOW.
DON'T GIVE ME AN EXCUSE!
YOINK!
MINUTES LATER...
UM...
BEAST BOY! ARE YOU DONE MINGLING WITH THE PLANTS?
...I THINK THEY LIKE ME MORE THAN THE DINOSAURS DID.
AW YEAH TITANS!
TIME TO DINE!
LET'S EAT HOT DOGS WITH A FRIEND OF MINE!

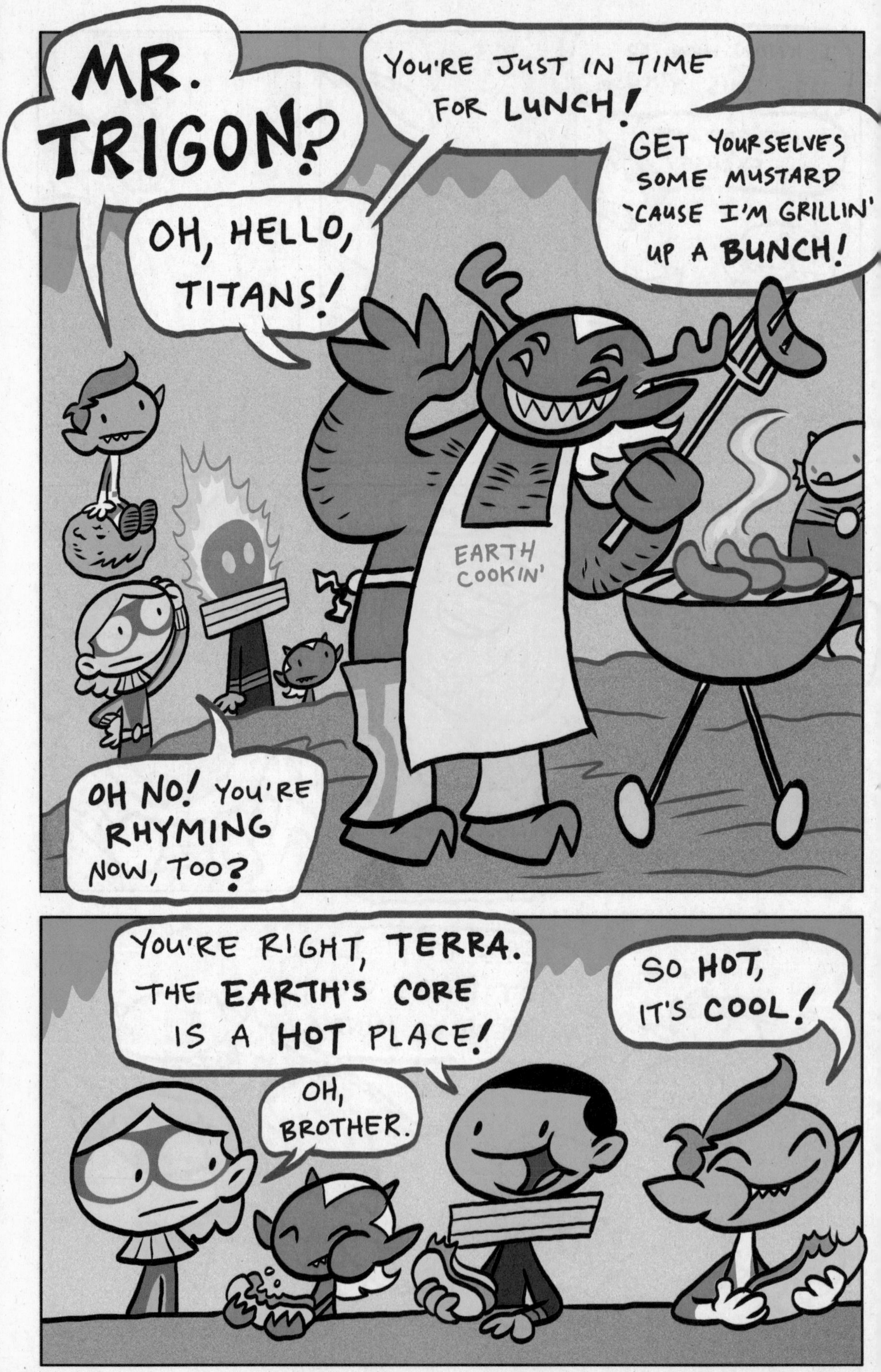
MR. TRIGON?
OH, HELLO, TITANS!
YOU'RE JUST IN TIME FOR LUNCH!
GET YOURSELVES SOME MUSTARD 'CAUSE I'M GRILLIN' UP A BUNCH!
EARTH COOKIN'
OH NO! YOU'RE RHYMING NOW, TOO?
YOU'RE RIGHT, TERRA. THE EARTH'S CORE IS A HOT PLACE!
OH, BROTHER.
SO HOT, IT'S COOL!

-RHYTHMATIC!

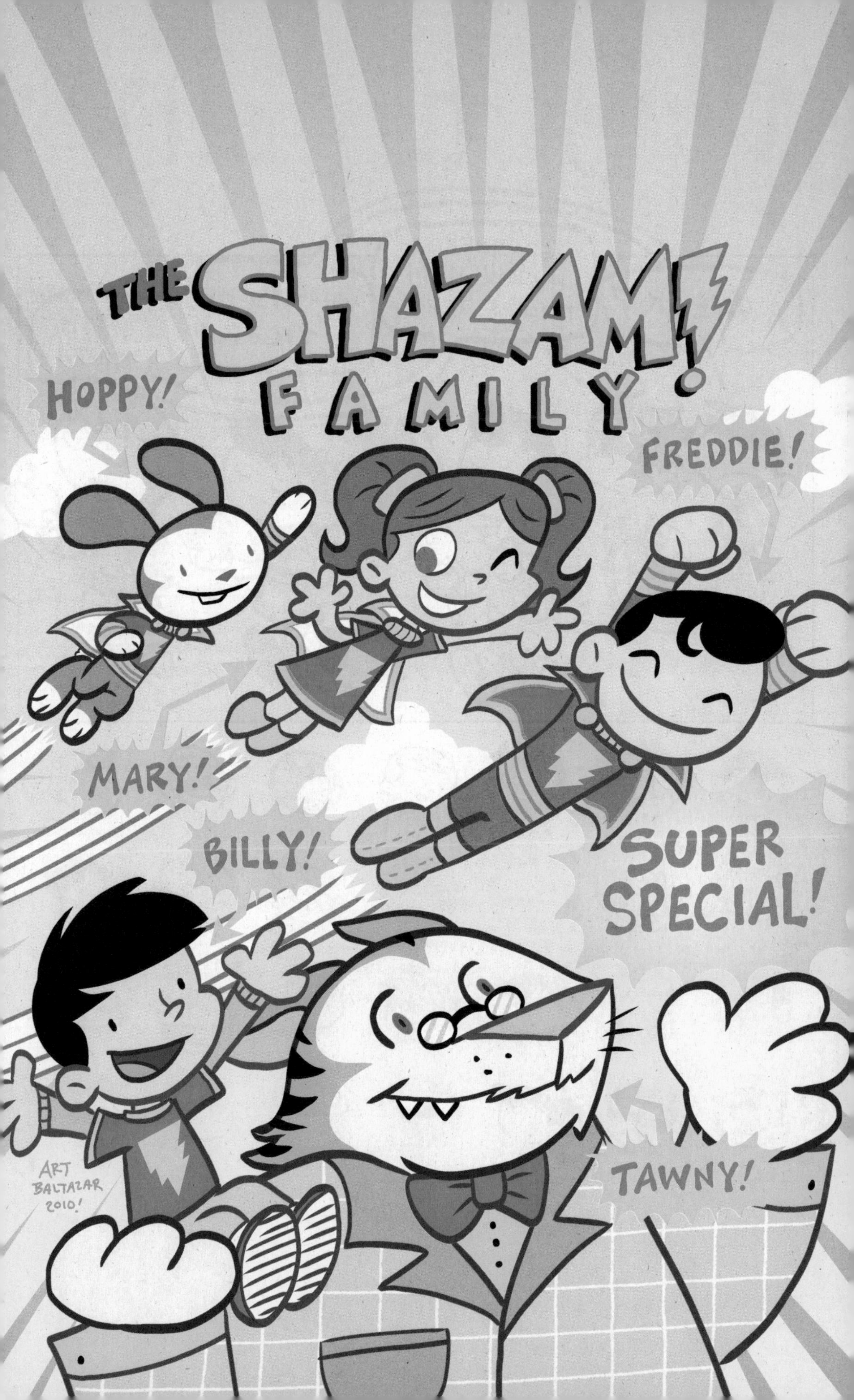
THE SHAZAM! FAMILY
HOPPY!
FREDDIE!
MARY!
BILLY!
SUPER SPECIAL!
TAWNY!
ART BALTAZAR 2010!

tiny titans

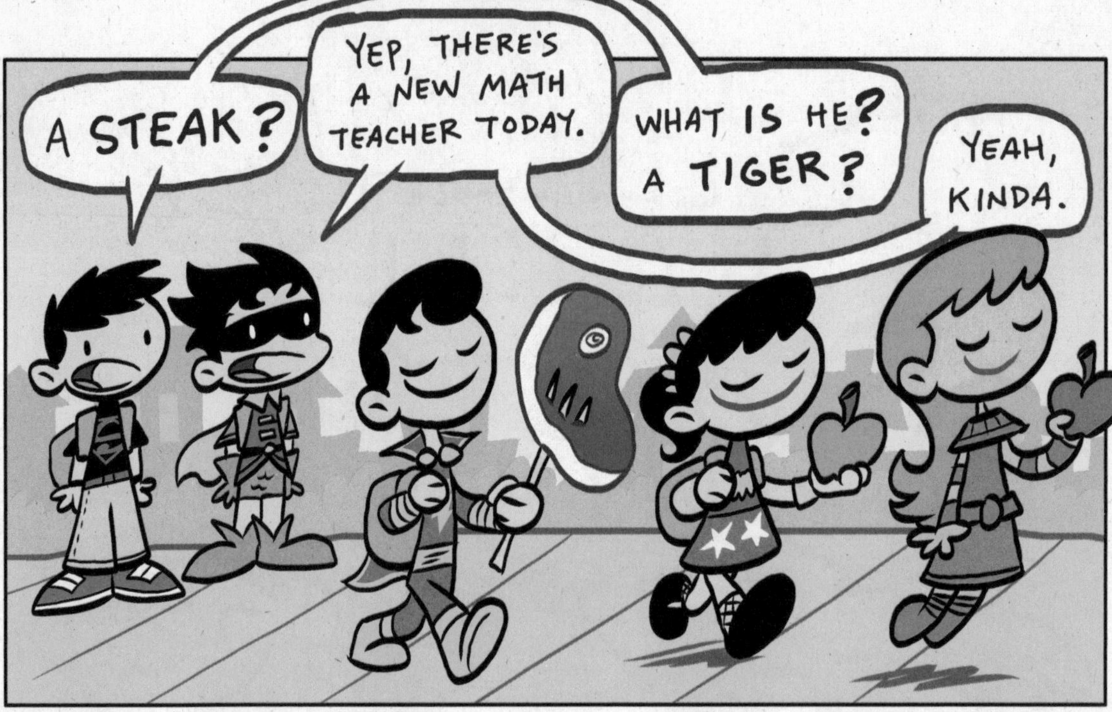
A STEAK?
YEP, THERE'S A NEW MATH TEACHER TODAY.
WHAT IS HE? A TIGER?
YEAH, KINDA.

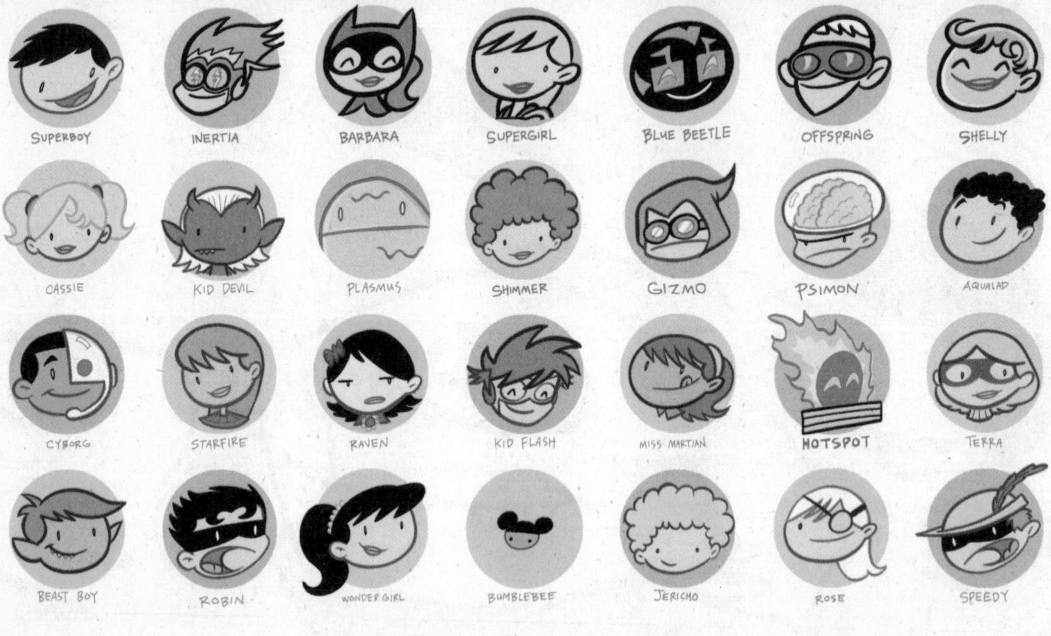
SUPERBOY
INERTIA
BARBARA
SUPERGIRL
BLUE BEETLE
OFFSPRING
SHELLY
CASSIE
KID DEVIL
PLASMUS
SHIMMER
GIZMO
PSIMON
AQUALAD
CYBORG
STARFIRE
RAVEN
KID FLASH
MISS MARTIAN
HOTSPOT
TERRA
BEAST BOY
ROBIN
WONDER GIRL
BUMBLEBEE
JERICHO
ROSE
SPEEDY

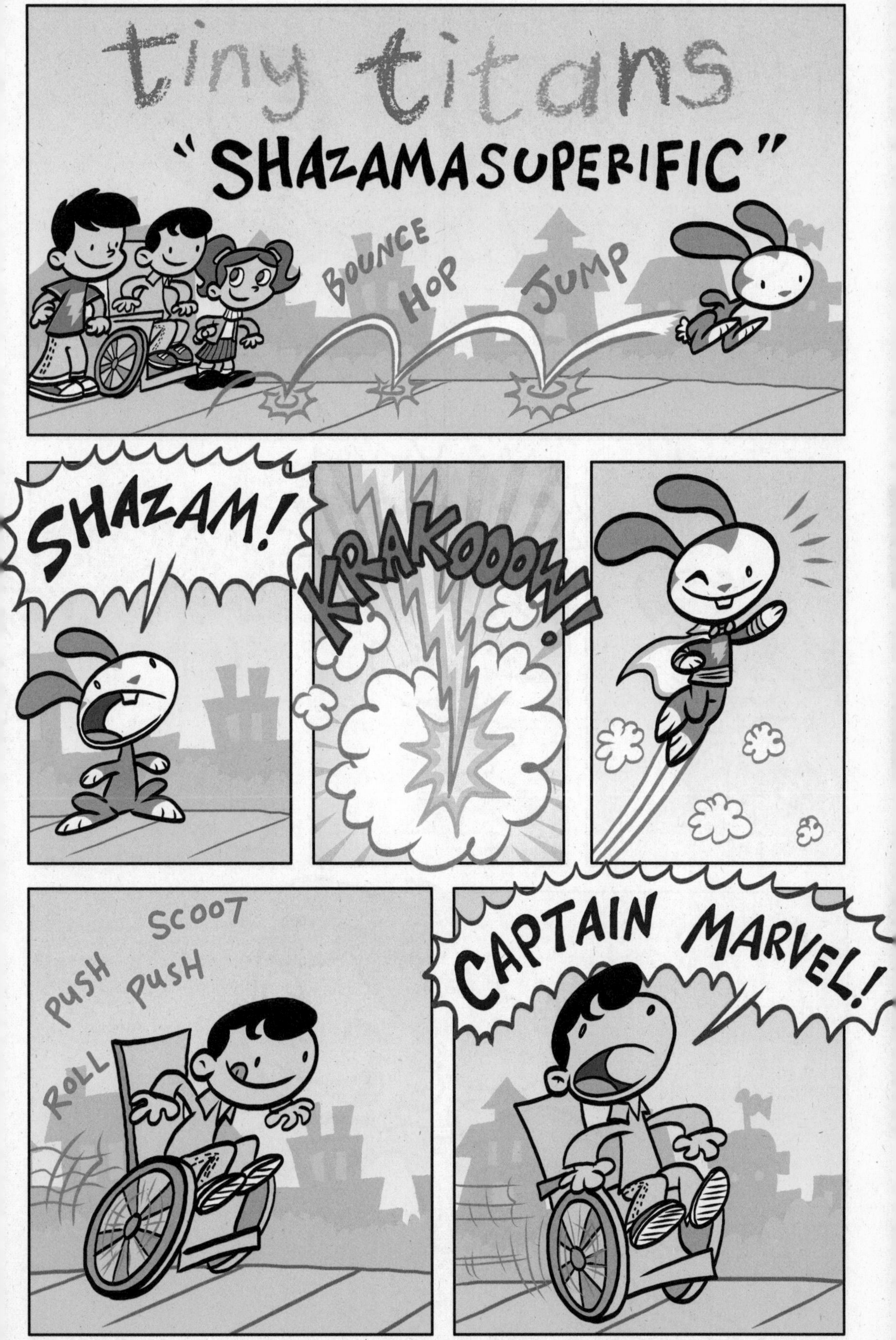
tiny titans
"SHAZAMASUPERIFIC"
BOUNCE
HOP
JUMP
SHAZAM!
KRAKOOOW!
PUSH
SCOOT
PUSH
ROLL
CAPTAIN MARVEL!

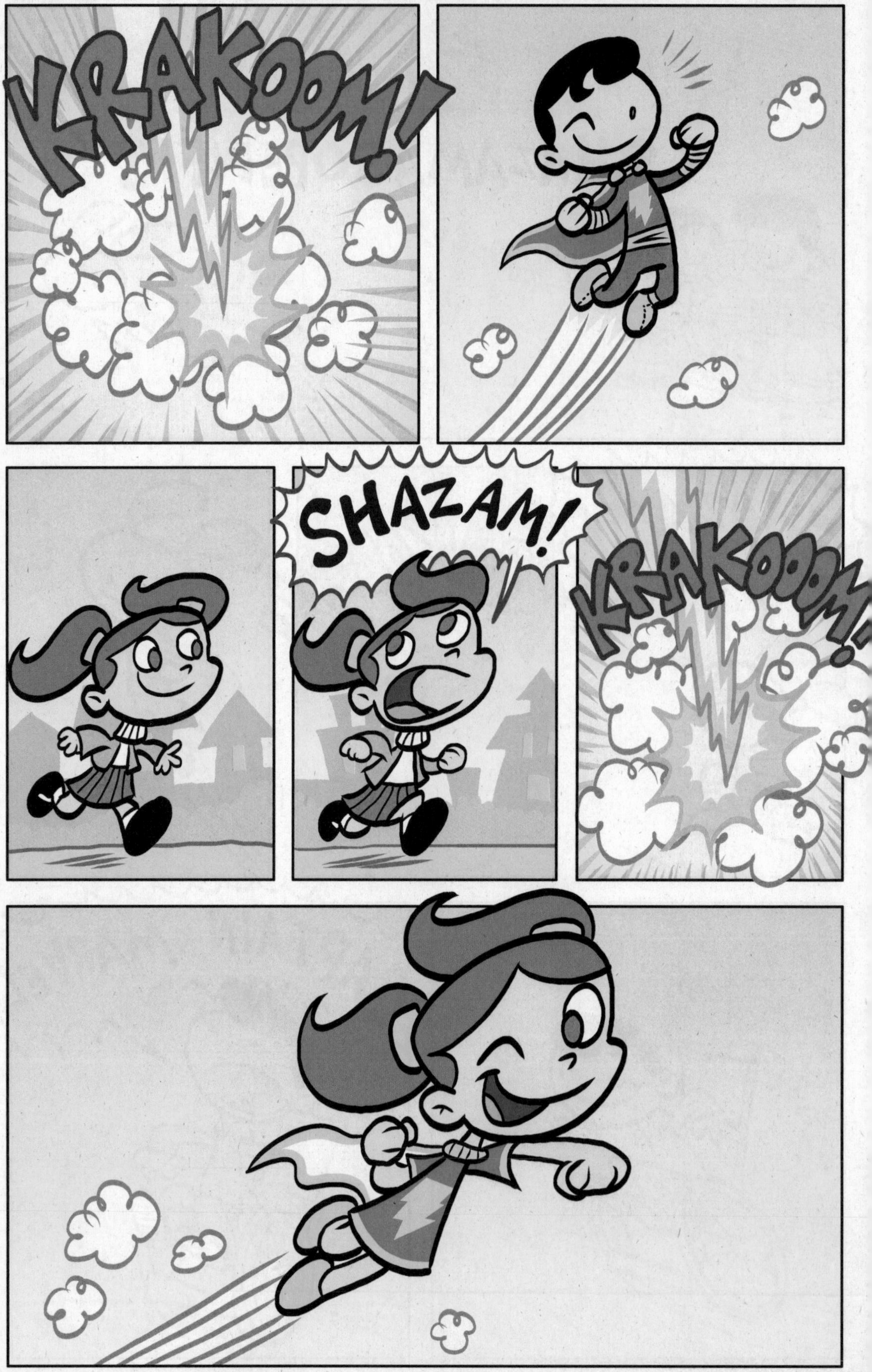
KRAKOOM!
SHAZAM!
KRAKOOOM!

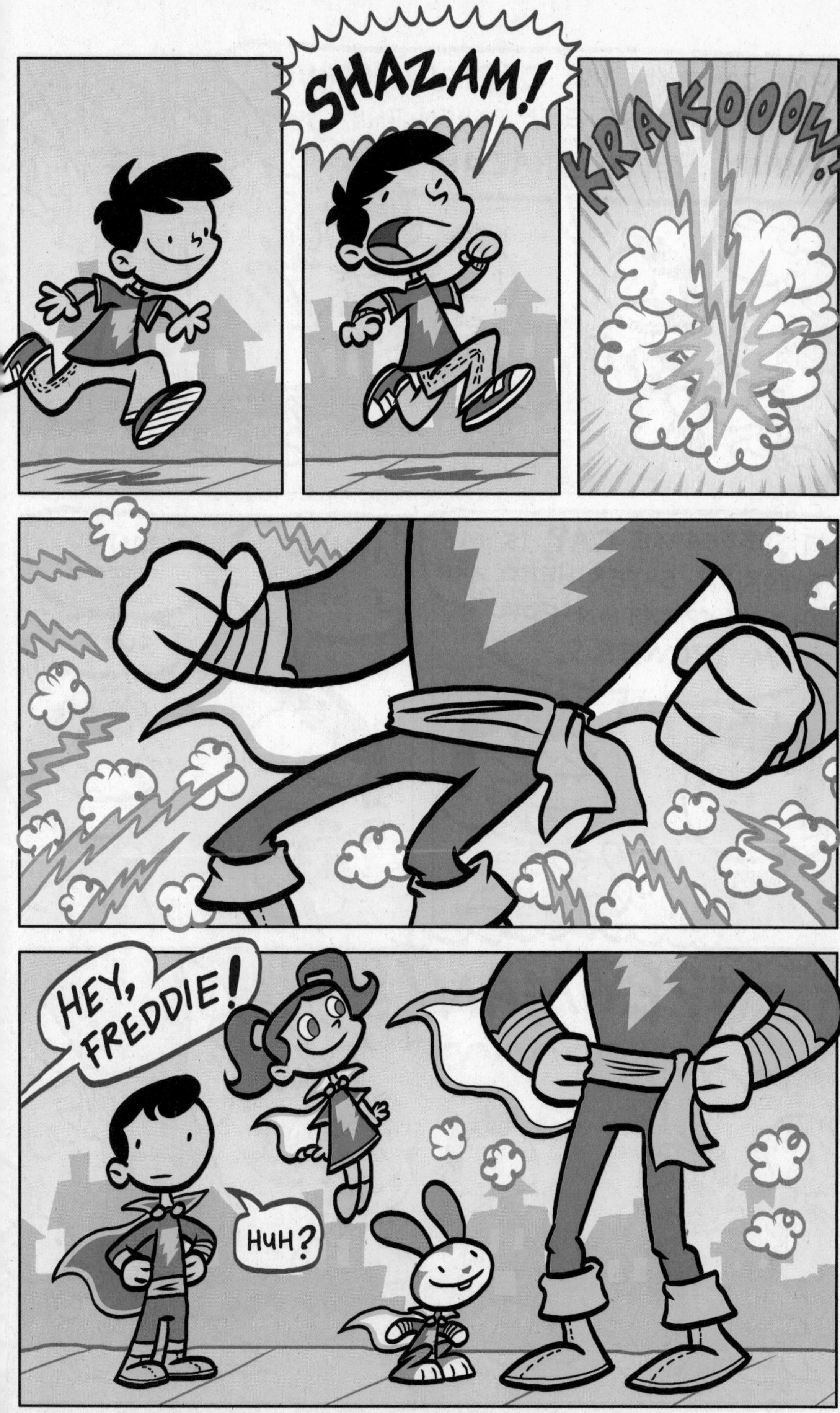
SHAZAM!
KRAKOOOW!
HEY, FREDDIE!
HUH?

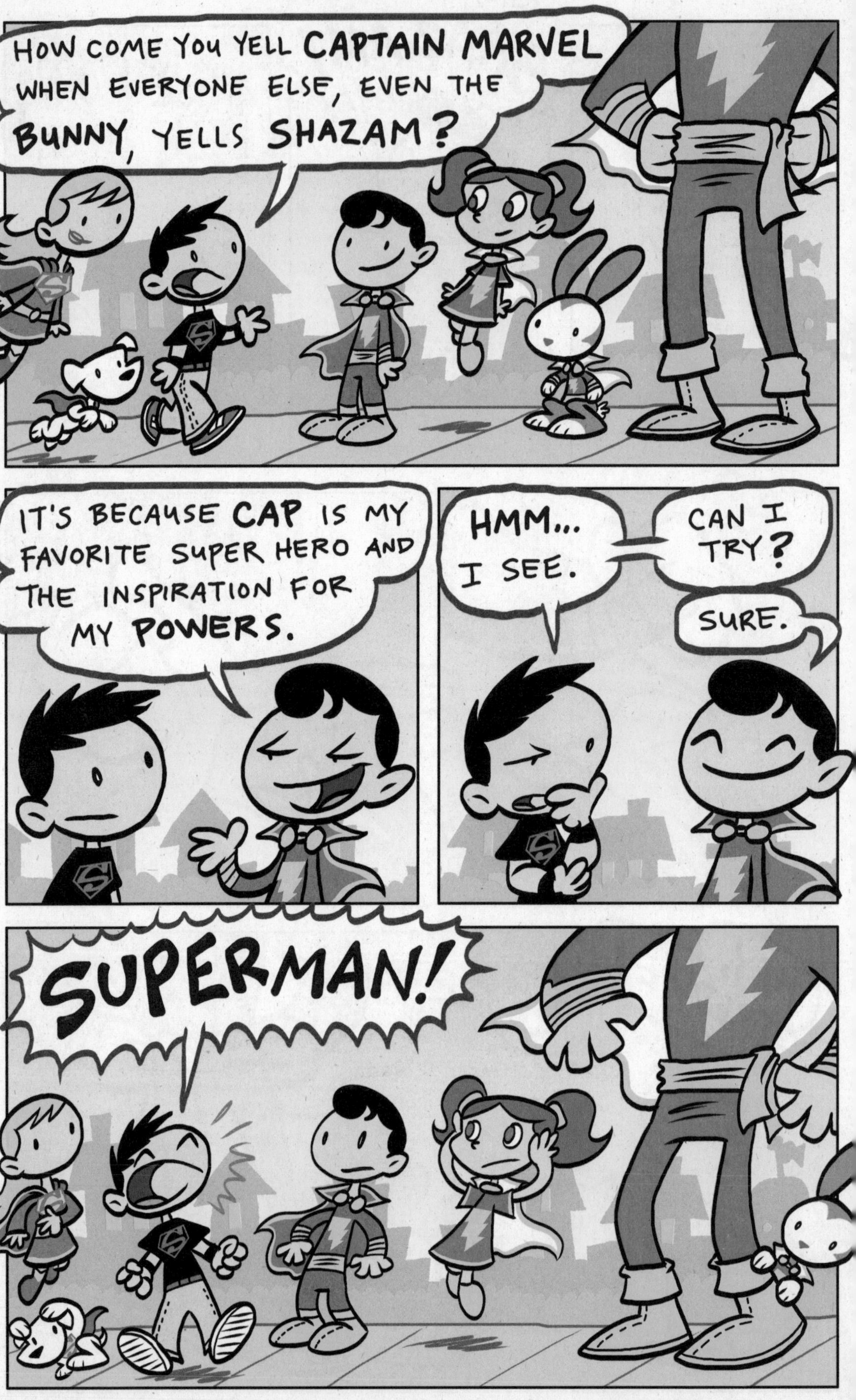
HOW COME YOU YELL CAPTAIN MARVEL WHEN EVERYONE ELSE, EVEN THE BUNNY, YELLS SHAZAM?
IT'S BECAUSE CAP IS MY FAVORITE SUPER HERO AND THE INSPIRATION FOR MY POWERS.
HMM... I SEE.
CAN I TRY?
SURE.
SUPERMAN!

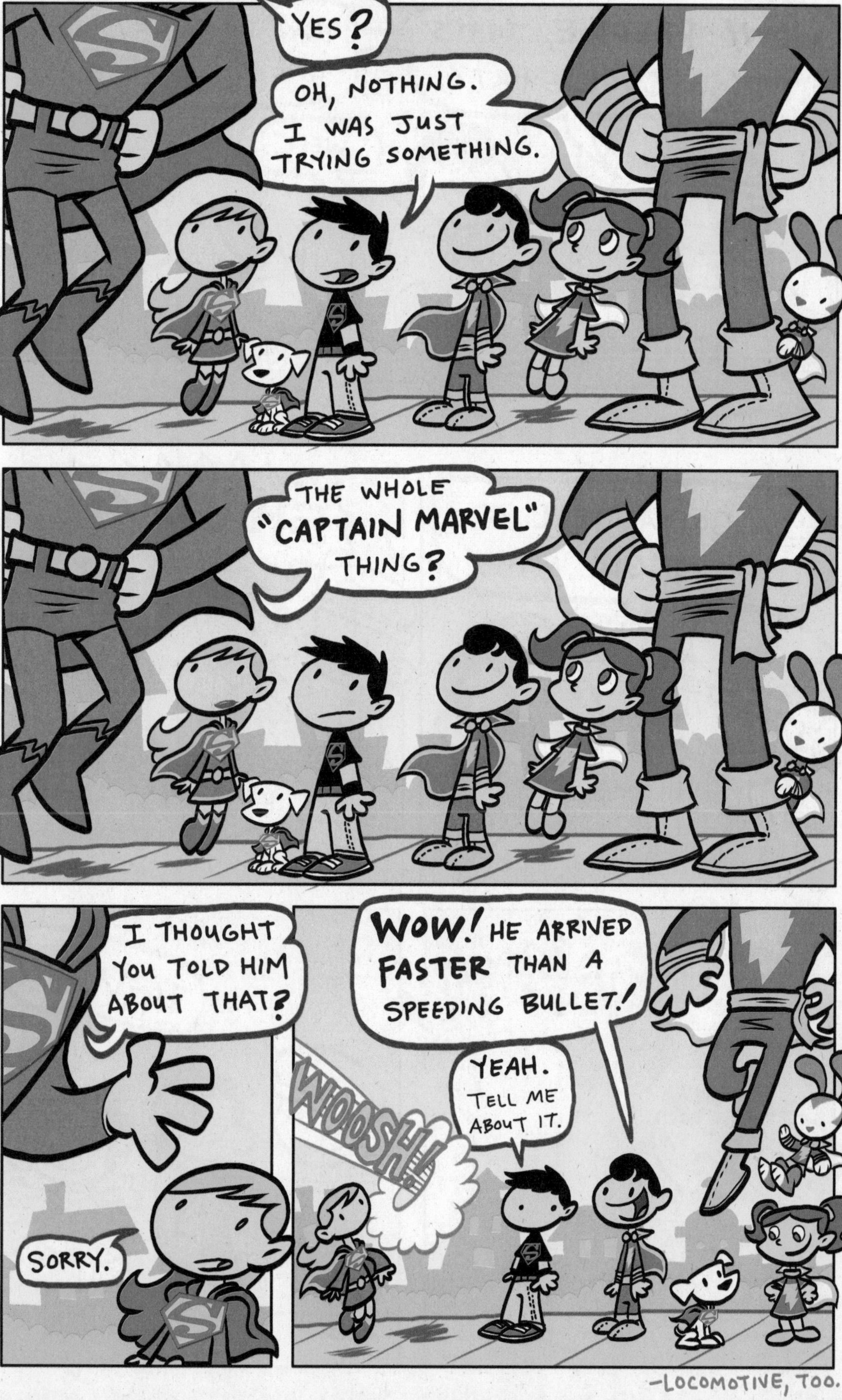
YES?
OH, NOTHING. I WAS JUST TRYING SOMETHING.
THE WHOLE "CAPTAIN MARVEL" THING?
I THOUGHT YOU TOLD HIM ABOUT THAT?
SORRY.
WOOSH!
WOW! HE ARRIVED FASTER THAN A SPEEDING BULLET!
YEAH. TELL ME ABOUT IT.

-LOCOMOTIVE, TOO.

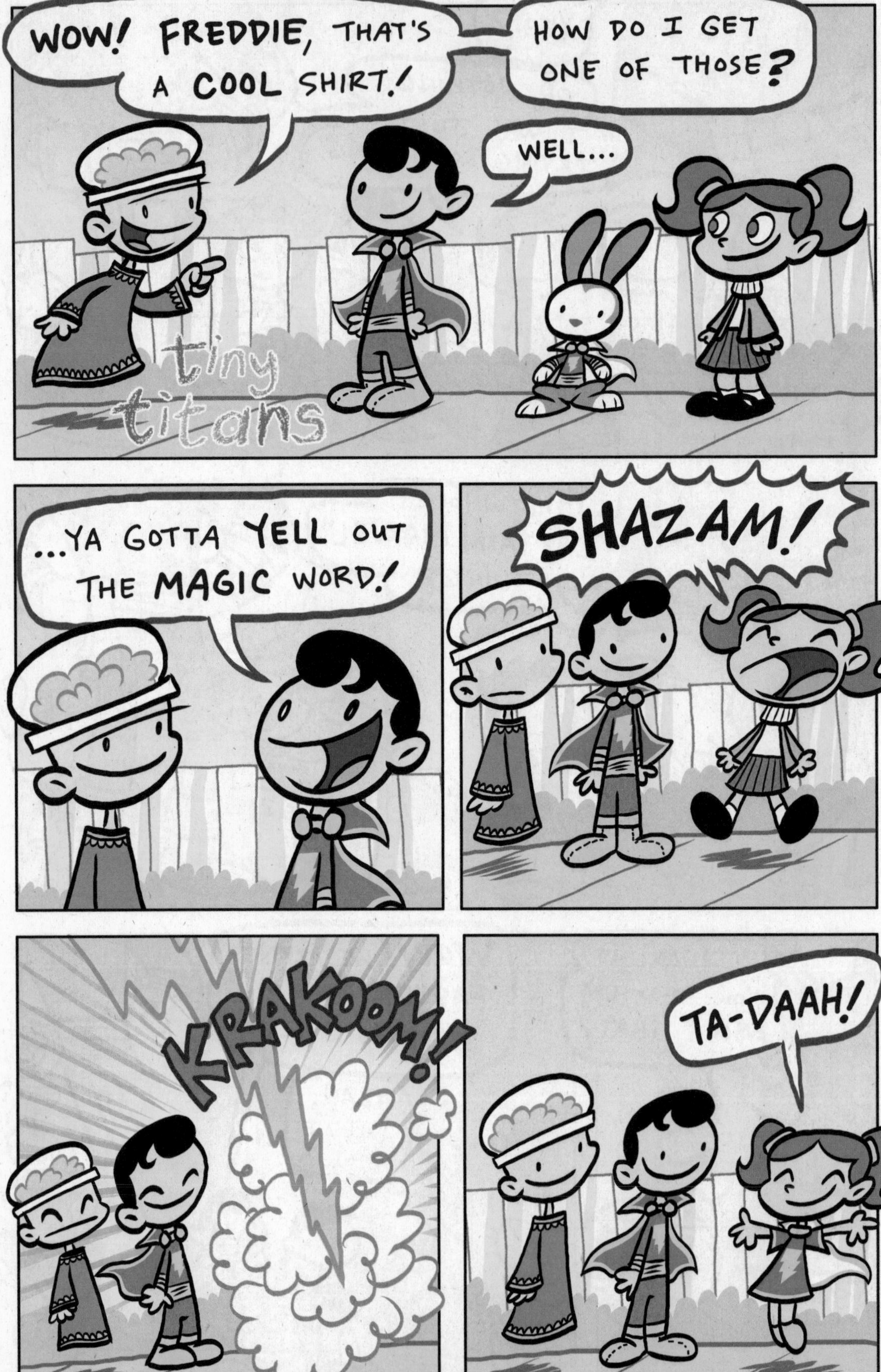
WOW! FREDDIE, THAT'S A COOL SHIRT!
HOW DO I GET ONE OF THOSE?
WELL...
tiny titans
...YA GOTTA YELL OUT THE MAGIC WORD!
SHAZAM!
KRAKOOM!
TA-DAAH!

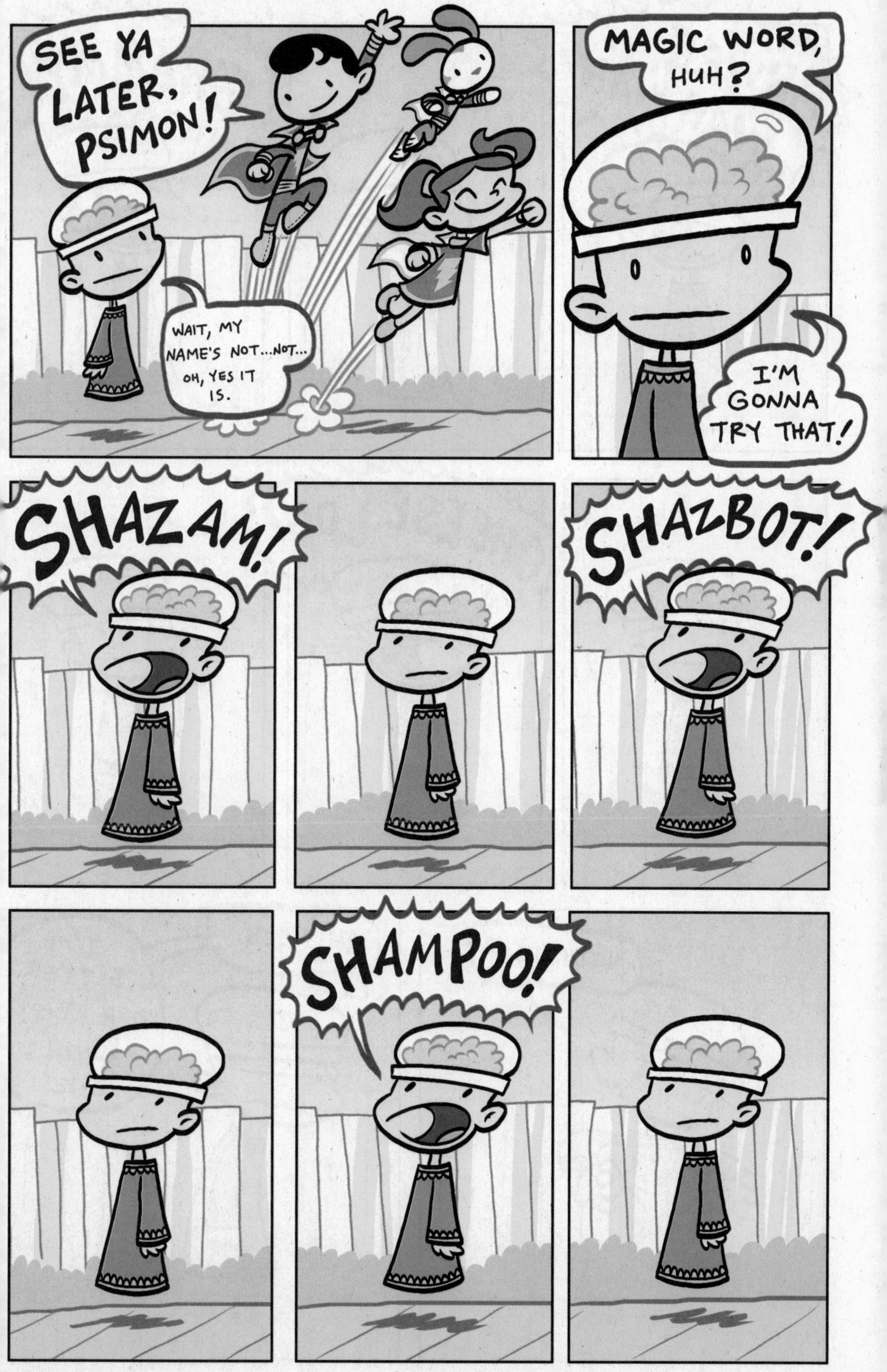

SEE YA LATER, PSIMON!
WAIT, MY NAME'S NOT...NOT... OH, YES IT IS.
MAGIC WORD, HUH?
I'M GONNA TRY THAT!
SHAZAM!
SHAZBOT!
SHAMPOO!

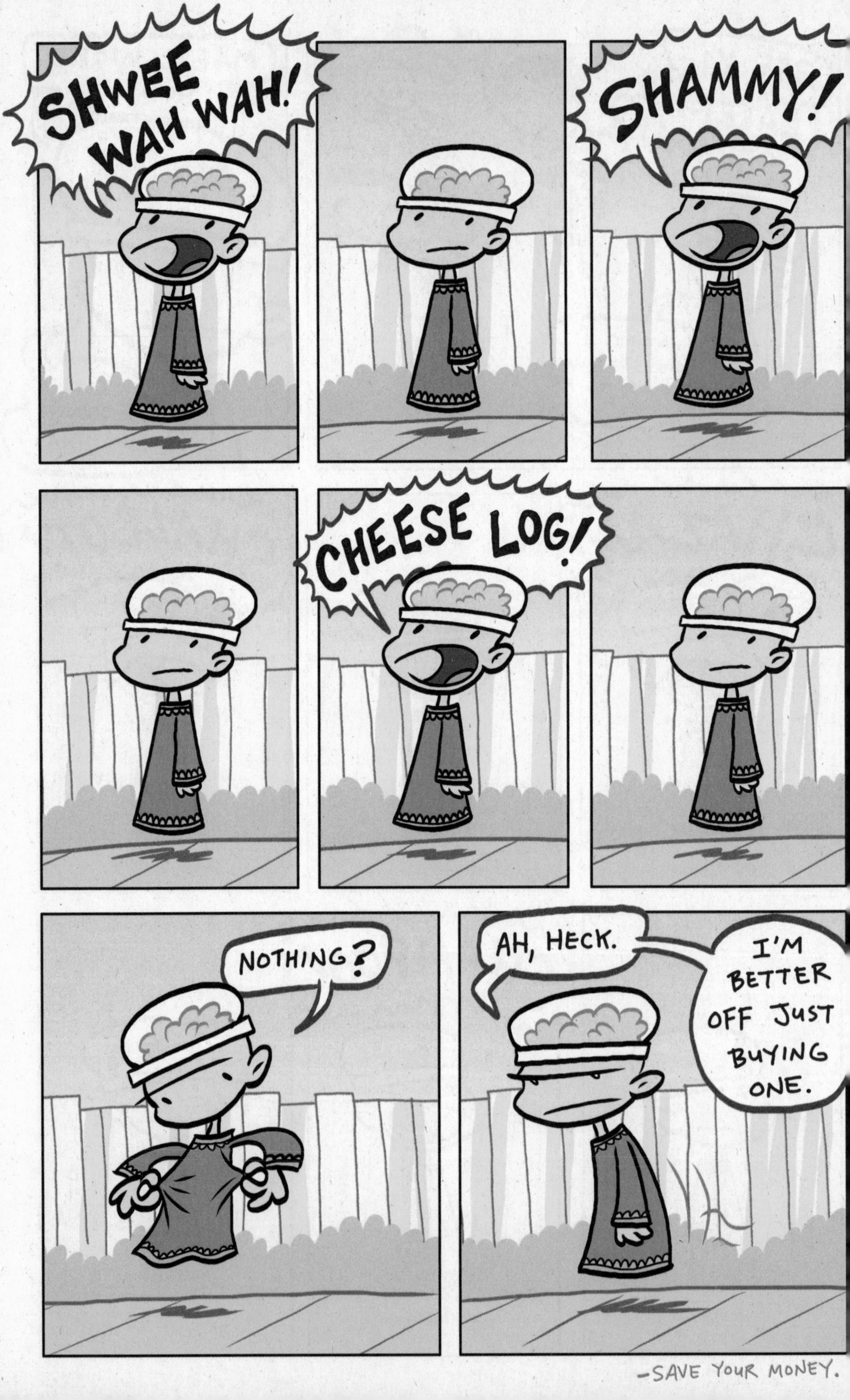
SHWEE WAH WAH!
SHAMMY!
CHEESE LOG!
NOTHING?
AH, HECK.
I'M BETTER OFF JUST BUYING ONE.
-SAVE YOUR MONEY.

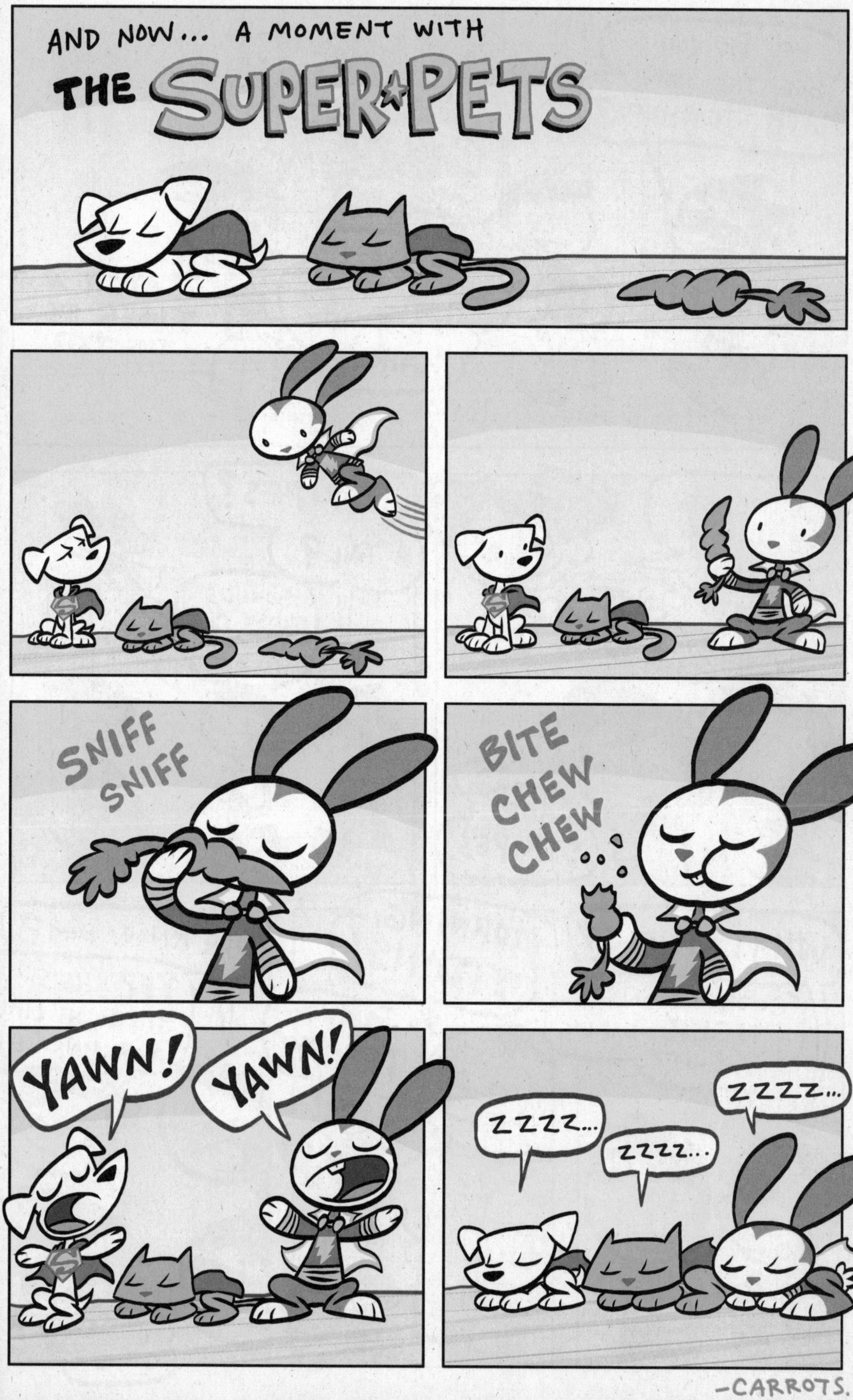
AND NOW... A MOMENT WITH
THE SUPER★PETS
SNIFF SNIFF
BITE CHEW CHEW
YAWN!
YAWN!
ZZZZ...
ZZZZ...
ZZZZ...

-CARROTS.

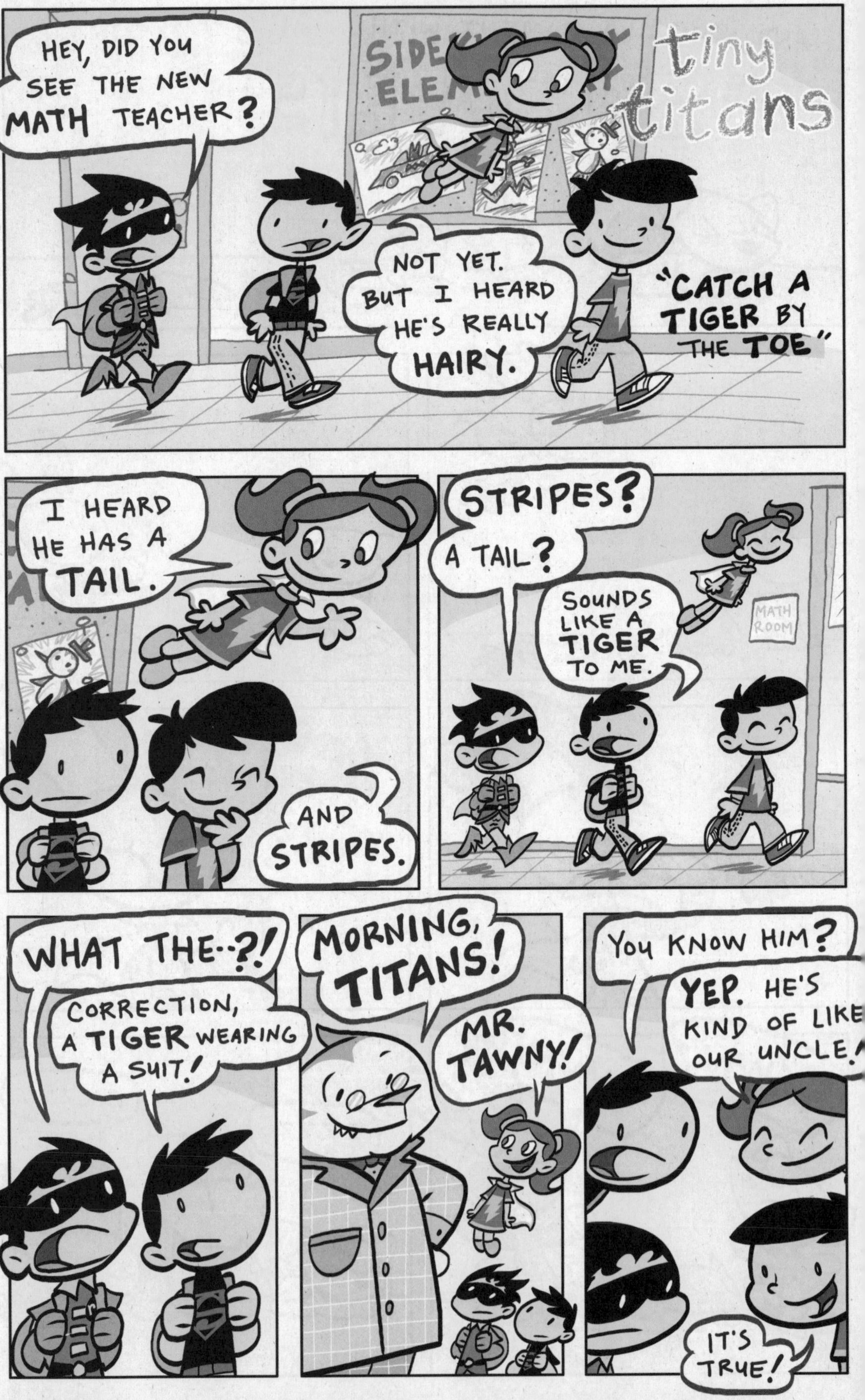
tiny titans
HEY, DID YOU SEE THE NEW MATH TEACHER?
NOT YET. BUT I HEARD HE'S REALLY HAIRY.
"CATCH A TIGER BY THE TOE"
I HEARD HE HAS A TAIL.
AND STRIPES.
STRIPES?
A TAIL?
SOUNDS LIKE A TIGER TO ME.
MATH ROOM
WHAT THE--?!
CORRECTION, A TIGER WEARING A SUIT!
MORNING, TITANS!
MR. TAWNY!
YOU KNOW HIM?
YEP. HE'S KIND OF LIKE OUR UNCLE!
IT'S TRUE!

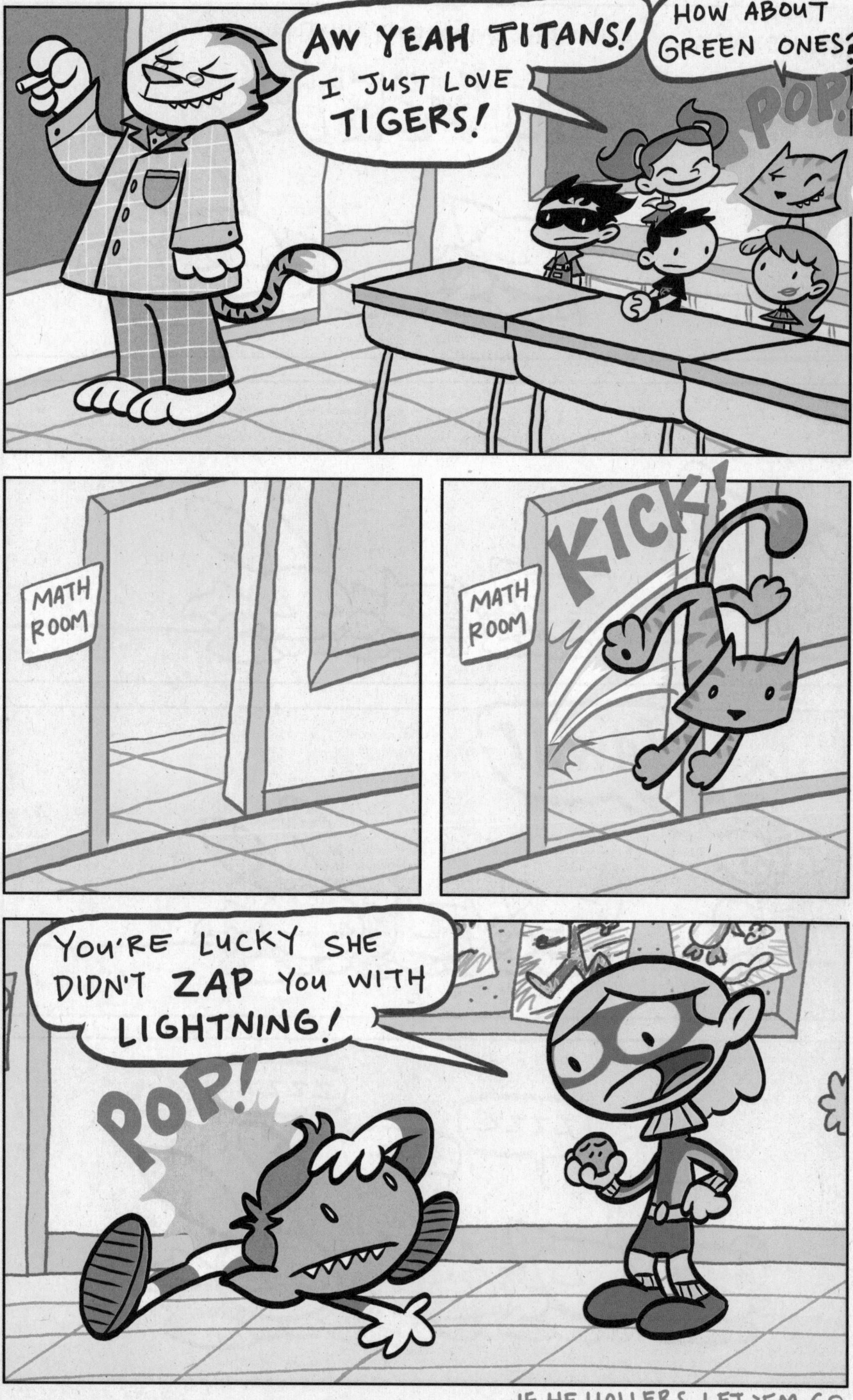
AW YEAH TITANS! I JUST LOVE TIGERS!
HOW ABOUT GREEN ONES?
POP!
MATH ROOM
MATH ROOM
KICK!
YOU'RE LUCKY SHE DIDN'T ZAP YOU WITH LIGHTNING!
POP!

-IF HE HOLLERS, LET 'EM GO.

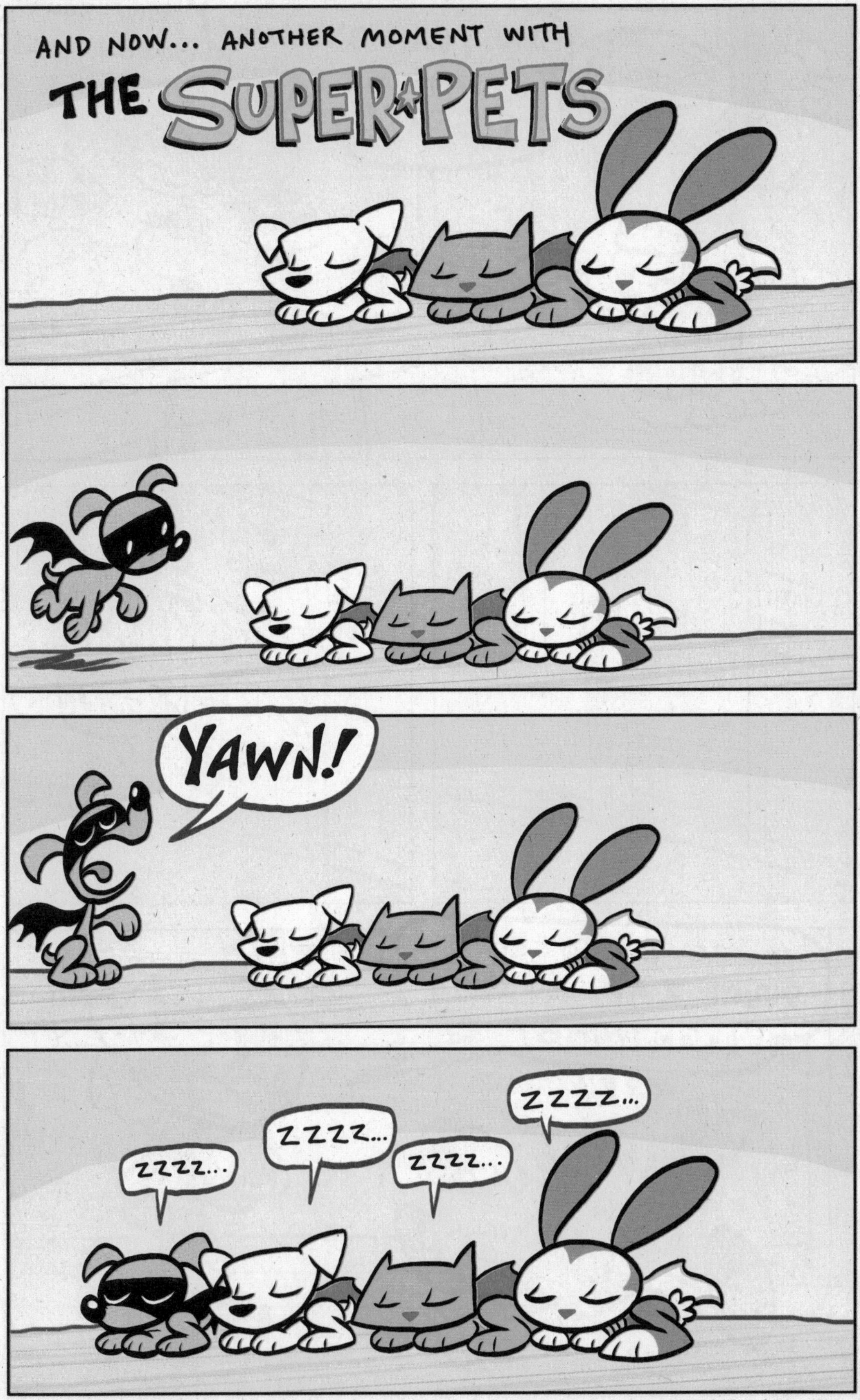
AND NOW... ANOTHER MOMENT WITH
THE SUPER*PETS
YAWN!
ZZZZ...
ZZZZ...
ZZZZ...
ZZZZ...

-SLEEPYTIME.

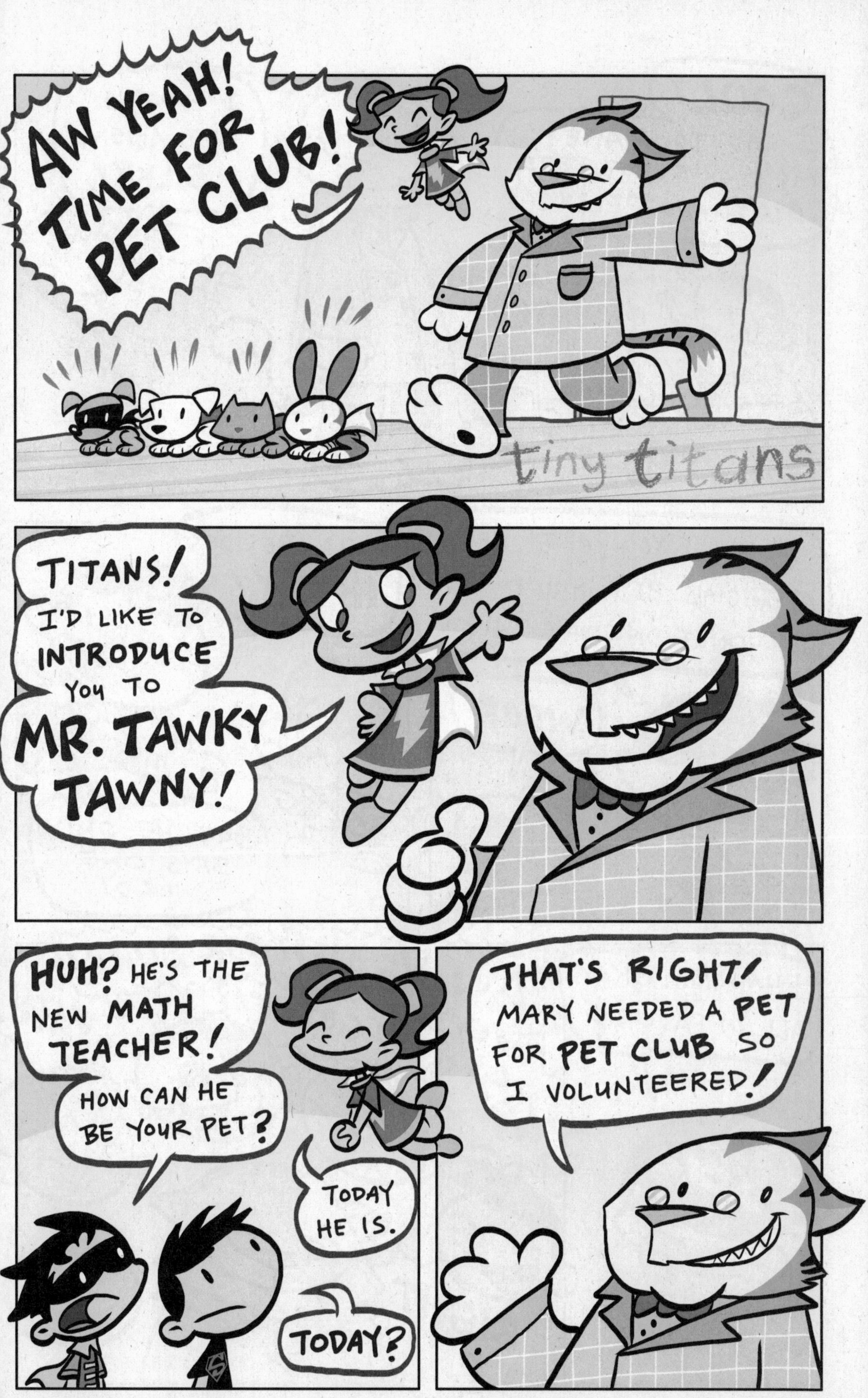

AW YEAH! TIME FOR PET CLUB!
tiny titans
TITANS! I'D LIKE TO INTRODUCE YOU TO MR. TAWKY TAWNY!
HUH? HE'S THE NEW MATH TEACHER!
HOW CAN HE BE YOUR PET?
TODAY HE IS.
TODAY?
THAT'S RIGHT! MARY NEEDED A PET FOR PET CLUB SO I VOLUNTEERED!

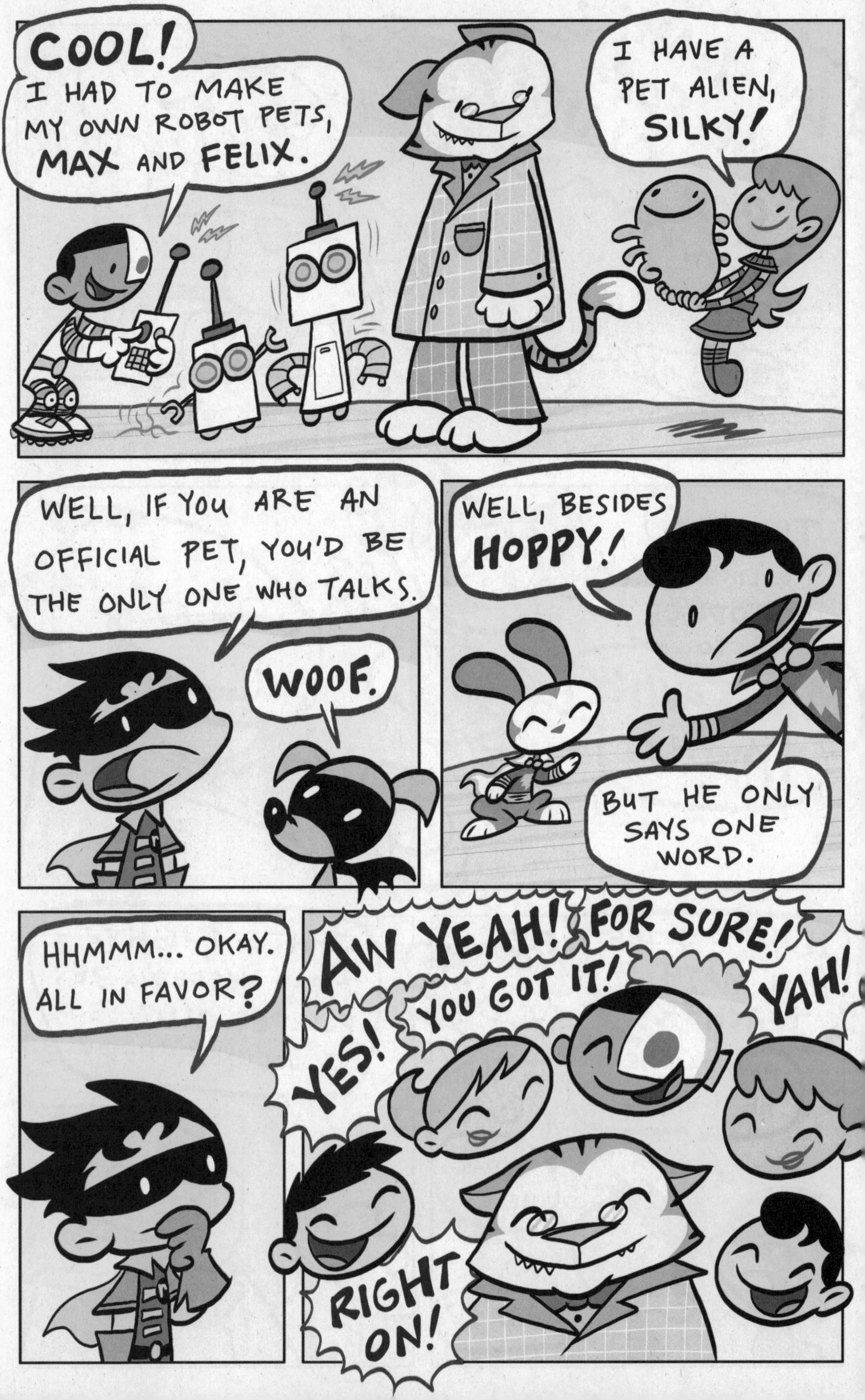
COOL!
I HAD TO MAKE MY OWN ROBOT PETS, MAX AND FELIX.
I HAVE A PET ALIEN, SILKY!
WELL, IF YOU ARE AN OFFICIAL PET, YOU'D BE THE ONLY ONE WHO TALKS.
WOOF.
WELL, BESIDES HOPPY!
BUT HE ONLY SAYS ONE WORD.
HHMMM... OKAY. ALL IN FAVOR?
AW YEAH!
FOR SURE!
YOU GOT IT!
YAH!
YES!
RIGHT ON!

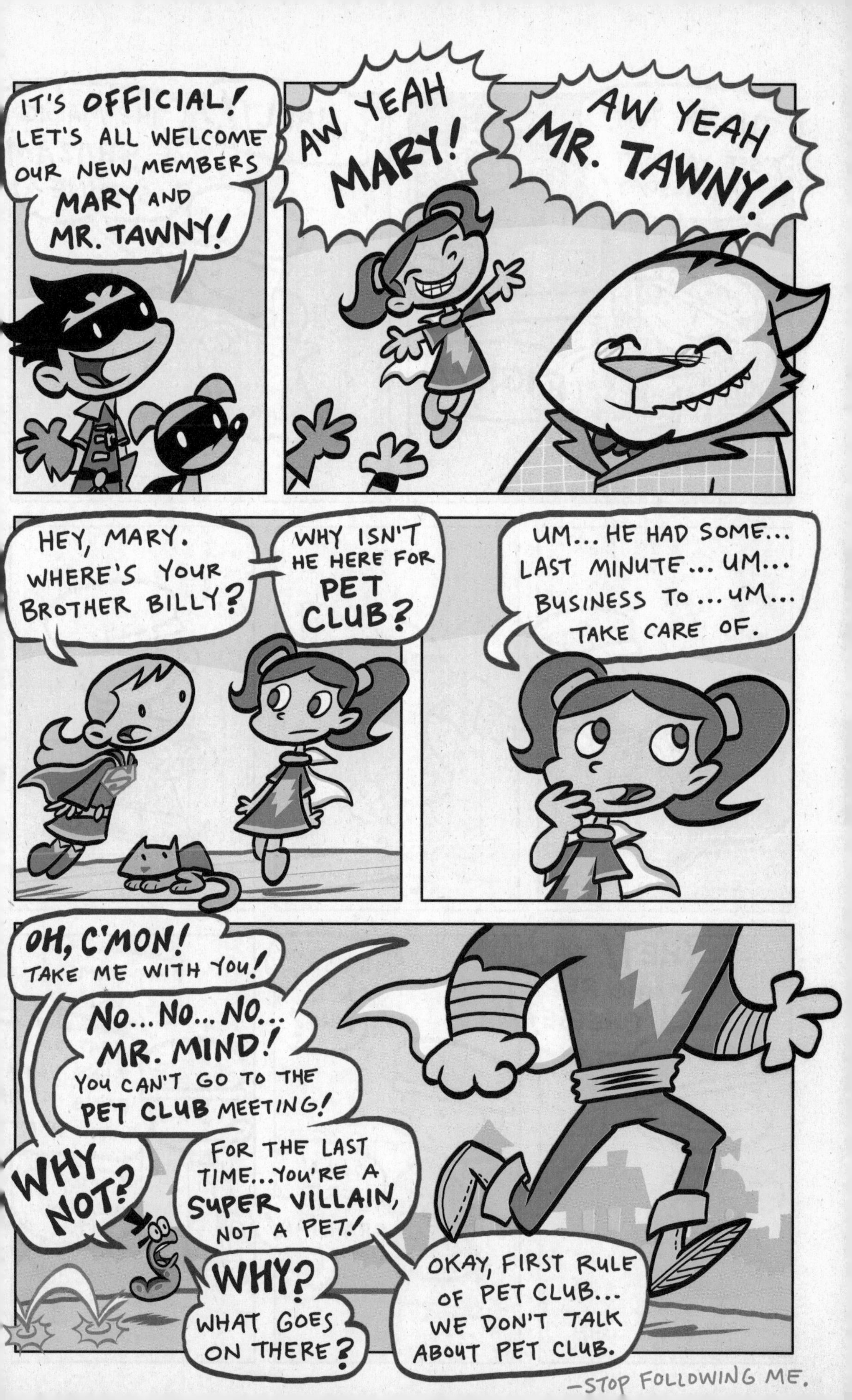
IT'S OFFICIAL! LET'S ALL WELCOME OUR NEW MEMBERS MARY AND MR. TAWNY!
AW YEAH MARY!
AW YEAH MR. TAWNY!
HEY, MARY. WHERE'S YOUR BROTHER BILLY?
WHY ISN'T HE HERE FOR PET CLUB?
UM... HE HAD SOME... LAST MINUTE... UM... BUSINESS TO ... UM... TAKE CARE OF.
OH, C'MON! TAKE ME WITH YOU!
NO... NO... NO... MR. MIND! YOU CAN'T GO TO THE PET CLUB MEETING!
WHY NOT?
FOR THE LAST TIME... YOU'RE A SUPER VILLAIN, NOT A PET!
WHY? WHAT GOES ON THERE?
OKAY, FIRST RULE OF PET CLUB... WE DON'T TALK ABOUT PET CLUB.
—STOP FOLLOWING ME.

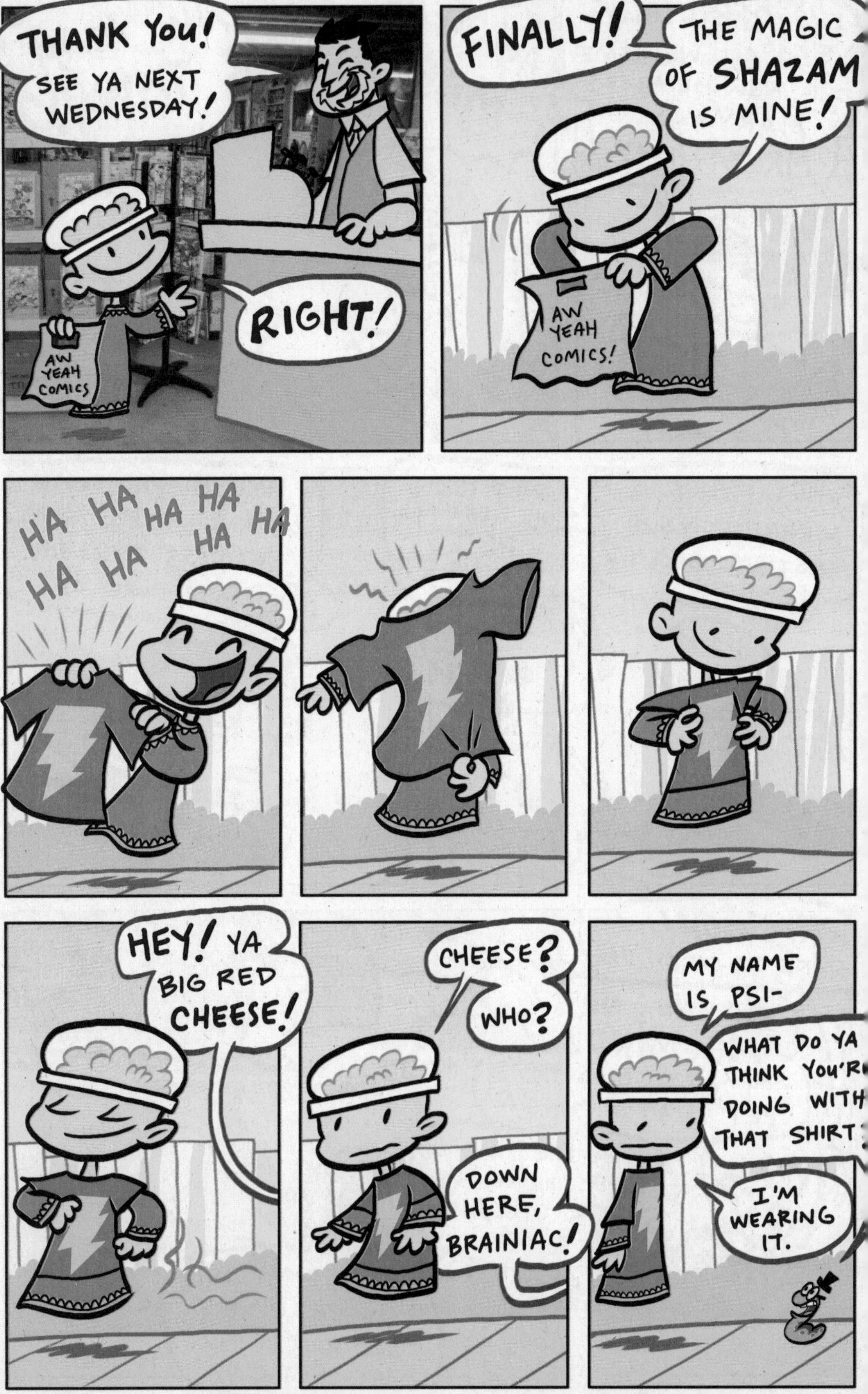
THANK YOU!
SEE YA NEXT WEDNESDAY!
RIGHT!
AW YEAH COMICS
FINALLY!
THE MAGIC OF SHAZAM IS MINE!
AW YEAH COMICS!
HA HA HA HA HA HA HA HA
HEY! YA BIG RED CHEESE!
CHEESE?
WHO?
DOWN HERE, BRAINIAC!
MY NAME IS, PSI-
WHAT DO YA THINK YOU'RE DOING WITH THAT SHIRT?
I'M WEARING IT.

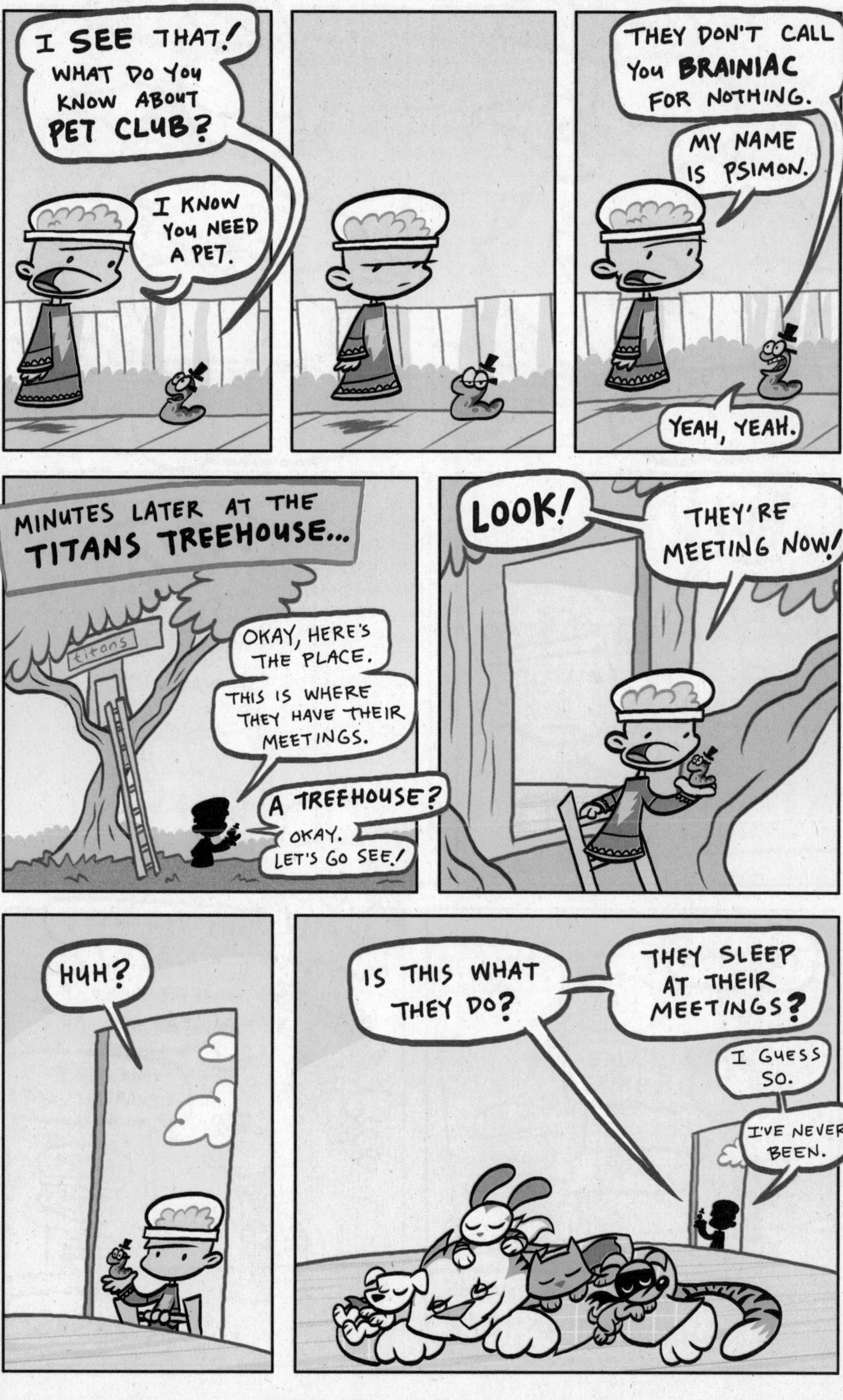
I SEE THAT! WHAT DO YOU KNOW ABOUT PET CLUB?
I KNOW YOU NEED A PET.
THEY DON'T CALL YOU BRAINIAC FOR NOTHING.
MY NAME IS PSIMON.
YEAH, YEAH.
MINUTES LATER AT THE TITANS TREEHOUSE...
titans
OKAY, HERE'S THE PLACE.
THIS IS WHERE THEY HAVE THEIR MEETINGS.
A TREEHOUSE?
OKAY. LET'S GO SEE!
LOOK!
THEY'RE MEETING NOW!
HUH?
IS THIS WHAT THEY DO?
THEY SLEEP AT THEIR MEETINGS?
I GUESS SO.
I'VE NEVER BEEN.

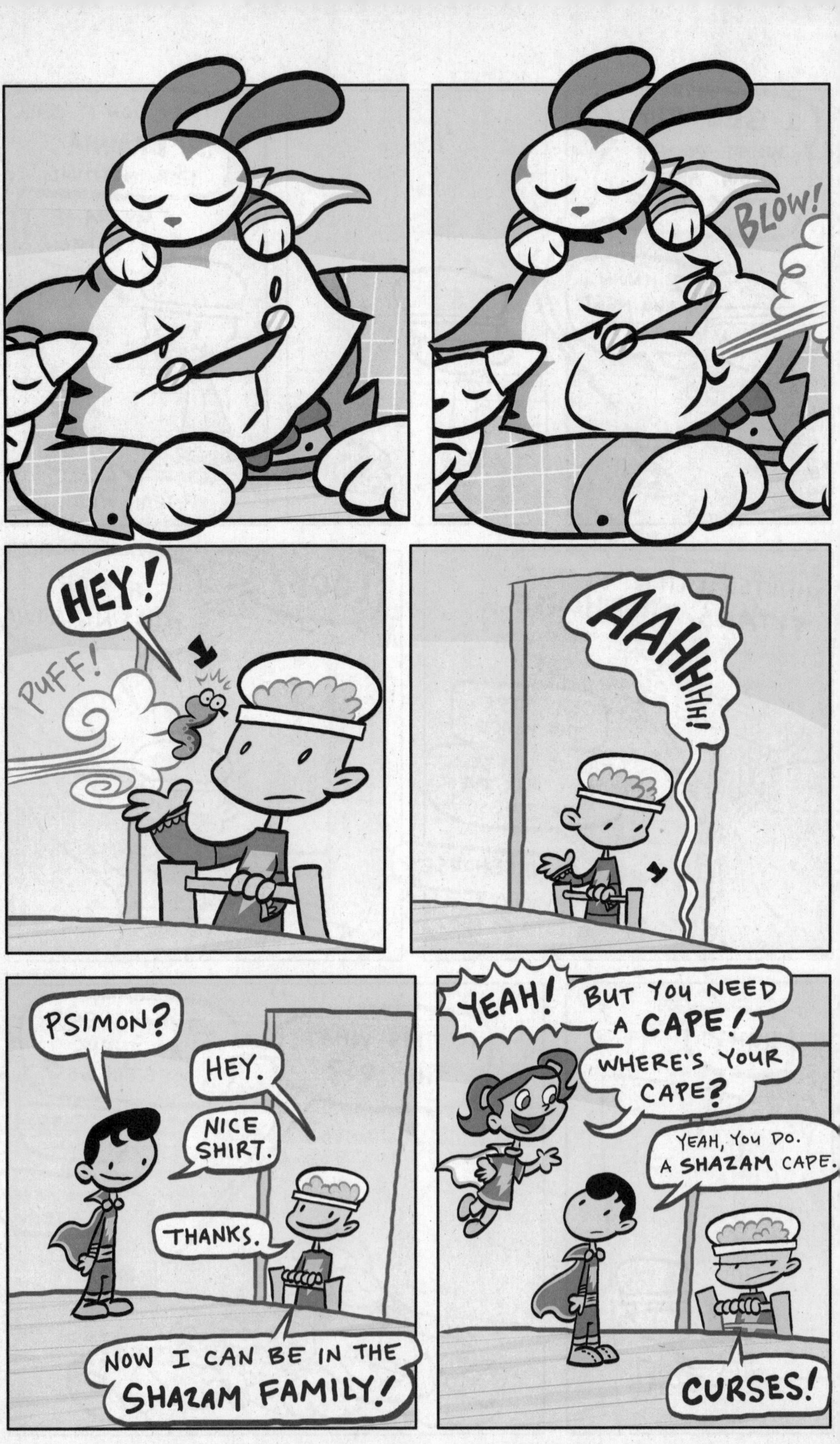
BLOW!
HEY!
PUFF!
AAHHHH!
PSIMON?
HEY.
NICE SHIRT.
THANKS.
NOW I CAN BE IN THE SHAZAM FAMILY!
YEAH!
BUT YOU NEED A CAPE!
WHERE'S YOUR CAPE?
YEAH, YOU DO. A SHAZAM CAPE.
CURSES!

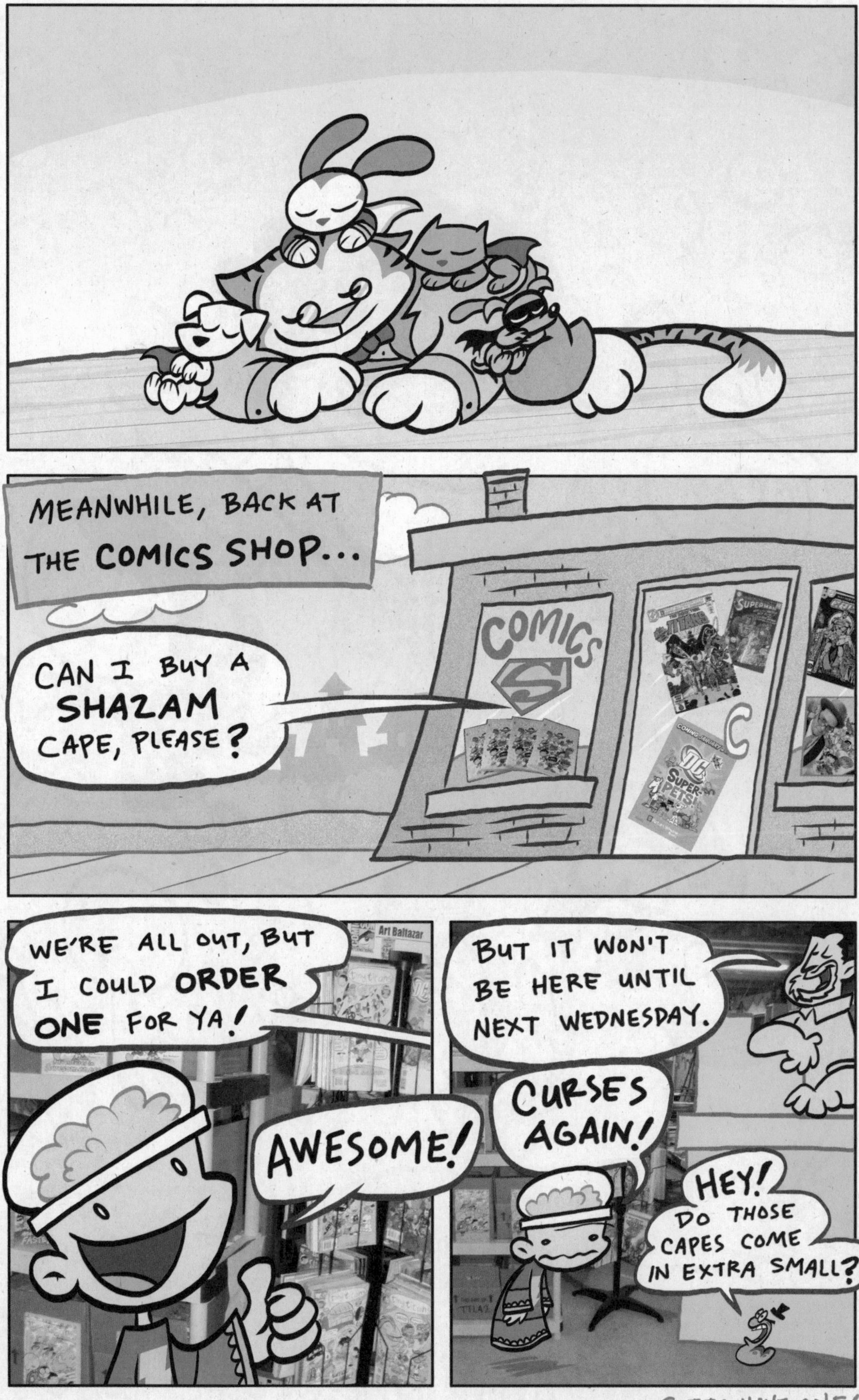
MEANWHILE, BACK AT THE COMICS SHOP...
COMICS
CAN I BUY A SHAZAM CAPE, PLEASE?
Art Baltazar
WE'RE ALL OUT, BUT I COULD ORDER ONE FOR YA!
AWESOME!
BUT IT WON'T BE HERE UNTIL NEXT WEDNESDAY.
CURSES AGAIN!
HEY! DO THOSE CAPES COME IN EXTRA SMALL?

- GOTTA HAVE ONE!

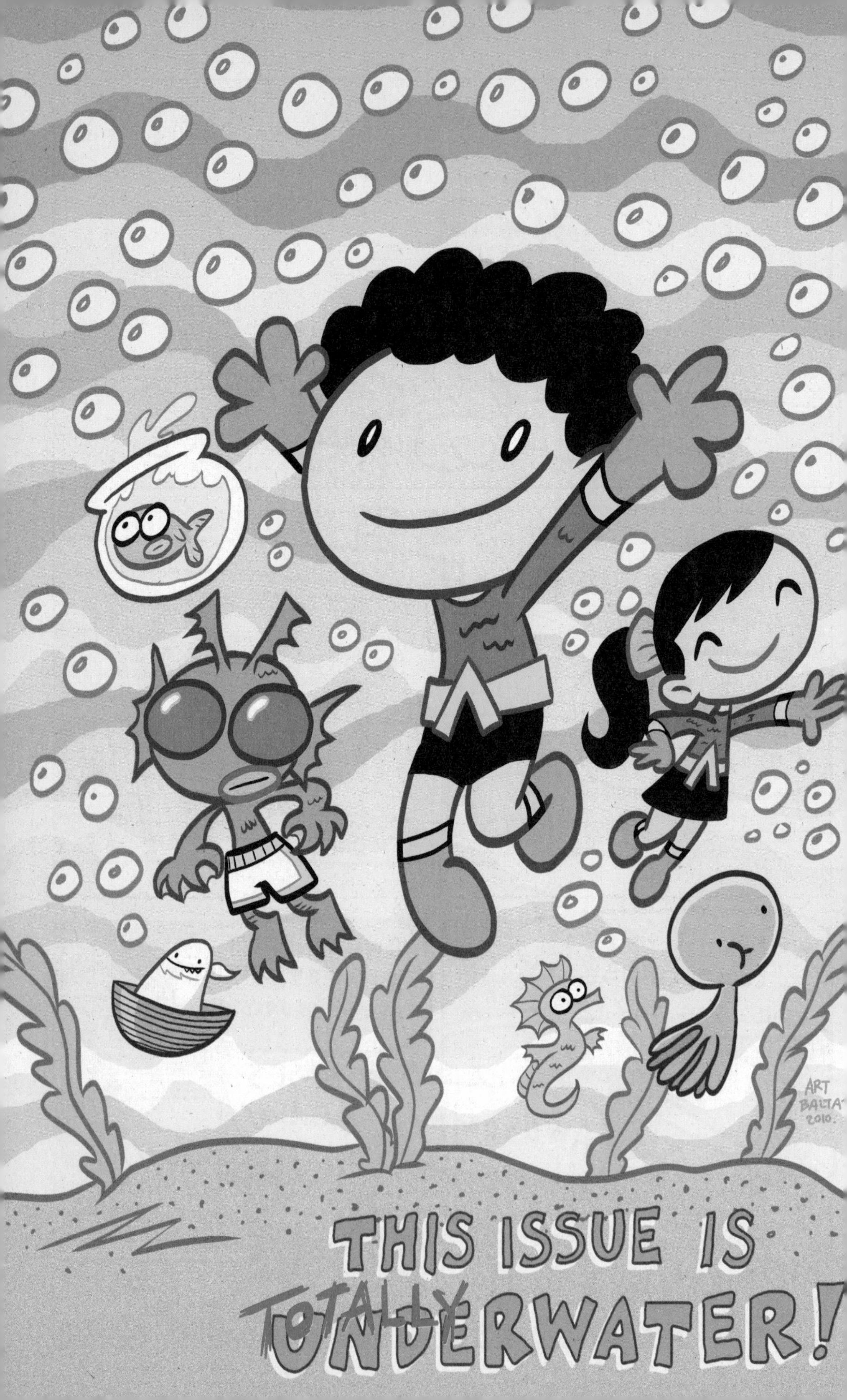
ART BALTA 2010.
THIS ISSUE IS
TOTALLY
UNDERWATER!

tiny titans

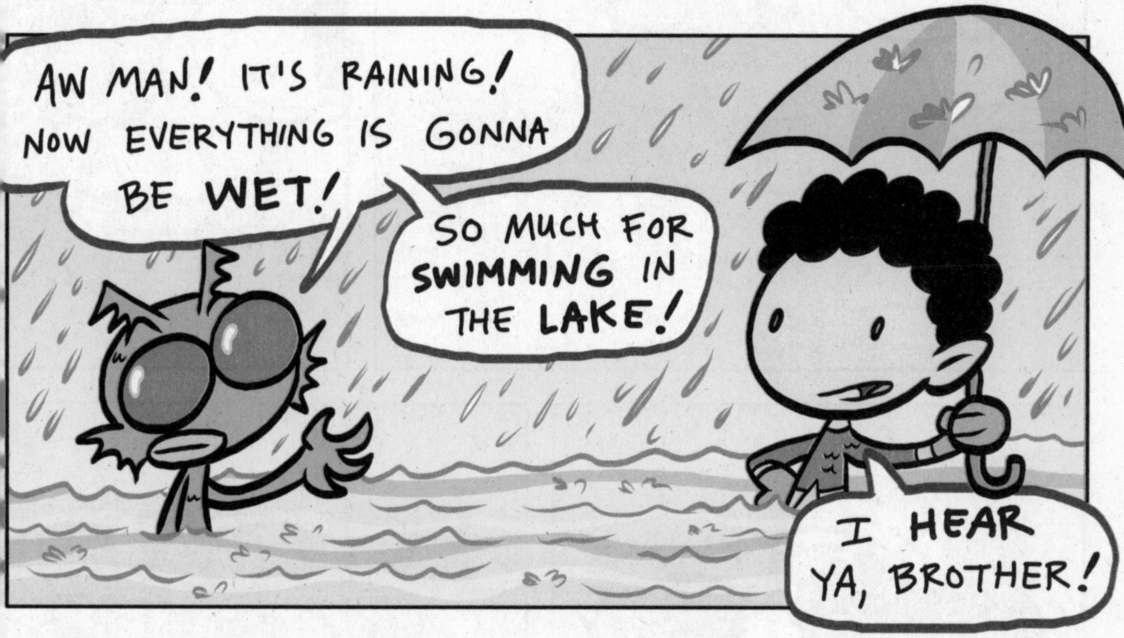
AW MAN! IT'S RAINING! NOW EVERYTHING IS GONNA BE WET!
SO MUCH FOR SWIMMING IN THE LAKE!
I HEAR YA, BROTHER!

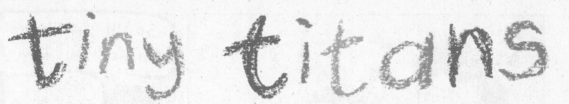

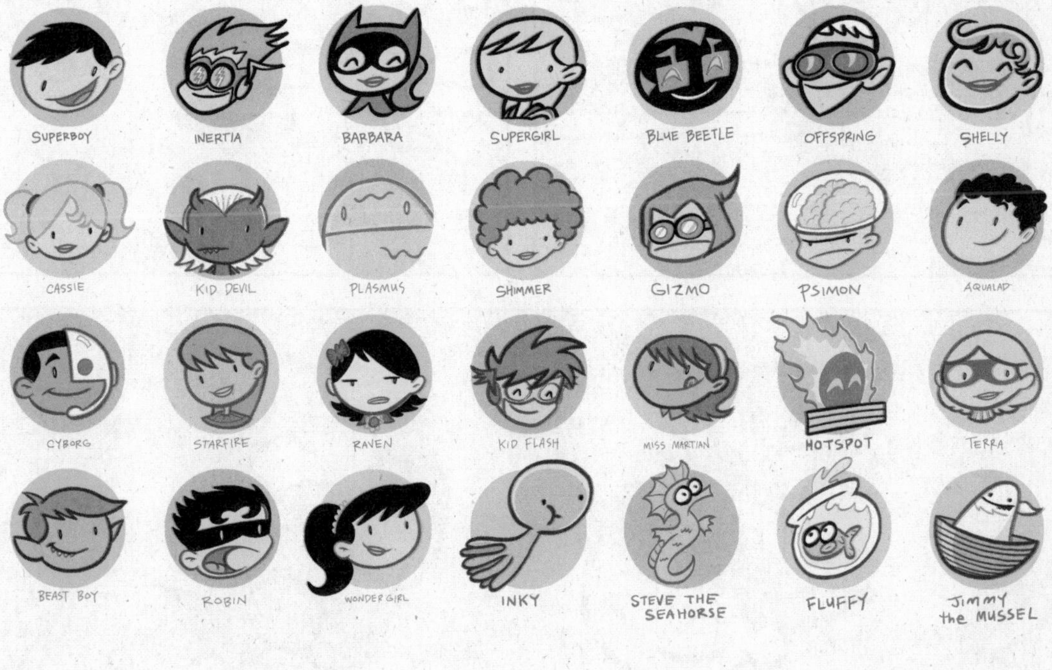
SUPERBOY
INERTIA
BARBARA
SUPERGIRL
BLUE BEETLE
OFFSPRING
SHELLY
CASSIE
KID DEVIL
PLASMUS
SHIMMER
GIZMO
PSIMON
AQUALAD
CYBORG
STARFIRE
RAVEN
KID FLASH
MISS MARTIAN
HOTSPOT
TERRA
BEAST BOY
ROBIN
WONDER GIRL
INKY
STEVE THE SEAHORSE
FLUFFY
JIMMY the MUSSEL

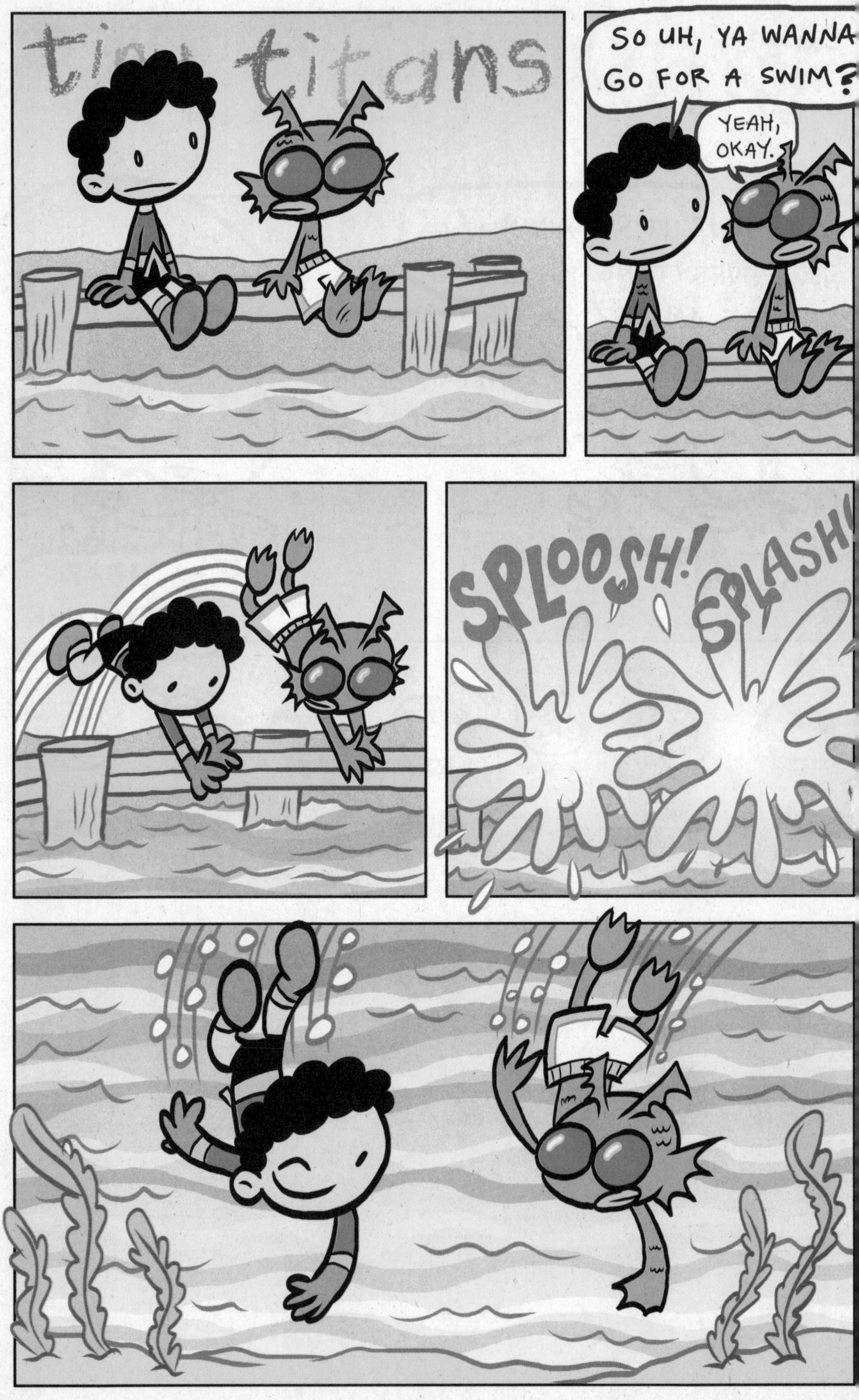
tiny titans
SO UH, YA WANNA GO FOR A SWIM?
YEAH, OKAY.
SPLOOSH!
SPLASH!

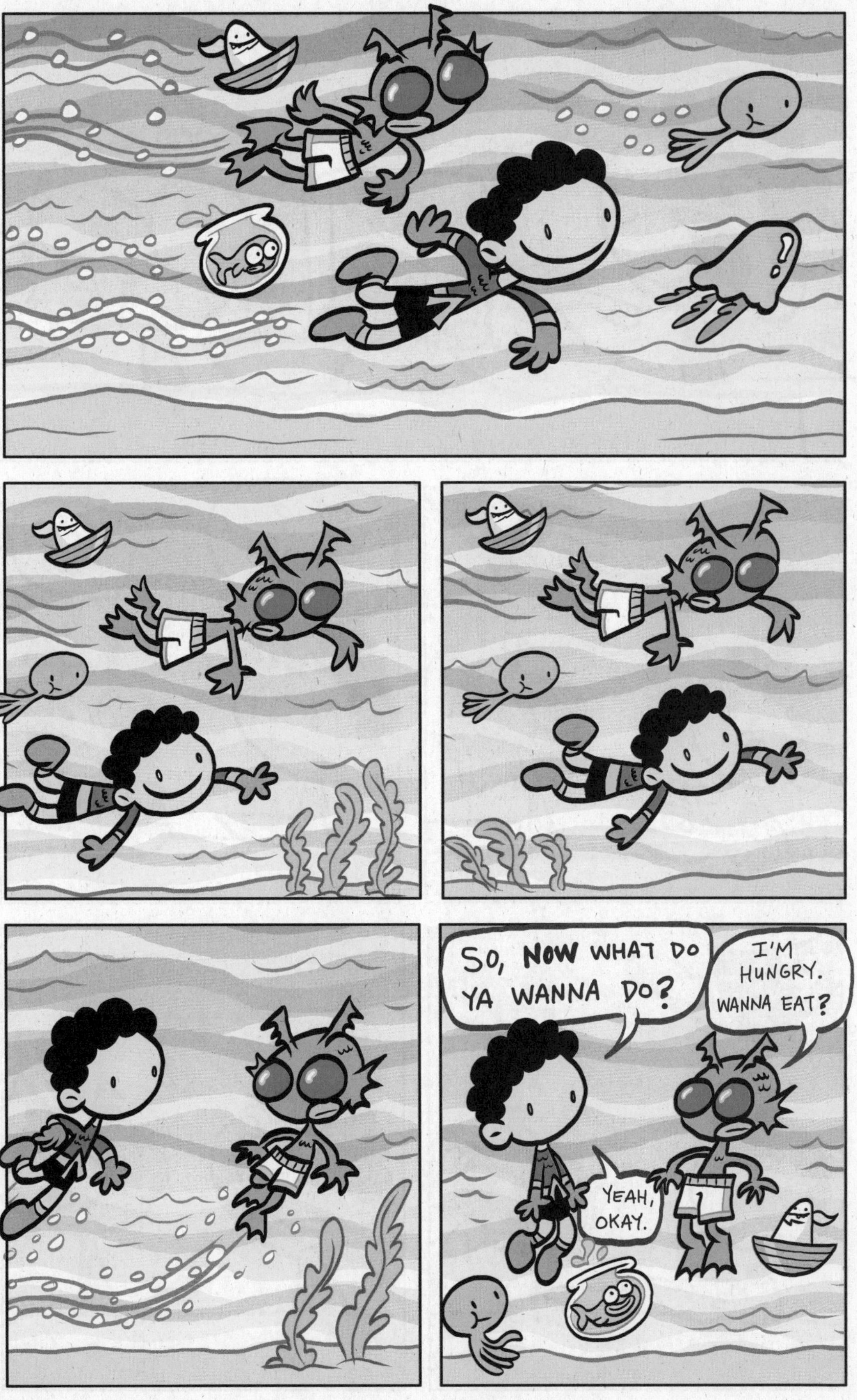

SO, NOW WHAT DO YA WANNA DO?
I'M HUNGRY. WANNA EAT?
YEAH, OKAY.

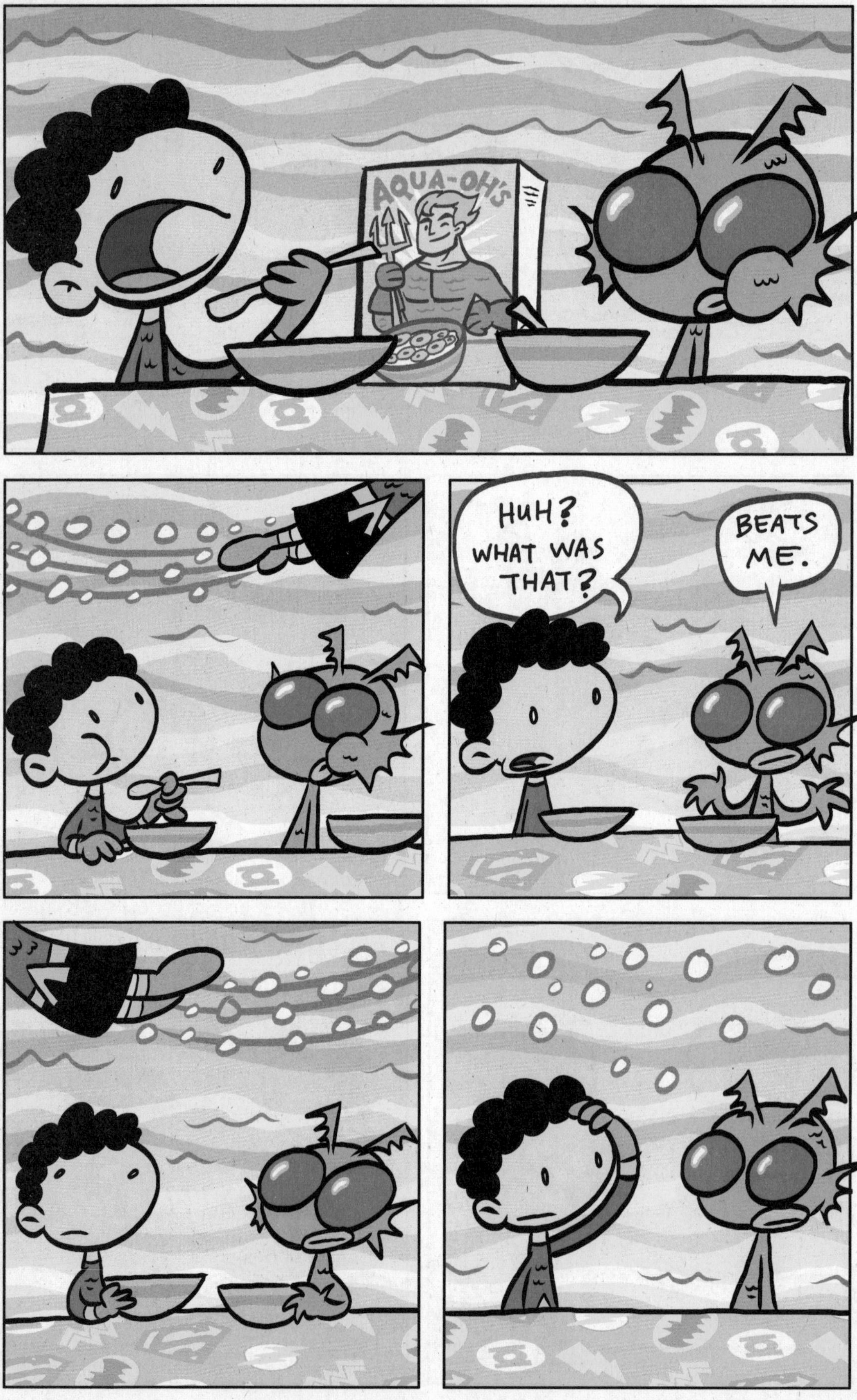
AQUA-OH'S
HUH? WHAT WAS THAT?
BEATS ME.

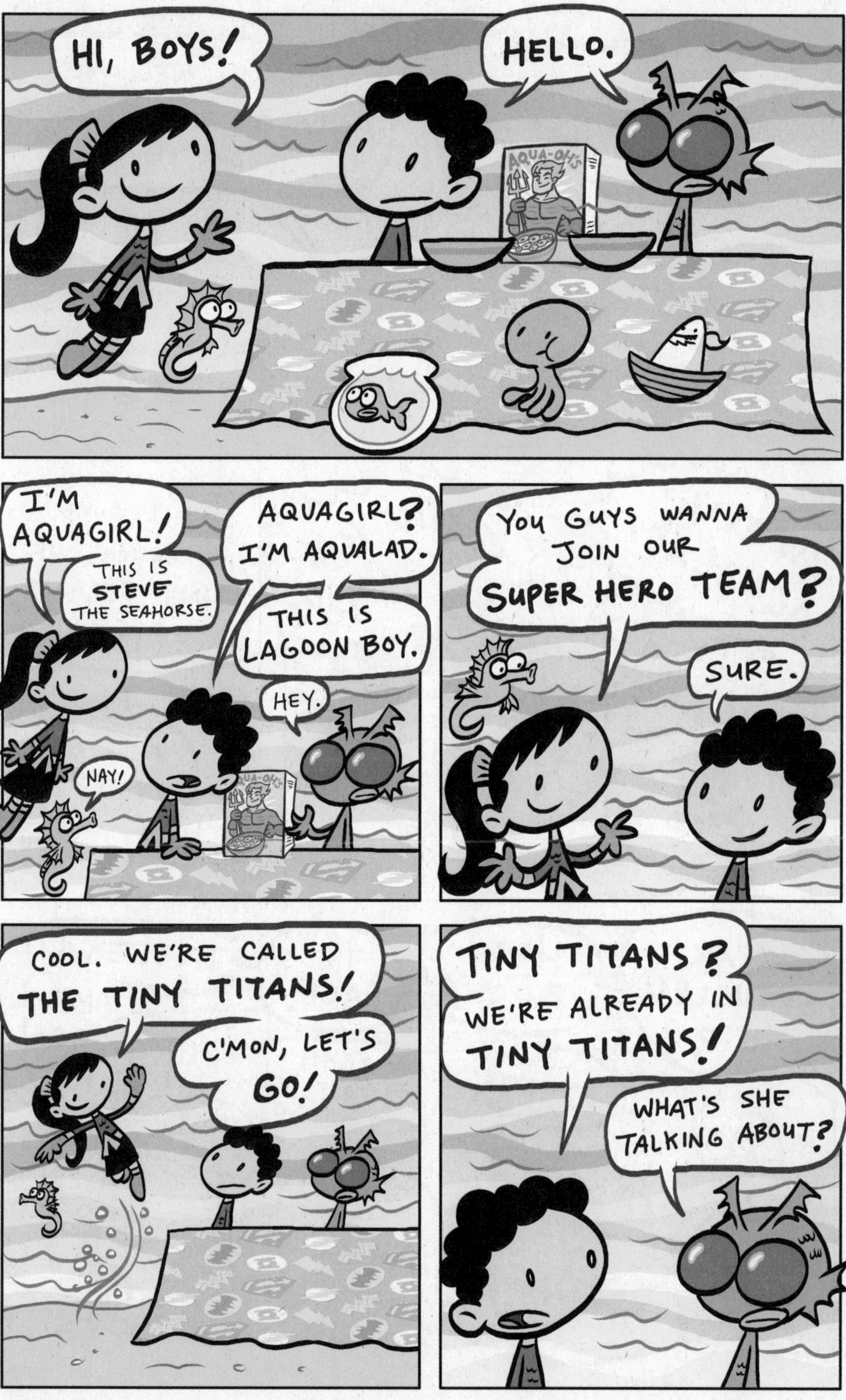
HI, BOYS!
HELLO.
AQUA-OH'S
I'M AQUAGIRL!
THIS IS STEVE THE SEAHORSE.
AQUAGIRL? I'M AQUALAD.
THIS IS LAGOON BOY.
HEY.
NAY!
AQUA-OH'S
YOU GUYS WANNA JOIN OUR SUPER HERO TEAM?
SURE.
COOL. WE'RE CALLED THE TINY TITANS!
C'MON, LET'S GO!
TINY TITANS?
WE'RE ALREADY IN TINY TITANS!
WHAT'S SHE TALKING ABOUT?

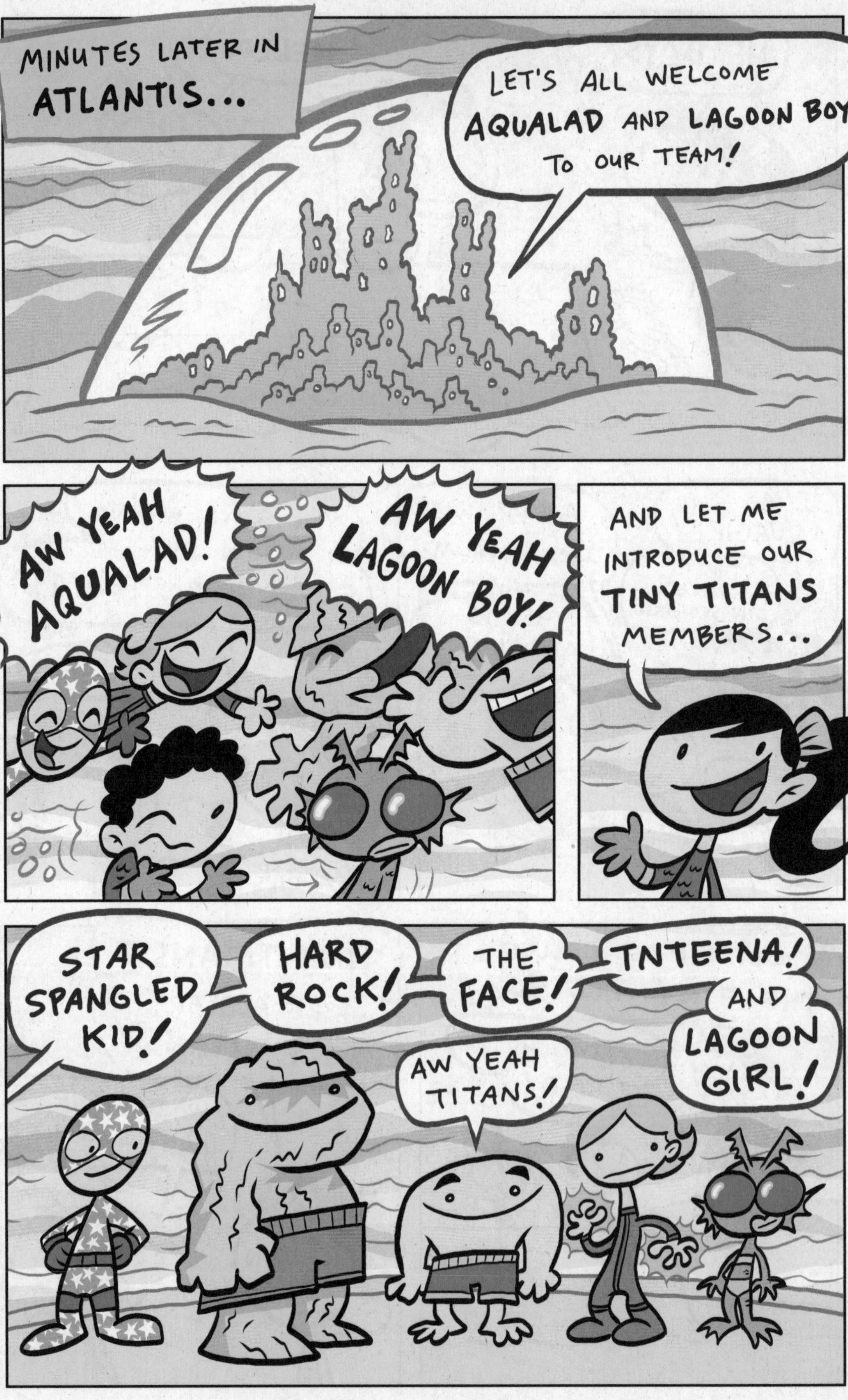
MINUTES LATER IN ATLANTIS...
LET'S ALL WELCOME AQUALAD AND LAGOON BOY TO OUR TEAM!
AW YEAH AQUALAD!
AW YEAH LAGOON BOY!
AND LET ME INTRODUCE OUR TINY TITANS MEMBERS...
STAR SPANGLED KID!
HARD ROCK!
THE FACE!
TNTEENA!
AND LAGOON GIRL!
AW YEAH TITANS!

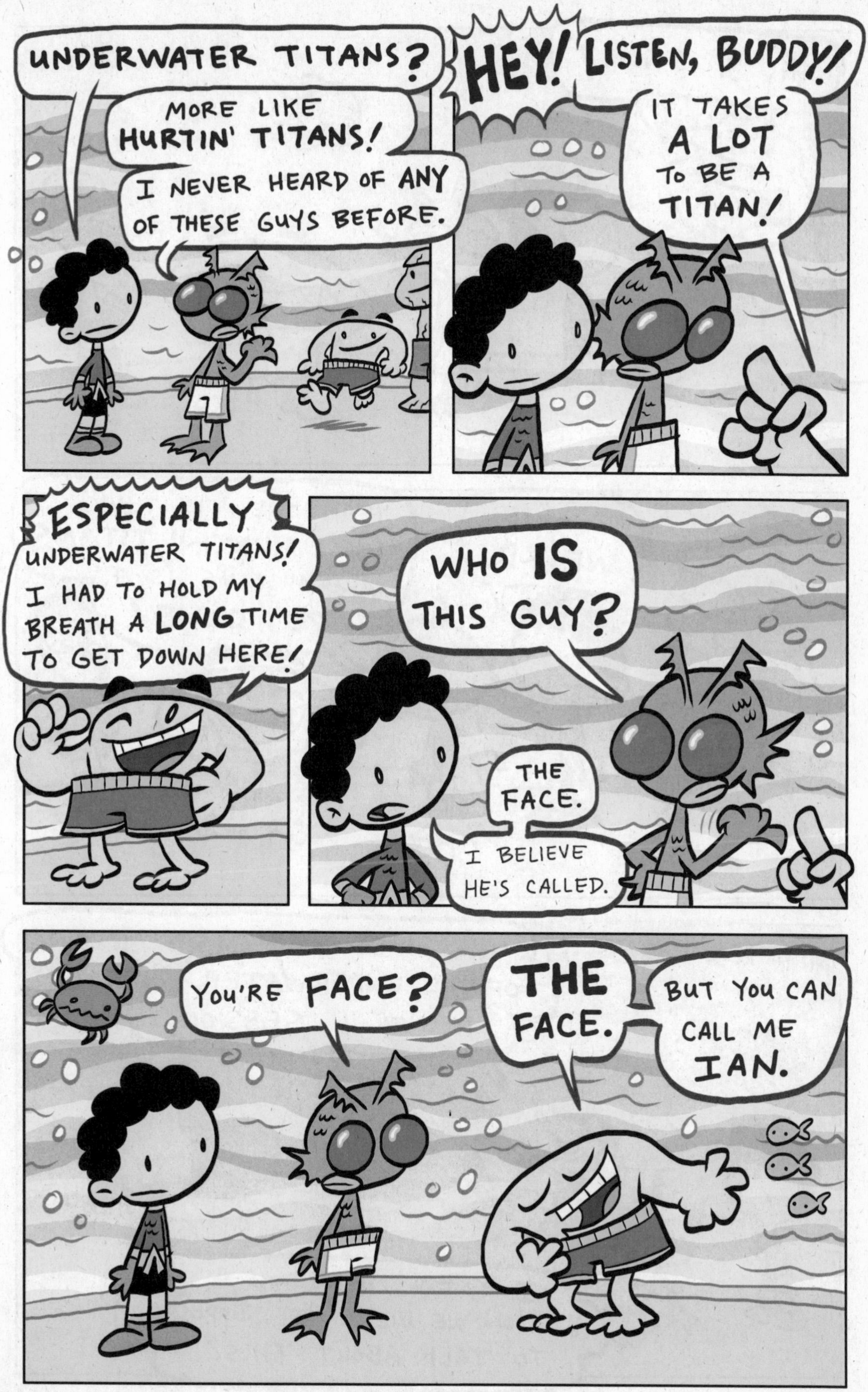
UNDERWATER TITANS?
MORE LIKE HURTIN' TITANS!
I NEVER HEARD OF ANY OF THESE GUYS BEFORE.
HEY! LISTEN, BUDDY!
IT TAKES A LOT TO BE A TITAN!
ESPECIALLY UNDERWATER TITANS!
I HAD TO HOLD MY BREATH A LONG TIME TO GET DOWN HERE!
WHO IS THIS GUY?
THE FACE.
I BELIEVE HE'S CALLED.
YOU'RE FACE?
THE FACE.
BUT YOU CAN CALL ME IAN.

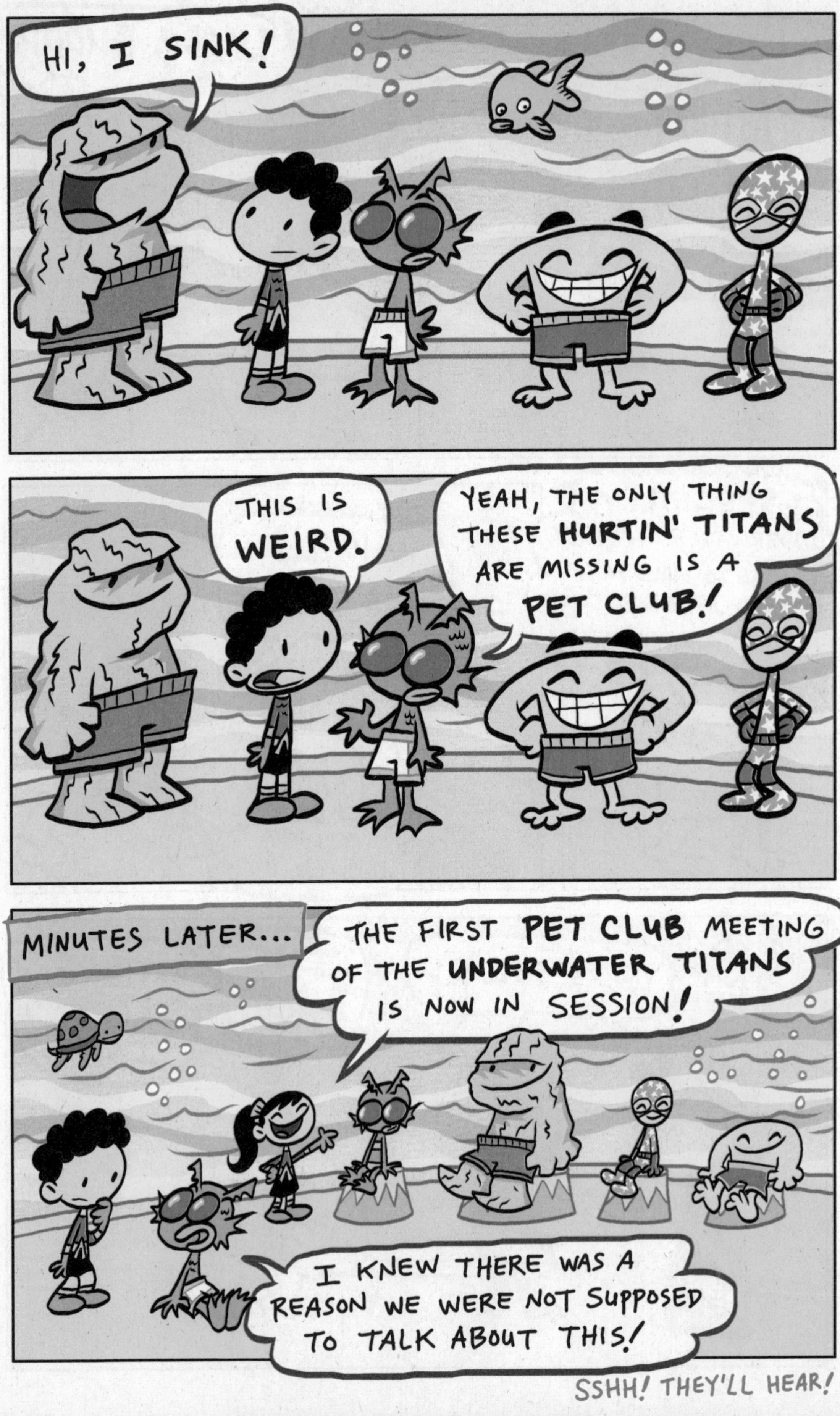
HI, I SINK!
THIS IS WEIRD.
YEAH, THE ONLY THING THESE HURTIN' TITANS ARE MISSING IS A PET CLUB!
MINUTES LATER...
THE FIRST PET CLUB MEETING OF THE UNDERWATER TITANS IS NOW IN SESSION!
I KNEW THERE WAS A REASON WE WERE NOT SUPPOSED TO TALK ABOUT THIS!
SSHH! THEY'LL HEAR!

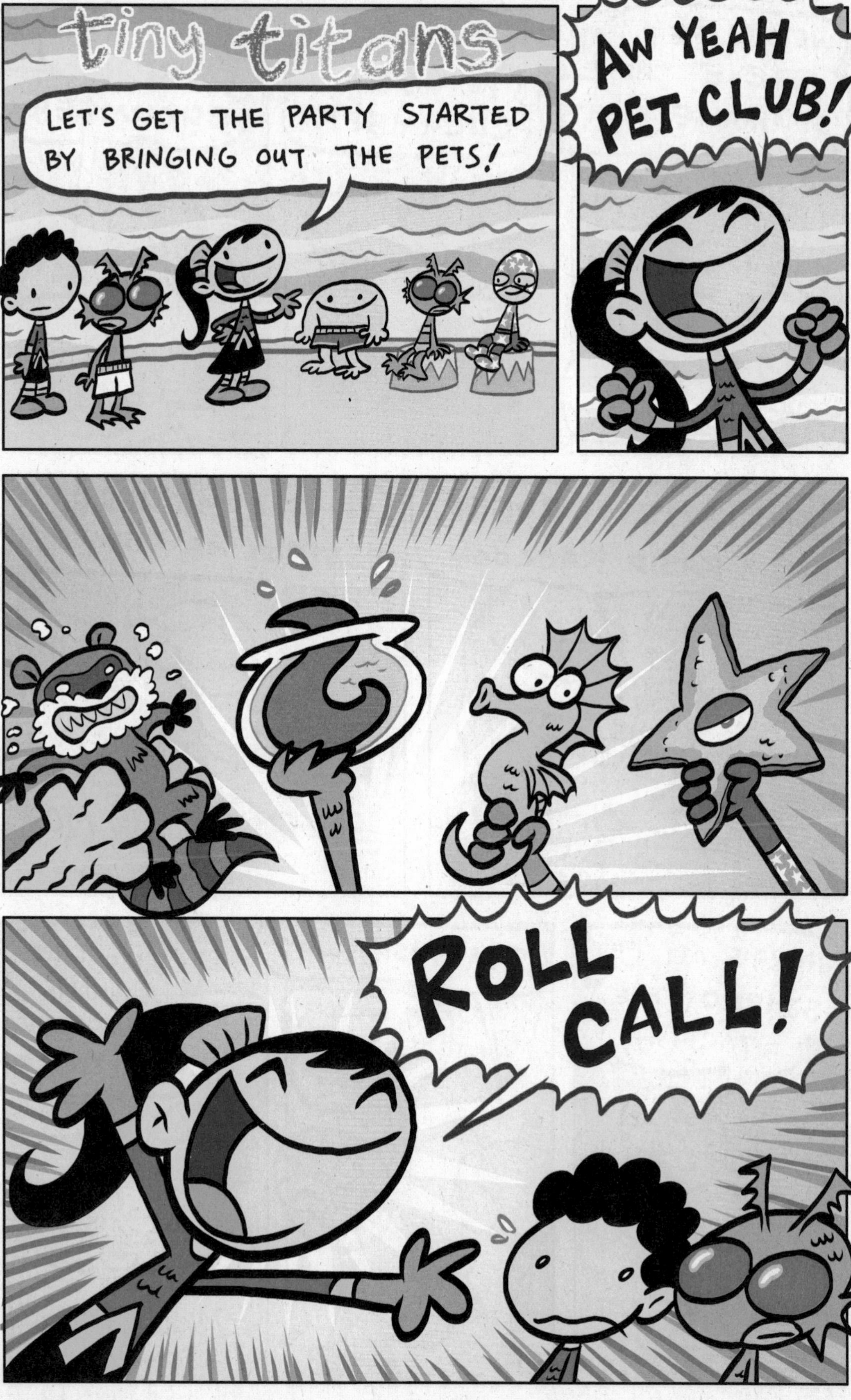
tiny titans
LET'S GET THE PARTY STARTED BY BRINGING OUT THE PETS!
AW YEAH PET CLUB!
ROLL CALL!

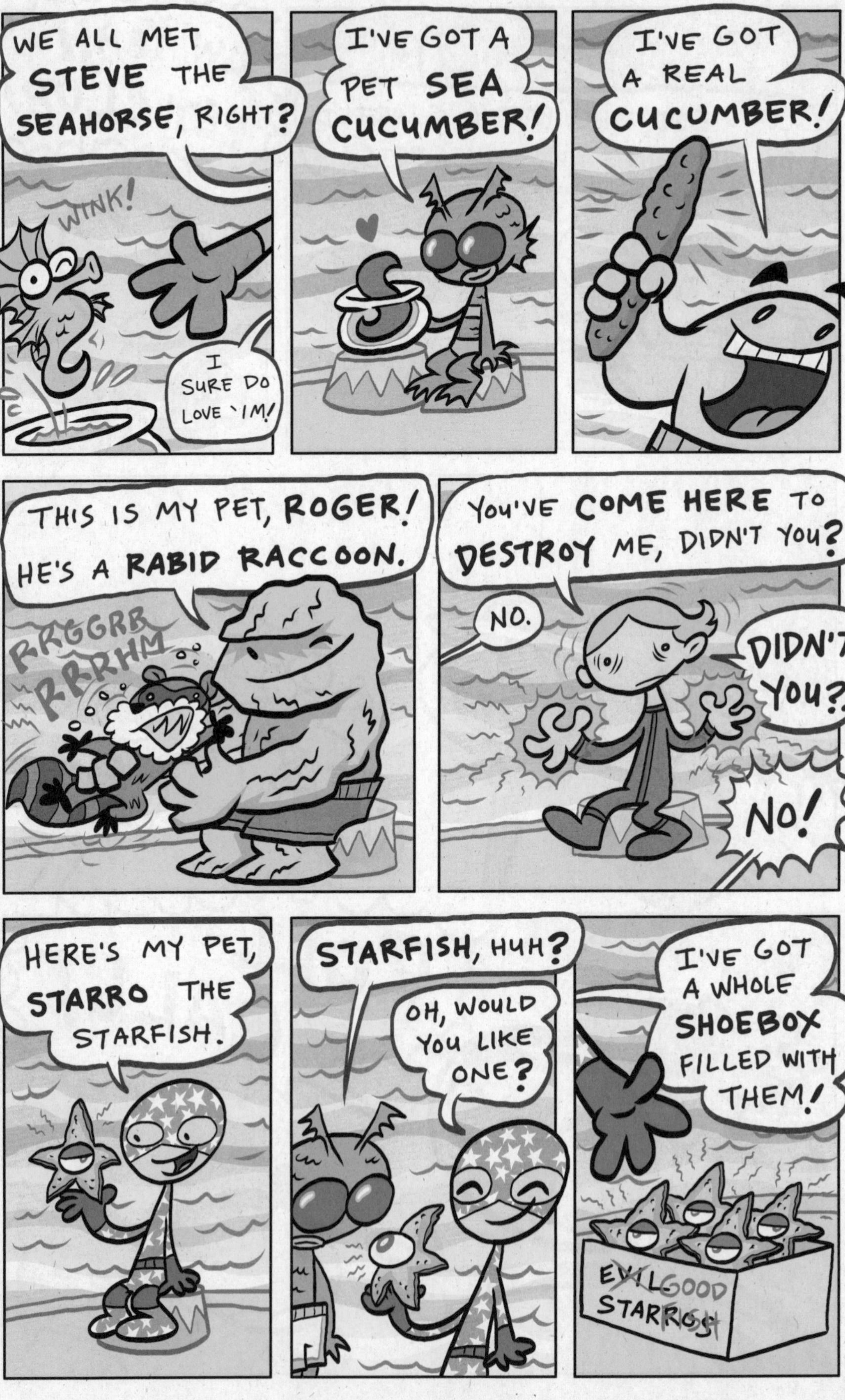
WE ALL MET STEVE THE SEAHORSE, RIGHT?
WINK!
I SURE DO LOVE 'IM!
I'VE GOT A PET SEA CUCUMBER!
I'VE GOT A REAL CUCUMBER!
THIS IS MY PET, ROGER! HE'S A RABID RACCOON.
RRGGRB RRRHM
YOU'VE COME HERE TO DESTROY ME, DIDN'T YOU?
NO.
DIDN'T YOU?!
NO!
HERE'S MY PET, STARRO THE STARFISH.
STARFISH, HUH?
OH, WOULD YOU LIKE ONE?
I'VE GOT A WHOLE SHOEBOX FILLED WITH THEM!
EVIL GOOD STARFISH

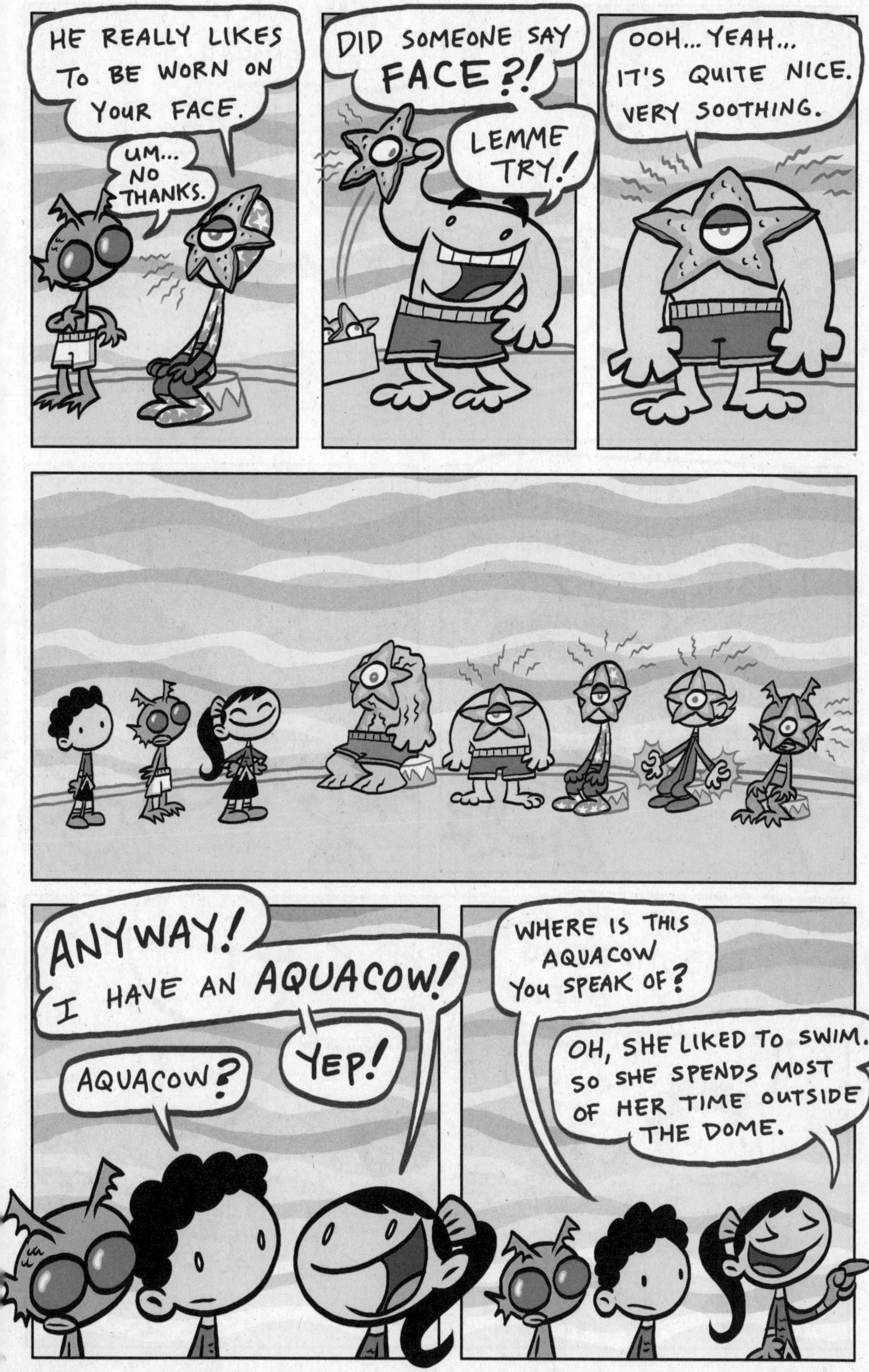

HE REALLY LIKES TO BE WORN ON YOUR FACE.
UM... NO THANKS.
DID SOMEONE SAY FACE?!
LEMME TRY!
OOH... YEAH... IT'S QUITE NICE. VERY SOOTHING.
ANYWAY! I HAVE AN AQUACOW!
AQUACOW?
YEP!
WHERE IS THIS AQUACOW YOU SPEAK OF?
OH, SHE LIKED TO SWIM. SO SHE SPENDS MOST OF HER TIME OUTSIDE THE DOME.

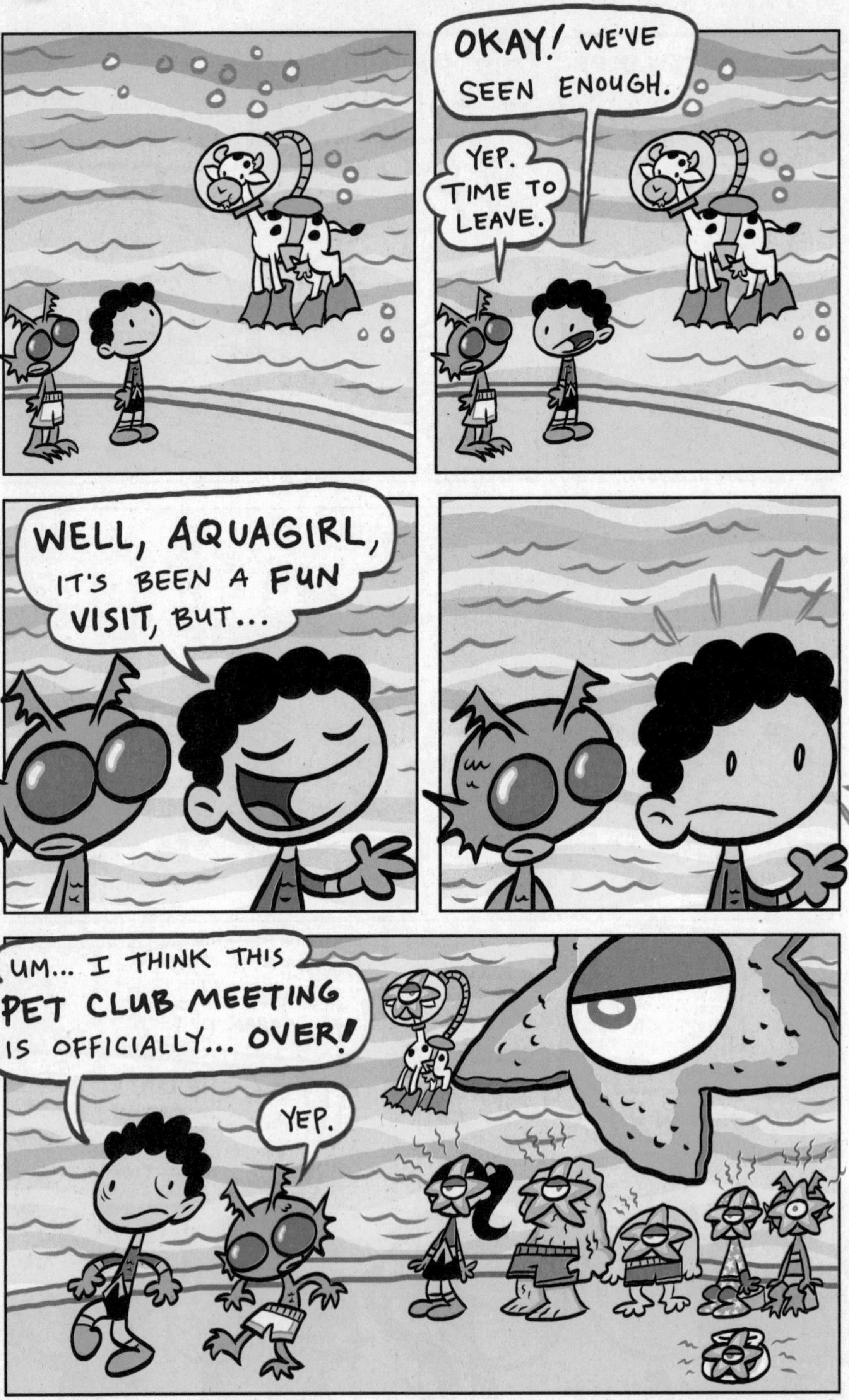
OKAY! WE'VE SEEN ENOUGH.
YEP. TIME TO LEAVE.
WELL, AQUAGIRL, IT'S BEEN A FUN VISIT, BUT...
UM... I THINK THIS PET CLUB MEETING IS OFFICIALLY... OVER!
YEP.

—OUTTA HERE, MAN!

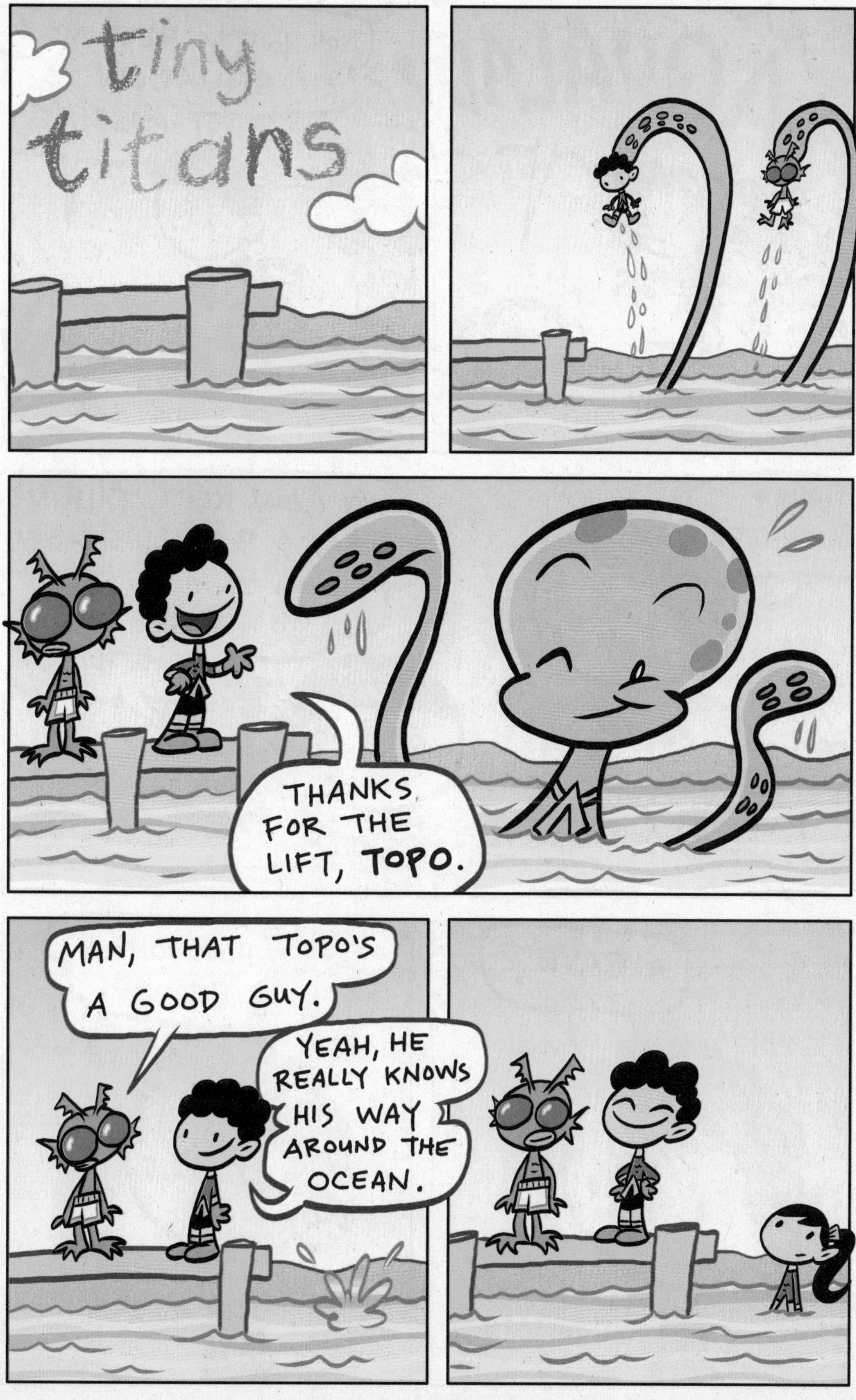
tiny titans
THANKS FOR THE LIFT, TOPO.
MAN, THAT TOPO'S A GOOD GUY.
YEAH, HE REALLY KNOWS HIS WAY AROUND THE OCEAN.

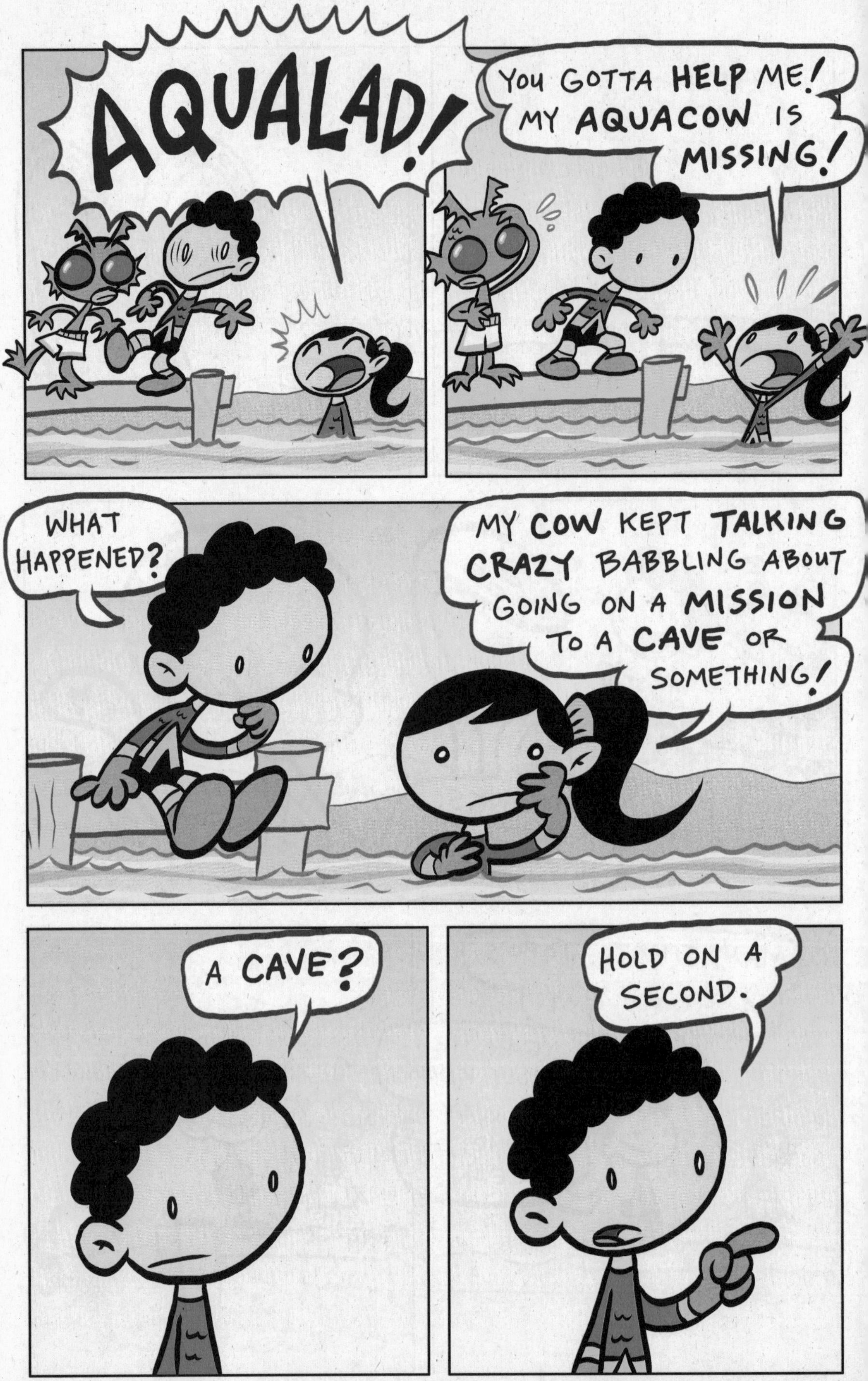
AQUALAD!
YOU GOTTA HELP ME! MY AQUACOW IS MISSING!
WHAT HAPPENED?
MY COW KEPT TALKING CRAZY BABBLING ABOUT GOING ON A MISSION TO A CAVE OR SOMETHING!
A CAVE?
HOLD ON A SECOND.

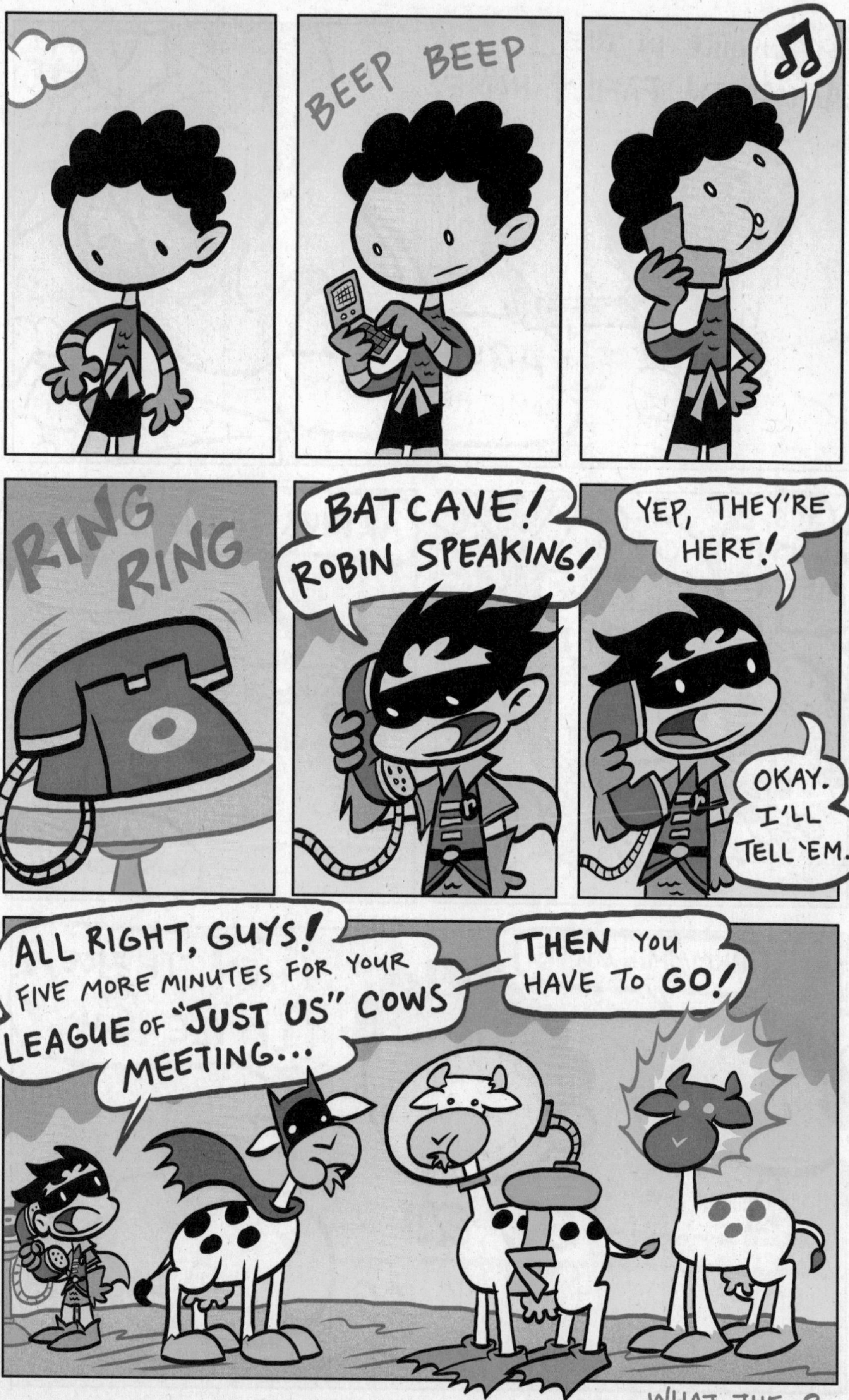
BEEP BEEP
♫
RING RING
BATCAVE! ROBIN SPEAKING!
YEP, THEY'RE HERE!
OKAY. I'LL TELL 'EM.
ALL RIGHT, GUYS! FIVE MORE MINUTES FOR YOUR LEAGUE OF "JUST US" COWS MEETING...
THEN YOU HAVE TO GO!

-WHAT THE--?

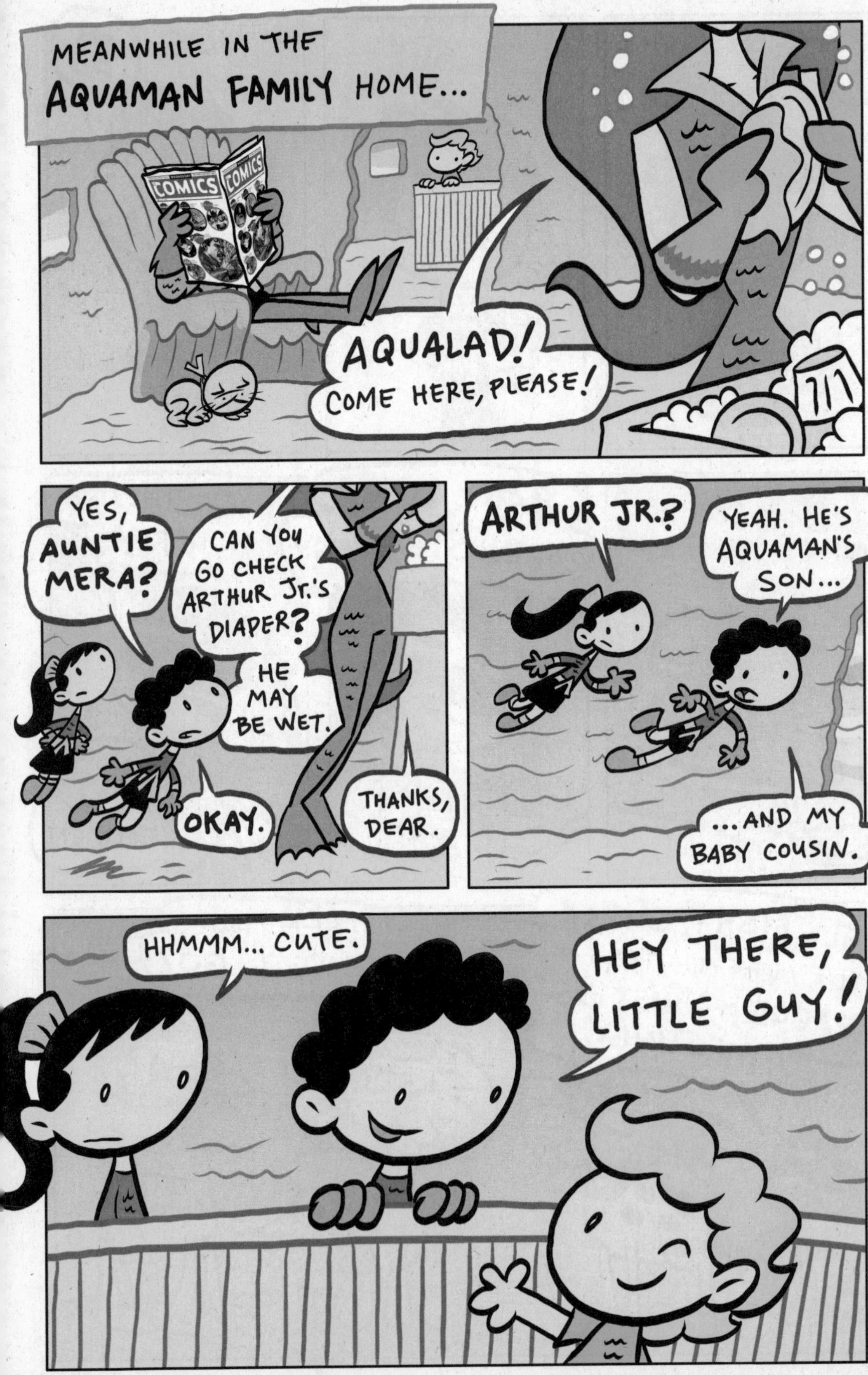
MEANWHILE IN THE AQUAMAN FAMILY HOME...
COMICS
COMICS
AQUALAD! COME HERE, PLEASE!
YES, AUNTIE MERA?
CAN YOU GO CHECK ARTHUR Jr.'s DIAPER?
HE MAY BE WET.
OKAY.
THANKS, DEAR.
ARTHUR JR.?
YEAH. HE'S AQUAMAN'S SON...
...AND MY BABY COUSIN.
HHMMM... CUTE.
HEY THERE, LITTLE GUY!

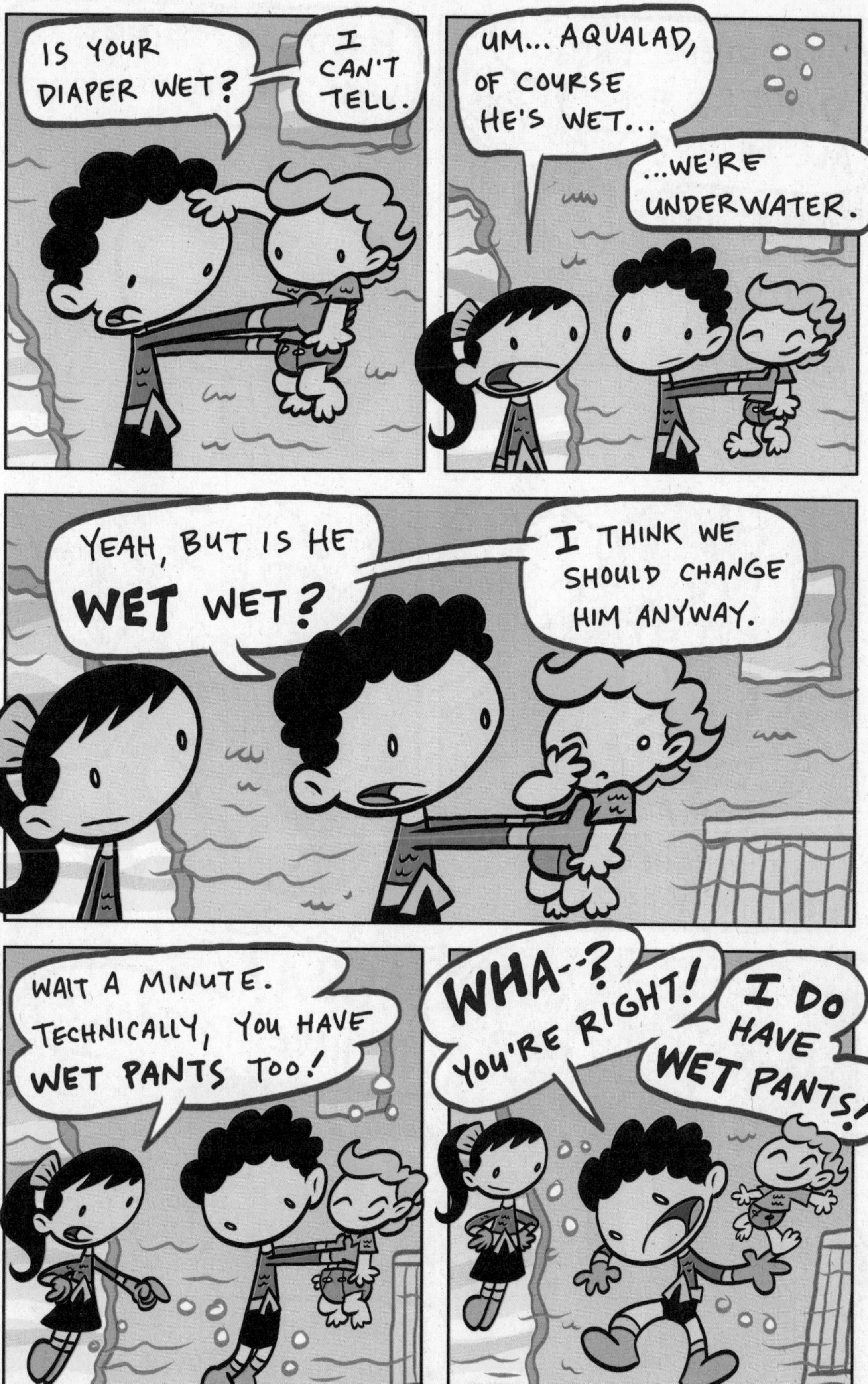
IS YOUR DIAPER WET?
I CAN'T TELL.
UM... AQUALAD, OF COURSE HE'S WET...
...WE'RE UNDERWATER.
YEAH, BUT IS HE WET WET?
I THINK WE SHOULD CHANGE HIM ANYWAY.
WAIT A MINUTE. TECHNICALLY, YOU HAVE WET PANTS TOO!
WHA--? YOU'RE RIGHT!
I DO HAVE WET PANTS!

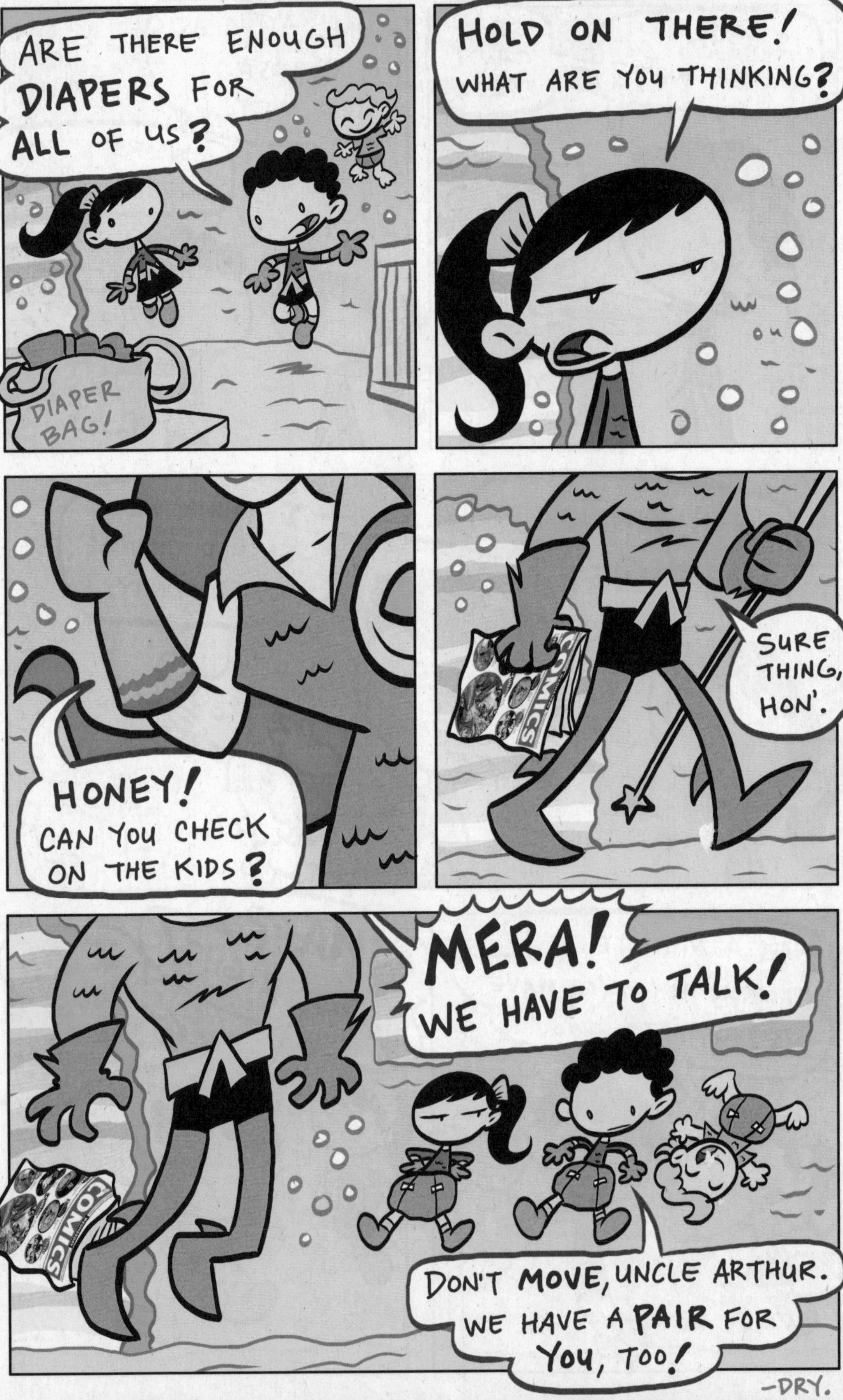
ARE THERE ENOUGH DIAPERS FOR ALL OF US?
DIAPER BAG!
HOLD ON THERE! WHAT ARE YOU THINKING?
HONEY! CAN YOU CHECK ON THE KIDS?
COMICS
SURE THING, HON'.
MERA! WE HAVE TO TALK!
COMICS
DON'T MOVE, UNCLE ARTHUR. WE HAVE A PAIR FOR YOU, TOO!
-DRY.

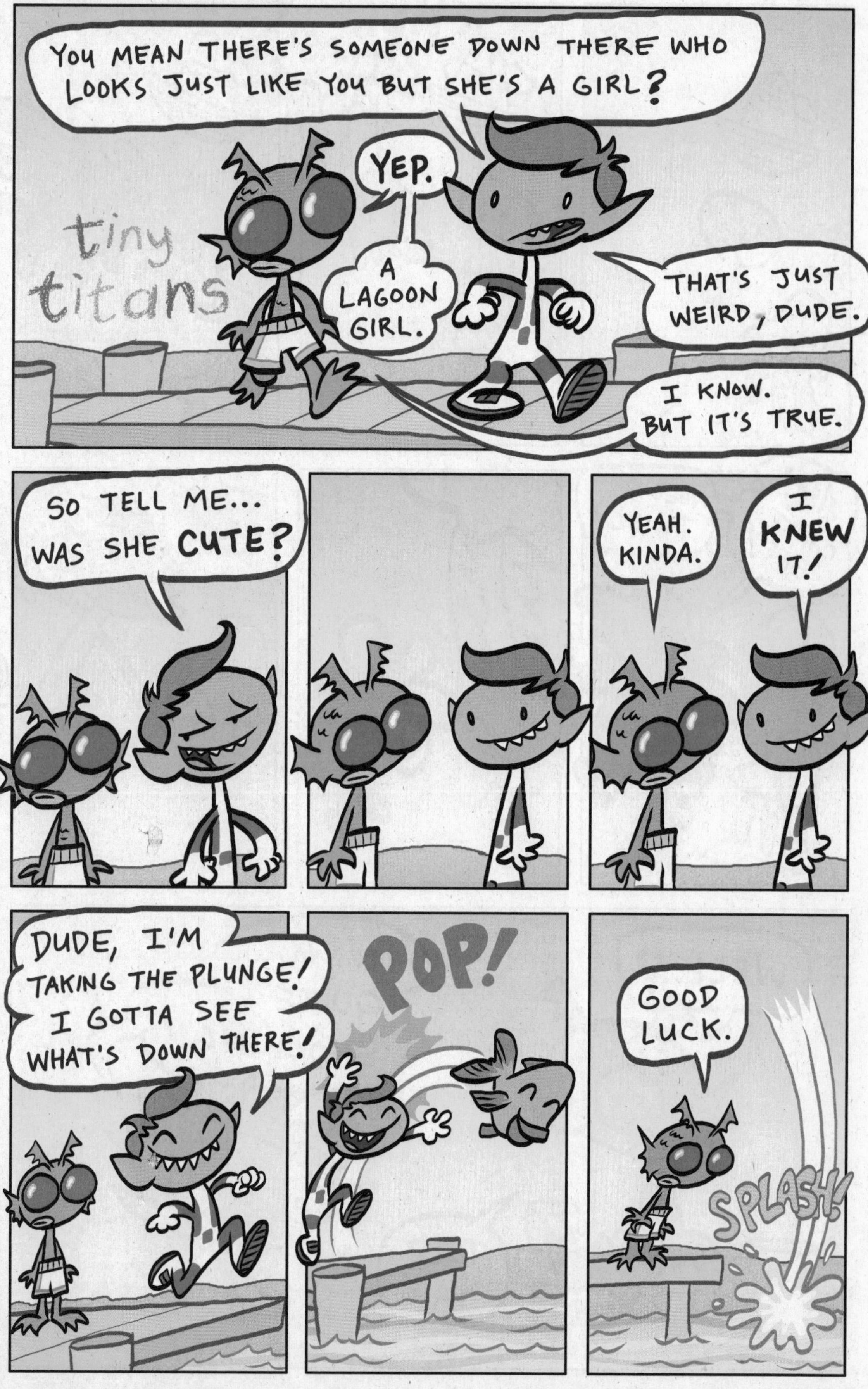
YOU MEAN THERE'S SOMEONE DOWN THERE WHO LOOKS JUST LIKE YOU BUT SHE'S A GIRL?
YEP.
A LAGOON GIRL.
tiny titans
THAT'S JUST WEIRD, DUDE.
I KNOW. BUT IT'S TRUE.
SO TELL ME... WAS SHE CUTE?
YEAH. KINDA.
I KNEW IT!
DUDE, I'M TAKING THE PLUNGE! I GOTTA SEE WHAT'S DOWN THERE!
POP!
GOOD LUCK.
SPLASH!

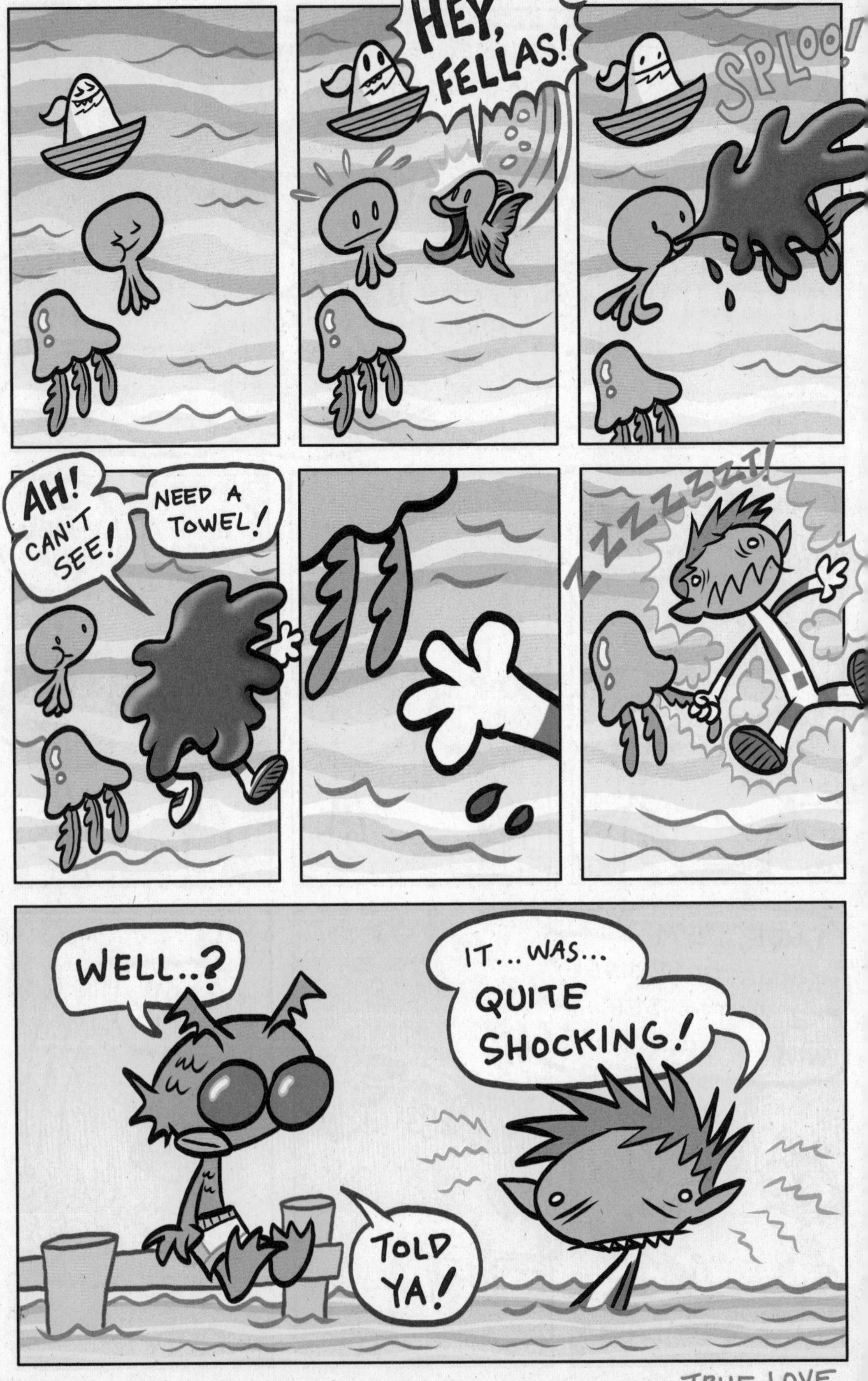
HEY, FELLAS!
SPLOO!
AH! CAN'T SEE!
NEED A TOWEL!
ZZZZZZZT!
WELL..?
IT... WAS... QUITE SHOCKING!
TOLD YA!

-TRUE LOVE.